MW01053765

Silvermoon Retirement Village

Cozy Mystery Books 1-3

Silvermoon Retirement Village

Cozy Mystery Books 1-3

Rodney Strong

© Copyright 2019-2021 Rodney Strong

Rodney Strong asserts his moral right to be identified as the author of this work.

ISBN 9780473563196

All rights reserved. No part of this publication may be produced or transmitted in any form or by any means, electronic or mechanical, including photocopying, recording or information storage and retrieval systems, without permission in writing from the copyright holder.

Published by LoreQuinn Publishing

This is a work of fiction. Names, characters, places, and incidents either are the production of the author's imagination or are used fictitiously, and any resemblance to actual persons, living or dead, events, or locales is entirely coincidental.

Editor: Anna Golden

Front cover design: Debbie Weaver, Weaver Creative

Printing by: YourBooks, Tawa

A catalogue record for this book is available from the National Library of New Zealand.

Also by Rodney Strong

Hitchhiker books
Murder in Paint
Murder in Mud
Murder in Doubt
Murder in Pink

Standalone books
Troy's Possibilities
The Second Chance of Joshua Messer

For children
Written as R.G Strong
Karmartha, The Last Garden
Escape from School

Welcome to the Silvermoon Retirement Village

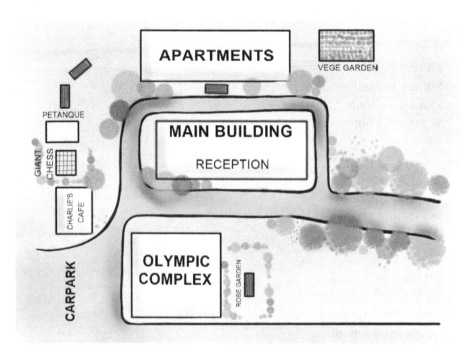

Contents

Poker Chips and Poison

A Silvermoon Retirement Village Cozy Mystery

ONΣ

Alice eyed her opponent. The next ten seconds were crucial. The next ten seconds meant the difference between ongoing torment or a swift end. It all came down to one thing:

Was that a poker face, or was she dead?

Alice had to admit, around here some days it was hard to tell.

Time was running out. She had to make a move.

With a confidence she didn't feel she looked at her hand, then lay the cards on the table.

'Flush.'

All eyes went to the woman sitting opposite Alice. The collective breaths of all four at the table stopped — a dangerous situation at the Silvermoon Retirement Village.

Teresa threw her cards down in disgust. 'All I had was a pair of tens.'

The others at the table laughed as Alice dragged the pile of chips towards her.

'Why on earth did you go all in on a pair of tens? I had more than that and I folded,' Owen said. A tall, solid man in his early eighties, he still dressed as if he was going into the office. White shirt, short-sleeved in summer, long-sleeved in winter (but never with the arms rolled up), a dark tie which could be anything from burgundy to deep blue (but nothing gauche like yellow or heaven forbid with pictures on it), and slacks.

'I thought she was bluffing. I was sure of it,' Teresa protested.

'And why were you so sure?' Betty asked in her soft Irish accent. Despite living in New Zealand for more than forty years, it was still there and became more prominent when she was accusing someone of something. Betty was short and leathery, a lifetime of working outside on a farm had dried and darkened her skin. Alice suspected that she and Owen were involved. If Alice had had anything more than a casual desire to know she could have found out in no time, but she figured everyone here had earned the right to some privacy just by making it this far in life.

''Well, she...' Teresa trailed off.

'Rubbed my earlobe?' Alice finished. She smiled at Teresa's open mouthed response. 'It's only a tell if you don't know you're doing it.' She winked and the table laughed again.

'I'll have to pay you when I get to the bank,' Teresa said with a scowl.

'None of that,' Owen replied. 'That's what internet banking is for.'

'I hardly think internet banking was set up to pay poker debts,' Teresa snapped, her fluffy brown hair bouncing as she shook her head.

It was always the same with her, Alice thought. Teresa always demanded her winnings straight away. However if she lost, which she more often did, there was some excuse about not having money on her, or being a little short until pension day. Given how much it cost to live in this place, no one believed she had to wait for her government pension to pay her debts.

Faced with stern expressions from her friends, Teresa adjusted her glasses, then meekly lifted her phone off the table, tapped on the screen, and a few seconds later Alice heard her own phone ping. It wasn't the first time she'd won money from those at the table. She might not know what a google was, but Alice made sure, with the help of her granddaughter, that she knew how to send money (and more importantly how to receive money) from her circle of friends.

She made sure to lose occasionally. Not that she was a card shark, but she had spent most of her working life reading people, and found it came in useful on occasion, even in a sedate place like the retirement village.

'I'm afraid I must go. This new woman is going to teach us how to make cats out of clay shortly,' Betty said.

Alice blinked. She could think of worse ways to spend the afternoon, but not many.

As her friends left the room, for a moment Alice had the shared space to herself. She looked out the large window that overlooked the back garden. The retirement complex sat on an acre of prime land on one of the many tree covered hills surrounding Wellington city. It was tucked away amongst all the suburban houses and many people didn't know the extent of the village that was at the end of the long driveway. A short trip down the hill would have taken her to a city filled with countless cafes and designer shops, but Alice didn't drive and had no great urgency for either coffee or clothes. When she was younger and had more energy it had been different. The population had been lower, and no one on the street had had their heads buried in their phones because phones were usually attached to kitchen walls. Or maybe what had changed was how she viewed them. Back then everyone, man or woman, was a potential target. Now that she was retired, her perception had changed. Mostly.

She sneezed. The simple act caused a different response now that she was approaching the century mark. She would never have guessed that a sneeze could cause her ribs to hurt, or a twinge to appear in her back, or occasionally make her pee. Somehow the fact she had almost no body padding left made it worse. Standing, she stretched one way, then the other and her muscles eased.

Alice considered sitting back down but there were several residents she preferred not to run into, especially Gordon, who considered himself God's gift to women over seventy. He was a bit handsy and at their last encounter she had only just resisted the temptation to put one of those hands in a cast. Breaking bones, unlike so many other things was more about angles and leverage than strength.

Following the plush carpeted hallway, brightly lit by sunshine through a skylight, Alice entered the waiting elevator and pushed the button for the second floor. From this side of the main building you could get to any level. From reception though, visitors needed to be buzzed in by a staff member. It wasn't so much an issue of security as it was the discretion that money bought.

Exiting into a small landing she punched her code into the panel next to the door on the left, one of only two on the floor.

Her apartment would have rivalled the poshest hotel. The open plan living area and kitchen was filled with modern comfortable furniture, and her floor-to-ceiling windows overlooked the perfectly manicured front lawn and driveway. To the left, past the kitchen, was a guest bathroom, and through a door at the opposite end of the lounge was the bedroom, complete with ensuite and walk in wardrobe, which Alice privately thought was a step too far. She routinely wore two outfits, one was on and the other in the wash, and had a third pair of pants and blouse for best. The rest was empty space.

The bathroom was another matter. She spent much longer in the tiled, walk in shower than she needed to get clean, because the multiple jets hit spots she couldn't anymore. Sometimes she considered carrying a chair in there and drifting off to sleep. After all, if her skin turned prune-like not many people would notice the difference.

Alice turned on the television, flicked through some channels, then turned it off again. Even with the movie channel available to all residents and playing the latest pictures from around the world, there was nothing that caught her fancy enough to sit through.

She thought about making a snack, or better yet, having one sent up from the restaurant kitchen. Glancing at the clock she decided against it. Brunch was never a meal she'd warmed to. That's what snacks were for, to bridge the gap between breakfast and lunch. No need to create new meals just for the sake of it.

Alice eased her wiry frame out of the chair and walked around the couch. It wasn't until the third rotation that she admitted to herself what was bugging her.

She blamed Oliver. Although technically she could blame her granddaughter Amanda for introducing Oliver to her. Or she could blame Violet Tumbleton, her long dead friend, for not staying dead. But Violet was gone again, Amanda away working, so Oliver squarely took the blame.

She thought she had been content pottering around, her previous life a fond memory, until Oliver Atkinson showed up at her door asking for help to solve a murder. Alice should have said no. He wasn't a detective, amateur or otherwise. He was a writer (and not a bad one judging by the books she had read), a father of two under-ten-year-olds, one of which showed great promise in a life of manipulation, and a husband to an incredibly patient wife. But a detective he was not, which was probably why he had asked for her help.

Yes, she probably should have said no. But she hadn't, because maybe she wasn't as content as she'd thought. And they had caught the murderer, which she'd found quite exhilarating. Now, at the age of 97, winning money from her friends at poker was no longer very satisfying.

With a sigh Alice sat back down in front of the television and randomly picked a movie. The leading man was handsome, but couldn't act to save himself (and had probably never had to).

TWO

The bright sunshine flooding through the windows did little to dispel her melancholy the next morning. Not needing as much sleep as she used to, Alice was up and dressed by 6:30. She cooked herself a poached egg on toast, took the many pills that her doctor had prescribed and that she grudgingly took, and was flicking through the morning paper that was delivered to her front door six mornings a week.

The murder case had made the front page, and there was a quote from Detective Wilson acknowledging the public for providing vital information which led to the arrest. Alice snorted, "providing vital information" indeed. She and Oliver had solved the whole damn thing for them. All the police had had to do was show up and slap on the handcuffs.

Alice turned to the crossword, picked up a pen and worked her way through from top to bottom. She was just working out a seven letter bird that started with B and ended in G when there was a knock at her door. Visitors were few, and those that did come were usually residents or staff of the village. There were a few of both she would be happy to avoid talking to.

She retrieved her phone from the coffee table and opened an app to a live stream video of the hallway beyond her front door. It wasn't something the management were aware of. Amanda had installed it for Alice when she first moved in. It made both of them feel better knowing she could check the door before opening it.

Owen stood in the hallway, shuffling back and forth on the spot. Alice put down her phone and went to usher her friend inside.

'Sorry to call around so early,' he said, once he was perched on a kitchen stool with a piping hot cup of herbal tea in front of him.

Alice thought he looked tired. And distracted. His top button was undone, a casual oversight to anyone else, but a concern to her.

She let him sip his drink and order his thoughts. Owen had been the chief executive of a bank before he'd retired a decade ago. She knew he liked to compose himself and consider all angles before making a decision. Most of the time it was an endearing quality, except for when they were playing poker. His tell was that he took longer than normal to decide on a bet when he was bluffing. Weighing risks versus rewards had been ingrained in him by a lifetime of management.

'Bunting,' she finally said to break the silence.

'Excuse me?' he said with wide eyes.

'Seven letter bird starting with B and ending with G. A bunting. It was in this morning's crossword.'

'Ah. I never had the time to do the crossword while I was working, and it's a bit late to take it up now.' He grinned briefly and she caught a glimpse of the handsome man he had been, before time and stress wore him out. The smile fell away and he looked troubled once more.

'Is it Betty?' she guessed.

He looked surprised. 'Is what Betty?'

'Whatever's on your mind.'

He hesitated, sucking on his teeth in a manner Alice found irritating.

'The thing is, I don't know if it's even a thing. Or if it is, whether it's a big thing or a small thing or nothing at all. Do you see?'

'Not the foggiest.'

He laughed. 'No, I'm doing a terrible job at explaining it. You see, it's this—' He broke off to cough, a chest-rattling sound that echoed off the walls, and took longer than Alice liked to get under control.

She had endured a similar cough recently. Colds definitely went in the cons column of growing old.

Owen cleared his throat. 'Sorry, some tea must have gone down the wrong way.'

'I never understood that saying,' Alice replied. 'There's only one way down and one way up.'

'Very true. It goes on the long list of strange sayings that don't make sense,' Owen said.

'Speaking of sayings, you were...?'

'Yes, well the thing is...' he trailed off, his face losing all colour. He swayed a little and shook his head slightly. 'You'll have to excuse me. I'm not feeling well, this damn flu. I think I'll go lie down for a while.'

Alice came around the end of the kitchen bench and put her hand on his arm. 'You're not looking the best, Owen. Would you like me to call Janice?'

Janice was the retirement village's nurse. Her office was discretely located at the back of Alice's apartment building. Any visit to the nurse was usually fuel for the gossips tongues so tucking the office away allowed for private consultations to remain private.

'No, no,' Owen said. 'I'm absolutely fine apart from this damn flu. I just need to lie down for a while.'

'Is the reason for your visit urgent?' Alice asked

Owen's face closed down as he considered her question, then with a small frown he shook his head.

'Look, it's probably nothing at all.' He laughed. 'I guess it was just something nagging at me, and I knew you were up and had the best tea selection in the village. It's fine.' He waved a dismissive hand.

Alice helped him to his feet and they shuffled to the door, where she told him to wait. On a small round wooden table next to the door was a phone with direct lines to reception, the nurse, the kitchen, and counsellor. Apparently old people got depressed, according to Silvermoon management. Alice wasn't an advocate for telling other people your problems unless there was alcohol involved. That was a by-product of raising a child alone in the fifties and sixties. Her motto for most of her life was "just shut up and get on with it".

She punched the button for reception. It was answered instantly.

'Yes, Ms Atkinson?'

'Vanessa dear, get someone to help Owen back to his room will you? He's in my apartment.'

'Really?'

'That's enough sass from you or I'll tell your boyfriend about the looks you've been giving Craig from the gardening staff.'

Vanessa laughed. 'I'll be right up.'

Thirty seconds later there was a soft knock and Alice opened the door. Vanessa was in her early twenties, with long brown hair and green eyes that winked at Alice when she saw her hand on Owen's arm. Smartly dressed in a dark green uniform, her name tag read Vanessa Carson, with the rather grand title of Concierge underneath.

'Come on, Mr Struthers. Let's help you on your walk of shame.'

'Oh really,' Alice said indignantly, but her smile ruined it. She was fond of Vanessa.

'I do want to talk to you, Alice,' Owen said to her. 'How about we have dinner later if I'm feeling better?'

Alice did her best to ignore another Vanessa wink and nodded. 'Of course. Get in touch if you're feeling better.' She watched them walk to the elevator. Owen's apartment was in the second building, which loomed over the main one. Twice the length and with an extra floor, it was home to the majority of residents.

'Vanessa?' Alice called as they disappeared into the elevator.

Her head popped back into view. 'I'll let you know when he's back home safely.'

'Thanks, and –'

'I'll set up a Dora.'

Alice smiled as the elevator doors closed. Dora Simmonds was a resident who had lain sick in her apartment for two days, too dazed and confused to call anyone and, because her family lived out of the country, no one had checked on her. The facility operated a policy of discretion, leaving residents alone unless they asked. No one here needed full time care, so it generally worked. Except in Dora's case. When they finally found her she was dehydrated and starving but had fully recovered. Since then management had asked all residents to check in every two days, but some of the staff had a more informal system. If they knew someone wasn't feeling well they'd arrange to pop in on them at least twice a day. They called it 'a Dora', much to the real Dora's chagrin.

Alice made a mental note to leave a tip for Vanessa at the end of the week. Then, because her mental note system wasn't as reliable as it used to be, she wrote it on a piece of paper and pinned it to the fridge with a magnet. Her fridge was covered in souvenir magnets. The few people she allowed into her home assumed they were from places around the world that she had visited, and technically they were. Alice had travelled far and wide in her working life, and each magnet represented a place she had visited, and a job successfully completed. It had been an exciting life, and as she studied the different shapes and colours it occurred to her that what she really missed, was working.

She was too old to get back into it. She couldn't trust her body, and although she was still more with-it mentally than many people her age, she wasn't as sharp as she had been fifty years ago. One rule about the con game was always be the smartest person in the room (and if you aren't the smartest, then be the most cunning).

It was mid-January. The morning was mild and bright, so Alice decided to go for a walk. Vanessa was behind the front desk and they exchanged waves before Alice exited through the doors of the main building, otherwise sarcastically referred to by residents as Colonel Mustard due to its colour. She went down the stairs, and onto the driveway. Turning left would take her along the tree-lined drive to the front gate. Instead, she crossed to the paved path, turned right and followed its curved direction around Colonel Mustard. She nodded to two residents who were pulling weeds out of the community vegetable garden. Up ahead she spied Betty going through the door to the

Wellbeing Centre, which was a fancy name for a place designed to keep your head and body from decaying too quickly. Residents had named it the Olympic Complex. She called out, but her friend didn't acknowledge her as she disappeared inside. Alice didn't think anything of it. Half the people here had some form of hearing difficulty. But Alice thought Betty had looked worried.

She stopped outside the complex and peered through the large window. No one was in the small heated pool. Beyond that she could make out the back of a figure on one of the treadmills. It made no sense to her. They had to walk to get to a machine that walked for them. There was no sign of Betty, so maybe she was in the gaming room (the name of which had excited Alice when she'd first arrived, only to find that it was a room with cards and board games rather than casino activities).

Alice hesitated, unsure whether to continue her walk or go in search of her friend. It was Tuesday, wasn't it? Alice and Betty had a regular coffee date at 10am on Tuesdays. She would talk to Betty then.

Continuing on the path, she looped past Charlie's, the small café just for village residents, where she saw Teresa deep in conversation with a woman Alice didn't recognise.

She marched the length of Owen's building, which was officially called Rimu House, and unofficially nicknamed Stumpy, rounded the corner and ended up where she started. Pausing on the top step, she leaned against one of the concrete columns (which seemed to be there for no reason other than to say "hey look how pretentious this building is"). She listened to her breath rattling. At least it showed she was alive, she thought, even as the disquieting thought crept in that it didn't sound quite right.

She pulled her phone from her jersey pocket and went to dial Amanda's number. She stopped. Her granddaughter was working, which meant calls to her were in case of emergency only. A vague feeling that something, somewhere might not be alright didn't constitute an emergency. Alice shoved the phone back into her pocket and slunk inside, ignoring Vanessa's greeting as the elevator doors slid shut.

'I guess ignoring people is catching,' she mumbled to herself.

In her apartment she stripped off the extra layers, made herself another cup of tea, and checked her emails. Most of the people she knew were dead or lived in the village, so she didn't get many messages. Someone had emailed to warn her that her computer had been hacked and someone had videos of her watching pornography which was quite amusing; someone else wanted to give her millions of dollars in gold, which made her want to respond to say if she wanted gold she'd steal it.. Mostly Alice used the email account as an alternative way to keep in touch with Amanda, but there was nothing from her. After her daughter Carol passed away, Alice took Amanda in and raised her to be smart, cunning, and independent. There was never any need to worry when Amanda was working. Which is why Alice only worried a little bit.

A few minutes before ten Alice walked down to Charlie's. The day had warmed up since her early morning walk and she stopped on the path to remove her jersey before arriving just in time to see Betty approaching from the other direction.

'Morning, Alice,' Betty said with a smile.

'It certainly is,' Alice replied with a grin, which turned into a laugh when Betty rolled her eyes.

Betty wore jeans and an apricot-coloured jersey. Her battered brown bag was slung over one shoulder.

Charlie's was small, comfortable and, most importantly, warm and quiet. A while back, when Alice had gone into Wellington city to meet Amanda, she'd found the cafes too noisy for conversation. Luckily Amanda knew of a quiet out of the way place where the only noise was their voices and the occasional hiss of a coffee machine. Here there was a gentle buzz of voices without any fighting for dominance. Three of the six tables were occupied, two by complex staff, and the other by Les and Freda, a couple Alice knew had been married for fifty years. As she watched, while Les was focused on topping up his cup from the teapot, his wife casually reached up and switched off her hearing aid. When Les looked back and resumed his discourse on the problem with society his wife nodded as if agreeing with everything.

At the counter Betty surprised her by saying, 'Order what you like Alice, my shout.'

Alice was about to respond that it was her turn to buy, but she paused when she saw how intently Betty was studying the selection of scones. Normally Betty was strict with schedules, whose turn it was to do things, what time to show up, what to bring. They had met for a coffee every Tuesday for eight months, always alternating who paid. This was the first time Betty had muddled up the order. For a moment Alice wondered if she herself had mistaken whose turn it was to pay, but she distinctly remembered Betty paying for her savoury scone and herbal tea exactly one week ago.

Determined to find out what had caused the lapse in routine, Alice told the man behind the counter her order, then sat down at one of the empty tables.

'I suppose you're wondering why I'm paying two weeks in a row,' Betty said when she joined Alice.

Alice nodded. That she realised the change was a good sign. Betty wasn't cracking up.

'There's no problem I promise you.'

'You looked a little worried this morning,' Alice replied.

'I didn't see you this morning.'

'I was out for a walk and I saw you go into the Olympic complex. You seemed preoccupied.'

Betty waved her hand. 'Ah I see. I was going for a workout with Peter and he told me last time he was going to try a new exercise with me. I guess I was nervous about it. I'm not used to exercise that doesn't involve moving livestock.'

Their scones arrived and they both smiled. Alice had chosen a cheese one with a small dollop of butter on the side, while Betty had gone for the more adventurous date and herb scone. The café had a suggestion box on the counter and every week they made one of the combinations suggested by residents. There had been some very interesting results, not all of them successful. Alice wasn't convinced about date and herb.

While they cut and buttered and sampled tiny bites, Alice considered why her friend was lying to her.

THREE

There might be another explanation of course, but a career of dealing with liars and thieves made Alice assume that everyone was lying until proven otherwise. She knew for a fact that Peter wasn't working that day. She'd run into him the previous evening and he'd mentioned he was taking Tuesday off to get a spray tan. Peter had been training for a body building competition and apparently getting his skin painted deep brown was part of the preparation process. Alice had never been a fan of artificial colouring, but she had to admit his muscles looked pretty good, even if she had to suppress a surprising urge to tell him to put some clothes on every time she saw him striding around the complex in shorts and a singlet.

She realised her thoughts were wandering and reigned them in while sipping the milky foam off the top of her drink. Betty had quickly moved on to talking about how Gordon had behaved in the dining room the night before. Alice nodded to show she was listening, which she wasn't.

Maybe it was nothing. Maybe Betty was secretly meeting a man (or a woman which, thanks to her granddaughter, didn't shock her as much as it may once have done). Maybe her friend was simply confused and her own mind was too used to nefarious explanations for simple behaviour. She smiled ruefully and tried to focus on the conversation.

'…honestly don't know why he bothers. We've all said no to him at one time or another. He reminds me of this ram we once had on the farm. He wouldn't leave the ewes alone. Would always find a way through the fence and start harassing them.'

'What did you do?' Alice asked.

'Took away his reason for visiting,' Betty replied, using her fingers to mimic scissors.

Alice shuddered. The closest she'd ever been to farm life was once staying at a bed and breakfast where the owners had three chickens and a pet goat. She preferred animals that were small and self-sufficient. Silvermoon had a resident cat that was constantly scamming food from the residents. Alice had once watched the little brown and white cat gobble up a bowl of food she'd left out for it, then walk straight to another door and meow pitifully until a second bowl was produced.

The staff called her Maddy.

Alice called her a hustler. She approved.

'…don't know what they are going to do about Gordon. Honestly, I've complained to management twice about him and they don't do anything.'

Alice looked at her friend, thinking it was ironic she'd used the word honestly twice while Alice believed she was lying about something.

'Did you know Owen is sick?' Alice said in the brief silence, while Betty sipped her drink.

'How sick?'

Alice smiled at her sharp tone.

Betty caught her expression and screwed up her face. 'I'm just concerned,' she grumbled. 'The same way I'd be worried if you were sick.'

'Not quite the same way.'

Betty shuffled in her chair and picked at the remains of her scone. 'Maybe not exactly the same.'

Alice nodded. Those words confirmed one thing and ruled out another. Betty wasn't the sort to cheat on someone so whatever she was lying about didn't have anything to do with a man.

'Perhaps I should check in on him,' Betty glanced at her watch.

'I'm sure he'll be alright, Betty. I spoke to Vanessa this morning. There's a Dora in place.'

Her friend's face betrayed her conflict and she picked up and put down her bag several times.

'Oh for goodness sake. Just go.'

Betty's face relaxed in relief and she was out of her seat in an instant as if afraid her friend would rescind the offer.

'I'll see you later, Alice.'

'Remember the big game tomorrow,' Alice called as Betty hustled out.

Unlike their more intimate game, the annual Silvermoon Village Poker Tournament was played for prestige rather than wealth. For Alice, it wasn't about the shiny trophy the winner got to flaunt for a year. Nor was it about the side bets that occurred between residents. For Alice, it was purely bragging rights, and a clear sign that she could still outthink and outwit a bunch of retired office workers and housewives. She had won the tournament for the past two years and knew there were some murmurings amongst the other competitors that she should be banned from future events. She had heard that several had looked her up on the internet, convinced she used to be a professional gambler. The thought had her grinning into her coffee.

'You look pleased with yourself, Alice,' Les called out.

'Leave her be,' his wife scolded.

'You haven't won that trophy yet you know,' Les said with a stern expression on his face. 'I've been practicing every day for the last month and I'm feeling confident.'

'Care to make it interesting?' Alice replied.

'No, he wouldn't,' Freda said before he could open his mouth.

Alice left the remains of her scone on the table and the bickering voices in her ears as she walked outside. Les was a good man, a little too self-important, and that was why he would never win the trophy.

25

He always adopted a smug expression whenever he had a good hand, and his eyes darted to wherever his wife was sitting in the room when he was bluffing.

The warm sun on her face and ceaseless cheerfulness of the bird-filled trees around her convinced Alice that she might have been mistaken about Betty lying to her. She took the long way back to her apartment, and by the time she walked through her front door she had almost forgotten it.

Almost.

Which was a mistake.

FOUR

On Wednesday, the poker tournament started at exactly 10am in the communal room. This year there were twenty players vying for the title, with an equal number of spectators. The players were split into four tables of five. Each table would play until a single player had won all the chips. Then the top players would assemble at one table to decide the overall winner. It was usually over by lunchtime, when the trophy was officially awarded to the winner by Tracey Miller, the manager of the complex. After which, Silvermoon put on a light lunch of sandwiches and cakes for everyone.

As they were milling around waiting to start, Vanessa sidled up next to Alice.

'Owen is feeling better.'

'I see that, dear.'

Owen was standing in a small cluster of people on the other side of the room. He still looked a little pale, but appeared much better than the previous day. Betty was glued to his side, ready to offer a steadying hand if needed.

'Of course you do,' Vanessa said, her eyes conveying the laughter she was suppressing. 'He was a bit brighter yesterday at dinner time. I don't think Betty has left his side since yesterday morning, so a Dora wasn't really necessary.' This time she did laugh, and dropped a wink in for good measure.

Alice snorted. 'Really, Vanessa. You ought to worry more about your own sex life and less about other peoples.'

'Unfortunately mine is on hold. Ben is away for a couple of weeks on some work thing, so it's just me and the roommate at home eating ice cream and binging on Netflix.'

'What's a Netflix?'

'You don't know about Netflix? Oh Alice, you should get it. It's amazing.'

A small bell rang to signal that the players should to go to their tables. Alice sat down opposite Les, who's face suggested he wasn't as confident as he'd stated the day before. On his left was a retired army general by the name of Gavin. They'd tried calling him General Gavin but the first stern look from him put paid to that. To his right was Sofia, a retired dance teacher whose body vibrated with excitement at everything, as if the very act of being alive charged her with electricity.

The fifth player took her seat and Alice thought it was good that she was already in poker mode, otherwise her surprise might have shown. She didn't know this woman, although she had seen her the day before with Teresa at Charlie's.

'Nanci Katz,' the woman smiled and shoved her hand out.

'Alice,' she replied, briefly but firmly shaking the offered hand.

She studied the newcomer while Nanci introduced herself to the others at the table. She was young, in her early seventies, with light coloured hair. There was a bit of padding to her face now, but Alice could see the beauty that would have had men drooling a few decades earlier.

A new player certainly made life interesting from a poker perspective, but it also raised some questions. And it changed Alice's game strategy. Her original plan had been to win as much as possible early on so she could take a break and watch the other tables. However now she would have to be more cautious, at least until she understood how Nanci played.

'...moved in?' Les was asking.

'No, I'm here for a week teaching sculpting classes to the residents and Tracey graciously said I could sit in and play. Not that I really know what I'm doing I'm afraid, solitaire is the limit of my card experience.'

Alice smiled. In her experience anyone who proclaimed a lack of knowledge on a subject was either exaggerating or outright lying. The obvious explanation of course was that Nanci genuinely didn't know anything about poker, but Alice hadn't often dealt with those types of people through the years. Honest people.

Regardless, the first few hands would tell her everything she needed to know.

She suddenly realised everyone at the table had gone quiet and were looking at her. 'Sorry, what?'

'I asked how you got so good at poker?' Nanci repeated.

'How do you know I'm good?'

'Pretty hard to miss it.' Nanci gestured to the plaque hanging on the wall next to the door, clearly showing Alice's name in the list of tournament winners.

'Of course,' Alice smiled, inwardly cursing herself. She preferred being the one pointing out the obvious, not the other way around. 'Well, I've had a slightly longer life than most of you, it gives me an advantage in some areas.'

'Life experience gives us everything, am I right?' Nanci looked at the others around the table and they all nodded enthusiastically.

Like getting up five times a night to pee, Alice thought.

Vanessa sat down in the remaining chair. Alice exchanged a smile with her before looking around to see Silvermoon staff taking their places at the other tables. Officially they were there to make sure the game ran smoothly. Unofficially, Vanessa had confided, they were supposed to stamp out the more obvious cheating.

Each player had an identical pile of chips in front of them. Yellow were worth one dollar, blue two dollars, red five dollars, and the black chips were ten dollars. Vanessa unwrapped a deck of cards and shuffled them with practised ease.

'You're getting quite good at that,' Gavin commented.

'Thank you, Gavin,' she replied. Her mouth twitched and Alice wondered if she was remembering their secret sessions where Alice had taught her tricks to impress her friends and win rent money.

Alice was of the opinion that every young woman needed a skill they could pull out of their back pocket, one that might come in handy in unforeseen circumstances.

Vanessa dealt the first hand and all other thoughts were pushed aside as Alice focussed on the game. She folded and sat back to watch what the others did. Les pushed forward two blue chips, then his eyes turned to where Freda was sitting in a chair under the window, her head in a book. Alice had already noted her location before they started. Les, for all his practicing, was a creature of habit. And he was bluffing. Sure enough when he finally showed his cards all he had was a pair of twos.

As the game progressed, Alice was pleased to see that the other players still had the same tells as well. The only one she was having trouble reading was Nanci. The woman lost as much as she won, and she didn't seem to have any obvious gestures or ticks that showed.

In no time at all Gavin was throwing his cards down and pushing his chair away from the table.

'Well done, all. A very enjoyable way to spend the morning.' He nodded briskly then walked, straight backed, over to the refreshments table to make himself a hot drink.

By the time Sofia bowed out ten minutes later, Alice had concluded that Nanci was as she appeared: a novice at poker. Nanci soon joined the others on the sideline and it was just Alice and Les left at the table. Alice's pile of chips was much bigger than Les's and he had taken to mopping his forehead with a large blue handkerchief.

Forty minutes after they started it was all over. Les pushed all his chips into the middle of the table and snuck a furtive look at his wife. Alice decided not to fold after all, and won the hand, and the table, with a pair of fours.

Les tried his best to hide his disappointment, and for the first time Alice felt a twinge of guilt.

It's not like I'm taking his money, she argued with herself.

'Well done again, Alice,' Les said.

'Thanks. I guess the coffees are on me at the café tomorrow, Les.'

His expression brightened at the mention of a free drink, and when she glanced over to him later he was cheerfully recounting his game to an increasingly bored-looking Freda.

'Normal programming then,' Vanessa said from across the table.

'Eh?'

'You winning. As expected.'

'I don't know about expected,' Alice replied, 'but it certainly beats the alternative.'

Vanessa grinned, then went in search of a drink. Alice knew she would be back to serve as dealer for the final game. She stood up slowly, her back stiff from sitting for so long. Her first few steps were tottering, but once blood started to flow everything eased and she moved more freely. She stopped by the refreshment table for a handful of chips, briefly eyeing up the cheese before dismissing it. Dairy products were problematic these days, and she only braved her beloved camembert on very special occasions.

Only one table was still playing. It was down to Teresa and Lawrence, a short man with an equally short temper. Alice had been glad not to have him at her table. Last year when he lost, he'd swept the chips off the table and stomped out of the room, refusing to speak to anyone for several days.

Teresa lay down her cards, revealing a full house of queens and tens. Everyone held their breath and looked to Lawrence. He shrugged, offered his hand in congratulations, and wandered off.

'I hear he's been told by his doctor that his blood pressure is so high he won't see another Christmas if he doesn't keep his temper in check,' Betty said.

Alice looked at her friend. 'It's not like you to gossip.'

'It's not gossip if it's true,' Betty replied.

Alice was about to argue the point when she spotted something curious. At least to her. Teresa had stood up from the table and was walking around the room, smiling, looking around her a little too much to be normal. Finally she stood next to Nanci. Teresa spoke to her briefly and a few seconds later both women disappeared through the door to the hallway.

'What are you looking at?'

'I'm not sure,' Alice admitted. 'But I have a feeling something is going on.'

'What?'

Alice frowned. 'I can't be sure. I'm suspicious by nature and I have a thought.'

'Thinking at our age is dangerous,' Betty laughed, slipping her arm through Alice's.

'It keeps me young,' Alice smiled.

'And being suspicious?'

'Kept me out of jail a few times.'

Betty's smile faltered, as if unsure whether Alice was being serious. Then she laughed and Alice joined her.

A bell rang indicating the start of the final round. Four players took their seats, but Teresa hadn't come back. Vanessa sat down and behind her, Tracey looked at her watch and tapped her foot. Alice had always found the woman a little officious. Tracey liked everything to run on time, which didn't work when you were dealing with children, animals, or stubborn old people.

As Tracey opened her mouth to speak, Alice reached out for her drink, accidentally sweeping her pile of chips onto the floor.

'Oh my goodness, I am so sorry,' Alice said to the table.

'Oh for–' Tracey stifled the rest of her sentence. She gestured for Vanessa to help pick up the mess.

'Oh my goodness?' Vanessa muttered as she knelt next to Alice's chair and began to collect the coloured chips.

'I refuse to win by default,' Alice whispered back.

'Oh my goodness, no,' Vanessa winked. She placed the chips back on the table and Alice had them sorted into piles by the time Vanessa had retaken her seat.

Luckily, before Tracey said anything further, Teresa came back through the door and took her seat.

'I'm so sorry. I was in the bathroom,' Teresa said, an excuse that shut down any potential comments about tardiness by anyone.

'Let's begin,' Tracey said, tapping Vanessa on the shoulder.

It didn't take long for Alice to realise that there was a new level of skill in her friend's poker playing that hadn't been there the week before. Teresa won three of the first four hands, once by bluffing, which Alice had not picked up on.

With renewed concentration Alice focused on the game.

And lost, badly.

Judging by the complete silence in the room, she wasn't the only one shocked by this result. Vanessa's mouth looked like she was readying to swallow an entire watermelon. Betty's face showed a similar reaction, and Owen's eyebrows were trying to meet his receding hairline. Amongst the shocked faces were the smiles of those Alice had beaten, this year and previously. Les's smile was the widest.

'Congratulations, Teresa,' Alice said.

'Thanks, Alice.' Teresa couldn't hide her delight, but she could barely meet Alice's eyes.

'That was the best I've ever seen you play,' Owen told Teresa, and Alice was pleased that *she* hadn't said it, though they were all thinking it. She didn't want to come across as bitter and she really was happy for Teresa. But her gut and Teresa's flushed cheeks suggested there was definitely something up.

'Ladies and gentlemen, if I could have some quiet?' Tracey said in a loud voice. She was holding the small trophy the winners got to keep.

After the brief presentation some people returned to their rooms, while others made their way to the refreshments table.

'Better luck next year,' Gavin said as he filled a coffee cup.

'I guarantee things will be different next year,' Alice replied. She was determined to learn the source of Teresa's sudden poker skills and she had a feeling it had something to do with Nanci.

A crashing sound startled her. Turning, she saw Betty slumped over a table, not moving.

'Betty!' Owen rushed from across the room. Alice hustled over as he attempted to lift Betty into a chair, but she slipped from his grip and fell back down.

'Betty? Are you alright?' Alice said, bending over to look at her face.

Betty's eyes stared back, unseeing. For a moment Alice hoped that it was just a fall, but when she pressed her fingers onto Betty's wrist in search of a pulse she couldn't find it.

Betty was gone.

FIVE

Death was a shock. Even in a place where the average age of the residents was in the high seventies. But it wasn't unheard of, and it didn't take long for the standard protocols of the Silvermoon Retirement Village to spring into action. The first step was to usher everyone out of the room, which they did successfully. Almost. Alice refused to leave her friend, and when Owen heard she was staying he insisted on staying as well. Teresa made a half-hearted protest too, but her face was pale and it didn't take much persuasion for her to go and have a lie down. Alice promised to pop by her apartment later to check on her.

Soon they were the only people left in the room apart from Tracey and Vanessa, who was on the phone arranging for an ambulance. Alice had always considered ambulances for the living, but the cynical side of her saw the reason behind the summons. No one wants to be the one to pronounce the death of a person. Or more importantly, to get it wrong. However in this case Alice was quite certain Betty was gone. She hadn't moved an inch and her eyes still had the same lifeless stare.

'I really think it would be best for the two of you to wait somewhere else until we can get this…' Tracey trailed off.

'Sorted?' Alice completed her sentence. 'This is Betty. My friend. She is not something to get sorted. You understand?'

Tracey's cheeks reddened. 'I was merely suggesting, for your sake–

'

'I'm staying. We're staying.' Alice turned to Owen who was sitting in a chair next to Betty holding her hand.

'It's funny, really. I was very fond of her, and was going to tell her. One day. Oh, who am I kidding? I was married for fifty years and I still get tongue tied when it comes to talking about my feelings.'

'Which is why your wife was a saint,' Alice replied.

Owen smiled ruefully. 'Most likely. I shall miss her.' He looked down at the hand he was holding and Alice followed his eyes.

She frowned. There was something about Betty's fingernails that didn't seem quite right. She bent down to take a closer look. Her fingernails had white lines across them. It triggered a memory somewhere in the back of Alice's mind, but she couldn't pin it down.

A hand touched her shoulder. 'The ambulance will be here shortly, Alice. I need to go and find her file so Tracey can let her next of kin know.' Vanessa squatted next to her. 'Do you need anything?'

Alice started to shake her head, then glanced across to Owen who was staring into nothingness. 'I think a situation like this calls for more than tea, don't you?'

'You know alcohol isn't allowed in the common areas.'

'Exceptional circumstances. Stop by my place on the way back. In the kitchen cabinet above the oven is a small silver flask.'

Vanessa nodded. 'Be back as soon as I can.' She gave Alice's arm a quick squeeze then headed out of the room.

Alice was turning her attention back to Betty's fingernails when Tracey blurted, 'I'm sorry about the loss of your friend.'

Privately Alice thought she should have said this earlier, but outwardly she nodded her thanks.

The door swung open and a stern young woman strode in. She looked in her early thirties, with short black hair, and was dressed in tight fitting jeans and a dark blue T-shirt.

'Judith? What are you doing here?'

Judith's eyes seemed to dart around the room, as if taking a series of mental pictures.

'We were supposed to meet for coffee when the tournament finished, remember? What's going on here, Aunt Tracey?'

'This poor woman has passed away.'

The way Judith's expression changed made Alice wonder about the sudden interest. She picked her way through the gaps between the tables and stopped next to her aunt.

'Suspicious?'

Tracey snorted. 'Judith, there are never suspicious deaths here. Few places have a higher death rate than retirement villages. It's the nature of the business. No offence,' she added, looking at Alice and Owen.

'That's why I came here,' Alice said, earning her a puzzled expression from Tracey before understanding dawned and she looked away in embarrassment.

'Mmm,' Judith replied. 'Judith Miller, detective, Wellington police.'

'Alice Atkinson, retired, Silvermoon Retirement Village.'

Judith's mouth twitched at the edges. 'Sorry, the detective thing is new. I'm still trying it on for size.'

'Congratulations,' Alice said. 'It seems to fit reasonably well.'

Another twitch of the mouth. 'If you don't mind me saying you seem to be taking this woman's death well.'

'Her name is Betty,' Owen said.

'I'm almost a century old,' Alice replied. 'You don't get this far without burying a lot of loved ones. You tend to become… pragmatic about death.'

'Alice!' Owen looked shocked.

She patted him on the arm. 'Of course I'm going to miss her.'

Judith seemed about to say something, but stopped herself, shifting her look between Owen and Tracey.

Vanessa returned, holding a folder. 'I've got the contact information for you.' She handed a slip of paper to Tracey, carefully filling the space between her and Alice. Sliding a small object out of her pants pocket, Vanessa held it behind her. Alice took the flask in her lap and covered it with both hands.

'Thank you, Vanessa. I'll need to go make some calls. Judith, would you mind waiting here? I won't be long.'

Judith waved a hand and sat down in a chair at the adjoining table. Tracey pulled her phone out and began dialling as she left the room.

'Vanessa, why don't you open a window,' Alice suggested. 'It's a little warm in here. Owen, would you mind giving her a hand? You know how the latches stick, I'm sure she could use a man's assistance.'

Owen seemed about to refuse, but chivalry overcame reluctance and he gently placed Betty's hand on the table and stood up.

Alice quickly poured a few drops from the flask into Owen's tea while everyone was distracted. Then she turned to Judith. 'Go on.'

'Eh?'

'You want to practice by looking at this as a crime scene. So go ahead.'

'How did you know?'

'I may not know how to post something on that Faces book, but I know people.'

'You don't mind? It's your friend.'

'Yes, she's my friend, but unless you're planning to autopsy her on the poker table, a close inspection isn't going to hurt.'

Judith jumped up from her seat and bent over Betty's body, clasping her hands behind her back as if the act of being near a recently deceased person would prove too much temptation and she was afraid she would poke and prod. Her stance reminded Alice of a chicken bending forward to peck at the ground.

'Deceased seems to be in her early seventies, approximately fifty kilograms,' Judith murmured. 'No medical bracelets indicating any known conditions. Did she…?' Judith turned her head to look at Alice.

'She'd spent her working life on the farm so she'd led a healthier life than most of us. She had some blood pressure problems, but that was it as far as I know.'

'And she fell?'

Alice frowned as she tried to recall everything that happened before Betty died. 'I think so. I had my back to her and heard a sudden bang, but before that she seemed fine.'

Judith nodded and resumed her inspection. Finally she stretched up tall. 'I'm sorry for your loss.'

'Thank you. You don't think it's suspicious then?'

A troubled look came across Judith's face, as if she wasn't sure whether she was being mocked. Alice made sure to keep her expression neutral.

'Difficult to tell without an autopsy, which is unlikely in these circumstances, but there's no outward sign of trauma so I think it's safe to say she died of natural causes.' Judith gave a little smile. 'Sorry, that sounds really officious.'

'Is speaking like that part of your training?'

'Actually, yes it is.'

'What are you two talking about?' Owen asked as he rejoined them.

'Just filling in time,' Alice replied, wishing he'd given them ten more seconds. She couldn't ask a police detective to look at Betty's fingernails now without awkward questions or upsetting Owen.

Soon the room got very busy.

First Tracey came back in, almost immediately followed by two ambulance staff. Then Owen insisted on accompanying them to wherever it was they took the recently deceased, and finally Tracey began quietly berating Judith for being disrespectful and treating Betty's death as a training exercise. For a moment everyone forgot about Alice. Sometimes she found if she sat still she became almost invisible, which was on occasion very useful.

She beckoned Vanessa over. 'Do you have your phone?' she whispered.

'Sure,' Vanessa replied in matching volume.

'Can you take a picture of Betty's fingernails.'

It was obvious by her face that Vanessa had questions, but rather than ask them she pulled out her phone, then looked at all the people crowding the body.

'Leave it to me,' Alice said. She stood up and took a few paces over to the adjoining table.

'Oh dear,' she said loudly, slumping into a chair. Everyone ignored her. 'OH DEAR,' she shouted.

Heads turned and conversations paused and suddenly she was the centre of attention.

'It's all too much. Another friend gone,' she wailed.

Tracey and Owen immediately stepped towards her.

'When will it all end?' Alice continued. 'Why must they be taken before their time?'

'Before their time?' Tracey repeated.

Now everyone was shuffling towards Alice, the ambulance staff looking a lot more excited about a *living* patient.

'Are you alright, Alice?' Owen's face was filled with concern and she felt guilty.

Behind everyone she saw Vanessa give a thumbs up.

'I'm fine. Just silly.' She sat up straight. 'It just became too much for a moment. I think I'd better go and lie down.'

'Of course,' Tracey said. 'Vanessa, will you escort Alice back to her apartment please.'

'Yes, Tracey. Come on, Alice.' Vanessa helped Alice to her feet. They were in the elevator before Alice let go of her arm.

'Are you going to tell me what's going on?' Vanessa asked.

'Do you know how to google?'

Vanessa grinned. 'Alice, I'm a millennial. You might as well ask me if I know how to breathe.'

'Good, because Betty didn't die of natural causes.'

'What?'

'She was poisoned.'

SIX

'What do you mean she was poisoned?'

They were sitting on the couch in Alice's apartment.

'Show me the picture of her fingernails.'

Vanessa pulled her phone out and tapped and swiped until a picture filled the screen.

'See those lines?' Alice said pointing to them.

'Oh yeah, that doesn't look right.'

'I don't think it is right. I've got this vague memory of lines like that but I can't recall exactly. Can you look up the possible causes of those lines on the google?'

On her phone, Vanessa brought up a search box. She typed in 'lines on fingernails' and selected the first item. They both scanned the article.

'It says here that slight vertical ridges commonly develop in older adults,' Vanessa said.

'That's the opening sentence, Vanessa. Read faster. It also says deep horizontal ridges may indicate a serious condition.'

'Health condition, not poison. You can't really believe Betty was poisoned.'

'I'm not sure what to think,' she admitted. 'But what if Betty's death *was* murder. No one is going to look into it. Everyone is convinced that it's just a case of another old person dying.'

'Murder?! Alice, that's crazy. Why would anyone want to murder Betty?'

Alice looked out the window at the leaves on the trees swaying a little in the breeze. It made them seem alive. 'I don't know.'

'Exactly.'

'But I'd be the first to admit I don't know everything. It couldn't hurt to ask a few questions.' She turned back to Vanessa. 'You said yourself, not much is going on at home, so you can help me.'

Vanessa dropped her gaze to her hands, turning her phone over and over. 'You don't think this has anything to do with...'

'With what?'

'Well, you've seemed a little bored lately, since you helped that writer out. Sort of... restless. Twitchy. You don't think you might be looking for things that aren't there? Just to do something exciting?' She looked at Alice, sadness and embarrassment mixing on her face.

Alice bit off the retort that sprang to her lips. Vanessa was right, she was bored.

But that wasn't it.

She patted Vanessa on the leg. 'You could be right. Maybe this whole thing will be a complete waste of time. So let's pretend it's a game, just between you and I. Humour me.'

Alice could tell Vanessa still wasn't convinced but she nodded. 'Where do we start?'

'We need to talk to everyone that was in the room and build up a picture of what Betty was doing just before she died.'

'Okay, I think I remember most of the people.'

'Why don't you go back to work. Tracey might be looking for you. Write down a list of everyone, and let's meet back here at the end of your shift. I'll shout for pizza.'

'I thought pizza gave you gas?'

'Honey, everything gives me gas these days.'

'TMI,' Vanessa leapt up and headed for the door.

'One more thing.' Alice waited for Vanessa to turn before continuing. 'There's a difference between humouring me and patronising me. Understand?' She realised the words would sound harsh so she tried to keep her tone light.

Vanessa's face flushed and she shrugged. 'Fair enough. See you soon.' This time she made it all the way to the door before she paused. 'Alice? Are you okay? About Betty.'

'I was fond of her and I shall miss her quite a lot, once I've had a chance to think about it. So let's delay that for a while, shall we?'

Vanessa nodded and disappeared through the door.

Alice got to her feet and went into the kitchen. She opened the cupboard next to the fridge and shifted a canister of flour. Tucked away in the back corner was a second silver hip flask.

She unscrewed the lid and sniffed the whiskey inside. Technically she wasn't supposed to be drinking with all the medication her doctor made her take. But if ever there was a time to break that rule it was now. Alice took a swig, swirling the liquid in her mouth, letting it kick all her taste buds into live before swallowing.

Her lips trembled slightly and she felt the corners of her eyes moisten. Alice took another drink. At least she could blame the alcohol for this uncharacteristic display of emotion.

Maybe this was more about her than Betty. She hoped that she was wrong, that Betty's death was natural. But she owed it to her friend to find out the truth. And if Betty's death wasn't natural, then someone was going to be in a lot of trouble.

SEVEN

The trouble with secret investigations was that you were prevented from asking a lot of the more obvious questions. Like, "did you know anyone who wanted Betty dead?"

Luckily Alice had spent a lifetime perfecting the skill of getting information out of people without them realising it. It was very useful, especially in the age of computers, where stealing passwords was often required before you could steal anything else (though Alice was mostly retired by the time computers really took off). However before she could ask any questions about Betty's death, Alice needed to ask one very important one. Which was why she was knocking on Owen's door.

He took a long time to open it and when he did his eyes were red and puffy. 'Hi Alice. Come in, please.'

He turned and she followed, closing the door behind her. His apartment was a smaller, although no less plush, version of hers. The biggest difference between the two were the mementos of his life scattered around the place. Framed pictures of family highlighting the passage of time, little knickknacks dotted along the windowsill and in the corner of the kitchen bench, and a truly hideous woollen rug underneath the coffee table. Alice had never been a knickknack type of person, she never saw the point, it was just another thing to dust or pack when you moved.

'Would you like a cup of tea?' Owen asked her.

She was about to say no, then thought it might be good for him to be busy so changed her mind. 'Yes please, but only if you'll have one too.'

He nodded absently and walked into the kitchen to switch the kettle on.

'How are you, Owen?' she asked as he busied himself with cups and milk and teaspoons.

'In a bit of shock, really. You know, I moved here when my wife died. We'd been married for fifty years and I didn't take her death terribly well. It was my children who suggested, insisted really, that I move in here. I think they wanted me to be around other people all the time so I didn't do anything silly.'

'Silly?' Alice asked.

'Oh, nothing permanent,' he shook his head. 'But you hear about it all the time, don't you? Married couples who have been together for so long, when one goes the other gives up. Not my sort of thing of course. I miss Karen very much, but life is like a job, you can't quit halfway through just because things get a little rocky.'

Alice nodded.

'Then I met Betty, and I grew fond of her, and I felt a little…'

'Guilty?'

Owen gave her a smile tinged with sadness. 'Yes, I suppose so. Anyway I think Betty felt the same, we hadn't really discussed it.'

'You mean you hadn't discussed it at all.'

'Well, no. You see it's been over half a century since I told a woman I was fond of her. I'm a bit out of practice.' He paused and straightened his tie a little before pouring the tea. 'Funny, really. I spent a lifetime working in offices, first hating the bosses, then admiring them, then copying them, and finally becoming them. I learned when to speak and when to listen and as a result I did fairly well for myself.'

Alice knew he was being modest. When he retired he had been the most successful CEO in the history of the bank, taking them to record profits and being universally admired.

'But talking to women in matters of the heart has always eluded me.' He smiled. 'Sounds a bit old fashioned doesn't it?'

'I hate to tell you this, Owen, but you're not exactly young anymore.'

'You can talk,' he shot back.

'A useful skill I've found,' she smiled back at him.

'Touché.' He handed her a cup of tea. 'Now be quiet and drink your tea.'

'Actually I wanted to ask you something. I was wondering if Betty had said anything to you about feeling unwell lately.'

Owen frowned and shook his head. 'No, but then she was the sort that didn't talk about her aches and pains. Remember last year with her ribs?'

She remembered well. Betty had cracked two of her ribs during a severe coughing fit, and lived with the pain for a week before going to the nurse. Not once had she complained and no one had noticed anything.

'I just wish she would have said something if she had been feeling ill. I wish I'd paid more attention to her today instead of worrying about poker.'

Owen patted the back of her hand. 'Don't you blame yourself. I spoke to her several times during the tournament and she looked and sounded fine. In fact she'd just made a friendly wager on you winning the whole thing.'

'Who did she make it with?' Alice asked.

'That new woman. What's her name now? Nanci?'

It was Alice's turn to frown. 'Who was Nanci betting on?'

'Teresa. Betty felt bad taking the bet, but not that bad, it was only for a hundred dollars, and she told me afterwards that anyone who bet on Teresa over you deserved to learn the hard way what a bad idea that was.'

Alice blew on her tea and took a sip, thinking. This woman's name kept popping up. Alice was beginning to have an inkling of how Teresa might have won the poker tournament, but to confirm it she would need to talk to both Teresa and Nanci. Besides, that had nothing to do with Betty's death.

'How are you feeling?' she asked.

'You already asked that,' Owen replied.

'I did? I mean physically. You weren't feeling well yesterday.'

He scratched his temple then shrugged. 'I feel fine. It must have been a 24 hour thing.'

'Good. At our age 24 hour things have a habit of developing into 24 day things, so I'm glad you're feeling better. Do you mind me asking what you wanted to talk to me about yesterday?'

Owen frowned and played with the knot of his tie. 'It doesn't really matter now.'

'Was it about Betty?' Alice guessed.

'Yes it was, but probably not how you think.'

Alice considered. If you dismissed matters of the heart then the next likely option was obvious. 'Money?'

'I did want your opinion on something, without going into the specifics, but now Betty has passed, circumstances have changed and I don't want to break confidences.'

Alice considered pressing the matter. If Betty had money problems it might point to a motive for her murder. She wasn't quite sure how but anything out of the ordinary might be relevant. She looked at the conflict on Owen's face and decided now wasn't the time.

'Of course. I completely understand.'

Owen's shoulders slumped a little and he let out a soft sigh. 'Do you think they'll tell us when they get hold of her children?'

'I'm sure they will. I would imagine Silvermoon will want to do some sort of memorial service here. And if they don't then we'll organise it ourselves.'

Owen was nodding. 'Yes good idea. Perhaps I should…'

'Why don't you leave it for today, Owen. Perhaps tomorrow you could start organising things. I'm sure Tracey would be more than happy for you to take the lead on this.'

He nodded again and Alice left him rummaging through a kitchen draw looking for a pad and pen.

Alice was halfway back to her place when Vanessa appeared from around a corner.

'Tracey gave me the rest of the day away from the front desk.'

'How did you arrange that?' Alice asked.

'I'm not sure I want to tell you,' Vanessa said, falling into step next to Alice.

Alice glanced at her. 'And yet I can tell you're dying to.'

'I may have told her I was worried about how you were taking Betty's death,' she grinned.

'Nice,' Alice replied.

'You don't sound surprised,' Vanessa said, disappointment obvious in her voice.

'It was the logical thing to say. Tracey would never have let you off work if you said you were upset by a resident's death, so it had to be one of us, and since you're helping me out it makes sense you used my name.'

She looked at Vanessa and added, 'but keep trying, one day you'll surprise me.'

'So where are we going, boss?'

'Back to my place. It's a bit early for pizza, but we can work on the list of who was in the room when Betty died. And for goodness sake can you slow down? These legs have seen a few more years than yours.'

Vanessa slowed and muttered an apology. Alice linked her arm with Vanessa's and they walked at a more leisurely pace back to her apartment.

'Let's see what our collective memories can recall,' Alice said once they were sitting on her couch. 'Here.' She held out a small pad and pencil, but Vanessa pulled her phone out instead.

'I can type faster than I can write,' she explained. 'Besides a tree died for that pad.'

'Well, it's already dead,' Alice waved the pad but Vanessa shook her head.

'What happens if I lose the paper?'

'What happens if you lose your phone?' Alice shot back.

Vanessa's face showed such genuine horror that Alice felt an urge to apologise and reassure her she was just joking.

'Alright, let's see. There was Gavin, Sofia, and Les at my table.' She paused as Vanessa's fingers sprinted across the screen of her phone. 'Then there—'

A knock at the door interrupted her.

Alice automatically reached for her phone to check the camera, then stopped herself. She trusted Vanessa, but only so far. As far as she knew Silvermoon management weren't aware of her extra security precautions and she preferred to keep it that way.

'I'll get it,' Vanessa said, jumping off the couch with energy that Alice hadn't felt in decades.

Alice was putting her phone back on the side table when she heard something that made her jaw clench.

'Hello, Mr Harrison. Come on in.'

Crap, she thought.

ƐIGHT

Gordon Harrison fancied himself the resident lothario. He had read somewhere that retirement villages were hotbeds for hook ups and that older people were experiencing a sexual revolution. Gordon wanted to be the poster boy for that revolution.

Alice knew he used to work for a government department, but she'd never had a long enough conversation to find out any more than that.

He wasn't aggressively pushy. Handsy? Yes. Relentless? Sometimes. Ever hopeful? Definitely. But he took every rejection with good grace. Even if it only resulted in a temporary reprieve for the lady in question.

When he stepped into her apartment, Gordon's slim body was clad in a pale blue tracksuit, with bright orange running shoes. What remained of his hair was slicked down with too much gel or something equally slimy, and dyed brown, which might have worked if he'd done the same with his bushy eyebrows and ever-present stubble, which were a more believable grey.

'Alice!' he exclaimed, as if surprised to see her sitting on her couch in her living room. 'I heard about Betty and I rushed right over to see how you were coping.'

It happened hours ago, she thought irritably. That's not rushing, even for this place.

Outwardly she smiled. 'Thank you, Gordon, I appreciate you stopping by.'

Gordon walked briskly over and took Vanessa's seat on the couch. He patted Alice's knee and she stifled an urge to break his finger.

'She was a lovely lady, Betty was. I didn't know her as well as I would have liked—'

I bet.

'But I know she was well-liked, and she always stopped to chat whenever I saw her.'

He left his hand on Alice's knee and it took every ounce of her will power not to hurt him.

'Mr Harrison, we didn't see you at the poker tournament this morning,' Vanessa said, as she drifted across the room and stood by the window.

Gordon had to turn away from Alice to look at Vanessa and he thankfully removed his hand. Alice took the opportunity to edge further down the couch.

'No, no, as I'm sure you know, I don't gamble, and watching other people do it is not my idea of a spectator sport.' He laughed loudly, his gaze flicking between the two ladies to see if they appreciated his humour.

Alice smiled politely but Vanessa matched his laugh with her own.

'When did you last speak with Betty?' Alice asked.

Gordon turned his attention back to her and seemed surprised at the new gap between them. 'Oh, well I saw her yesterday morning. She was coming out of the recreation building. We chatted briefly. I invited her to have coffee with me but she had another appointment.'

'How did she seem?'

'Seem? How do you mean? She seemed like Betty.'

'I mean did she seem well?'

'I suppose so,' he smoothed one of his eyebrows with his fingers. 'Why?'

Alice took a deep breath to calm herself. 'Well her death was very sudden, I guess I was just wondering if she'd been feeling ill lately.'

'Ah, well you would know better than I of course, but no she seemed well. In fact she seemed happier than I'd seen her in a while. If I didn't know any better I would have thought she'd just…you know.'

She did.

'No. What?' she asked with raised eyebrows.

Gordon's face flushed and his eyes flicked to Vanessa who was trying and failing not to look amused.

'I know, Mr Harrison. I'll explain it to Alice later.'

Alice shot her a look which called her a spoilsport, and Vanessa returned it with one that may or may not have told her to stop torturing the old man.

'Well anyway, she looked very happy.'

Alice decided to change tack. 'Gordon, have you met the new woman Nanci?'

'Nanci Katz? Yes, wonderful woman. I've invited her to dinner, and I think we've got it booked in for one day next week,' he replied excitedly.

Poor woman, Alice thought.

'Had you ever seen her and Betty together?'

'What? Not that I recall, why?'

Alice waved her hand casually. 'No reason. I haven't had a chance to talk to her yet and I just wondered how social she was.'

'Oh right. I can't say, although she was very friendly towards me, and I do remember seeing her talking to Teresa one time, and Owen too come to think of it.'

Alice frowned. For a newcomer, Nanci seemed to have talked to a lot of the residents. She shook her head to try and dislodge her suspicious nature. There's nothing odd about being friendly and trying to fit in. Not everyone had an ulterior motive. Although there was the poker game. There was definitely something weird about that. Or maybe she was a sore loser.

She heard Vanessa clear her throat and Alice realised her thoughts had been wandering again. That had been happening a lot recently.

Between that and the damned cough she'd had forever she was beginning to think that maybe she was getting old.

'So,' Vanessa began and Alice snapped back her attention to the room, 'Alice is feeling a little overwhelmed with everything from today Mr Harrison so perhaps we need to let her rest.'

Alice turned a tired looking face towards her visitor. 'Sorry, Gordon, but I am feeling a little tired.'

'Of course, my dear.'

Gordon used the arm of the couch to steady himself as he stood up. He swayed a little, then beamed down at Alice.

'Let's catch up soon, once you're over this shock.'

Alice nodded which apparently satisfied him and Vanessa escorted him to the door, closing it firmly.

'Overwhelmed! I'll have you know I once stood in a room with ten people, nine of whom wanted me dead, and walked out with their wallets, and two of their phone numbers. Overwhelmed,' she repeated disgustedly. 'I have never been that in my life.'

'Noted,' Vanessa replied. 'And one day I definitely want to hear that story. But it worked, didn't it? He's gone.'

Alice looked at her for a moment, then nodded. 'It was quick thinking. You saved me from doing something he'd regret. However next time, can we use a different word?'

'You're the boss,' Vanessa grinned.

'Good. Now what do you know about Nanci Katz?'

'Not a lot. Management handles all the paperwork for residents, I'm just the pretty face that greets them,' she laughed.

'Could you take a peek at her records?'

'All that stuff is confidential. I'm not supposed to talk about anyone's personal information.'

'I don't need to know her weight or her bra size, just where she came from.'

'You don't need to look at her records to know that. Just google her.'

'The google can tell you stuff like that? I thought it was just medical articles and cat videos.'

'That's YouTube,' Vanessa replied.

'What the heck is a YouTube?'

'A copyrighter's worst nightmare.'

'What are you talking about?' Alice said.

'Nothing. Anyway we can just type her name in and if she's ever been tagged in anything or been in the news at all it will come up.'

Vanessa looked at Alice who stared back.

'Well? Get on with it!'

Vanessa tapped away on her phone with two thumbs, faster than Alice had ever been able to do with all her fingers.

'Okay. Luckily her name isn't that common. Here's something. A Nanci Katz used to live in Christchurch. There's an article here that… Wow.' She looked at Alice.

'What wow?'

'It says here that twenty years ago a Nanci Katz was banned from the Christchurch casino,' Vanessa read.

Alice's mind raced as she connected the dots. 'Let me guess, for cheating at poker.'

'*Allegedly* cheating at poker.'

'Ha, allegedly is just a word the police use so they won't get in trouble with judges. She was cheating, and if she's a gambler then that confirms my suspicions.'

'You think she cheated at the tournament today? But she lost.'

Alice leaned forward, and placing her hands on the coffee table for support she eased herself onto her feet.

'Yes. That was the whole point.'

'You've lost me,' Vanessa said, standing.

'The point is, never con a con artist. We need to talk to Teresa.' Alice started walking to the door.

'You're not going to do or say anything stupid are you?' Vanessa asked.

'Vanessa, all my stupid days are behind me.'

'Lucky you,' Vanessa muttered. 'My day's not complete unless I've done or said something I regretted.'

Closing her front door, Alice walked to the elevator and pressed the button to summon it.

'Tell me something. You can use that google to look up anyone, am I right?'

Vanessa nodded and her cheeks turned pink.

'That's what I thought.'

'I do it for everyone, it passes the time when it gets quiet. I can't tell you the number of times I've googled myself.'

'What did you find out?' Alice asked as they stepped into the elevator.

'If even half the stuff I read was true then you are my hero.'

Alice sniffed. 'Don't believe everything you read.'

The doors opened on the ground floor and they walked into the lobby.

Alice paused on the top step.

'But it was probably true,' she winked.

NINE

Teresa wasn't at her apartment, but as they left Stumpy they ran into Les who told them he'd just seen her at the café.

When they walked in they saw her huddling with Nanci at one of the tables furthest from the door. Teresa looked strained, and then guilty when she spotted them approaching.

'Alice! We were just leaving,' Teresa said, then followed Alice's eyes to the full coffee cup on the table in front of her. 'I mean…'

'Won't you join us?' Nanci asked.

'Thank you,' Vanessa replied.

No one spoke until the two of them were seated. Alice noted that Teresa refused to look her in the eye, suddenly finding her coffee cup the most fascinating thing in the world.

'It's a great shame about your friend,' Nanci said.

'Yes. It's never easy when someone close to you passes away.' Alice studied Nanci, who in turn was studying her back.

'It makes the whole poker tournament seem a bit silly,' Teresa said.

'It was always a silly thing,' Alice retorted, then sighed when it looked like Teresa was about to burst into tears. 'I mean it was always just a bit of fun,' she continued in a softer voice.

Teresa looked at Nanci and her cheeks darkened. 'Of course.'

Alice sighed again. 'Look, I don't care that you cheated, Teresa. I even respect you a little more for it. But I am curious as to whether it was your idea, or yours,' she turned to Nanci.

'Cheated!'

'It was mine,' Nanci replied calmly.

'Nanci!'

'No sense denying it, Teresa, especially in light of what happened and what Alice just said. The tournament was just a bit of fun.' She turned to Alice. 'Teresa and I were talking and she said she didn't see the point of entering this year because you were bound to win again, so I offered to help her.'

'How'd you do it?' Vanessa asked.

Nanci just stared at Alice, with an almost challenging look on her face.

'This is a complete shot in the dark, but I'd imagine she got herself assigned to my table and lost on purpose, lasting just long enough to learn how I played. Maybe found some tell that I don't know about. Then she told Teresa what it was, and I'm guessing also told her what her own tells were. Close?'

'I'm glad it wasn't a real shot in the dark, or there'd be an extra hole in my head about now,' Nanci said wryly.

'How do you possibly know all that?' Teresa demanded.

Alice inwardly enjoyed the amazed expression on her face. Being underestimated had proven extremely useful over the years.

'I imagine she used to be like me,' Nanci said.

'A gambler?' Teresa asked.

'I had quite a few jobs during my working life,' Alice admitted.

'I *am* sorry about your friend. I only spoke briefly with her but she seemed nice. And I'm sorry about the tournament. As you said, it didn't mean anything so I didn't see any harm in helping Teresa win. And it's not like I taught her to count cards or anything.'

Teresa choked on her drink and quickly hid her mouth with a tissue as she coughed.

I bet you tried.

'No, quite right, there was no harm other than to my ego. I'm glad that Teresa won, and once the shock of Betty's death has passed I'm sure her victory will make a nice distraction from everything else that happened this morning.'

'Thank you, Alice. I'm sorry my competitive nature forced me to take such drastic action. I was just tired of losing to you. I so desperately wanted to win for a change.

Alice waved her hand dismissively, then patted Teresa on the arm. 'It was very cunning and I'm proud of you.'

'So no hard feelings?' Nanci asked.

'Not at all. Although one day we will have to sit down and play another game of poker, now that we understand each other a little better.'

Alice and Vanessa left the two women to finish their drinks and walked out into the sunshine.

'Was that like looking in a mirror?' Vanessa commented as they made their way back towards the main building.

Alice snorted. 'I was a lot of things over the years, but common gambler was never one of them.'

'She beat you, so obviously she wasn't that common.'

That earned Vanessa an elbow to the ribs and she stepped away laughing. As they reached the Olympic building, Alice stopped.

'Time for a quick swim?'

'No,' she muttered. 'But what was Betty really doing here yesterday morning?'

'I can't understand you when you mumble.'

'I'm not mumbling, I'm thinking quietly with words.'

'Sure, my mistake.'

Alice opened the door to the building. Immediately inside was a small reception area with a desk that wasn't usually… *attended* or *peopled* or whatever the politically correct term for *manned* was. Alice struggled to keep up with what was and wasn't allowed anymore, but then she'd never paid that much attention to it when she was younger either.

To the right was a glass door, through which she could see the heated pool with a head and two arms visible, ploughing through the water.

Directly ahead was a wide corridor that led to the rest of the complex. Alice marched past doors leading to massage therapists, physiotherapists, changing rooms, and the large recreation room filled with games and books and a massive television.

'What are we doing?' Vanessa asked as Alice pushed open the glass door leading into the gym.

'I saw Betty come in here yesterday morning. When I asked her about it she lied and said she was seeing Peter.'

'But Peter wasn't working yesterday. Garth was.'

Alice nodded as she scanned the room. The weights might have been a little lighter, but otherwise it was just like any other gym, except there were fewer mirrors. Retired people had less desire to watch themselves in the mirror as they exercised. Stationary bikes and treadmills were lined up against one glassed wall, where users could watch people swim or, twice a week at 8am, partake in water aerobics. Her friends raved about it, but Alice couldn't see the point of dressing to come to the pool, getting into your swimsuit to work out, then dressing again to go home. It seemed more work to get to the exercise than to actually do it.

Against the opposite wall were the weight machines, and at the end were some dumbbells and other free weights. A man stood with his back to them, a weighted bar at his feet. She couldn't see the number written on the weights, but they looked heavy. He squatted down, carefully grasping the bar in his hands, then gave a little wiggle of his bottom as he set himself, before shooting upright, hauling the bar with him. Seconds later his arms were directly above his head and he held the pose for a moment before dropping the bar in front of him.

He turned and Alice's mouth dropped in surprise. It was Les.

'Well done,' Vanessa said.

Les rubbed the side of his face, leaving a smudge. Looking at his hands Alice saw they were covered with white powder.

'I didn't know you came here, Les,' Alice said.

His face flushed, although it could have been from the exertion. He glanced towards the door and out to the pool before crossing the gym floor.

'The thing is, I don't really want Freda to find out.'

'That you're coming to the gym?' Vanessa asked.

'What I'm doing at the gym.'

'Why on earth not?' Alice said. 'I would have thought she would love the idea of her man becoming a muscle bound He-man.'

Les's cheeks darkened further. 'It's just I'm… I'd just rather she didn't know, for now.'

Alice put her hand on Vanessa's arm. 'Of course, Les. It's your secret to have, and ours to keep. Although we surely can't be the only ones that have spotted you here.'

Les shot another look towards the door. 'No, but you're the only ones who know Freda well enough to mention it to her.'

'We understand,' Alice replied. 'But tell me something. Do you come here the same time every day?'

'No, I'm usually here in the morning, but Freda was a little upset over Betty so I stayed with her this morning.'

'Two morning's ago I saw Betty come into the building at about 8am. Were you here?'

Les nodded, dislodging a strand of slicked hair, which draped across his forehead. Alice resisted an urge to reach out and push it back into place. 'I was, but I didn't see Betty. She didn't come into the gym or the pool. After lifting I sit on the bike for a while and then have a spa. It helps with my recovery. I would have seen her.'

'Which means she went into the rec room, or to the physio,' said Alice.

'Or she got a massage,' Vanessa suggested.

Alice shook her head. 'No. I tried to persuade her to go and see Georgina one time and she said she'd rather lay in a field and let sheep run over her than take her clothes off and have a stranger poke and prod her.'

Les shrugged. 'I know what she means. Sorry, I can't be of any more assistance, but I need to get back to my workout before I seize up.'

'Of course. Be careful, Les, I wouldn't want you to hurt yourself with those weights.'

'Don't worry about me,' Les smiled. 'It's all about technique, and mine's perfect.'

'What now?' Vanessa asked as they left the gym.

Alice poked her head through the door of the recreation room, but it was empty of people. The doors to the other rooms were firmly shut. 'Now I need you to try and find out if Betty had an appointment with the physio.'

'I thought you said she hated the thought of strangers touching her.'

'She hated the thought of a massage. Physio is different, it's medicinal.'

'Okay, so let's say she did have an appointment. How could that possibly be related to her death?'

Alice enjoyed the warmth of the sun on her face. The soft breeze carried a hint of freshly cut grass, which overrode the smell of chlorine from inside. 'Everything's relevant until it's not,' she said.

'That's like saying everything's hot until it's cold,' Vanessa replied.

Alice grinned. 'Nothing like that at all. Can you find out or not?'

'Of course I can. All the appointments are run through a central system. I just need to be at my desk.'

'Right, you go do that, and keep working on the list of who was at the tournament. I'll see you at my place at 5pm.'

'What are you going to do?'

'I'm going to chat with Freda before Les gets finished here. She's always more chatty when her husband isn't around.'

'Sneaky,' Vanessa said.

'Practical,' Alice replied.

'See you later, and don't forget the pizza you promised.' Vanessa walked away with the sort of walk that said *I could skip or even run if I wanted to and it wouldn't be a problem*. It had been a long time since Alice had walked like that.

A short time later she was being ushered inside by Freda. As they sat on the couch, and Alice declined the offer of tea, she thought that Freda appeared to have been crying. It made her feel guilty that she hadn't shed more tears herself for Betty.

'It's just such a tragedy,' Freda said. 'And I feel so guilty, like I was the one who killed her.'

TƐN

Alice stared at Freda, trying to get a sense of whether the woman was being literal. She looked so upset. Something was definitely going on.

'What on earth do you mean by that?' Alice asked.

Freda reached over to the coffee table and plucked a tissue from the box. She dabbed at her eyes before replying. 'I did something silly. Les has been going out a bit more than usual recently and I happened to see him one day with Betty. They were sitting on that bench by the rose garden and, oh I don't know, I assumed something was going on.'

She stopped to blow her nose.

'You confronted them,' Alice guessed.

'The thing is, Les has always been faithful, through everything over the 54 years we've been married, so I have no right to think that anything was going on. But I've started feeling a little insecure lately, and he's been secretive about something. He's started plucking his nose hairs again. It's been years since he's done that. When I saw him and Betty talking and looking so cosy I put two and two together and got—'

'An affair.'

Freda smiled at her sadly. 'Silly, isn't it?'

Alice thought it was, but daren't say it aloud. 'So what did Les say?'

If possible Freda looked more miserable. 'I didn't confront him. I waited until he left and I said something to Betty.'

'I can imagine how well that went,' Alice replied.

'She denied it, which of course she would, but I was too angry, and I told her to stay away from Les. I stormed off and a day later she was dead. I can't help thinking what if it was my fault for some reason that she…'

Alice placed her hand on Freda's arm as she dissolved into tears.

'Unless you have some supernatural powers I'm not aware of, Betty dying had nothing to do with you. You're not a witch, are you?'

Freda laughed which turned into a cough and then back into a laugh. 'My mother-in-law did always accuse me of putting a spell on Les, but I think she was just being a bitch.' Her mouth dropped open as she looked shocked. 'I mean… I can't believe I said that.'

'Why not? She probably was.'

Freda looked around, then nodded slightly. 'Maybe a little bit. I know I was being silly, this whole being jealous thing is new to me.'

'You have nothing to be jealous about,' Alice reassured her.

'Do you know what his secret is?' Freda looked at her sharply.

'It's not my place to say anything, but I can tell you it has nothing to do with another woman.'

'Oh.'

Freda looked like she had a million follow up questions and was struggling to decide which one to ask first, so Alice quickly changed the subject.

'Freda, yesterday at the tournament, did you see Betty acting strangely just before she died?'

'Strangely? I don't understand.'

'I'm just trying to find out if she was feeling unwell beforehand or if it was sudden. I'd hate to think she wasn't herself and I missed it.'

'Yes, I see.' Freda wiped her eyes and stared into the distance, considering. 'She seemed fine to me, although I didn't pay much attention to anything other than Les's table at the start. After Teresa beat you (I still can't believe that by the way) I did spot Betty stacking some poker chips on the table. I turned around to talk to Les and that's when she must have collapsed. Such a tragedy.'

'Do you know whose chips she was tidying up?' Alice asked with a frown.

'No idea,' Freda replied, pulling a fresh tissue from the box, deftly folding and tucking it in her sleeve. 'Does it matter?'

'No, no, just an idle thought.'

They chatted for a few more minutes, then Alice left Freda looking miserable. Having concluded that her sharp advice to "Stop moping over a man" wouldn't help, Alice had wisely kept it to herself and instead departed with a less helpful: "It'll all be fine".

Her next port of call should have been to the dining room, the scene of the tournament. She wanted to check out the tables to see if she could figure out whose chair Betty died beside. However, as soon as Alice stepped into the lobby her stomach growled so loudly she was surprised the replacement concierge's head hadn't shot up from the phone or book she was engrossed in.

Deciding a snack was required before further investigation, Alice returned to the elevator. As she pressed the button she felt something soft slide past her. She looked down to see Maddy sitting there. When the cat saw Alice looking she produced her trademark meow of starvation.

'Never con a con artist,' Alice told her, earning a second more pitiful noise from the feline.

The doors slid open and Alice stepped into the elevator. She turned to see the cat still sitting there waiting.

'Oh for goodness sake, come on then.'

As if understanding her, Maddy sprang inside before the doors could shut.

'I must be losing my touch,' Alice muttered.

Maddy yowled in agreement.

The cat stuck close to Alice until they were inside her apartment, where it jumped onto the kitchen counter and sat down. Alice picked her up and moved her to one of the stools. By the time she had retrieved a can of tuna from the cupboard and turned back around,

Maddy was sitting on the bench again. Alice hissed at her, receiving a yawn in return.

'Fine, but you're not eating up there. And you better have a clean ass.'

Maddy proceeded to prove it by licking herself in that exact area. Alice wanted to believe the cat could understand her, but thought coincidence was a more likely explanation.

She opened the tuna can and placed it on the floor, barely getting her hand out of the way before the cat jumped down and shoved her mouth inside.

With the sound of slurping in her ears, Alice fixed herself a sandwich and sat down to watch a game show on television. As she answered another question correctly her phone beeped. A message from Amanda. Being raised by Alice it was no wonder she'd gone into the family business, persuading other people to give her their things. She was often absent for weeks at a time, and out of contact for a lot of that, but Amanda tried to check in with her grandmother whenever she could.

As usual her text was simple: "I'm still alive. Are you?"

Alice sent back an affirmative and switched off the television, deciding she was more intelligent than the contestant on the game show. She looked at Maddy who was lying in a patch of sun.

'Time to go, cat.'

The only response was a lazy tail twitch.

'I don't blame you. It looks nice. Only trouble is I wouldn't be able to get up again.'

This time there wasn't even a twitch, just the rhythmic rise and fall of a temporarily full stomach.

'If I leave you here how do I know you won't pee on the carpet while I'm gone?'

Maddy opened one eye as if to say, please stop talking to me.

Short of bending down and picking her up, Alice had no choice but to leave the cat where she was and hope for the best.

Taking the elevator back to the lobby, she made her way into the dining room, and found that she wasn't alone.

In the middle of the room Gavin stood staring into space. When he heard the sound of the door he turned, his face devoid of emotion.

Alice shivered.

ELEVEN

Gavin blinked and seemed to see her for the first time.

'Hello, Alice. Sorry, I was somewhere else for a moment,' he said and his face relaxed into a smile.

'That's quite a stern face you've got there,' Alice replied.

He laughed, 'I was in the military, Alice. A good death stare was mandatory if you wanted to climb the ranks.'

'Yes, I imagine it came in handy. With that skill, I'm surprised you're not better at poker.'

'So am I,' Gavin admitted with a shrug. 'But it was never my thing.'

Alice stepped further into the room. All the poker chips had been cleared away and a stack of clean plates and cutlery sat on the side table ready to set the tables for the next meal.

'Are you waiting for dinner?' she asked.

He glanced at his watch. 'No, I'm going over the events of the poker tournament again. I thought it would be easier to do if I was in the room.'

'Why?' Alice came closer.

He gave her another shrug. 'Call it professional habit. During my career I was responsible for sending a lot of men into potential war zones, and every single one of them that didn't come home, I made damn sure I knew why. I realise that this place is just a halfway house while we wait to head off into the great beyond, but when someone

68

dies unexpectedly I get an itch in the back of my brain that can only be scratched when I have answers.'

'People of your age die all the time,' Alice said.

'Your age? I hate to tell you this Alice, but we're in the same category.'

She flapped her hand dismissively. 'I passed your age a long time ago and I intend to attend all your funerals.'

'Morbid.'

'But not sinister. Not intentionally anyway.' She grinned at him. 'Do you suspect foul play?'

'Foul play? I may have been alive at the same time as Agatha Christie but the words *foul play* have never crossed my lips. Of course I don't believe anything untoward happened, I just like to know things, to have things resolved. In this case I'd like to know if poor Betty was suffering from something undiagnosed, or if it was a case of food poisoning or something else that might require us to be on guard.'

Alice nodded. She also liked to know things, and right now she wanted to know if Gavin was telling the truth. His tell in poker was quite obvious, but in life she had yet to get a sense of him.

'Have you discovered anything?' she asked.

'Everything had been cleared away by the time I got here, so there's not much to see.'

She thought he seemed put out, but then he was probably used to people not doing things without his permission.

'Do you remember who was sitting at the chair Betty was beside when she collapsed?' Alice asked.

'What? No, can't say I do, not exactly. Everyone was paying attention to your table towards the end and no one was sitting down. I think Gordon was at that table when the tournament was going but can't be completely sure.' He smiled ruefully. 'I was too busy getting my rear flank handed to me by you.'

Alice inclined her head at the compliment, then moved around the table. There was a time when she would have remembered every person that had been in the room, where they sat, what they were wearing, and probably the value of any jewellery. But the years had taken the edge off her memory, and she no longer had any interest in stealing the jewellery.

Gavin's comment had jogged something loose, but it was just out of her grasp. Alice walked over to where she had been sitting for the first round, pulled the chair out and lowered herself into it.

Slowly Alice scanned the room, trying to recall the tournament. A clear picture snapped into her mind.

Gordon had been sitting at the table, next to him had been Owen, then a woman she knew in passing, Judy or Jackie something, the dealer was a member of staff, and the fifth player...

Alice frowned, she couldn't recall who the last person was. Vanessa would be able to find out from the sign-up sheet. The important thing is that she remembered whose chips Betty had been tidying when she died.

'Everything alright, Alice?' Gavin asked.

She smiled at his concern. 'I'm fine. I guess I got tired from jogging all those memories.'

Gavin sat down opposite her. 'Have you met the new woman, Nanci?'

'I have.'

'I've only talked to her for a short time, but I find her intriguing,' Gavin said.

She's a con artist, was what Alice wanted to say, but instead she said, 'She seems an interesting character.'

'I might ask her for coffee.

Alice struggled with the right reply. It wasn't her place to say anything, but then she didn't want to see anyone taken for a ride (unless she was the one doing the driving).

'Gather your intel first.'

'What do you mean?'

She shrugged. 'You like to know things. We don't really know anything about her. I'm just suggesting you find out a little bit more before getting involved.'

Gavin replied briskly. 'Goodness me, I'm not talking about getting involved. Just getting a coffee. But I see your point, always better to know more.'

'Are you done here?' Alice gestured around the room.

'I'm not sure what I expected to find, but it's probably preposterous to think that Betty's death was anything but her time to go.'

Alice pondered his words after he left the room. The same doubts persisted, a new one popping up every time she tried to squash one. Perhaps he was right and this whole thing was a foolish quest by a silly old woman. Alice frowned. She'd never called herself silly before. Stupid, yes, occasionally an idiot, but never silly.

Alice made her way back to her apartment and scrubbed the already clean kitchen bench. Even Maddy's presence, crawling along the carpet chasing the slowly fading patch of sunlight, wasn't enough to bring her out of the funk.

Such was her distraction that she didn't even check the security camera when there was a knock at the door.

'Pizza time yet?' Vanessa asked when Alice opened the door.

She looked at the clock on the stove and saw it was after five. 'Go ahead,' she waved at the kitchen counter where the landline sat.

Vanessa tucked her hair behind her ears. 'Already ordered it. I got you a no cheese, gluten free, vegetarian pizza.'

Alice gave her a dirty look. 'There are several words in there that should not be in the same sentence as the word pizza.'

Vanessa's grin dissolved into a laugh. 'Actually I ordered lots of meat, not so much cheese on yours, with garlic bread and potato wedges.'

Alice's eyes narrowed. 'How did you know what I normally order? We've never had pizza together before.'

'Did you forget? All deliveries have to come via the front desk.'

'Of course. Good detective skills,' Alice said. 'What else have you learned?'

Vanessa went and sat on the couch. She tapped on her tablet, then showed the screen to Alice, who sat down next to her.

'This is all the people who signed up for the tournament, and the tables they were at.' She swiped upwards on the screen and a new list of names showed up. 'And these are the people who were watching. Although I can't be sure that's all of them. I was a bit busy for some of the time.' She cast a guilty look in Alice's direction.

'Don't worry, Vanessa. This was better than I was expecting,' Alice said. Then she heard her granddaughter's voice in her head reminding her that sometimes she could come across as blunt. Actually her exact words had been, "stop being a mean old lady".

'What I mean is most young people can't see past their cell phones.'

The look on Vanessa's face suggested that wasn't much better.

'Because young people are all about me, me, me.'

'Riiiight,' Vanessa said in a disappointed tone. 'If that's the way you feel…'

Alice stifled a sigh. Things were so much easier when people didn't get so easily offended. 'Not you personally, just…'

'Just all my friends and everyone I know,' Vanessa finished.

'Yes, exactly. Now back to this list. It looks pretty complete to me, although…were there any other staff there? Apart from the ones working the tables.'

Vanessa's eyes widened. 'Only Tracey from what I can remember. Why?'

'Just being thorough.'

'You don't suspect Tracey do you? I know she can be a pain sometimes, but she's not evil. I don't think.'

'We don't even know if there's a crime, so no point in excluding suspects just yet,' Alice said.

'For the possible crime.'

'I know how it sounds.'

Vanessa shrugged. 'Tracey declined my annual leave application for next week because I didn't give her enough notice. Even though I don't think she killed anyone, I'd be happy if she was slightly dodgy.'

'Alright then. This is the table that Betty died at. She was stacking poker chips at Gordon's chair.'

'Gordon! So d'you think he was the target?'

'I think we need to find out how Betty died,' Alice said. 'Do you know what happened to her body?'

'It's at a funeral home in the city. They're waiting for her family to make the funeral arrangements.'

Alice leaned back against the couch and rubbed her fingers and thumb together on her left hand. It was a habit she'd picked up years ago. The rhythmic motion helped her think.

'We can't ask the family to get an autopsy because we think Betty was murdered,' Vanessa said into the silence. 'They'll never believe us, and I'll probably get fired.'

'What for?' Alice asked.

'For bringing the Silvermoon Retirement Village into disrepute.'

'Tell me the truth. Is that the first time you've used the word *disrepute*?'

'Yes, I feel so grown up.'

'We don't need the family to authorise an autopsy.'

'Ew. We're not doing it ourselves,' Vanessa said with wide eyes. 'I'm happy snooping, but draw the line at dissecting.'

'Dissecting! Betty isn't a frog in a biology class.'

Vanessa's face flushed and she looked towards the window.

'Do you own a suit?'

'A suit? Like a business suit?' Vanessa asked, still facing away. 'I've got a white blouse and a jacket at home that could work. Why?'

'Because I need you to be a lawyer,' Alice said.

'What?'

Alice always enjoyed the look of surprise she could elicit on other people's faces. Vanessa's was a classic combination of confusion, puzzlement, and surprise.

'A lawyer. We're going on a field trip.'

TWELVE

'I want to go on record as saying this is a really bad idea.'

'See, you're talking like a lawyer already.'

The previous evening when Alice had outlined her plan, Vanessa had seemed excited, but standing outside the building of McDonald and Hope Funeral Home, she was having second through to a hundred thoughts.

'They'll never believe I'm a lawyer,' Vanessa argued. 'I'm not smart enough.'

Alice gripped her arm tightly and glared at her.

'You listen to me. I never want to hear you say you're not smart again. It's that sort of thinking that will hold you back from what you really want to do in life. Self-belief is the most important tool in any woman's arsenal.'

'Tool belt.'

'Eh?'

Vanessa smiled. 'You don't have tools in arsenals, they go in tool belts.'

Alice loosened her grip and smoothed the fabric on Vanessa's sleeve. 'And you say you're not smart. You don't have to be a lawyer, you just have to look like a lawyer.'

Which she did, in a short black skirt, white blouse, and a black jacket. Her hair was swept back in a pony-tail and Alice thought it was a good thing Vanessa hadn't managed to find some glasses on a string. It was a fine line between lawyer and librarian.

Alice had borrowed some clothes from Teresa, supposedly to try them for size before she bought her own. Teresa had impeccable taste in clothing, and although she had a bit more meat on her bones than Alice, the grey dress and jacket, accompanied by a silk scarf and diamond brooch that Alice had acquired during her working days, meant that she looked the part of grieving friend.

The building they entered was on the edge of Wellington city, an old concrete structure backing onto the railway lines, and beyond that the large sports stadium. A smartly decorated reception was painted in muted colours and furnished with soft chairs on one side, and a desk on the other. A subtle bell rang as they walked through the door, and a woman in a pale green uniform popped out of the door behind the desk.

'Goodness me, please take a seat,' the woman said when she saw Alice.

Alice stifled her irritation. Everywhere she went these days people treated her like she was about to take her last breath just because she looked old, when she'd rather make the most of being alive to keep on moving.

'Thank you, dear,' she said in a frail voice, allowing herself to be guided by the arm to one of the soft chairs.

'May I get you something? Tea? Coffee?' the woman asked. She appeared to be in her late forties, and the name tag on her uniform declared to the world that her name was Beatrice.

'Nothing for me, thank you,' Alice replied with a smile.

'If you'd like to wait here I'll get one of our sales managers to come and talk over our package options with you,' Beatrice said.

'My client is not here for her own funeral arrangements,' Vanessa began. 'She has a more delicate matter to discuss with a manager.'

'Your client?'

'Viola is my lawyer,' Alice informed her. 'She's a bit officious, but she is, on this occasion, correct. I would like to speak with your manager about something.'

'Of course. I'll see if Mr Watford is free.' She hurried to the desk and picked up the phone.

'Well done, Vanessa,' Alice murmured.

'I think I'm going to throw up.'

'Later, dear.'

'Mr Watford will be out in a moment,' Beatrice relayed to them from across the room.

As if waiting for the introduction, a door opened and a young man walked through. He wore the same uniform as Beatrice, and his name tag read "Greg Watford, Assistant Manager".

'Good morning. Would you come this way please,' he said in a deep voice full of assurance.

He led them through the door, down a short corridor, and into a small room with four chairs and a coffee table. He gestured to the chairs, and closed the glass door behind them.

'How may I help you?' Greg asked once he'd taken his seat, addressing his question to Vanessa.

This could be easier than I hoped, Alice thought.

'Two days ago a woman was brought here from the Silvermoon Retirement Village,' Alice began.

Greg held up his hand. 'I'm sorry, it's against company policy to discuss the deceased.'

'A wonderful policy, which gives me a great deal of comfort should I find myself in your care after…' She studied his face without appearing to, so she could gauge his reaction. Sure enough his eyes narrowed slightly and he straightened his tie.

'Of course,' he said.

'The thing is, this woman, Betty, there is a possibility that she might be my long lost sister.'

'Oh?'

'Yes, it's a complicated family history that I won't get into. However I need to be sure as I'm…'

She waited to see if Vanessa would jump in as planned.

'My client is wealthy and she has no other family, and she is 97 years old and suffering from terminal liver failure.'

'Why don't you tell him all my secrets,' Alice grumbled loudly.

'You're the one who wanted to come here,' Vanessa reminded her.

Alice glanced at her in time to see the eye role Vanessa gave Greg, who grinned at her.

'As it stands Mrs Harper has two choices for her vast estate. Leave it to her cat, Mr Wigglesmith, or find the sister she last saw 70 years ago. We uncovered some information that suggested Betty might be her sister and we went to the retirement village yesterday, where they told us the bad news.'

'That's terrible,' Greg said. Alice watched him not so subtly checking out Vanessa's legs.

'Exactly.'

'I understand that Betty has children, and if she turns out to have been my sister I want to make sure they get some money. But I'm not giving it away to strangers. I need to be sure she's my spaghetti,' said Alice.

'Your what?' Greg asked.

'Betty spaghetti,' Alice said in a tone that suggested her own eye roll.

'Ah, I see. What I don't see is how I can help.'

'I realise that she would have changed a lot over the decades, but I'm sure I would recognise her if I saw her.'

'I'm afraid that's not possible,' Greg replied with a frown.

'Technically it's possible, just not permitted,' Vanessa chimed in.

'Well, there's the wishes of the family,' Greg began.

'Of which, my client is saying she might be one. Tell me, will it be an open casket funeral?'

'That hasn't been arranged yet, we're waiting for the deceased's daughter to fly in tomorrow.'

'However, if it was an open casket then the body would be visible to anyone, correct?'

'Well, yes but—'

'So all we're really asking for is a preview,' Vanessa said.

'But we are still preparing the deceased,' Greg protested.

'Betty,' Alice wailed, covering her face in a dainty handkerchief she pulled from the sleeve of her jacket.

'It's just...'

Vanessa put her arm around Alice and shot Greg a disapproving look. Then, to completely shatter his defences, she reached up with her other hand, pulled her hair free from the ponytail and ran her hand through it.

'I suppose a short, off the books, viewing would be alright,' Greg said in a weak voice. 'I'll just go and set things up, if you will please wait here for a minute.'

As soon as he closed the door Alice uncovered her face to reveal a smile.

'The hair thing was a nice touch, although a bit premature,' she said. 'He was about to cave anyway.'

'Sorry,' Vanessa answered with reddening cheeks. 'I got caught up in the moment and to be honest, I've always wanted to try that with a man.'

'You never have before?'

'It always seemed so corny.'

'It is, but also highly effective. I used it when I was your age. Nice to know men haven't changed that much,' Alice said with a soft laugh, before adopting a solemn look.

A split second later Greg opened the door. 'This way ladies.'

He led them through the door opposite the meeting room, down another short corridor and into a small windowless room. It was empty except for a table in the middle covered in a body shaped white cloth.

Alice walked over to the table and folded the cloth down, revealing Betty's face. She heard Vanessa gasp, and felt a twinge of sadness at seeing her friend's still, pale face.

She felt Vanessa step up next to her.

'What are we looking for again?' she whispered.

Alice wasn't quite sure. Any signs of foul play seemed a bit general, even if she knew what those signs were. She already knew there was something odd about Betty's fingernails.

Alice wished she'd done some of that googling thing, or at least got Vanessa to do it.

'Is it...' Greg asked.

'I think so. It's been a long time but...' Alice paused and leaned in closer to study Betty's face. She shuffled sideways a little to block Greg's view, then reached out a hand and gently pried open one of Betty's eyes. The pupil stared unresponsively at the ceiling and told Alice absolutely nothing except to confirm that Betty was dead. Something that had undoubtedly already been confirmed by several more qualified people.

As she was straightening up Alice noticed several tiny sticks lying on the table in the space behind Betty's neck. They looked like stray white hairs but the way they lay it seemed like they were stiff, like they were covered in hairspray.

'Oh dear,' Alice said in a wavering voice. She pulled her handkerchief out again on the pretext of wiping her eyes. As Vanessa put an arm around her shoulders Alice scooped up the hairs with the handkerchief, before turning to face Greg.

'It's not my sister. I was so hoping it was her, but this poor unfortunate lady is a stranger.'

'I am sorry to hear that,' Greg replied. 'Let me show you out.'

The way he hustled them out of the building it was obvious Greg was relieved to avoid the complications associated with a long lost relative.

Before he closed the front door he did make a final attempt at a charm offensive on Vanessa, who responded by retying her hair into a ponytail and turning her back on him.

'I feel a little bad at being rude,' she said after he'd closed the door. 'But he was being a sleezy pig.'

'Then don't feel bad.'

They started the slow walk back to the car.

'How do you do it?' Vanessa asked.

'What's that?'

'The way they treated you, like you were a child that needed their help. It would drive me crazy.'

Alice slipped her arm through Vanessa's and leaned on her a little as they walked.

'I'm sorry, are you alright?'

Alice grinned and straightened up.

'Bugger, I just did the same thing,' Vanessa said with red cheeks.

'To be honest it does irritate me. I guess that's one of the reasons I don't like leaving the village anymore. I might still be the oldest there, but at least they're all less than a half century younger than me.'

'You've got way more patience than I have.'

'Of course I do,' Alice replied as they reached the car. 'But I've had more practice at it.'

'So did we learn anything? Apart from the fact that I don't like looking at two day old corpses, especially ones I know.'

'Let's hope you don't have to see too many then,' Alice said.

Vanessa indicated and pulled out into traffic. She made a noise like she wanted to say something but cut herself off.

'Out with it.'

Vanessa glanced across at Alice in the passenger seat. 'It's just, I don't know much about what you used to do, and I wondered if…'

Alice filled in the blanks. 'Not too many but seeing dead bodies was occasionally an occupational hazard.'

Vanessa nodded.

'What exactly do you think I did for a living?'

'Exactly? I don't know,' Vanessa admitted. 'But presumably something that wasn't always legal. I mean you called yourself a con artist but what does that actually mean?'

Alice looked out the window at a city vastly different to the one she grew up in. She still had vivid memories of this place during the Second World War when she'd been young and full of confidence and together with her best friend Violet they had taken their destiny into their own hands with some morally questionable, but extremely fun, choices.

But they weren't all happy memories from back then, and suddenly Alice felt tired, not just her body, but her mind as well. She slumped in the seat and stared at nothing.

'Did I say something wrong?'

Stop this melancholy you silly woman, Alice thought. 'No you didn't. Sorry, just thinking about something. We don't have time to go over the full job description of what I was, but when this is all over I promise we'll sit down and I'll teach you everything I know.'

'Teach? I just wanted to know what it was like, not to become you.'

Alice looked at her. 'Are you sure?'

'Of course,' Vanessa replied in a tone that wasn't quite convincing. 'My parents would kill me if I turned to a life of crime.'

Alice snorted at her use of the cliché.

'Back to my original question. Did we learn anything from that?'

'I'm not sure. Maybe. There's these strange things I found by her neck.'

Alice carefully unfolded the handkerchief and stared at the thin white hairs. She reached out her fingers to pick one up and accidentally stabbed herself with it.

'Damn!' she said as she tried to extract the object with her other hand.

It was only once she'd successfully removed it that she realised she had lost the feeling in her finger. She waggled it and it seemed to work fine, but when she tapped it on the window her brain didn't register any sensation.

'Damn,' she repeated.

'What happened?' Vanessa asked.

'I think I may have just poisoned myself.'

THIRTEEN

'Well I don't know what you stuck yourself with, but the effects seem to have worn off and all your blood tests came back normal.'

'That's not good enough,' Vanessa told the ER doctor. 'Do you mean to tell me you can't find what caused this? That's ridiculous, what sort of doctor are you?'

'A busy one. However I can assure you that we have ruled out any immediate danger, and if Mrs Atkinson still refuses to stay the night…?'

Alice nodded. Staying a night in the hospital was a slippery slope at her age. It starts with one night, then suddenly it's two, and eventually you never leave.

'Then there is nothing more we can do at the moment. Your blood pressure is a little low, but that's not unexpected at your age. Do you have someone at home that can look after you?'

'I can take care of myself,' Alice said firmly.

'I'll make sure she's alright,' Vanessa replied.

'Right, then I'll arrange the discharge papers.'

'Before you go, any idea what the little white hair things are?'

The doctor shook his head. 'No idea, although they look organic to me.'

'Organic?' Alice asked.

'Plant. You could try asking at a garden shop. Palmers garden shop in Miramar, the staff there might know. Someone will be in shortly with your discharge papers. '

The doctor left the room, sliding the curtain closed behind him.

'See, I told you I was alright,' Alice said.

Vanessa stared with a look of disbelief. 'You were the one who said you'd been poisoned.'

'I said I *might* have poisoned myself.'

'You said the word poison, that's all I heard. After Betty, what did you think I was going to do? Drive you back home and give you a cup of tea?'

'That's what you can do right now. I'm fine. I can feel my finger again, and you heard the doctor, I'm in no immediate danger.'

'That doesn't mean there isn't something nasty working its way through your body right now.'

Alice shuffled to the edge of the bed and slid her feet to the floor. 'I'm closing in on a hundred, dear. It'd be a miracle if there wasn't something nasty working its way through my body. Now, let's get the piece of paper from the cute doctor and go ask someone about these hairs that aren't hairs.'

Vanessa threw her hands up in disgust. 'You're so…'

'Stubborn? Frustrating? Annoying? Yes.'

Before Vanessa could argue further the curtain slid open and a nurse handed them the discharge papers.

'Take it easy for a few days, Mrs Atkinson, and if any further symptoms appear then please come back in.'

They thanked her and the nurse hustled out of the room, followed by the women at a more sedate pace.

'I'm taking you home,' Vanessa said.

'Yes, dear. Right after we go to Palmers.'

'No, I'm taking you home now. Then I'll go to Palmers by myself.'

Alice considered continuing the argument, but the truth was she was tired, and Vanessa could easily find out the information without her.

'Okay.'

Vanessa frowned at her with suspicion, then nodded and marched towards the car, only to come back after a few paces to offer her arm to Alice.

'You know, you make it hard to exit triumphantly,' she muttered.

'Yes, dear.'

'Stop it,' Vanessa grumbled.

So Alice did, remaining quiet the rest of the way home, and not even objecting when Vanessa insisted on accompanying her up to her apartment, although she drew the line at the suggestion of a Dora.

Alice felt that a cup of tea was in order, but decided to just sit on the couch for a few minutes.

She was woken by a loud thumping on the door. Alice checked the door camera to see Vanessa standing outside, and went to open it just as Vanessa's arm was stretched backwards ready to bang on the wood panel again.

'Why did it take you so long? I was about to break the door down. Or at least go get the override code from reception.'

'You only knocked twice, you know how long it takes me to get to the door,' Alice replied, stepping aside to let Vanessa enter.

'I was knocking for five minutes!'

'Oh. Well what did you forget?'

'Nothing, Alice. I've been to Palmers. I've been gone for almost two hours.'

Alice looked at her watch, which confirmed Vanessa's story.

'I must have drifted off.'

Vanessa's face went pale. 'Can you not use that term? Especially after what I found out.'

'Tell me all about it while I make us a cup of tea.'

Vanessa perched on one of the kitchen stools while Alice put the kettle on to boil and pulled cups and teaspoons from the cupboard.

'It turns out that what you found are spines from the Ongaonga plant. It's a stinging nettle found all over New Zealand.'

'Really? Then why did my finger go numb?'

'Because it's a highly poisonous plant.'

Alice paused what she was doing and stared at Vanessa.

'Deadly?'

'The person I spoke to had to do some research as they don't normally sell deadly plants, but they said not usually. There are some reports that people have died from being stung.'

Vanessa tapped on her phone, then slid it across the countertop to Alice. It was a picture of a long thin green leaf edged by sharp white needle like hairs.

'What are the symptoms?' she asked.

'It can be quite painful, and cause the area to go numb.'

Alice rubbed her finger. 'So why did it kill Betty and not me?'

'I don't know for sure, but according to the research I did one of the side effects from getting stung is a drop in blood pressure. Didn't the doctor say your blood pressure was low?'

'He did, but it's always been a little on the low side.'

'Maybe the effects aren't as severe the second time around. If these had already poked Betty then maybe she got the worst of the toxin. Did she have low blood pressure?'

Alice looked at Vanessa.

'You want me to look at her records, don't you? Are you trying to get me fired?'

Alice laughed. 'No, I'd miss you too much. Besides I know she had low blood pressure. She had to take pills for it every day. Used to drive her crazy, she hated having to remember taking them. She had one of those pill containers with the days of the week on them, but she would say to me that it only worked if she could remember what day of the week it was.'

Vanessa took off her jacket and let her hair loose from her ponytail. She caught Alice watching her.

'I actually prefer it loose,' she smiled. 'Only sometimes it gets in the way. So was Betty confused about the days of the week on Wednesday?'

'Not in the way you're implying.' Alice snorted. 'She was a farmer all her life, weekdays and weekends didn't mean much on the farm. The cows still needed to be milked on a Sunday.'

'Oh.'

Alice finished making the tea and handed Vanessa hers. She blew the steam away from her cup, then set it down on the counter.

'I never saw the point of blowing on drinks. Like your breath is magically going to cool the tea enough so you don't burn your lip on the boiling water,' Vanessa said.

'It does seem a bit silly.'

'It's like when people give you food and tell you it's hot, and you take a bite anyway and they look at you like you're a little crazy for not listening to them and...'

'What?'

Vanessa sighed and drummed her fingers on the counter. 'I'm trying not to consider what this all means, because there were no stinging nettles in the room when Betty died. In fact there are none on the property, at least none I've ever seen, which means her getting spiked wasn't an accident, which means that someone killed her, which is crazy because who would want to kill Betty? And if someone did kill her then that means...'

'That someone we know killed her,' Alice finished. She looked at the miserable expression on Vanessa' face. If you want to forget all this and go back to work—'

'What! Of course not. It's just. Shouldn't we tell the police?'

-'Tell them what?' Alice asked. 'That we think our friend was poisoned by a leaf by someone unknown for some reason unknown?'

'Okay, so not the police. Why don't we ask Tracey's niece? She just became a detective and we could talk to her off the record.'

'I don't think there is such a thing, despite what television would have you believe.'

'Please?'

Alice shrugged. 'If you think it would help then sure, go ahead.'

Vanessa looked at her watch, then gave Alice a rueful smile.

'You already called her didn't you?' Alice said.

'She'll be here in five minutes.'

'I don't know whether to be annoyed or impressed.'

'Hopefully more impressed than annoyed.'

'We'll see. But Vanessa, whether or not the police take this seriously, I'm not going to stop until I find out who killed my friend. And when I do they better pray that the police get there before me.'

FOURTEEN

'It's pretty thin,' Judith said.

Alice shot a *told you so* look at Vanessa who seemed to be deliberately avoiding her gaze.

'Like wafer thin,' Judith continued. She was wearing a grey suit, and had made a point of telling them she was squeezing them in during a break in her work day.

They'd explained what they'd learned, and what they suspected, and it was going about as well as Alice had expected.

'You were the one who thought it might be suspicious earlier,' Alice reminded her.

Judith held up a hand. 'Actually I asked the question and was reassured by my aunt that it was unlikely to be suspicious.'

'And now we're telling you differently,' Vanessa said.

'No, what you're telling me is a bunch of ideas loosely connected by one giant leap.' Judith's expression softened as she looked at Alice. 'Look, I get it. You've just lost a friend. It's hard, but that doesn't mean this was anything but natural causes. She was in her eighties with low blood pressure and who knows what else wrong with her. And to be honest, from what my aunt has said, no one had a motive to kill Betty.'

'You checked!' Vanessa said in triumph.

'No,' Judith replied gently. 'I simply asked Aunt Tracey what sort of person Betty was. It was a polite conversation. She was upset by the death.'

'Well, we won't take up any more of your valuable time, detective,' Alice said getting to her feet.

'But—'

'Will we, Vanessa?'

Vanessa shut her mouth and glared in response.

Judith paused at the door. 'And I don't want to hear about either of you harassing residents with your theories, understood?'

'Of course, detective,' Alice replied.

They waited until the elevator doors closed on Judith before shutting Alice's front door.

'We're going to harass some residents with our theories, aren't we?' Vanessa asked.

'Of course. She didn't tell us not to.'

'She just did,' said Vanessa as they walked back to the couch.

'No, she said she didn't want to hear about it. So we make sure she doesn't hear about it,' Alice replied.

They stared at each other for a moment then laughed, which for Alice rapidly turned into a coughing fit.

'Stop it,' she said to Vanessa when she had herself under control.

'Stop what?'

'Looking at me like I'm going to expire any second. It was just a cough.'

'Sorry, can't help caring,' Vanessa told her.

'And I appreciate it, but this is going to get tiresome very quickly if you call for a stretcher every time I sneeze. I promise to tell you if I'm not feeling well. Good enough?'

'Depends. Do you mean it?' Vanessa asked, tucking her hair behind her ears.

'You're catching on.'

'You're worse than my grandmother.'

'Thank you.'

'It wasn't a… Never mind. Alright, so the police aren't interested. What now?' Vanessa asked.

'Now we think we know *how*, so the next questions are *who* and *why*?'

'According to all the shows on Netflix it's either to do with money or sex and I don't think it was...' Vanessa stopped, her face red.

'It's alright Vanessa, you can say it. Betty didn't have much of one and even less of the other.'

'I didn't mean...'

'Yes you did, and that's fine, because you're mostly right. Mostly. But just to spare your poor cheeks from turning permanently into beetroots, let's look at the possibility that money was the motive. Betty was comfortable, but not rich, as far as I know. Although she was pretty taciturn when it came to money, so she might have been loaded. I think we need to take a look around her apartment.'

Vanessa sighed. 'Why not? I've seen her dead body twice. Breaking into her apartment doesn't seem like much of a violation.'

'Excellent attitude. Although, as you can legally obtain the key and she's dead, it's not technically breaking in,' Alice said.

'Do you want me to call Judith back here and you can try that theory with her?'

'Just go get the key and I'll meet you at Betty's.'

When Alice opened the front door, Maddy, who had been sitting next to the elevator, stretched and walked slowly into Alice's apartment.

'How did she get up here?' Vanessa asked.

Alice shrugged. 'That's our next mystery.' She watched the cat stroll over to the patch of sun by the window and flop down. 'Now that's retirement,' she mumbled, closing the door behind her.

In the lobby they split up, Vanessa heading behind the reception desk and through the door to the back offices, while Alice exited through the front door. She spotted Owen walking towards the rose garden and followed him.

When Alice had first moved into the complex and heard there was a rose garden, she'd had visions of a couple of rose bushes tucked away in a corner. While it *was* tucked away beside the Olympic complex, that was about the only thing she had been right about. Surrounded by a waist-high hedge, the rose garden was home to dozens of rose bushes of different colours, sizes and (according to the small signs planted in front of each bush) species. Alice had made the mistake of saying out loud that she hadn't realised there were multiple species of roses and had spent the next hour being lectured by Freda, the resident anthophile. She'd had to ask someone what that word meant and had decided it fit Freda exactly.

In the middle of the rose garden were two wooden benches, back to back, both with small brass plaques advising who had donated them. Alice had heard that it was a tranquil place to sit, surrounded by colour and quiet, but stopping to smell the roses was never a saying she'd had much use for.

Alice entered the garden through the gap in the hedge and saw Owen standing before a bright yellow rose bush. As she approached he reached out and broke off a flower.

'I'm pretty sure they don't like you doing that,' Alice said.

Owen turned with a sad smile. 'The roses?'

'They probably don't like it either, but I was talking about management.'

He stared at the flower in his hand, then shrugged. 'Unless they're keeping a tally I don't think they're going to miss one.'

'Do you mind if we sit?' Alice asked. 'I've been doing far too much walking today and my legs are reminding my hips that they never liked exercise much.'

They settled themselves onto one of the benches, the sun warming Alice's back. She had to admit it was peaceful. The concrete and glass structure of the recreational building loomed over the tops of the rose bushes, and to their left past the edge of the small hedge was a bigger hedge that guaranteed the residents privacy from their neighbours and the rest of the world.

'Owen, I think it's time you tell me about Betty and the money,' Alice said firmly.

Owen raised his eyes from the rose and looked at her with a troubled expression. 'There's the matter of confidence.'

'Betty is dead. And I'm not convinced it was by natural causes.'

She'd been going for a gentle push, but by the look of shock and disbelief on his face, Alice had achieved that with all the subtlety of a freight train.

'What on earth are you talking about?'

She quickly told him what she and Vanessa had discovered. By the end the shock had worn off but disbelief was still firmly in place.

'You can't possibly think someone killed Betty. I'm sorry but that is just..'

'Preposterous? Ludicrous? Outrageous?'

The corner of Owen's mouth twitched.

'I've gone through all the *ous* words Owen, but there's no way that she got stung by Ongaonga nettles naturally.'

'But why would anyone want Betty dead?'

'Which brings us back to Betty's secret. It could be a motive.'

Owen nodded slowly. 'I see. Well I guess telling you can't hurt now. It *was* to do with money, in a manner of speaking, as you guessed earlier. I wasn't really helping her myself, it was never my area of expertise, and it had been a long time since I'd worked directly with customers, so I just provided her with one of my old contacts.'

'In the bank.'

'Yes, at the bank.'

'Contacts for what?' Alice asked, finding it increasingly difficult to stifle her impatience.

'Gold. Buying and selling, specifically.'

'Gold,' she repeated.

'Yes, you know, that yellow stuff, worth a bit,' Own replied with another twitch of his mouth.

'Yes, I've heard of it. What *specifically* did Betty want help with? Buying or selling?'

'Selling. She had recently come into a quantity of gold and wanted to know how to sell it. Banks don't really handle that sort of thing, it's usually done through gold dealers, but a man I had worked with had some experience in that area so I gave her his name and number.'

Alice sat back in her seat and considered the implications. 'So why did you want to talk to me about it? It seems a straightforward thing.'

Owen nodded. 'The transaction wasn't the problem. I was just hoping that you could persuade Betty to put the gold into the safe in the main office here.'

'She had the gold with her? In her apartment?'

'Yes. She told me she'd had a lifetime of fighting with banks and other institutions and that she didn't have the strength to do it now so she was keeping the gold with her.'

'Where did it come from?'

'She didn't tell me. She just said that it arrived recently, and she was grumbling about how much the courier cost.'

The skin on the back of Alice's neck prickled and she rubbed it with her hand. 'How much gold are we talking about?'

'I'm not sure exactly. Roughly about ten kilograms, I think?'

'Ten kilograms?'

'Yes, roughly.'

'Unless roughly means you're nine and a half kilos out, that's a lot of gold. What's that worth?'

'It depends on the day's price of course.'

'Roughly,' Alice said, earning a proper smile this time.

'Roughly... I would say about half a million dollars.'

'Bloody hell.'

'Yes.'

'No, you silly boy. Bloody hell, you've just described the perfect motive for murder.'

'Oh...' Owen responded as her words sunk in.

'And bloody hell, where is it now?'

FIFTEEN

Considering she out-aged him by at least a decade, Alice should have been struggling to keep up with Owen as they hurried to Betty's apartment, but it was Owen who was puffing to catch up.

'You were walking two strides to every one of mine, how did you beat me?' Owen said, wheezing as they reached the big front doors.

'Because you're old and slow and I'm just old.'

When they approached Betty's front door, Vanessa was leaning against the wall, tapping on her phone. She looked up as they got closer and Alice immediately saw that something was wrong.

'I don't want to talk about it,' Vanessa said, shoving her phone into her pants pocket.

'Talk about what?' Alice asked.

'About…. Oh. Nice try. Hi, Owen.'

'Good morning, Vanessa.'

Vanessa looked at Alice.

'I told him our suspicions and he told me something interesting. Let's talk about it inside.'

Vanessa unlocked Betty's front door using her key and pushed it open, stepping aside to let Alice go in first.

The room didn't look like they did on crime shows, with furniture torn apart, pictures smashed and lamps overturned, but Alice could see that someone had definitely searched the apartment. Betty hadn't been a neat freak, but she wasn't a slob. Cupboard doors were ajar, the coffee table had been dragged to an odd angle as if someone had moved it so they could look under the couch.

A quick check in the bedroom revealed similar disturbances. The wardrobe doors were wide open and several shoe boxes had been pulled out and opened.

'What's wrong?' Owen asked.

'Someone's searched the place,' she replied.

'I was here yesterday and it wasn't like this,' Vanessa said. 'Tracey asked me to check the apartment was secure and I popped my head in. That coffee table was definitely straight and the kitchen cupboards were closed. What were they looking for?'

'At a guess, about ten kilos of gold.'

'That's a hell of specific guess.'

'It seems our mild-mannered Betty was a gold tycoon,' Alice told Vanessa. 'Recently anyway.'

Vanessa looked thoughtful. 'That's a hell of a motive for murder,' she said, looking around the room. 'What would ten kilos of gold look like?'

Owen shrugged. 'It depends on the form it takes. It could be in bars or coins or nuggets....'

'Or one big piece?' Vanessa asked.

'Well,' Owen scratched his cheek and adjusted his tie, 'the largest nugget ever found weighed 78 kilograms, so it's not unheard of.' He saw Alice's expression. 'I was curious when Betty told me about the gold so I did some research. Anyway that was found in Australia. The heaviest nugget ever found here was only three kilos. I'd be surprised if it was all in one piece.'

'Could it be flat?' Vanessa looked over at the bookcase. 'Like in a book?'

'A very big book perhaps,' Owen conceded.

Alice had visited Betty several times, but had never paid close attention to the titles on display, assuming they were romances or the cosy mystery books most people her age read. She was basing this on the two women she'd seen in the dining room reading books with topless men on the cover.

When Alice stepped closer to inspect the bookcase, she was surprised to see that Betty preferred the horror genre (unless romance had changed considerably over the years). All of the titles on Betty's shelf included either *blood*, *death*, or *vampire* (and in one case all three).

'That's unexpected,' Vanessa said as she pulled one of the books off the shelf. '*Too Many Vampires*, mmm the movie was better.'

'I guess you never really know someone until they're dead,' Alice replied.

'Don't tell me you have books like this,' said Vanessa as she replaced the book.

'I prefer stories that make you think rather than blink.'

Vanessa smiled. 'I like that. I'm going to use it.'

'Be my guest,' Alice muttered as she ran a finger along the tops of the books. There didn't seem to be any missing and none felt different to her touch, like their pages might be glued together. She checked the other shelves but they all appeared unremarkable as well.

'I'm not sure I feel comfortable with this,' Owen said. 'We shouldn't really be going through Betty's things.'

Alice turned to face him. 'Then wait outside, because we need to figure out if the murderer got what they came for and the only way to do that is to search for it.'

The troubled expression on his face increased.

'Owen,' Alice said with a sigh. 'You knew Betty, as well as anyone did. She was very pragmatic so do you honestly think she would mind us doing this?'

Owen took his time replying before finally nodding. 'I suppose she wouldn't. What can I do to help?'

'You search out here. Vanessa and I will take the bedroom. Call out if you find anything.'

With Vanessa doing all the heavy lifting, it took them 30 minutes to search the entire apartment. There was no sign of the gold. Vanessa even checked the freezer, although Alice advised that it was traditionally diamonds that were hidden in the ice tray. And just to be certain the gold wasn't hidden in a tub of cookie dough ice cream, Alice tasted several spoonfuls.

Alice stood in the middle of the lounge, while Owen straightened the couch cushions and Vanessa nudged the coffee table back into place.

'They must have taken it,' Owen said.

'It looks that way,' Vanessa replied.

Alice wasn't convinced. She had more faith in her friend's sneakiness. The question was, if it wasn't hidden here, then where was it.

She turned to Owen. 'You said you recommended that Betty put it in the office safe. Do we know that she didn't? Vanessa?'

Vanessa shook her head. 'She would have asked Tracey.'

'Can you find out?'

'I could say I need to do a complete inventory of Betty's belongings before her children get here and did she have anything in the safe.'

'Good. Off you go. We'll regroup at my place at dinner time and compare notes.'

'What are you going to do?' Vanessa asked.

'We have the motive, now I need a suspect. It has to be someone who was in the room during the tournament. With all the residents and staff, I think there were thirty names on the list.'

'You suspect the staff?'

'The only two people I don't suspect, apart from myself, are you and Owen,' Alice told her.

'But I know the staff.'

'Do you? Or do you just chat to them at work?' Alice said. 'How well do you actually know them?'

She could tell she was making Vanessa uncomfortable, but now that she was sure it was murder, and why, Alice was more determined than ever to get revenge for Betty's murder. *Justice*, she corrected herself.

'I'm not particularly happy with the idea that it was one of the residents either,' Alice said. 'These are people we see every day and though they are many things (liars, thieves, boring), I never pegged any of them as killers.'

'Right, well let's hope it's one of the residents.' Vanessa's face took on a panicked look as she realised what she'd said. 'I mean—'

'It's alright, dear, we know what you meant, don't we, Owen?'

Owen nodded.

Vanessa left the apartment looking more troubled than ever.

'That girl seems more upset now that the murderer could be someone she works with than the very idea that there was a murder in the first place,' Owen remarked.

Alice looked around Betty's apartment one last time, trying to identify the nagging feeling she had that there was something she was overlooking.

She nodded absently. 'No one likes to think that their colleagues are capable of killing. It could make staff morning teas quite awkward.'

They closed the door and Alice checked that it had automatically locked behind them. She thought about installing one of her old tricks so that she'd be able to see if the door was opened again, but decided against it. For one thing she didn't have a match, and secondly it looked like the apartment had already been searched so it was unlikely the person would come back. Unless there was more than one person after Betty's gold, but that thought made her head ache. Briefly she wondered if she was up for all this investigating business. Her legs hurt, her head hurt. She was exhausted.

'If I'm hurting I'm breathing,' she murmured to herself.

'What's that?' Owen asked.

She flapped her hand to indicate it was nothing. What she needed was to talk to her granddaughter.

'I'll catch up with you later, Owen,' she said as they stopped outside Stumpy. The sun sat low in the sky casting long shadows over the lawn. 'In the meantime don't talk about this with anyone.'

'Don't worry. It's not the sort of thing that casually comes up in conversation.'

She nodded grimly. 'We don't know who did this and until we do, assume everyone is out to kill you.'

'What?!'

'I'm kidding. But let's just say someone has already killed for the gold. If they hear you talking about it they might assume you know more than you do. Best to keep quiet.'

She left Owen wearing a troubled expression. It seemed she was dispensing fear everywhere she went today.

As she walked past the café she glanced in and happened to see Nanci sitting at a table by herself.

Alice changed direction and stepped through the open door.

'The usual, Alice?' Connor asked from behind the counter.

'Takeaway, please,' She pointed at the table where Nanci was sitting.

'Alice, join me,' Nanci said with a wave at the seat opposite her. She waited until Alice was settled in her seat before asking, 'How are you holding up?'

'Oh, it's never easy to lose a friend, is it?'

Nanci shook her head. 'Lord knows I've lost enough people close to me over the years. It always gets to you.'

Alice hesitated then decided to press ahead. 'Nanci, I think you and I are similar, at least in our previous working lives.' She paused to watch Nanci's response.

'I'm flattered that you think we're in the same league,' Nanci replied.

'So you know who I am,' Alice said with narrowed eyes.

Nanci sipped her coffee. 'Let's just say if you're who I'm pretty sure you are then you were the gold standard in our business.'

Alice snorted dismissively, but couldn't help inwardly flinching at the mention of gold.

'My reason for talking to you is twofold,' she said, 'although perhaps they're the one and the same. Teresa is my friend, and she can be a pain in the behind, but I'd hate to see her get taken in. If she is part of your long game then it's best you stop now.'

'I'm retired,' Nanci said.

'So am I,' Alice replied. They both waited to see who would twitch first.

Nanci sighed. 'Alright,' she said. 'Teresa is a fool and I could easily take her for everything she's got. But I really am retired. This is where I'm planning to live out the rest of my hopefully long life. I'm not going to mess that up. That thing with the poker tournament was a favour. For a new friend. That and I wanted to see if you were as good as I'd heard.'

Alice decided to accept her words at face value, or at least give the woman that impression. Her tea was delivered to the table and Alice stood up.

'Just out of curiosity, what would you have done if I *was* up to something?' Nanci asked.

'You've done your research on me?'

Nanci nodded.

'London 1972.'

Nanci's face paled. It was a satisfying response.

SIXTEEN

Alice read the list of names again. It was pointless trying to strike anyone off it, because every time she did a nagging doubt surfaced and she immediately put the name back on again. The trouble was that none of them struck her as a cold-blooded killer. Or a warm-blooded killer for that matter.

The only two people she could cross off the list with any certainty were herself and Vanessa. In theory she should also remove Owen as a suspect because he was in love with Betty and because he'd told her about the gold, but then love was also a powerful motive.

Moodily she watched Maddy, who was lying on the other end of the couch. As if sensing she was under scrutiny the cat opened one eye.

'Who did it?' Alice asked her.

'Rowl,' Maddy replied.

'Are you sure?'

'Mraw.'

'That's not helpful. Now if this thing could translate cat,' she waved her phone.

Maddy closed her eye again and Alice went into the kitchen in search of inspiration. A couple of sips from one of her many hidden flasks later and she had no more answers but was feeling calmer.

There was a soft knock at the door and the camera revealed Vanessa standing outside with several containers of food.

'I thought pizza two nights in a row would be bad for my figure,' she said when Alice let her in.

'What on earth are you talking about? You're gorgeous.'

'Well thanks, but I'm not going to stay that way if I stress eat and pizza is my stress-eating go-to. Even now I'm craving a chicken and bacon pizza with camembert.'

Alice began unpacking the food onto the kitchen bench, opening the first container to find noodles and vegetables.

'What do you have to be stressed about? Well, apart from the whole murder thing.'

'I don't want to talk about it,' Vanessa replied as she rummaged in the top drawer and pulled out two forks.

Alice took one of the forks and began loading wontons onto a plate. 'What did Ben do?'

Vanessa gave her a sharp look. 'Who said he did anything?'

'Because most of the time when people don't want to talk about something, it relates to what a man has done. Or hasn't done but was supposed to do.'

Vanessa chewed a piece of broccoli while Alice waited patiently for her to decide how much she want to reveal.

'It's Ben,' she said finally. 'He texted me to say he wasn't sure about our relationship.'

'Dump him,' Alice replied firmly.

'Alice!'

'Do you love him?'

'I really like him and we've been going out for a while,' Vanessa said.

'Right so you don't love him, and he obviously doesn't love you or else he'd say something to your face instead of over text. So I repeat, dump him.'

'But—'

'You are a confident, beautiful young woman and if he doesn't realise what he has then dump him faster than I dumped the Beverley Diamond Ring in '68.'

Vanessa tilted her head to the side and narrowed her eyes. 'Very quickly.'

'You're right, I know. I do like him though.'

'Does he challenge you?'

The head tilt was back. 'I don't understand. To a duel?'

'No, fool girl, does he challenge you to be a better person? Does he try and be your knight in shining armour or does he push you to be better?'

Vanessa answered by forking noodles into her mouth, leaving a tiny trace of sauce on her lip which she wiped with a napkin before speaking. 'I guess… he tries to make everything better.'

Alice waved her hand. 'Then dump him. You deserve someone that makes you better, not safe.'

Vanessa frowned. Then there was a slow nod and Alice wasn't sure whether her message had got through. She hoped it had.

'I've got something for you,' Vanessa said through a mouthful of food. She dug a slip of paper out of her back pocket.

When Alice opened it she saw there was a telephone number written on it along with the name Zoe.

'Betty's daughter. I thought the best way to find out about the gold might be to ask a relative.'

Alice nodded approvingly and fetched her phone from the coffee table.

Dialling the number, it connected after one ring. 'Zoe speaking,' came a strong voice down the line.

Alice fumbled with the phone and put the call on speaker.

'Zoe, this is Alice Atkinson speaking. I was a friend of your mother's at Silvermoon.'

'Yes, Mrs Atkinson. She mentioned you several times. Thank you for calling.'

'I'm sorry for your loss, dear.'

'Thank you. I don't mean to be rude, but I'm just about to head to the airport.'

'I was at your mother's apartment today to water the plants and I'm afraid it looks like someone has been in there without permission.'

'Oh hell. Was anything missing?' Zoe asked in a resigned tone.

'It's hard to tell. It doesn't look like it, but I could be wrong.' Alice paused, wondering how to proceed. 'There is one other thing…'

'Yes?'

'Betty mentioned before she died that she had a quantity of gold in her apartment.'

There was silence on the other end of the phone line.

'We can't seem to locate it,' Alice finished.

More silence, then finally Zoe asked, 'How much gold?'

'I think roughly ten kilograms.'

Still more silence, then a swear word that had both Alice and Vanessa nodding in appreciation.

'She bloody told me it was a family heirloom,' Zoe muttered.

'The gold was?' Vanessa asked.

'Who's that?'

'Sorry, Zoe. My name is Vanessa, I work at Silvermoon and I knew your mother too. I was supervising Alice while she was in Betty's apartment. Management rules.'

Alice was impressed and made a circle with her finger and her thumb and held it up to Vanessa.

'Oh, I see. Well I didn't know it was gold. There was an old locked wooden box that had been in the family for decades. Longer probably. I think it originally belonged to Mum's grandfather. Mum asked me to send it to her because we're selling the farm.'

'Do you think she knew what was in it?' Vanessa asked.

'I'm not sure. I don't think so, otherwise she wouldn't have been happy for it to go via courier.'

Alice felt her mouth open slightly at the thought of a half million dollars bouncing around in the back of a courier van.

'And now you say you can't find it?' Zoe asked.

'How big was the box?' Alice said.

'Uh, a bit bigger than a loaf of bread, I suppose. The proper big loaves, not those little gluten-free things.'

Alice had never seen or eaten anything gluten-free in her life, and wasn't even sure what it meant, but she assumed a gluten-free loaf was smaller than a normal loaf.

'I should report this to the police,' Zoe sighed again.

Vanessa nodded to Alice who shook her head.

'You absolutely should, although I think it might be better to wait until you get here. It might just be that we overlooked it and I wouldn't want to waste police time,' Alice said.

'I suppose so. I'll be there first thing in the morning. Could you meet me at Mum's apartment at 9am?'

'Of course,' Alice replied.

'Thank you. I'll see you then.' There was a click followed by silence.

'Why didn't you tell her Betty was murdered?' Vanessa asked.

Alice refilled her plate with more noodles. 'Is that really the sort of thing that should be done over the phone?'

Vanessa hid her embarrassment behind a forkful of rice.

'Anyway, we've got until tomorrow morning to try and solve the murder and find the gold. Zoe doesn't strike me as someone who will let the police dismiss our suspicions.'

'Which is a good thing, right?'

'It's messy.' Alice sighed. 'Worst case scenario they ignore her and she kicks up a fuss around the village, panicking the murderer who takes off, probably with the gold. Best case scenario the police believe her and cause a fuss around the village causing the murderer to take off, probably with the gold.'

Vanessa paused, her fork half-raised towards her mouth. 'Either way we're screwed.'

'Not quite. Like I said, there's a third option: we solve the case and find the murderer before Zoe turns up here in the morning.'

'And how do you propose doing that in…' Vanessa glanced at the oven clock behind Alice, 'the next fifteen hours?'

'By spending the first part of it eating and thinking,' Alice replied, crunching on a wonton.

SEVENTEEN

It took the rest of dinner and several sips from the hip flask usually hidden in the container marked flour before Alice formed an inkling of a plan.

'Why hide the hip flasks?' Vanessa asked, disrupting her thoughts. 'You're the only one who lives here.'

Alice grinned. 'Two reasons. One, it's an old habit that I don't have the desire to break. I always hid valuable things around the house and I like to stay in practice.'

'And the second reason?'

Alice's smile grew wider. 'Because I like the thought that when I finally stop breathing, the person who goes through this place will find a seemingly endless supply of hip flasks in the most unusual of places.'

Vanessa cracked up laughing and that's when the inkling turned into a half-plan.

'Did we check the freezer? That's a good place to hide things, although it's best for diamonds. What?' she said, realising Vanessa had stopped laughing and was looking at her strangely.

'We've already had this conversation,' Vanessa said.

Alice frowned, then remembered they had talked about it in Betty's apartment.

'Right,' she waved her hand in irritation. 'I'm allowed to forget things occasionally without being accused of senility.'

'I didn't accuse you of anything.'

'You were thinking it,' Alice shot back.

'All I said was we've already had that conversation. And if you're going to get grumpy every time I look at you then I can just leave now.'

They glared at each other and it was Alice who blinked first.

'Fair enough,' she said. 'I'll try to keep the grumpiness to a minimum.'

Vanessa nodded, 'Thanks. And I'll try and avoid looking at you.

'We're beginning to sound like an old married couple.'

'Who are you calling old, grandma?'

'You've got too much sass. Why don't you go to the gym and work it out?'

Alice stopped.

'What?' Vanessa asked.

'Maybe I am losing it.'

She got up and started walking towards the door.

'Where're you going?'

'To the Olympic complex. I saw Betty go in there on Tuesday and she was carrying a bag.'

Vanessa caught up with her at the door. 'You didn't tell me that.'

'I just remembered. If she wasn't going to the gym, then why did she have a bag?'

Vanessa pushed the elevator call button. 'Because she was hiding the gold.'

'Right.'

'Why was she hiding it? Why not just leave it in her apartment.'

Alice pondered that all the way to the ground floor until they stepped through the front door and paused on the top step. Freda and Les were walking hand in hand towards the rose garden. Freda must have talked to him.

A thought suddenly came to her.

'Because she told someone about the gold,' Alice said. 'And then Betty didn't feel it was safe in the apartment, so she decided to hide it.'

They began walking towards the recreation building.

'But… the only person she told was Owen,' Vanessa said in a low voice. 'Are you saying…'

'I'm not saying anything,' Alice replied. She refused to believe her friend was responsible for murder.

'Besides,' she continued, having thought of something. 'He was the one who told me about the gold. Why would he do that if he was the one who killed Betty for it? It would have been smarter to keep quiet and look for it once he'd got her out of the picture.'

'Good point,' Vanessa said, relief evident in her voice. 'Although the cynical voice in my head says that maybe he just needed you to get him into her apartment.'

'Never listen to the cynical voice,' Alice replied. She wished she could believe her own words, but a lifetime of lying to other people had left her with the ingrained assumption that everyone else was doing the same.

As they got to the front door of the recreation centre Alice looked towards the café. Teresa and Nanci were standing outside talking. As she watched, Nanci walked away and Teresa headed in her direction.

'I've got a better idea,' Alice muttered to Vanessa. 'Teresa!' she greeted her.

'Hello, Alice, Vanessa,' Teresa said with a wary smile. 'What are you two up to?'

Alice looked around as if to make sure no one was listening, then leaned in closer. 'Teresa, I think you should be careful of Nanci. I don't trust her. I wouldn't want you to be taken in.'

Teresa squeezed Alice's arm. 'Don't worry, Alice. You're a dear to be concerned, but I know all about Nanci's background. I had my lawyer do some digging before I agreed to let her teach me card tricks.' She laughed at the surprise on Alice's face. 'I know I come across as a bit, shall we say, *frivolous* sometimes, but I have no intention of giving my money away. You don't know how painful it is handing over my poker losses each week. If someone shows up and decides they want to be my best friend I always get them checked out.'

'Just how rich are you?' Alice asked bluntly.

Teresa winked. 'Let's just say that I can see rich when I look in my rear-view mirror.'

Alice only just managed to conceal her irritation. If she'd known the woman was that wealthy she would have raised the stakes in poker a long time ago.

'Speaking of rich, did you know that Betty had left a considerable sum of money when she died?'

She did her best to ignore Vanessa's look of shock, while focussing on Teresa's expression.

'Really?'

'Yes,' Alice confirmed with a nod, 'a valuable heirloom.'

'Oh really?'

Alice watched her closely. There was no sign of greed, only curiosity.

'Yes, a family heirloom. Betty told us she left it in the games room in a special hiding spot. Vanessa and I are going to check it's safe and hand it over to Betty's daughter at 9am when she arrives.'

'Why not put it in the office safe?' Teresa frowned.

'Well the thing is…' Alice stopped. She hadn't actually thought this far through.

'The thing is,' interjected Vanessa, 'there's no room in the safe right now, and we're going to make sure the object is secure where it is. It's just as safe where it is, especially since no one knows it's there.'

'Right,' Alice said shooting Vanessa a look of appreciation. 'Don't tell anyone, Teresa, understand?'

'Of course. Lips sealed and all that.'

'Thank you. Now we'd best press on. Remember, not a soul.'

'Absolutely. If there's one thing I know how not to talk about it's money.'

Teresa walked away towards her building while the others walked inside.

'Why did you tell her?'

'What's Teresa's reputation in the village?' Alice said.

'She's tight with money,' Vanessa replied.

'And?'

'She's loose with gossip,' Vanessa finished with a grin.

'I guarantee you she's heading for the dining room right now to not tell everyone she can find about Betty's heirloom.'

'So how does that help us?'

They walked down the hallway to the games room, and Alice pushed open the door.

'How does a flood of people coming to search for the gold help us find it?' Vanessa asked again, as they stepped into the room.

'I think most people will treat Teresa's story as nothing more than a curiosity. As far as we know there are only two people that know there's really any gold. Owen, and the murderer.'

'And you're hoping that the murderer will come and try and find it.'

'Exactly.'

Vanessa looked at her suspiciously. 'And we'll jump out at them and shout *Gotcha*?'

'Exactly,' Alice repeated.

'Got to say, I hate this plan.'

'You don't have to stay,'

'Oh sure, I'll just leave an old woman by herself to wait for a murderer. Mum will love hearing that when I go around for Sunday dinner. "What did you do this week, darling?" "Oh I let one of the residents get herself killed while I went home and ate rocky road ice cream and watched Netflix."'

'Are you finished?'

Vanessa's eyes narrowed, then she shrugged. 'Sure.'

'You know you get quite testy when you're mad.'

'Then stop making me mad,' Vanessa shot back.

'Why? It's entertaining. Now that the issue of you staying is settled, let's look for the gold.'

The communal room was about the size of Betty's entire apartment. At one end was a pool table and table tennis table, while the other end had several tables for card and board games. A full-length built-in cupboard ran along one wall, and large windows let in plenty of natural light.

There were limited places to hide a box of gold and once they'd searched behind all the books and inside all the game boxes they reluctantly concluded it wasn't there.

'Now what?' Vanessa asked.

Alice surveyed the room trying to identify anywhere they might have missed. 'The plan doesn't change. The gold might not be here, but the murderer doesn't know that, so we wait.'

'And what if someone comes in to play a game of pool?'

'It's Thursday night. Everyone is either glued to that cooking show on Channel One, or the rugby match. No one will be coming here,' Alice said.

They chose seats which allowed them to see the door clearly, but meant anyone would have to step right into the room to see them. To pass the time Alice showed Vanessa some more card tricks, then beat her six poker hands in a row. Slowly the room grew dark as the sun disappeared behind the hill.

Vanessa switched on the overhead lights.

'This is a waste of time,' she said as she shuffled the cards.

'It wouldn't be if we were playing for money.'

'That's not what I—'

The door swung open.

EIGHTEEN

'Oh,' said Nanci. 'I wasn't expecting anyone to be in here at this time.' She had stepped confidently into the room and had frozen on seeing the two women.

'No? Then what are you doing here?' Alice asked.

Nanci's eyes darted around. 'I just came to play some solitaire,' she said fixing on the deck of cards.

'I'm sure a woman of your life experience would have some cards in her apartment,' Alice said in a deliberately casual tone.

'Yes,' Nanci nodded, her eyes still roaming the room. 'Of course I do, but sometimes I like a change of environment.'

'Oh absolutely.' Alice nodded.

'What are you two doing in here?'

Alice looked at Vanessa who was sitting rigidly in her seat, her knuckles white as she gripped the edge of the table. She patted Vanessa's arm.

'You haven't just talked to Teresa, I suppose,' Alice said, ignoring Nanci's question.

Nanci's eyes rested on Alice's face. She licked her lips.

'Teresa?'

'Yes, and of course she didn't tell you about Betty's missing heirloom and how it might be hidden in this room.'

Nanci seemed to be struggling with how to respond, then her body relaxed. She nodded. 'Alright, yes. Old habits and all that. I thought it might be worth a sniff.'

'To give it to Betty's family?' Vanessa suggested.

Nanci smiled, then looked at Alice. 'Remember when we were that naïve?'

Alice shook her head. 'I never was. Anyway we're settling in for a long game of cards, we might be here late into the night, or even early morning.'

'Perhaps I could…'

'No, you couldn't,' Alice replied firmly.

Nanci sighed. 'Oh well, easy come easy go. Enjoy your game.'

After Nanci left the room, Vanessa turned to Alice. 'What are you doing? She could have been the killer!'

'No,' Alice shook her head. 'She's a con artist and shady as all hell, and she might have conned Betty out of the gold, but she wouldn't have killed her for it.'

'How can you possibly know that?' Vanessa demanded, her eyes flicking to the closed door as if expecting Nanci to pop back through any second waving a killer plant.

'Because she's me. A slightly younger less polished version of me. And I wouldn't kill anyone.'

'That's lame.'

'Are you dead? No? Then trust me, it's not her,' Alice replied.

They settled down again but Alice quickly realised Vanessa's heart was no longer in the game. She looked at the big clock on the wall with its exaggeratedly large numbers and saw it was edging towards nine o'clock. Outside darkness had reduced the world to shades of black with glimpses of streetlights through the trees that lined the edge of the property.

'I'm getting thirsty. Would you be a dear and go and fetch one of the hip flasks from my apartment?'

'But what if… what if someone comes while I'm gone?'

Alice looked at the clock again. 'You won't be long, and I'm sure if anyone shows up before you get back I can stall until the cavalry arrives.'

Vanessa looked unconvinced so Alice pressed on. 'I've got my phone. I'll call you and you can come running. It'll be good for you to get some fresh air because we're likely to be here all night and I don't need you falling asleep on me.'

'Okay, but I'll be right back,' Vanessa said.

She paused at the doorway and looked back, as if about to change her mind, then disappeared into the hallway and the door slowly shut.

Alice got up from her chair and searched the room again. The gold had to be somewhere and this was the only place it could be.

A little later she slumped back into the chair, tired and still without the gold. She looked back at the clock and saw that Vanessa had been gone for almost ten minutes. She felt her eyes slide shut and yawned. It had been a long time since she'd attempted to stay up all night and she was beginning to think she might have overestimated her ability to do so.

She closed her eyes once more. Vanessa would be back in a few minutes. It wouldn't hurt to rest until then.

NINETEEN

She dreamed that the door opened and someone entered the room. The person towered over her chair.

With a start she realised she wasn't dreaming. Her eyes snapped open and blinked a few times, adjusting to the light.

'Shame. I was hoping you'd stay asleep, it would have made this a lot easier.'

'Sorry to complicate your murder plot,' Alice replied. Her eyes darted to the clock. She'd been asleep for almost thirty minutes. Where was Vanessa?

'Your friend won't be coming to help. She's been detained.'

'What did you do to her, Gordon?' Alice snapped. 'If you've killed her I'll—'

'You'll what?' Gordon smirked. 'Overpower me and race to her rescue?' He gave a short laugh that sent a chill down her back.

'No, I'll do this.'

Gordon obviously felt that his superior size and the fact that he was a man meant an ordinary woman like Alice would be automatically intimidated by his presence. He didn't consider three important factors. One, he had killed one of her close friends. Two, he might have harmed a girl she was very fond of. And three, she had never been an ordinary woman. As such, Gordon was completely unprepared when Alice's hand shot out, grabbed one of his fingers and wrenched it sideways.

There was a loud snap, and an even louder scream.

Staggering out of her chair, Alice hobbled to the door, silently cursing her old body for seizing up every time she sat for more than a minute.

In the dimly-lit hallway she should have turned right and headed for the entrance. Instead she turned left and slipped into the dark gym. Ducking down, she shuffled along the wall until she was sheltered by one of the machines. Every muscle and joint reminded her of her age.

Alice heard a door opening and held her breath, then let it out slowly when she realised it must have been Gordon going into the hallway. She reached for her phone to text for help, but it wasn't in her pocket. With a groan she realised it was still on the table in the games room.

'I know you're in here, Alice,' came Gordon's muffled voice. She was pleased to note the pain in his voice. 'There's no one coming to help you. I've got all night.'

He moved further down the hallway. She knew it wouldn't take him long to realise she wasn't in the pool or changing rooms and come back her way. Hopefully she would have enough time to arm herself.

In the dim light she made out the weights at the other end of the gym. Stepping out from behind the exercise machine she began to quietly cross the room. The minute she took a step forward the sensors caught her movement and the gym lights came on full.

Alice froze, then looked through the glass door into the hallway, where Gordon was smiling at her.

'Should have broken his face,' Alice muttered.

Willing her legs to move she walked as quickly as she could towards the weights stacked neatly against the wall. As she reached them she heard the door open.

Reaching down she attempted to pick up a five kilogram disc. Her arms and back issued a fresh protest, so she ditched that idea and picked up a two kilo weight instead. Turning to face Gordon she gripped the weight in both hands and held it in front of her.

'What are you going to do with that?' Gordon asked. She could see a thin layer of sweat on his forehead and he was cradling his injured hand against his body.

'Do you remember the last time you asked me that?' Alice said brandishing the weight.

Gordon glanced down at his broken finger then gave her the angriest look she'd ever seen. If that look had been a physical thing it would have been a rabid dog crossed with a gorilla.

'Where's the gold?' Gordon asked.

'How do you know about that?' Alice replied.

Gordon glared. 'I overheard Betty talking to Owen about it. So I went snooping, trying to butter her up, but she wasn't having it. Told me to get out. Said I needed castrating. Then had the nerve to complain to Tracey about me.'

'So you thought you'd kill her and steal it.'

'It's alright for you,' Gordon raged, his voice bouncing off the walls. 'For all of you. I'm a retired civil servant. I had to sell everything I owned to afford this place. I needed that money or I was going to have to move. Betty didn't need it. Why shouldn't I have it?'

'Because it didn't belong to you,' Alice said. 'Didn't you learn that lesson in kindergarten?'

Gordon took a step forward and she waved the weight again. It was getting heavy.

'What gave you the idea about using the Ongaonga plant?' she asked.

Gordon edged forward. Now he was halfway across the floor. Alice's eyes darted around the room, identifying and dismissing possible options.

'I used to work for the Department of Conservation,' Gordon said. 'I knew the nettle's sting could be used to lower blood pressure. I didn't really mean to kill her. I just wanted her out of commission while I took off with the gold.'

'Why do it in a room full of people? Why not wait until you were alone?'

'I didn't know how long she was going to hold onto the gold for so I had to act fast.' He smiled grimly. 'No one was paying attention to me, so it was easy to slip up behind her and brush the spines against her neck. Her skin was so leathery from working outside all her life she barely felt it. I was worried I'd stick myself, even with my hand wrapped in a handkerchief. By the time she collapsed I was on the other side of the room, just another bystander concerned about poor Betty.'

Alice wished she had the strength to throw the weight at Gordon's head, but she doubted it would go even a quarter the way.

'So then Teresa told you about our conversation,' she said.

'Over dinner,' Gordon said. 'I'd searched Betty's place and knew it wasn't there. When Teresa said you thought an heirloom was hidden in this building I knew immediately what you must be talking about. I was on my way here when I saw Vanessa leave, so I followed her and made sure she wasn't going to come back.'

Alice felt anger bubble up and she swallowed it back down. She needed her wits sharp, not dulled with fury.

'You've overstepped, Gordon. You killed Betty, attacked Vanessa, and now you're after me? The police will figure out it's you.'

'Who cares,' Gordon replied with a shrug. 'I'll have the gold. With half a million dollars I can disappear and start again. So where is it?'

'No idea,' Alice admitted. 'I was sure Betty hid it in the games room but it isn't there.' She inched towards him.

'You're lying.'

'No, I... Owen, now!' she yelled.

Gordon whirled around and Alice took a big step forward, closing the distance between them. Gordon realised he'd been tricked and turned back as Alice swung the weight as hard as she could, connecting with the soft bit between his legs.

Gordon let out a strangled cry, his eyes bulged and he fell to the ground.

'Not quite castration, but it'll do,' Alice said as she dropped the weight and stepped over him.

She hustled to the door. She heard her name being shouted, as the door in front of her burst open and Owen strode in with Tracey right behind him.

'Alice, are you alright?' he asked.

'Absolutely fine,' she lied, ignoring the pain in her chest and the burning in her lungs.

'Alice!' Gordon yelled from the gym.

Owen looked over her shoulder. 'He sounds in pain,' he commented dryly.

'I hope so,' Alice replied.

'What on earth is going on?' Tracey asked, bewildered.

'Betty was murdered. Gordon did it. You'd better call the police.' Alice pushed past her and hobbled towards the door.

'Where are you going?' asked Tracey.

'To find Vanessa.'

TWENTY

'My head hurts,' Vanessa said.

'My everything hurts' Alice replied.

They were sitting in Alice's apartment with Betty's daughter Zoe, Tracey, Owen, Judith, and stretched out in a patch of sun, Maddy.

'It was very unwise,' Judith told her. 'You should have come to the police.'

'Excuse me, but we did,' Vanessa said angrily. 'You blew us off.'

Judith's face went red and she mumbled an excuse, earning another scowl from Vanessa.

'I'm glad you're alright, Vanessa,' Owen said.

'So am I. I can't believe that dickhead gave me a concussion.'

When Alice had returned to her apartment she'd found Vanessa lying on the floor, a nasty cut to the back of her head. After she came to and was seen by a paramedic, she told Alice how Gordon came to the door just as she was leaving, forced her inside and hit her with a vase from the side table.

'After you called yesterday I dug through some old family journals,' Zoe began. 'It turns out my great grandfather dug up two giant gold nuggets back when he was a gold prospector. He kept one and sold the other, which is how my family could afford the land for the farm. The remaining nugget was passed down from generation to generation until Mum decided to sell it and divide it amongst us kids so we could afford to buy our own houses.'

'That sounds like Betty,' Owen told her. 'Practicality above sentimentality.'

Zoe smiled at him. She looked exactly like a younger version of her mother.

'We still don't know where it is,' Vanessa said.

Alice struggled to her feet. She was covered in bruises and her arms and back protested. She winced as she straightened up.

'You should book in for a massage when Georgina gets back tomorrow,' Tracey told her.

'Maybe,' she replied as she slowly made her way to the kitchen. 'Wait, what?' She turned to Tracey.

'When Georgina gets back from her leave,' Tracey expanded. 'She's been on leave all week but she'll be back tomorrow.'

Alice felt the beginning of the feeling she got when she'd been stupid.

'How long has she been on leave?' she asked casually.

'For the last five days,' Tracey replied. 'Since Tuesday. Why?'

'Sometimes I want to kick my own butt. Vanessa, come on.'

'Where are we going,' Vanessa asked when she joined Alice at the front door.

'To get the gold.'

'Huh?...Oh. Oh!'

'Exactly.'

In a slow procession everyone followed Alice to the recreation building, where she stopped outside the massage room. She tried the door but it was locked. Vanessa leaned in and slid her card over the security reader. There was a click, and the handle turned under Alice's hand. She pushed the door open to reveal a small windowless room. Off to the left hand side was another door. A massage table sat in the middle of the room and at the far end was a small table with lots of bottles on it.

Alice stepped into the room, closely followed by Vanessa. Owen crowded into the doorway and watched as Alice stood still, her head swivelling from side to side.

There didn't seem to be many places to hide a big chunk of gold. Vanessa opened the second door but it led to a small closet, containing a rail and some empty coat hangers.

Alice's brain was working hard. She tried to think like someone who didn't have a lot of experience hiding things. It had to be somewhere easily accessible.

At the end of the room, next to the table holding all the bottles, was a large wicker basket. A crumpled white towel was visible on top of the basket.

'Too simple,' she muttered.

She walked across the room and pulled out the towel, revealing another used towel. She pulled that out as well and found another one. The basket was half empty now. One more towel came out… revealing a wooden box. Alice reached in to pull it out, then remembered it would weigh at least ten kilos.

'Vanessa, a little help?' she gestured the girl forward.

Vanessa lifted the box out and placed it on the table. Alice fumbled with the latch, then lifted the lid, suddenly aware that the others had crowded into the room.

As gold went it was pretty unspectacular, not bright and shining like you'd expect, but dull. Yellowish. It didn't detract too much from the fact they were looking at half a million dollars.

'Whoa,' Vanessa said.

'Quite,' Alice replied.

TWENTY-ONE

'Are you sure you want to do this?' Nanci asked.

'Well, it's one way to pass the time, don't you think?' Alice replied.

They were sitting on opposite sides of the table in the dining room, a deck of cards and several neatly stacked piles of poker chips between them.

'I've already beaten you once,' Nanci reminded her.

'Well then, you have nothing to worry about.'

Nanci shrugged, picked up the deck of cards and shuffled them. She dealt five cards to each of them.

'This is going to be fun,' Nanci said with a smile.

Alice watched her opponent pick up the five cards and fan them out in her hand. It was small, but there was the tiniest hint of a twitch from her left eyebrow.

'Yes it is,' Alice agreed.

THE END

Author's Note

The Ongaonga plant is a real plant from New Zealand. Its spines are poisonous and there has been at least one death attributed to being stung by the plant, although it isn't usually fatal.

The largest nugget of gold found in New Zealand was 3 kilograms, but why go small when you can go big. It was important to make it worth enough money to spur someone to murder (which I know these days could be any amount at all).

Rodney Strong

Hip Flask and Hanging

A Silvermoon Retirement Village Cozy Mystery

Hip Flask and Hanging

ONƐ

'Are you sure she said to meet you here?' Vanessa asked.

Alice looked up at the front of the old brick railway station. Both it and she used to be a lot younger and shinier.

'You read the message,' she replied. 'She said Platform Nine at 10:30.'

They both looked at the giant clock above the main doors of the building. It was 10:20.

'Let's sit while we wait,' Vanessa suggested.

They walked a few paces to one of the bench seats that lined the walkway to the doors, and Alice eased herself down, stifling the groan that threatened to escape from her mouth.

She'd never had a problem admitting she was getting old. But for Alice there was a difference between *being* old and *feeling* old, and lately she'd been feeling old.

Simply walking around the Silvermoon Retirement Village left her tired and achy. It didn't help that she was still recovering from someone trying to kill her, and that was months ago. The doctor had suggested she avoid strenuous activity for a while. Actually what he'd said was, 'You're 97 years old, don't be in such a bloody hurry to die'. With the life she'd led it had never been a case of being 'in a hurry to die', more death popping in to knock on the front door occasionally.

Alice looked at her companion. Vanessa's long brown hair was pulled back in a ponytail and her green eyes sparked with humour that was never far below the surface. She could have been looking back through time at a younger version of herself. Alice was still as thin as the girl, although she suspected there were more muscles under Vanessa's work uniform than under her own pants and jersey.

Vanessa Carson worked for the Silvermoon Retirement Village as a concierge. Alice intended to change that. This girl was too smart and had too much potential to sit at the beck and call of residents with an average age 50 years older than her 23.

Alice didn't think it would take much persuading. Vanessa was already showing signs of being restless, which is possibly why she jumped at the chance to escort Alice to the train station this morning. Lately she seemed to spend more of her time with Alice than at her desk.

'Were you here when this was built?' Vanessa asked with a wave at the three storey building with a steady stream of people moving through the doors.

'Cheeky,' Alice replied.

Vanessa grinned and Alice shook her head in mock disgust.

'Alright, yes I was. I was fifteen when it opened.'

Vanessa's grin widened and Alice rolled her eyes.

'This is why I don't take you places, you just like reminding me how old I am,' Alice grumbled.

'No one else is going to drive your grumpy butt,' Vanessa laughed.

The ever-present Wellington wind ruffled Alice's hair and she shivered. Though the sky was clear, there was no heat in the May sun. The short, cold days of winter were just around the corner.

Alice looked up at the clock again. It was time to get moving. She had no idea why her granddaughter had asked to meet here, but given Amanda was in the same line of work Alice had been in, strange requests were not unusual.

Alice and Vanessa made their way slowly through the high-ceilinged foyer and past the internal doors to the train platforms. Platform Nine was closest to the road so they turned right and made their way around the corner onto the platform.

Alice scanned the crowd, searching for Amanda and (from a lifetime of habit) for potential victims and threats.

A few feet away a man stood with his back to her. He looked vaguely familiar, which was a description she attributed to half the population.

'Oliver!' she called out.

The man turned and surprise flitted across his face before he nodded.

'Hello, Alice. I assume you're here for the same reason I am?'

'I suspect so.' She considered the implications of him being there. Amanda had been the one to first introduce them, and Alice knew that he'd helped her granddaughter out of a nasty situation recently in Australia. In a way, it made sense that he was here.

What didn't make sense is why they were both there.

'Oliver, this is Vanessa. She drove me here.'

Vanessa thrust out her hand, 'You're Oliver Atkinson, the writer.'

'Uhh, yes. Have you read my books?' Oliver asked.

Vanessa laughed, 'Oh no, I don't read. Not enough time.'

Alice saw a pained expression flash across Oliver's face, then he said, 'I guess those real housewives won't watch themselves.'

Vanessa smiled at him.

'Are you here alone, Oliver?' Alice asked.

He nodded. 'Jennifer's at work and the kids are at school.'

'Not quite what I meant,' she tapped the side of her head.

'Oh,' Oliver replied, his cheeks reddening. 'No.'

'Am I missing something?' Vanessa asked.

'Just an inside joke, dear,' Alice told her.

Before they could say anything else, a bus pulled up next to them and the doors swooshed open. A stream of cruise ship tourists stepped onto the pavement. Alice spotted the sign on the side saying *The Emerald Princess* and it was cruise ship season. It didn't take a genius to put two and two together.

She'd been on a cruise ship once, persuaded in her early sixties by a friend. It had been one of the worst experiences of her life, stuck on a ship with a bunch of old people pretending they were still young by making fools of themselves. Still, the scenery had been spectacular, with the pristine wilderness of Alaska had meant the trip wasn't a complete disaster.

Someone jostled Alice's arm as they passed. The man turned his head and for a moment stared directly into her eyes as he mumbled an apology, before continuing on his way.

A deep chill ran through Alice as she watched him join two women, slipping his arms in between theirs. One of them said something and they all laughed.

'What is it?' Vanessa asked.

'We need to follow that man,' Alice replied.

'Why?' Vanessa turned to where Alice was looking.

'Because he just stole my watch.'

TWO

'Are you sure you were wearing a watch today?' Vanessa asked, as they crossed the street.

The man and his companions were 30 feet in front of them. Fortunately for Alice they didn't seem to be in a hurry.

'I might not always remember your name, but I remember putting my watch on this morning,' Alice said.

'You don't–.'

'I was joking,' Alice reassured her. 'Look, I know he took my watch. Besides, there's something else about him.'

Up ahead the trio stopped at a pedestrian crossing, allowing Alice to slow down. Her hips were protesting the pace, which was still slow enough to let everyone else casually pass them.

Something had been nagging her since the man had caught her eye on the platform. She couldn't shake the feeling that she knew him. Not a good kind of knowing, but one that unsettled her.

He appeared to be in his mid to late 70s, with silver grey hair. His eyes were a dull grey colour and under the blue jacket his frame looked to be all bone and sinew.

They stopped a few feet behind the man, and Alice wracked her brain, wishing it wasn't so full of memories, which made picking one out harder than it used to be.

'Like I always say,' the man's voice drifted in their direction, 'time waits for no man, but will slow down for a lady.' He laughed heartily, joined by the two ladies.

Alice swallowed the bile that rose to her throat. From the look of Vanessa's face she found his banter equally nauseating.

'Oh Richard, you are full of it sometimes,' one of the ladies said with another laugh.

Alice's eyes widened and she spun on the spot and headed in the opposite direction.

'What's happening?' Vanessa asked as she caught up.

'We need to go home, now.' Alice tried and failed to keep fear out of her voice.

Vanessa touched her shoulder. 'Alice, what's wrong?'

'I thought I recognised him, but I didn't think it was possible, because he's dead, or supposed to be dead. But the eyes...' she mumbled. 'The eyes and the name. It has to be him.'

'Him who?' Vanessa asked as they got to the car.

Alice didn't reply until they were both inside the car with their seatbelts done up. 'Richard Dankworth.'

Vanessa put the key into the ignition. 'And who is Richard Dankworth?'

Alice closed her eyes for a long time, and when she opened them again Vanessa was looking worried. For once she didn't have a glib reassurance to give her.

'Richard Dankworth quite likely wants me dead,' Alice said.

'What?'

Alice took several deep breaths and felt herself regaining control.

'Alice, why would that man want you dead?'

'Because he thinks *I* want *him* dead,' Alice replied with a hint of a smile.

'And why would he think that?'

'Probably because I told him.'

THREE

'Is it at all likely that you're going to tell me what's going on?' Vanessa asked, pacing around Alice's living room.

Despite several follow up questions Alice had refused to discuss the matter any further until they were back in her apartment at the Silvermoon Retirement Village.

For some, the word *apartment* wouldn't do the place justice. It was more penthouse, than apartment, with high-end furniture, a kitchen that would make a professional chef weep with envy, and windows with views to Wellington city across the harbour, and to the hills beyond.

Alice sat on the couch watching Vanessa march from the coffee table to the kitchen bench and back again.

After her initial shock, Alice had recovered enough to think more clearly about the implications of what she'd discovered, or what she thought she'd discovered. She wasn't quite ready to believe that Richard Dankworth was alive. But if he was, the odds of him being on the same bus as Amanda being a coincidence were low.

'Alice! You tell me that a guy you thought was dead isn't dead but you wanted him dead and you told him you wanted him dead and so he might want you dead…?' Vanessa flopped down on the couch next to her and sighed. 'That's a lot of dead in one sentence.'

Alice patted her on the knee. 'Would some tea help?'

Vanessa gave her a sly grin. 'No, but some of what's behind the flour container might.'

'That's for special occasions. Try the back of the cutlery drawer.'

Vanessa sprang off the couch, walked into the kitchen and rummaged through the drawer, before returning with a small silver hip flask.

'You know, one day you'll have to tell me how many of these you have hidden around this place.'

'Around the apartment? Or the complex?' Alice replied.

She enjoyed the wide-eyed response, almost as much as she enjoyed hiding the hip flasks. There was no policy banning alcohol at Silvermoon so there was technically no reason to hide them, especially in her own apartment. It was her lifetime-habit of concealing things, and her amusement at imagining those clearing out her apartment after she passed, that spurred her to hide them. Only she knew how many there were.

She took a sip from the flask.

FOUR

London, March 1969

'Maureen? Are you going to answer my question? What are you doing with my favourite flask?'

Alice (also known as Maureen Stratler) looked at the man asking the question. 'Isn't it obvious? I'm having a drink, darling,' she replied with a smile.

William Partridge, Earl of Oxfordshire, 53 and greying, looked uncertainly at the flask in her hands, at her face, then at the bedside drawer she'd retrieved it from.

'But how did you know where to find it?'

'You told me, obviously. It's not like I went snooping.' Which is precisely what she'd done. She knew his nervous reaction had less to do with the hip flask than it did with the envelope filled with questionable pictures.

'Why the troubled face, William?' Alice pouted. Despite being a professional she hated acting like a simpering helpless woman. 'All I did was take a drink. I've got no interest in what else is in that drawer.' She waved a hand dismissively and draped herself over the end of the bed. Though her face was relaxed she watched him carefully. He was supposed to be playing tennis. She'd thought she had plenty of time to work with, but on hearing his voice outside the bedroom door she'd barely had time to snatch the flask, shove the drawer shut and spring away from it.

William took a step towards the bedside table. She could sense his conflict – should he check the drawer while she was there, or laugh it off like it didn't matter?

'It was locked,' he said with narrow eyes.

'Obviously not,' she replied with a smile. 'Otherwise how could I have this?' She raised the flask and took another sip. The liquid burned her throat, she'd never been a fan of whiskey, and she stifled the urge to cough.

She watched his body relax. 'Well, no matter. I just came back to get my wallet. Garth and I are making a little wager on the match. You should come and watch.'

'That sounds like fun,' Alice said. She rose to her feet, enjoying the way his eyes stayed glued to her cleavage. A distracted man was a man who'd already lost. She handed him the hip flask and walked to the door, giving him a smile over her shoulder.

She watched him throw the flask on the bed and follow her out.

She might take it with her when she left, as a souvenir.

FIVE

'Alice?'

Lost in memories, Alice took a sip and handed the flask back to Vanessa.

'Now what would be the fun in telling you how many there are?'

Vanessa put the flask on the coffee table, then sat back and looked at her. 'Fine, let's get back to Richard Dankworth and death.'

Alice opened her mouth to reply, when there was a knock at the door. It swung open and for one horrible second she expected to see Richard Dankworth walk in. The person who entered was friendlier and definitely more welcome.

'You took your time,' Alice said sourly.

'You left before I could talk to you,' Amanda replied.

'I got distracted.'

'Hello, Vanessa. Keeping well?' Amanda asked.

'Pretty good, thanks. You?'

Amanda walked into the kitchen and switched the kettle on. 'Nothing's broken and I'm breathing, so no complaints,' she said.

'I'd better go,' Vanessa said, standing up.

'Stay. I have a feeling I'll need a witness,' Amanda replied.

'What have you done?' Alice demanded.

Vanessa hovered, half-standing half-sitting, before settling on the edge of the couch.

'I'm not sure,' Amanda said with a frown. 'Probably nothing, but I've suddenly got a feeling I may have made a mistake.'

Alice studied her granddaughter, and considered coincidences and odds and dead people. 'Richard Dankworth,' she said.

Amanda nodded. 'He was on the ship (or someone calling himself that was), but I remember you saying Richard Dankworth was dead.'

'I heard he was,' Alice said. 'Then I saw him get off the bus.'

'If you knew he wanted to kill her, why did you put her directly in his path?' Vanessa interjected.

'Who said anything about him wanting her dead? Alice? You just said there was unfinished business between you.'

'And what do you think that meant?' Alice asked. 'That he owed me money?'

Amanda started pacing up and down the kitchen. 'Funnily enough, Gran, even with our shady background, my mind didn't automatically go to murder.'

'Don't call me *Gran*, you know I hate that.'

'Shady?' Vanessa asked in the following silence.

Alice and Amanda looked at her and her face flushed. 'Sorry, none of my business.'

'All in good time, dear,' Alice said.

'Which *dear*?' Amanda replied.

'Both of you. Amanda, I taught you everything you needed to know to survive in this world, but never assume that means I told you everything. And Vanessa, if I told you a quarter of the things I've got up to in my life you'd never believe me.'

Amanda stopped pacing and took a deep breath. When she let it out, her face was calm and her voice steady. 'Okay, so I'm guessing you saw Richard get off the bus and followed him?'

'It took me a while to figure out who he was exactly,' Alice replied. 'It's been a long time since I last saw him, but his eyes were the same.'

'You got close enough to see his eyes?'

'He caught my eye as he passed. That's what made me follow him,' Alice said.

'And your watch,' Vanessa chimed in.

'What?'

'You said he stole your watch.'

Alice's hand went to her wrist and for a moment she frowned. Had she been wearing a watch this morning? Then her brain turned over and the memories settled.

'Yes, my watch, obviously, that's what tipped me off. He brushed past me and snagged my watch. Probably on the wrist of one of those…' she searched for an appropriate word and settled for a good enough one, 'airheads.'

'My, my, such strong language,' Amanda said in mock horror.

Alice shot her granddaughter a dirty look. 'I can think of stronger,' she said sourly. 'I wasn't completely sure, but then we heard one of the women call him Richard.'

She caught the exchange of glances between Vanessa and Amanda. She sighed as unpleasant long-buried memories nudged their way forward. 'Richard Dankworth is a nasty piece of work I ran into in England in the late sixties. He was young and stupid and I was not quite as young and not stupid at all and I made some mistakes. But I'd made mistakes before him and I definitely made mistakes after him so… that's life.'

'That's life,' Vanessa repeated.

Alice smiled and patted her on the knee. 'I think it's time you got back to work, dear. Thank you for helping me this morning.'

Vanessa's cheeks brightened and she stood up straight away. 'Of course, sorry. Tracey will be docking my wages if I don't get back. See you later, Alice. good to see you, Amanda.'

Vanessa strode to the door and Amanda met her there.

'What my grandmother means,' Alice heard Amanda say, 'is she doesn't want to talk about it, and the best way to avoid questions is to be alone. She'll be getting rid of me next.'

Vanessa looked at Alice, then nodded. 'I'm worried about her,' she whispered.

'Me too.'

Despite her advanced years, Alice's hearing was good enough to hear everything and she had to stifle her irritation as Vanessa gave her a small wave and left.

'What a good idea,' Alice said as Amanda walked over to the couch. 'You can leave too.'

'Sure,' Amanda replied, sitting down.

'I'm pretty sure that's not leaving.'

'I need you to tell me how dangerous he is.'

Alice felt a slight tremble in her hands and clasped them tightly together, before looking at Amanda. 'When I knew him he was borderline psychopathic. I can't imagine the years have cured him of those tendencies.'

Amanda's face didn't show any emotion. 'Then it's just as well he doesn't know you're still alive. Besides he should be safely back on the ship and leaving the city.'

'Yes,' Alice replied, thinking that her voice was as full of doubt as Amanda's was.

SIX

London, March 1969

'Maureen, let me introduce you to Richard.'

Alice painted a smile on her face as she turned and wove through the sun drenched tables to where William was waiting. With him was a handsome young man with dull grey eyes and a bored expression. They were both dressed in tennis whites, and beyond the table Alice could see players of varying shapes and skill attempting to hit the ball over the net.

She'd never played tennis, preferring less rigorous games, and luckily for her William was old school English, and didn't believe that men and women should play against each other, which had saved her from discussing why she refused to don the whites. Alice was content to mingle with the bored trophy wives that frequented the terraces of the Whitestone Tennis Club.

If Alice had been a thief, then the bejewelled fingers and necks of those present would have been easy pickings. No one became a member of the club unless their family came from money.

'Richard Dankworth, may I present Ms Maureen Stratler, a friend. Maureen, Richard is the son of an old school chum.'

Alice waited. Introductions were always a good way to assess the character of a man, especially when meeting a woman for the first time. The more progressive offered their hand for a formal handshake. The more traditional inclined their head politely. The more arrogant did neither.

Richard Dankworth offered her his hand which she took as a good sign. Until her fingers were grasped in his, then she felt him squeeze harder than necessary. His eyes sparked a little as she grimaced.

Maureen Stratler was a society lady, recently home from abroad, and wouldn't know how to react in a situation such as this.

Alice was not a society lady, and had to smother a desire to kick him in the inner thigh with her expensive, pointed high heels.

'Pleased to meet you, Ms Stratler,' Richard said in a smooth voice. He gripped her hand for a moment too long before releasing it.

'The pleasure is all mine,' Alice replied, wriggling her fingers to check for broken bones. *I'm going to find a way to make you pay for that little display*, she thought.

SEVEN

Amanda had barely gone when there was a knock at the door. Alice unlocked her phone and checked the front door camera. Not a feature the Silvermoon Retirement Village typically offered, or in fact knew about, but it was a handy way for Alice to avoid talking with those she wanted to not be at home for.

A tall, distinguished man stood in the hallway. As she watched, he adjusted his tie and raised his fist to knock again.

Like most things these days it took Alice longer to cross the apartment to the door than it used to, but just after the third rapping she shucked the deadbolt and pulled the door open.

'Hello Owen, what a lovely surprise,' she stepped aside to let her friend in.

'Really? Am I early?' Owen's face creased as he checked his watch. A lifetime in the corporate world had instilled a habit for punctuality. Although long retired, he still dressed for the boardroom. It wasn't just him – half the residents in the retirement village wore a shirt and tie year round.

Distracted by the morning's events, she'd completely forgotten that she and Owen were scheduled for their weekly coffee catch up at the village café. It had started as a way to fill the void left by the murder of Betty earlier in the year. Betty had been one of Alice's closest friends, and was being pursued by Owen, woo'd sounded to 18th century but was probably a better description.

She thought about pleading tiredness and cancelling, but the last thing she wanted was someone else looking at her like she had one foot in the grave.

'No, you're right on time,' Alice reassured him. 'I just meant sometimes you open the door to people you'd rather avoid. It's always a pleasant surprise to see a friend.'

Owen's face smoothed and he smiled back. 'Are you ready?'

'I just need my phone.'

He remained at the door while she picked her phone up off the couch and returned to where he was waiting.

They chatted in the short elevator ride down to the ground floor, where Alice deliberately avoided looking at Vanessa behind her desk. Vanessa thought matchmaking was part of her job description, despite Alice's insistence that she had no further use for matches, literal or figurative.

Silvermoon Retirement Village, like so many things in Wellington, was built on a hill. From her second-floor apartment Alice could see for miles, but at ground level they were cocooned by a subtle ivy covered wall and trees as old as some of the residents.

Owen and Alice walked down the steps and turned right. The main building, containing a restaurant, the administration offices, and several apartments on the upper levels, was one of three that housed and fed everyone.

They passed a large building cheekily known as The Olympic Complex, containing an indoor pool, gym, and games room. Through the wide windows Alice saw an instructor taking an aqua jogging class. Alice had reluctantly tried it once. The sensation of being kept afloat by a belt strapped to her waist wasn't something she was interested in feeling again.

Beside the Olympic complex was Charlie's, a small café exclusively for residents.

Five of the ten tables were empty when they walked in and placed their orders at the counter.

The muffin of the day was orange, sesame and pecan. The café had a box where residents were encouraged to leave suggestions for flavour combinations. Some were quite delicious, while others were more challenging.

Alice bypassed the muffin of the day and ordered a plain scone. Owen decided to be adventurous which, by the look on his face when he took the first bite, he immediately regretted. She sipped her drink and watched him struggle with the dilemma of whether to swallow or eject the mouthful into a tissue. She averted her gaze and by the time she turned back his mouth was empty.

'So, what's new in your world, Alice?' he asked.

Owen knew nothing of her working life, and telling him about her encounter earlier in the morning would likely result in many more questions than she was prepared to answer. 'Not much. My granddaughter is back in town.'

Owen nodded. She knew from previous conversations that *his* family visiting was a happy time. He had been lonely since his wife of 50 years had died, and having chattering grand and great grandchildren around always perked him up. 'How long is she here for this time?'

Alice shrugged. Amanda kept her own schedule, and was increasingly becoming unpredictable, relying more on her own skills and less on Alice's knowledge. It gave Alice a sense of pride tinged with sadness that Amanda might have outgrown her.

'A few days I imagine,' she replied.

'I envy her. What is it she does again?'

'She's a freelance security consultant.'

Owen sipped his coffee and nodded approvingly. As the ex-chief executive of a bank, he had spent a great deal of his career ensuring customers' money and records were kept secure.

Alice had never tried to rob a bank, and she thought the term *thief* was crass, even if plenty of people had accused her of being just that.

'You know, you never talk about your daughter. Is she…?'

'No, she isn't.'

'I'm sorry,' Owen straightened his tie in a nervous gesture before quickly changing the subject. 'You seem a little distracted today. Care to talk about it?'

She considered her response carefully. With the exception of Vanessa (who only knew a fraction of the truth), no one at Silvermoon had an inkling of Alice's past. She'd deflected their questions by saying her husband had made a fortune in real estate while she stayed at home raising their daughter. The only truth in that story was the fact that Alice had raised her daughter. Other than that, she'd never been married and had never owned anything larger than a car in her nine decades on the planet. She'd had several things in her possession over the years that were infinitely more valuable than a house, but that was part of the past she wouldn't tell anyone about.

She had thought about confiding in Owen several times, however in the end a cast iron inclination to keep things to herself won out.

Now, part of Alice wanted to tell Owen all about London and Richard Dankworth. She ignored it. 'It's nothing really,' she said with a smile. 'I thought I saw a ghost from my past this morning. It brought up some unpleasant memories.'

Owen nodded. 'Yes they can do that. I read somewhere once that ghosts are just memories that won't go away.'

If that was the case Alice had enough ghosts to fill the largest graveyard. She grinned to herself. At least she didn't have Oliver's problem.

The front door opened, letting in a cool breeze and two people. Les and Freda had been married for half a century, and were still mostly happily married. There had been a few bumps on the way, the most recent of which was when Freda thought Les was interested in another woman. That little misunderstanding had been cleared up, and for the past few months Alice hadn't noticed Freda using a single weapon in her arsenal of happiness. (Alice knew she used to turn off her hearing aid whenever Les got onto his soap box about something that was wrong with the world.)

The four friends exchanged greetings and Owen offered them a seat at the table. While Les ordered their drinks, Freda took the chair opposite Alice.

'I suppose you've heard the latest?' Freda said.

'You'll need to be a bit more specific.'

Freda glanced over at her husband, then sighed. 'He wants to take up tennis. He's convinced his new muscles would allow him to produce a killer serve.'

ƐIGHT

London, March 1969

'… killer ace,' William said.

'Do you play, Ms Statler?' Richard asked.

'Goodness me, no. I haven't touched a racket since school. I'm afraid my father never believed physical pursuits were appropriate for a lady.' Which was technically true, even if it applied to her real father, the book keeper from Wellington, and not her fictional father, the owner of an American bank.

During one of their fights, she had considered telling her real father about her physical activities during the war, but despite their clashes she had no desire to break his heart.

She watched Richard's eyes scan her body and she had to strongly resist the urge to pull her light blue cardigan tightly across her chest. Alice wasn't used to being put off balance so quickly and she didn't like it. Aside from anything else, Richard's presence might prove to be an unnecessary complication. She was close to getting what she needed from William and then she'd be gone, Maureen Stratler consigned to the 'I wonder whatever happened to her' category.

'And what do you do, Mr Dankworth?' Alice asked.

'Richard is being groomed to take over the family business,' William said, clapping the man on the shoulder.

'Which is?'

'Cars, Ms Stratler–'

'Call me Maureen,' Alice deliberately interrupted. She watched his eyes narrow slightly before he smiled and continued.

'Maureen, then. My family owns one of the largest car manufacturers in England. Next year we start exporting to Europe. And the year after that my father will step down and I will take over as chairman.'

There was something in his tone that made Alice think the two year wait was going to feel like a lifetime for the man.

'Richard will be the youngest chairman in the country,' William said.

Richard himself didn't comment, but a smirk played briefly across his face.

'Richard and I were about to have a drink. Please join us,' William continued.

'Of course,' Alice replied. She allowed him to pull out her chair, then watched him beckon the waiter over and order for her. She wanted to remind him she had a voice of her own, but decided now was not the time to use it.

They chatted about inconsequential things while they waited for their drinks. Alice made sure to apply all her charm to both men. By the time the drinks were half empty, she could tell Richard had dismissed her almost entirely.

She drained her glass and stood up too quickly, stumbling slightly as she caught her foot in the leg of the chair. She grabbed Richard's arm to prevent herself from falling.

'Are you alright, my dear?' William asked, half rising.

'Yes, I'm fine,' she replied with a smile. She released Richard and bent down to pick something up off the ground. 'Is this yours?' she asked, holding out a small locker key.

Richard patted his pants pocket then took the key from her. 'Must have fallen out. Thank you.'

'I'm going to powder my nose,' she said to the air in between the two men. They were already deep in conversation.

Alice wove between the tables and into the bar. Once she was out of sight of the two men, she slipped off her heels and picked up the pace. From the bar she walked down the hallway to the changing rooms. Despite Richard's question earlier about her playing, Whitestone didn't allow women members, but they did allow discrimination based on wealth. There were two changing rooms, and although they weren't labelled as such, one was for those who made their own money, and the other (more opulently furnished) room was for those that came from money.

Just past the changing room doors was a trolley stacked with neatly folded white towels. Alice picked up a stack and went back to the second of the two doors. She knocked and pushed it open slightly, calling out, 'Towel service.' When there was no reply, she slipped through the door. It was a small wood panelled room with ten lockers lined up against the opposite wall, and another door to the right that lead to the showers.

Alice crossed to Richard's locker. Her stumble had been designed to dislodge the key from his pocket. She didn't need the key itself, just the number on it.

Fifteen seconds later she replaced her hair clip and pulled open the locker door. An expensive-looking suit hung from a metal rod, above which was a shelf containing a wallet, gold watch, and a set of car keys.

Alice rifled through the wallet. There was some money, one or two business cards, and a slip of paper with a telephone number on it, and a series of other numbers underneath that.

She memorised the numbers then returned everything to where she found it. A quick search of his suit pockets failed to reveal anything of interest and she was about to close the locker door when she noticed a thin sliver of paper on the ground outside the locker.

She picked it up. There was nothing on it but it seemed out of place in the otherwise immaculate room. She remembered a spy novel she'd once read where the hero placed a piece of paper in the locker door to know if anyone had opened it in his absence. For a moment she hesitated. There were too many variable factors. Even if it had been a makeshift security device she had no way of knowing where it had been in the door.

Thinking quickly she summarised everything she knew about Richard already, and concluded he might be paranoid, but he was undoubtedly arrogant enough to think no one would break into his locker. Just in case, she pocketed the piece of paper. Better it vanished than stayed on the floor.

Picking up the stack of towels, Alice exited into the hallway, first checking no one was there. Replacing the towels on the trolley, she retraced her steps to the terrace. She missed a step when she saw William was alone.

Trying to appear casual, she scanned the crowd, There was no sign of him.

'I thought you'd disappeared forever,' William smiled when she retook her seat.

'Don't exaggerate, William. I was only gone for a few minutes,' she returned his smile. 'Where is your friend?'

William waved a hand dismissively. 'He had to make a phone call. Besides, I don't think tennis is his game.'

NINε

'...think tennis is his game,' Owen said.

Alice shook off the memory and refocussed on her friends. She wasn't sure how long she'd been away but no one was giving her strange looks and Les looked like he'd just sat down, so it couldn't have been long.

'No, that's what I tried telling him.'

'Tried telling me what?' Les asked.

He was a medium-sized man in his seventies who earlier in the year had decided to try his hand at body building. To everyone's surprise, including his own, he had placed second in his age group. Since then his long suffering wife had endured a flood of suggestions on what he could do with his new found strength.

'That you've never played tennis in your life, and you can't just pick up a racket and expect to be an expert. Besides, where are you going to practice? Silvermoon doesn't have a tennis court,' Freda said.

Les flashed his wife a mildly patronising look. 'There's a tennis club just down the road. I could walk there – helps with cardio.'

Alice caught Freda's exasperation and decided to help her. 'You know what else muscles are good for? Singing. Something to do with a strong diaphragm letting you hold the notes for longer. I heard a rumour that Tracey is thinking of starting a Silvermoon choir.'

'Really? I hadn't heard that,' Les replied. He looked thoughtful. 'I can hold a note, but Freda here is the better singer. She should have been a professional.'

'There you go,' Alice said. 'Something you can do as a couple.'

Freda mouthed a thank you and soon they were all engaged in a discussion about who at Silvermoon might be interested in joining a choir. By the time Alice and Owen finished their drinks and said goodbye, their friends had half the residents grouped into alto, bass, and soprano. (Alice politely declined to be involved. She had many skills but singing was not one of them.)

Outside, Alice headed towards the main building.

'Are we not having our walk today?' Owen said in surprise, falling into step next to her.

'Oh yes, but first I need to warn Tracey about the choir. It was a spur of the moment thing, and if Freda and Les have their way we'll be singing at the Town Hall next week.'

Tracey was out, but Alice left a message with an amused Vanessa who was back behind the reception desk. She had assured Alice on several occasions that she enjoyed welcoming people. It helped satisfy her natural nosiness by letting her keep track of who came to see whom (or in her own words, 'it's like a reality show and I'm the camera').

Duty completed, Alice and Owen slowly navigated the grounds of the complex. Behind the main building was a taller and longer one where the majority of residents lived. It was officially called Rimu House (and unofficially called Stumpy, thanks to its general likeness to a brick). The gardens were colourful and immaculate, thanks to one full time professional gardener, and several retired amateurs.

Completing their loop, they crossed the grass in front of the main building and entered the small rose garden. There was a bench in the middle and they both eased down. Alice felt her muscles twinging like the pinging of an old car when its engine is switched off.

'You were talking about ghosts,' Owen prompted.

Alice sighed. She'd hoped he'd forgotten about it. Finally she said, 'You don't get to my age without meeting a few nasty pieces of work. Even bankers must come across a few, Owen.'

Owen smiled at her. 'I'd wager there are more nasty pieces of work in banking than any other industry in the world.'

'True. I never met a banker I liked – until you, of course. Well, this morning I saw a man who reminded me of someone I met almost fifty years ago.'

'A nasty piece of work?'

'The nastiest,' Alice agreed.

'That must have been unsettling,' he replied, patting her on the arm.

She knew she was guilty of it herself from time to time, but she still had to stifle a mild irritation at this gesture. Patting was for dogs, not people.

'Let's talk about something more pleasant,' she suggested.

'Alright. I heard that woman Nanci was moving in.'

Alice looked at him in surprise. Nanci Katz had visited Silvermoon earlier in the year to teach some sort of pottery class. While here she'd also taught Teresa, a friend of Alice's, enough poker skills to make the annual poker tournament far more interesting than it usually was. Alice and Nanci had developed an understanding when she left.

'That could liven things up a bit,' Alice said.

Owen's eyes sparkled as a smile tugged at his lips. 'I'm not sure we need the sort of livening up that occurred last time she was here.'

Alice stretched her fingers out, feeling the breeze catch them.

'Are you going to the movie night this evening?' Owen asked.

She didn't understand the need for community movie nights, especially in the age of streaming television where everything could be easily accessed in her own apartment. Unless she pushed the wrong button. However, management had decided that once a month it would be a good idea to gather everyone in the dining room and play a classic movie. Some of the residents enjoyed the opportunity to reminisce about where they were or how old they were when the movie came out.

Alice had enough reminders of her age, like having to pee five times a night. Watching a black and white movie wasn't her idea of fun.

'What is it again?'

'The Great Escape.'

At least this one was in colour. Alice shook her head. 'Probably not, war movies are a bit harder to take when you've lived through one.'

Which wasn't the real reason, but she found mentioning World War 2 was usually an effective way to end a conversation.

'Fair enough, but I'll save you a seat in case you change your mind.'

TEN

London, April 1969

'… change your mind?' William asked.

'I'm afraid not,' Alice replied. 'It has been wonderful, William dear, but the time has come for me to go home.'

They were in the drawing room of his London apartment, although apartment didn't do the space justice given it took the entire floor of the building.

He took her hand. 'But I thought we were having fun.'

She squeezed his hand. 'Believe me, this has been incredible fun. But, William, I made it clear right at the start, this was never going to develop into anything further. Besides,' she extracted her hand and stroked his cheek, 'you can do better than a 40-something widow. The moment I walk out that door you'll have a line of firm young ladies waiting to take my place.'

William had the good sense to nod. Alice knew there was no shortage of eligible London ladies waiting to relieve him of his money. At least she was only interested in one thing from him, and it didn't involve love or sex.

'They're all young and shallow,' he complained. 'None of them have your beauty or depth of character.'

She might have believed him on the character compliment. Most of women's interests were limited to how they would look with diamonds hanging off their ears or draped around their wrists. But in regards to beauty, she knew he was lying. She considered herself attractive, and perhaps in the right light, with the right clothes, very attractive. But some of the ladies circling William were knock out gorgeous.

'William, my heart belongs to a ghost. You could never compete with that.'

She walked over to the window and looked out on the busy street below. People scurried from one place to another in the misty rain and cars kicked up tiny waves of water.

'I'm sorry if I upset you,' William said from behind her. 'You haven't really talked about your husband.'

Alice took a deep breath and let it out slowly. She hadn't meant for her words to carry so much emotion. It had been years since John died, and technically he hadn't even been her husband, although she did love him.

'You didn't upset me,' she turned with a smile. 'It never pays to look back for too long, William. In a few weeks you will have forgotten all about Maureen Stratler.'

William looked at her in a way he hadn't before, and for the first time she caught a glimpse of the shrewd business mind lurking underneath.

'I haven't gone yet,' Alice told him. 'It's such a horrible day outside, how about a game before dinner?' His eyes flicked to the card table. A fresh deck of cards sat neatly on top, next to two equal stacks of poker chips.

'Are you sure?' he said, his eyes sparkling. 'You haven't had much luck so far.'

'I've won a few times,' she protested.

'Ah, but I've won more,' he replied, taking her arm and guiding her to the table.

That was the point, she thought as he pulled out her chair.

'Shall we up the stakes then?' Alice suggested.

'What did you have in mind?' William picked up the deck and expertly cut the cards and shuffled them, his hands a blur.

'We each put up something we hold dear, five hands maximum.'

His hands paused and he looked thoughtful. 'What would you be putting up?'

She slid her shawl off her shoulders to reveal bare shoulders. 'Every hand you win, I'll take an item of clothing off. And if you win over all then we retire to your bedroom.'

'If your virtue is what you hold dear,' William said with a smile playing across his lips, 'then you've already given it to me.'

She reached up and pulled her hair loose from its neat ponytail. 'William, you've only seen a fraction of what I can do. If you win, I'll show you it all. And I mean, all.'

His eyes widened and she could see him considering what that might entail. 'And in turn, what do I put up? Money?'

'Is money really what you hold most dear?'

'What else is there?' he asked.

'Trinkets, mementos, heirlooms.' Alice's eyes roamed the room, settling on the antique sideboard for a moment, before returning to William. She was pleased to see him glance over before refocusing on her.

'Alright then, shall we begin?'

He dealt them each five cards. Picking his up, his expression went blank. Alice checked hers. A pair of threes.

'Opening bids? I wager the gold cigarette case.'

'I wager my stockings,' Alice replied.

William clearly didn't think it a fair trade, but he looked at his cards again and his expression settled.

Less than a minute later he triumphantly laid down a full house, jacks over tens. Alice stood up and placing one leg on her chair slowly rolled her stocking down her leg to the ankle…

ELEVEN

'That'd take me about ten minutes these days,' Alice muttered.

'Sorry?' Owen said.

They were standing outside the entrance to Alice's building.

'Nothing, just thinking about how everything takes longer than it used to.'

'That's if you can still do it at all,' Owen quipped.

She smiled at her friend, feeling lucky that she had someone in her life to commiserate with on the downfalls of getting old. Out of the hundred or so residents and staff she could count on one hand those she could honestly say were friends.

'It's almost lunchtime. Care to join me in the dining room for some slop and leftovers?' He was joking. Only the best food was served at Silvermoon, and with what they paid to live there the cuisine was expected to be many steps above jello and custard.

'I'm feeling a little tired. I think I'll eat at home.'

'Right,' Owen replied, worry etched his face. 'I might check in on you later.'

She stifled her irritation at the sudden concern, knowing it came from a caring place. 'I'm fine, Owen. I will take you up on movie night though. Save me a seat.'

He beamed and promised he would, before striding off at a pace that made Alice feel exhausted just watching. Now she'd have to sit through the movie. The things she did for friendship. Or, if she was going to be honest with herself, to avoid vultures of concern. She wasn't dead yet and had no plans to change that.

Vanessa was on the phone as Alice passed, and she gave her a small wave on the way to the elevator.

A short time later Alice was inside her apartment. The thought of food made her stomach turn, but maybe that was because she hadn't had breakfast. Or maybe she had. Sometimes it felt like she'd had so many breakfasts in her life it was hard to tell which was today's and which belonged to thirty years ago.

A quick check of the dishwasher showed no dirty dishes. Her pantry was full of interesting and tasty looking items, none of which appealed to her, so she settled for a sliced tomato on toast. She knew the tomato would give her gas, but that was the benefit of living alone.

Retrieving butter from the fridge, she spotted a hip flask in the back of the vegetable cooler. Pulling it out she pressed the cold metal between her two hands. She might not have remembered to eat that morning but she knew exactly where and when she'd obtained this. She clearly remembered how the whole hip flask thing had started. William's was the first, the little memento, she'd watched enough crime shows to know it was called a *signature* – always taking one thing from each scene. Only instead of murdering someone, she was just helping them out of ownership of some possessions. The flask was a keepsake, held onto long after the other items had been sold off.

There were some things that only Alice knew, such as exactly how much money she had invested or hidden away, and how many hip flasks were in her apartment. She had left explicit, sealed instructions for Amanda regarding the money, but the other matter always made Alice smile, imagining the look on her granddaughter's face when she learned how many there were.

Alice carefully buttered a piece of toast and added a sliced tomato. The juicy red fruit was almost off the menu for her, it was starting to give her acid reflux.

She took a bite and savoured the taste, before leaving the plate on the bench and crossing to the bookcase. She didn't have photo albums, hers wasn't a conventional life that resulted in holiday snaps and happy family portraits. There were pictures of her daughter somewhere, and of Amanda when she was a baby, but precious few of Alice existed.

If anyone looked close enough though, they would see a series of books that seemed out of place. History books detailing places: England in the 1960s. She pulled that one from the shelf and retired to the couch, toast forgotten on the bench.

The pages crackled slightly as they were turned for the first time in decades. The books were another of Alice's reminders of her working life. She usually found just looking at the spines enough to recall memories, but now she needed something more concrete. Like the photos on page 140. Black and white images of London that she remembered in full colour.

A knock at the door pulled her back. She checked her phone and saw Teresa standing outside.

'Sorry to bother you, Alice.'

'Not at all. Tea?'

'Got anything stronger?' Teresa asked hopefully.

Alice looked at the clock. Midday wasn't too early for her, but she hadn't pegged Teresa for a daytime drinker. She retrieved the fridge hip flask and poured a healthy dose into two glasses. Prior to Betty's death earlier in the year, Alice had written Teresa off as a harmless, slightly shallow woman. But events around Betty's death had given her a new appreciation for the shrewd mind that lurked under the carefully styled hairdo.

Teresa was dressed as always in a classy outfit of light grey slacks and a light blue blouse. Her outfit undoubtedly cost more than Alice's entire wardrobe. Throw in the gold wristwatch and diamond earrings and the ensemble probably cost as much as an apartment at Silvermoon.

Alice's guest took a sip of her drink and gave a little grimace. 'I normally stick to wine these days,' she commented, downing the rest of the drink. 'But this reminds me of something my husband kept in his desk drawer for emergencies and guests.' Her eyes twinkled as she looked at Alice. 'He had a lot of emergencies and guests, judging by the empty bottles in the trash every month.'

'A man after my own heart,' Alice said.

Teresa held out her empty glass and Alice's interest peaked. A two-drink visit pointed to something other than a casual drop in. She drained the hip flask into Teresa's glass and took another sip out of her own.

'I think Joshua is stealing from me.'

Alice had to sift through a lot of names and faces to place Joshua. Finally, more slowly than she would have liked, she figured it out.

'Joshua the new cleaner?'

Silvermoon Retirement Village retained a staff of cleaners whose job was to ensure residents didn't have to touch a cleaning cloth (unless they wanted to of course. Some found it hard to let go of a lifetime of household chores, while others seemed infinitely relieved at the thought of never having to scrub a toilet ever again). Alice had never been anyone's idea of a domestic goddess, but she also didn't like strangers going through her things. While she would have loved someone to come in once a week, she instead pulled on the rubber gloves and did the bare minimum to maintain hygiene.

She had been vaguely aware that a new cleaner had recently started. The fact that he was a *he* had caused plenty of gossip amongst the older generation of residents (which was pretty much all of them). A male cleaner wasn't as scandalous as an affair or a murder, but it ranked above the latest way their grandchildren had disappointed them.

'What makes you think he's stealing from you?' Alice asked.

Teresa's glass clattered against the bench as she put it down and started pacing. 'I usually keep some cash in a bowl on the kitchen counter.'

Alice didn't think she meant loose change.

'Joshua came this morning while I was out, and when I got home some of the cash was gone.' Teresa must have read the doubt on her face because she hastily carried on. 'I know it's a bit tenuous, but there're other things as well. Thing have been moved.'

'If someone has been cleaning then surely that would explain things moving.'

Teresa's face flushed and she fiddled with her glass, scraping it across the counter top between her hands. 'I sound senile. I don't suppose you've ever been in a situation where everyone would rather believe you're crazy than entertain the possibility you're telling the truth?'

Of all the things Teresa could have said, that hit home the hardest. Alice had had a hard time convincing anyone that Betty's death was murder, but she'd known it. She couldn't explain how she'd known, she just had.

'Alright, let's work on the basis that you're right. Has anything else been taken from your apartment?'

Teresa started to shake her head, then paused and gave a little shrug. 'I'm not sure, to be honest. I don't think so but I was a bit too shaken to look closely.'

Alice asked the question that had been nagging at her. 'So why tell me? If you're sure Joshua took the money why not tell Tracey?'

'Because I'm *not* sure. Suspicion is not the same as proof and if I'm wrong…'

'Then an innocent man is fired,' Alice finished.

'And possibly worse. What if Tracey involves the police?'

Alice doubted she would. Tracey was the village manager and was as straight as they came, but something like this would be a scandal, and scandals weren't good for business. She had barely recovered from the fact there had been a murder at Silvermoon. The resulting investigation, even though Alice had done most of the work actually solving the case, had resulted in a ton of negative press. No one wanted to move into a village where people were murdered.

'I thought, given what I know about your background, that you might… take a look.'

Alice nodded. It would probably do her good to focus on something other than bad memories. 'Well, I'm not sure what these tired old eyes can do to help…' Alice said in a sad voice, then grinned, seeing that Teresa wasn't buying the poor-me act. 'Okay, let's go.'

Teresa lived one floor down in the same building. From what Alice knew of Teresa's wealth, she could easily have afforded a penthouse apartment (in fact probably the entire top floor), but she was beginning to appreciate that Teresa liked to keep quiet about her money.

The layout of Teresa's apartment was virtually identical to Alice's, only smaller and with a view of trees rather than the city.

Alice had been inside the apartment a few times and had been struck by how neat it was. Never a cushion out of place, or book with its spine upside down. The kitchen bench gleamed and Alice was certain if she opened the cupboards the plates would have a never-used gleam to them.

'Show me what was moved,' Alice said.

Teresa went around the room pointing at several objects that to Alice looked to be fine where they were. According to Teresa though, the lamp with the picture of a cat on it had been facing the other way, while the couch had been moved back slightly. When she looked closer Alice could see the indents in the carpet where it had previously stood.

'Nothing is missing?' she asked.

'Not that I can tell,' Teresa answered. 'I've checked all my valuables and they all seem to be here.'

Alice frowned as she scanned the room, looking at it not as a friend, but as a con artist. Things that could be taken without being missed, or that she could easily convince their owner that the object would be better in someone else's hands. There were too many of them to narrow down.

'Alright, there's three possible explanations,' she said. 'First, this is all innocent and the moved objects are the result of a new cleaner learning the ropes. Second, someone is going to rob you and hasn't gotten around to it yet, maybe they're scoping the place first.'

'And third?' Teresa asked when Alice paused.

'Third, someone is looking for something.'

'But what?'

Alice smiled at her friend. 'That's what makes it interesting. I have no idea.'

TWELVE

London, April 1969

'Are you sure about this?' William asked.

'In for a penny, in for a bra,' Alice replied. She was down to her underwear, but had made sure to win some hands as well. Currently piled in front of her was a silver cigarette holder, a gold engraved lighter, and a crystal wine goblet.

William smiled back, but he wasn't looking at her face. His attention had been wandering with the more hands she lost, which was entirely the point. He dealt her two cards and himself one. She added a nine and a jack of hearts to the rubbish hand she held, and noticed his left eyebrow twitch slightly. He was happy with what he had.

'I'll raise you,' William said, looking around the room for something else to wager.

Alice looked at her hand again. Unless something had gone horribly wrong then everything still could work out fine.

'I'm all in,' she said.

'All in!' his eyes bulged. 'As in…'

'As in winner takes all. If you win, I will…' She proceeded to describe an act that she would never perform but had heard about from some working girls during World War 2. Apparently it drove men wild and by the look on William's face they weren't exaggerating. 'And if I'm all in then your matching bet has to equal mine in value.'

'What do you suggest?'

'One thousand shares in your company.'

William started to shake his head, then looked at his cards again. Then across to her. 'Why on earth would you want shares in my company?'

'William, dear, I couldn't care less about your company. I merely thought that it was something of considerable value to you. After all, if I'm prepared to lose something important to me, then so must you be.'

He looked at his hand one more time, then nodded. 'Alright. If you win I'll sign over 1,000 shares of my company to you. And if I win you'll…'

'And more,' Alice said with a sly smile.

He looked at her questioningly and she held up one finger. He slid a card across the table and her hand was transformed from rubbish, to a straight.

William stayed with the cards he had, and his hands tremored with excitement as he no doubt imagined what they were shortly going to be doing.

Alice felt a twinge of guilt, but it was too late now.

William took the loss admirably, his good breeding preventing him from swearing and throwing things around the room. Instead he crossed to his desk and lifted the telephone receiver. When the call connected he instructed his lawyer to assign 1,000 shares to Maureen Stratler. It was a significant amount and she could hear the protests on the phone, from her place across the room. William was a man of his word, and it wouldn't make a material difference to his wealth or to the company, so he insisted it be done. She heard him mention Richard and she stifled a sudden flood of nerves. She'd pondered the numbers she found in his locker at the tennis club, and had finally found out they were bank account numbers. As she had no reason to investigate further, she'd left it there, but there was something about Richard that made her tense.

When William hung up, he showed surprise that she was still in the same spot, still in her underwear.

'You may have lost the bet, but no reason to miss out altogether,' she said. They spent the next hour having a pleasurable romp in the bedroom. But she didn't do the act she'd suggested during the poker game. She wasn't even sure she knew how to do it.

THIRTEEN

The next obvious question from Teresa had been, 'Looking for what?'

Alice couldn't answer that yet.

'It must be something particularly valuable,' Teresa said.

They were sitting on her couch sipping tea. Teresa had wanted to break open the gin, but it had never been Alice's drink of choice and another alcoholic drink would have written off the rest of her day.

'That doesn't narrow it down,' Alice pointed out.

'That's what's confusing. If they wanted to steal something then they could take their pick.'

'Maybe not,' Alice mused. 'If you found something was gone, what's the first thing you'd do?'

'Go straight to Tracey.'

'And there'd be an investigation and fingers would be pointed.'

'Quite right.'

'So what if the thief was trying to be more subtle? What if they stole something that wouldn't be immediately missed? It might take days or weeks before you discover it missing, by which time the number of people coming through here (and therefore suspects) would have increased tenfold.'

'I'm not running a train station,' Teresa said sourly. 'But I take your point. So what do I do?'

'Go through the place again. Focus on small items, jewellery, things like that. Items you might have overlooked the first time. There might be something you missed.'

Teresa looked dubious, then thoughtful, then determined. Finally she put her tea cup down on the coffee table and stood up. 'Right, let's get started.'

Alice stood a little more slowly, shaking her head. 'I don't know enough about your belongings to be useful.'

'Good point. Alright, leave me to it and I'll give you a call if I find something. Or don't find something.'

Alice left the apartment feeling less than sure that there was anything for Teresa to find. Someone had evidently been there, but given that Silvermoon had a new cleaner it was most likely him who'd moved things around. There was nothing to suggest anything sinister had happened.

It was only lunchtime and a long day of bad memories stretched out before her, so maybe there was no harm learning what she could about Joshua, the new cleaner.

The best place to start was with Vanessa. Alice walked into the elevator and pressed the button for the ground floor. It was lucky she was already friendly with the person that knew everything about the staff.

The doors opened and she smiled as she approached the front desk. Vanessa was on the phone, by the sounds of it sorting out tickets for someone.

Alice waited until the call finished, then smiled again.

'Not that I don't enjoy your company Alice, but when you smile at me like that I get very nervous.'

'Like what?'

'Like you know things I don't, and I won't like finding out the things that you know that I don't.'

'Vanessa,' Alice replied. 'Of course I know more than you do, I'm almost five times your age. However, in this instance my smile was supposed to say, "You know something that I don't and I need your help"'.

Vanessa looked surprised, then pleased. 'Oh, alright then, how can I help?'

Alice looked around. She knew there was no one else in the lobby but it never hurt to add a sense of intrigue to any situation. 'What do you know about the new cleaner, Joshua?'

'That he's too young for you,' Vanessa grinned.

Alice snorted. 'He's too young for my granddaughter. Get your mind out of the gutter and answer the question.'

'He seems alright. A bit quiet. Why? Don't tell me you're finally going to allow a cleaner into your apartment?'

'Not a chance. Does he seem trustworthy?'

Vanessa tucked a stray hair behind her ear and stared at Alice. 'What does that even mean? If you're asking if he wears black and has a handle bar moustache that he twirls then no. If you're asking if I'd trust him to deliver my baby, then the answer is also no. I guess he's somewhere in the middle.'

'That's a big middle,' Alice replied wryly.

They laughed, then Vanessa said, 'So let's narrow it down. What exactly do you want to know?'

Alice told her about Teresa's theory and by the time she was finished Vanessa was frowning and shaking her head. 'Every employee has to undergo a background and police check before they're hired. If there was anything dodgy about Joshua he wouldn't be working here.'

'Police checks are only good for people who've been caught,' Alice pointed out.

'Were you ever caught?' asked Vanessa.

'Don't be ridiculous.'

'My apologies.' Vanessa did not look in the least bit sorry.

Not caught by the police anyway, Alice thought.

'I haven't talked to him much, but he's always smiling, and I've heard some of the residents saying nice things about him. Honestly, I think Teresa has got it way wrong if she thinks he's stealing from her.'

She was probably right, but Alice decided to reserve judgement until she had at least spoken to Joshua. 'Is he working today?' Alice asked.

Vanessa tapped purple nails on her keyboard and nodded.

'Can you tell him I'm considering employing the cleaning service but want to meet him first.'

'I can, but…'

Alice waited for her to decide whether to finish her thoughts.

'Do you really want to encourage Teresa's…'

'Is that what I'm doing? I thought I was interviewing a prospective cleaner.'

'You know,' Vanessa's expression was sour, 'I think I hate your innocent look more than your knowing smile.'

'Wait until you see my innocent smile,' Alice said sweetly.

'Oh joy,' Vanessa said as she picked up the phone.

FOURTEEN

New York, June 1969

Alice stood at the window of her hotel room. She could have stayed in the penthouse suite, but very rich people are more memorable than moderately wealthy ones. She planned to come back and work in this city one day and didn't want to be remembered.

New York had many similarities to London, but there were marked differences as well, mainly in the way people behaved. Men strode these streets like they were kings and women here were embracing a more progressive age of feminist freedom. From what Alice could see, that involved mini-skirts and no bras.

She turned back to the small dining table, picking up and absentmindedly nibbling at the remains of a breakfast roll as she read the paper. A music festival was to be held in up-state New York in a couple of months. She turned the page, thinking it sounded like a dud.

Halfway through the paper there was a small international news section and she froze upon spotting a picture of William. The headline read, *Earl Hangs Himself.*

The following article was frustratingly short on details, other than to say William had been found by his staff, and a funeral was planned for the coming Friday.

Alice squashed her first instinct to reach for the phone, and continued reading the paper. After a few minutes she realised she wasn't taking anything in. With a sigh she picked up the phone and asked reception to book her a flight to London, leaving as soon as possible.

It went against everything she'd learnt. Once a job was completed you got out and stayed gone. But something was niggling at her. She held a soft spot for William, he was a nice man, and she knew him better than most. And the thought of him hanging himself didn't sit right.

She wasn't a trained investigator and had no proof that anything wrong had occurred. Just a feeling that something terrible had happened. And if it had, then someone was going to pay.

FIFTEEN

'Nice to meet you, Mrs Atkinson.'

Alice shook the offered hand and was pleased to find the grip firm but not crushing. A good sign.

'Come in, Joshua,' she said, stepping aside to let him enter the apartment.

He looked around as he walked to the centre of the room, then turned to Alice.

'Thank you, Vanessa,' Alice said.

'You're welcome,' Vanessa replied, before entering after Joshua and closing the door behind herself. She gave Alice a sly wink.

Alice was pleased that Vanessa wanted to stay. If she was going to teach her everything she knew then the first lesson was intelligence gathering, which was always better first hand.

Alice waved for them to sit on the couch while she took the armchair opposite. As she settled herself, she studied Joshua. He appeared to be in his early twenties, Polynesian, with short black hair. His uniform was clean and seemed well looked after so he evidently took pride in the way he looked.

'I understand you're thinking of using our services,' Joshua said in a soft voice.

'Yes. Why do I detect an undertone of surprise in your voice?'

Joshua dropped his gaze and looked at his hands. 'Sorry.' He grinned at her. 'The cleaning staff talk and the story is you're the only one at Silvermoon who has consistently refused to use our services.'

'And that may still be the case,' Alice replied. 'But my doctor has advised me to slow down a little and since slowing down is the first step to stopping altogether, I think the best way to delay the inevitable is to get other people to do the things that are less important.'

Joshua frowned.

'Someone else can clean her toilet before she dies,' Vanessa translated.

'Which is what I just said.'

Vanessa returned her irritated look with a bland smile.

'Oh.' Joshua shifted in his seat and looked everywhere but at Alice.

'Joshua, if you're going to work at a retirement village the first thing you need to learn is death is never far away.'

'*O le ola e taupule-esea*,' Joshua said. When he saw the blank looks on their faces, he added, '*Our lives are decreed to be taken by the gods.*'

Alice nodded thoughtfully. 'Nicely said. Samoan?'

'Yes, most people get it wrong and think it's Tongan.'

'I won't profess to know all the differences between the languages, but I did know a Samoan chief once who taught me to speak a little.'

'I didn't know you were multi-lingual.' Vanessa looked impressed.

'Hardly,' Alice snorted. 'But I know the essentials in most languages: where's the toilet, where's the nearest bank, give me the good bottle of wine, that sort of thing.'

Vanessa opened her mouth to say something else and Alice stopped her with a tiny wave of her hand.

'As you can understand, Joshua, I don't like the idea of strangers in my home, especially if I happen to be out when they arrive. So I'd like to know a little about you before making my decision.'

Joshua inclined his head. 'Of course.'

'Why are you working here?'

Joshua's eyes widened at the direct question. He hesitated, his face showing he was struggling to find an answer.

'Let me help you out,' Alice said. 'The appropriate answer is, "None of your business." But I'm guessing you were raised to respect your elders.'

Joshua's body relaxed and he smiled. 'Well, that and not to annoy the clients.'

'I'm not a client yet, so relax and tell me why you're wasting your time working in this place.'

'Hey!' Vanessa said.

'I'll get to you later,' Alice informed her.

Joshua laughed. 'I'd heard about you two.'

'Oh?' Alice raised an eyebrow.

'Apparently you solved a murder together? And you act like you're related, lots of arguments I think one person said.'

'Witty banter,' Vanessa said, 'Not arguments.'

'At least from one of us.'

'Don't be hard on yourself, you can be funny when you want to be.'

Alice and Vanessa glared at each other long enough to make Joshua squirm uncomfortably, before they both grinned.

'I'm working here because my mum needs the money,' Joshua said softly. 'She got scammed and lost all her life savings and is struggling to pay her rent.'

Alice's eyes narrowed at the word scam. 'How did she lose it?'

Joshua sighed. 'One of those phone ones where they pretend to be from the internet company. They got access to her computer and transferred all her money. The bank is trying to recover it, but in the meantime…'

'She's in trouble,' Vanessa said.

'Yeah,' Joshua nodded. 'It's funny, she's always told me to be careful of strangers offering things, not that she's not friendly, just cautious. But when it comes to computers she's a bit gullible.'

'So you need money fast.'

Joshua shrugged at Alice. 'This wasn't my first choice, but I'm in my final year at university and work experience is pretty limited. It was this or McDonald's, and this place pays more.'

'What are you studying?' Vanessa asked.

'Bachelor of Architectural Studies,' Joshua replied. 'I like the idea of building things.'

Alice asked him a few more questions and promised to let him know.

After he left, she turned to Vanessa. 'Tell me about this phone scam.'

Vanessa had filled her in on the basic concept of how they worked. People call up pretending to be from the internet provider saying their computer had been hacked, then talked them through a series of actions that supposedly made the connection safe again but in reality gave the scammer access to be able to get banking passwords and other valuable information.

Alice's brain started whirling as she considered the possibilities.

'Is that what you used to do?' Vanessa asked in a light tone.

Alice pulled herself back into focus. 'Vanessa, there is a vast difference between a scammer and a con artist. Scammers are common thieves. The same as someone walking into a store with a knife and demanding cash. What I did required skill and finesse and only hurt people who could afford the loss of property and pride.'

'Of course. Sorry.'

'One day soon I'll give you some more details, then maybe you can do something with your life other than being a palaeontologist.'

'What?'

'Working with fossils.'

Vanessa smiled. 'Don't you know I'm writing my thesis. In no time at all I'll be world famous for working with actual dinosaurs.'

'Just remember one thing dear. Not all dinosaurs were plant eaters. Some ate meat.'

'What does that mean? Are you threatening to eat me?'

'No I—'

'Because I'm pretty sure that's against Silvermoon policy.'

'You know that's— '

'And it's gross.'

'You can go,' Alice said sourly.

'What? You don't like my witty banter?'

'Careful it doesn't escalate to an argument. Find out where Joshua's mother lives.'

'Why? Are you going to eat her too?'

'Then can you get away for another trip into the city?'

Vanessa looked at her watch. 'I haven't had lunch yet, so as long as it doesn't take more than an hour.'

'It won't,' Alice promised.

'Where are we going?'

'To see a man about a computer.'

SIXTEEN

London, June 1969

Alice sat in the back of the cathedral. She was dressed entirely in black and she had a good view of the massive space. The death of an Earl was a big thing and the place was packed with family, friends, dignitaries, and those there out of obligation rather than any particular attachment to William.

She'd arrived early and could have taken a seat further towards the front, but she wanted to observe people arriving. She'd spotted several she knew, although with their eyes firmly fastened to the coffin next to the altar, none thought to turn their heads.

Richard Dankworth strode in a few minutes before the ceremony began. He arrogantly marched to the front and she saw someone give up their seat to him after some terse words. She couldn't hear what was said but the elderly woman who rose to her feet looked flushed. Alice gritted her teeth and gripped her handbag tightly. There would be plenty of time for him later.

She didn't recall much of the service, but after what seemed like too short a time to recap a man's life, it was over and people were filing out. Alice was one of the first to exit. She stood to the side of the doors and watched people filter into the sunlight, some left straight away, while others formed little clumps, talking in hushed tones.

Richard Dankworth emerged and focused on a small group of important looking men. She knew one of them was the manager of William's company, but didn't recognise the others.

'Thank you for coming, Ms Stratler.'

She turned to find a small well-groomed man dressed in a formal suit.

'I'm Edward Calthrop, the Earl's butler.'

'I'm sorry, I didn't recognise you,' she replied.

He inclined his head slightly, 'I wouldn't be doing my job if you did, Ms Stratler. I wanted to let you know the Earl was very fond of you.'

'He was a dear man.'

Edward nodded. 'I was the one who found him.'

Alice looked at him sharply. 'That must have been awful,' she finally said.

'It was very distressing.'

She watched doubt cross his face.

'Had William been upset about anything recently?' Edward seemed to be grappling with something, so she continued, 'I'm not asking you to break employer confidentiality, Edward, I'm just trying to understand why this happened.'

His face softened. 'There had been several visitors to the house, all suited men, none who stayed long. And on occasion I entered a room filled with angry words.'

She looked across to Richard. 'Are any of those men here today?'

She turned back in time to see Edward give an almost imperceptible nod.

'I'm sorry I can't be of more assistance to you, Ms Stratler.'

Alice barely supressed the urge to grab his shoulders and shake the decorum out of the man. He was doing a waltz with propriety when he obviously had something important to say. Edward shifted his feet as if he was getting ready to leave. Alice said the first thing that popped into her head. 'I'm glad there was someone else in the house for William. I'm sure he wouldn't have wanted anyone else to find him like that.'

'The Earl was aware of the importance of his position,' Edward replied with a faint touch of pride. 'He was careful to hide his shortcomings. If he didn't want you to know he couldn't do something, the only way you would find out is if he told you himself. The Earl once told me that he regretted not being able to do some of the things the other boys did growing up, like scouting for example.'

She had the feeling he'd just told her something vital, but before she could question this further the sound of laughter distracted her. Richard obviously found something humorous and was clapping a man on the shoulder. When she turned back Edward was gone.

Alice waited for most of the crowd to leave before walking slowly back to her hotel. A mix of emotions bubbled inside her. Seeing William's coffin brought back unpleasant memories. She had been fond of William. The conversation with Edward had raised more questions about William's death than it had answered, and there was something in his last comment that was nagging at her. A clue? Or maybe just a misinterpreted cryptic comment that was simply an innocent observation on his employer's life.

Back in her hotel room she poured a drink and sat on the windowsill as she considered her next move. For the first time in a very long time she doubted herself. She wondered whether Richard was involved in William's death or if she had just hoped he was so she could make a man she intensely disliked pay.

She was still sitting there when the sun went down and the bright lights of the city drowned out the stars.

Sometime around the fourth drink an idea came to her.

By the time she'd stripped her clothes off and slipped between the soft sheets of the king-sized bed the idea was forming into a plan.

With a sigh, she realised that she should have peed before getting into bed.

SEVENTEEN

'Alice?' Vanessa said.

'I need to pee,' Alice replied.

'Okay, good to know, but what I actually asked was is this the place?'

Alice looked up at the shop sign. *Computer and Phone Repairs,* it stated in faded letters.

'This is it.'

She pushed open the door and a soft buzzer sounded to announce their arrival. A young man looked up from his laptop and smiled when he saw them.

'Alice! You're not dead yet!' he exclaimed.

'Hang on!' Vanessa started in an indignant tone.

Alice put her hand on Vanessa's arm. 'It's fine. What he lacks in social skills he makes up for in rudeness.'

'That doesn't…that's not how that saying goes,' Vanessa protested.

The man stood up and came around the counter.

'I need to use your bathroom,' Alice said after he kissed her cheek.

'You know where it is,' the man replied.

'Vanessa, this is Troy. Troy, Vanessa. Play nice, at least until I'm back. I don't want to miss the show.'

Troy was in his mid-twenties, slim with long brown hair that might have seen a brush sometime in the last five years. He was clean shaven and wore a black short sleeved shirt.

When Alice reappeared from the back of the shop Vanessa was carefully studying phones in a display case, and Troy was back behind the counter.

'I don't think she likes me,' he said to Alice with a grin.

'Must be your winning personality,' Alice replied. 'She likes everyone.'

'*She* is standing right here,' Vanessa interjected. 'And *she* is wondering exactly why we're here.'

'Troy is the best computer guy I know.'

'It's true,' Troy said.

'Which would be impressive, except I'm guessing you only know about two computer people.'

Alice smiled. 'Just the one actually. Luckily he's very good at what he does.'

'Computer repair?' Vanessa said looking around the shop.

'Sometimes,' Troy replied with a wink.

'Alright, enough flirting. There's a young man at Silvermoon whose mother has just been scammed out of her life savings.' She ignored the choking sounds coming from Vanessa.

Troy's eyes brightened. 'You want me to get it back?'

Alice shook her head. 'No, I'll cover her losses. I want you to make it look like the money came from the bank. Then I want you to find out where the scammers are and pay them a visit.'

Troy nodded. 'The first one I can do no problem if you give me her details. The second will be a little harder. These things are all run offshore and are virtually impossible to track down.'

'Virtually is different from actually,' Alice said.

She and Troy stared at each other, waiting to see who would blink first. Finally Troy looked down at his hands and sighed. 'I can't promise anything but I'll take a look.'

Alice smiled and patted him on the arm. 'Of course you will. Now before we go there is one other matter I need your help with.'

They left the shop a short time later with a small package and Vanessa asking non-stop questions. 'How is it that most people in their nineties don't even know how to turn on a computer and you have your own personal hacker?'

Alice felt a twinge in her knee and slipped her arm through Vanessa's for extra support. 'For a start, that's a little offensive to old people. Besides, an important lesson you need to know if you want to become a con artist is that you don't need to know everything, as long as you know people who do.'

'I don't want to become a con artist,' Vanessa protested.

'We'll talk later,' Alice replied. She eased herself into the passenger seat of the car and felt all her tendons and bones creak and pop like a cooling car engine.

'Why are you so intent on fixing my life?' Vanessa asked when she was settled in her own seat.

'Because it's too late to fix mine,' Alice muttered.

'How are you going to persuade Teresa to install the camera outside her front door?'

Alice snorted. 'Vanessa. Sometimes it's like you don't know me at all.'

Vanessa pulled out into traffic before replying. 'The easy way would be to play on her fears that someone is breaking into her apartment.' She glanced across at her passenger. 'But the Alice way would be...'

Alice watched Vanessa consider the options.

'Installing the camera without telling her about it,' Vanessa said.

Alice nodded approvingly. 'Seems you do know me after all.'

EIGHTEEN

The camera Alice had bought was small, wireless, and easily hidden. Installing it should have been a ten second job, but Vanessa made it awkward and displayed all the finesse of a puppy playing with a ball. Alice gritted her teeth and reminded herself a few times that the girl wasn't experienced in this line of work. (Although as a girl, Vanessa must have had plenty of experience sneaking out of the house as a teenager.)

With urgent whispering from Vanessa, interspersed with barely supressed nervous laughter, and forgetting to turn the camera on, it was an excruciatingly long five minutes before they stepped back onto the elevator and ascended to Alice's floor.

Troy had set up some sort of application on her phone so that all Alice had to do was open it and they were staring at a clear image of Teresa's door.

Alice and Vanessa stared at the screen for a little while before Vanessa commented, 'It's like watching a painting and expecting it to move.'

'I've seen worse shows on television,' Alice replied.

'Does it notify you when there's movement? Or is it recording the whole time?'

Alice put the phone on the kitchen counter and walked over to switch the kettle on. 'Have you heard of a cloud?'

'Sure, it's the white, sometimes grey thing that hangs out in the sky. But I think you're talking about *the* cloud, which is a virtual storage place for your data.'

'My what?'

'Data, like pictures, and documents and stuff.'

'Oh. Then yes, *the* cloud. Apparently, the video is stored there and we can access it anytime. Well, *you* can access it anytime. I have no idea how to do it,' Alice admitted.

Vanessa opened her mouth to say something, then closed it again.

'Out with it,' demanded Alice. 'I don't have you around to be reticent.'

Vanessa gave a little shrug. 'I just wondered what it was like, having to rely on other people so much when the way I see it your entire life has been relying on just yourself to get things done.'

It was a good question with a tricky answer that Alice wasn't sure how to word without sounding cold-hearted. With anyone else she wouldn't have worried but she liked Vanessa.

'I have never claimed to know everything. Even at my peak there were always skills I needed from other people. That hasn't changed.'

'I guess I get that,' Vanessa replied. 'Can I ask another question?' She hurried on before Alice could answer. 'How did you end up... in your line of work?'

Alice hesitated before replying. 'Life wasn't always plush apartments and catered meals. In the early-fifties I was a single mother with a young daughter, fighting for everything that seemed to be handed to men with ease. One day the wrong man took one of the few things I had of value. So I took it back.' She smiled at the memory. 'I enjoyed the planning and scheming, so everything went from there.'

'You started as a thief?' Vanessa said.

'It's not theft if the item belonged to you in the first place,' Alice snapped.

Vanessa's face flushed. 'Sorry.'

'No,' she sighed. '*I'm* sorry. That's a silly old woman's pride talking. What I meant was, anyone can steal things, what I did took skill.'

Vanessa met her eye again. 'Now I know you're playing with me. You'd never call yourself silly unless it was to deflect.'

Alice grinned. 'Good girl. Amazing what a bit of humility does to defuse a situation.'

Vanessa stood up. 'Okay I need to get back to work or Tracey will dock my pay. Let me know if anything exciting happens on the Teresa Cam. And don't think I don't have plenty more questions for you.'

Alice sat at the bench a while longer, staring at the phone screen, her mind fifty years in the past. *Some lessons come the hard way.*

NINETEEN

London, June 1969

'I have a knot problem,' Alice said.

'Yes, madam. Physical or metaphorical?'

Alice adjusted her glasses and smiled nervously at the shop assistant. 'Physical. You see, I need to tie a knot strong enough to hold a body.'

The man blinked several times before his manners took over. 'Is the problem one of restraint or something more… permanent in nature?'

'Permanent, I'm afraid. I need to know how to hang someone. Or more specifically, how someone could hang themselves.'

The shop assistant, who's name tag read Albert, nodded thoughtfully and tapped the display case counter with one perfectly manicured finger. For the moment they were alone in the small shop. High-end camping gear lined the walls and a small sign above the front door stated that Grimwall and Sons had been supplying London with goose-lined sleeping bags and tins of caviar since 1895. This was not the place to come if you wanted to rough it in a field somewhere. This was the place you sent your manservant to ensure that roughing it was restricted to having to use two forks for dinner rather than the usual five.

However, Alice had discretely asked around and, despite the wealthy clientele, word was that the staff knew their stuff. And she needed information.

'How heavy is the person?' Albert asked.

Alice thought for a moment. 'Around 180 pounds.'

'Rope?'

'Yes,' she replied.

Albert gave her a ghost of a smile. 'Naturally. I meant what type of rope?'

She didn't have a clue. The scandal of a suicide had been enough to rule out any police enquiry and William's butler had already signalled his reluctance to betray is employer's privacy, so the actual details, such as the thickness or length of the rope, were vague at best.

Her hesitation was enough of a response for Albert.

'Presumably madam wishes it to be successful?'

'The plot requires it,' she confirmed.

Alice had introduced herself as the private secretary of a well-known crime author who was having some problems writing a scene in his latest novel. Albert had accepted the explanation with barely an eyebrow raise, as if it were perfectly normal for a camping store sales assistant to be asked such questions.

'You probably need a climbing rope, specifically designed to hold a weight for long periods of time.' He reached up to the shelf behind the counter and brought down a looped rope, showing her the end, perhaps believing that the very sight of it would be enough to prove his point.

All Alice saw was a rope. 'I'll trust your judgement on that,' she smiled. 'However it's really a question of knots. Would any knot do the trick?'

Albert appeared horrified. 'Goodness me no, madam. While most knots will *appear* strong, not many will hold significant weight for the required period of time.' He coughed, a tinge of red colouring his cheeks. 'I'm told it's not always a quick process.'

Alice felt her own face flush, but in her case it was supressed anger. She wasn't convinced that someone had murdered William, but the thought that he may have suffered regardless of whether it was self-inflicted or not, made her more determined to discover the truth.

'My apologies, madam. I didn't mean to… become too descriptive,' Albert said.

She sighed and stifled irritation at another man attempting to protect her from the horrors of the world. She'd seen and done things that would likely have him going straight to church to pray for her soul.

'Not at all,' Alice patted him on the arm. 'My employer makes me read his manuscripts and some of them are very… descriptive. So a specific knot would be required?'

'Not necessarily, but more likely than not.' He chuckled at his play on words.

'And therefore specific knowledge on how to tie the knot?'

'Well, a simple slip knot would do the trick, any man who was in the scouts or the navy could probably rustle it up. But generally speaking, if your character had no experience with ropes and knots, then it could be a problem.'

Alice thanked Albert for his time and stepped out onto the cobblestone streets of North London.

The sun was hidden behind buildings and long shadows stretched over uneven surfaces. She set off in the direction of her hotel, unbuttoning her suit jacket and releasing her hair from the tight bun. By the corner, her hair was free, jacket and glasses gone, and her appearance had been altered enough to give any followers a moment's hesitation.

She only looked behind her once, which would later prove to be one of many costly mistakes.

TWENTY

Alice cooked herself dinner. She was in too reflective a mood to suffer the often banal conversations that littered the dining room.

She would have loved to grill a nice juicy steak, with salad and new potatoes. Unfortunately steak was more troublesome to eat than it used to be, from the chewing, to the stomach and out the other end, so she settled for a poached egg on toast.

She ate while watching a game show. The news was on the other channel but none of it interested her anymore, she usually stuck with lighter entertainment where she could.

Occasionally she glanced at her phone, but there was no movement. Troy had mentioned setting up an alert to let her know when the camera was activated, but she didn't totally understand it and therefore didn't fully trust it.

At 7:20 she turned the television off, deciding that company was what she needed after all. Specifically the type of company where no one was allowed to talk. Movie night was due to start in ten minutes and Owen would be saving her a seat.

Pulling on a sweater, she picked up her phone and made her way out of the building. There was no one behind the reception desk, Vanessa having left for the day. The front doors of the building locked at seven and only residents with the appropriate access codes could get in.

Day was fading into night and the pale lights lining the driveway were beginning to take hold, helping keep darkness from taking over. As she approached the Olympic Complex it seemed like every light inside was on.

She heard a scuffling behind her. Turning quickly she felt her head drift in a moment of dizziness as she peered first at the path, then at the grass on either side of it. There was nothing there. She stayed motionless for a moment longer, annoyed at how fast her heart was beating. Finally convinced it was a bird or perhaps Maddy, the village cat, she turned back at a more sedate pace and completed the journey to the Olympic Complex.

Inside, the bright lights dispelled any remnants of disquiet at the sound, and her reaction to it. Immediately to her right was the indoor pool which she could see was currently empty. She'd never used it herself, but had been told it was always comfortably warm, and not too deep. Past the reception area was a hallway leading to the gym at the back, and the games room.

'Casing the joint?'

She didn't need to turn to know the owner of the voice, but her heart still reacted to the sudden sound. Maybe going outside wasn't good for her health.

'I heard you were moving in,' she said as Nanci stepped next to her

Nanci Katz fancied herself as a younger version of Alice. In her early seventies with light coloured blonde hair she still held glimpses of the beauty that would have been an asset and a liability in her youth. Alice had thought her a passerby, but now that Nanci was moving in, she might need to remind the younger lady that the residents of Silvermoon were off limits where it came to pulling a con.

'I liked the place so much, when the opportunity came up I jumped at it,' Nanci said, with a smile.

'And right over everyone ahead of you on the waitlist,' Alice replied dryly.

'I got lucky I guess,' Nanci shrugged. 'Going in to watch the movie?'

'Yes, I thought I might.'

'Me too. I'm hoping that dish Owen will be there.'

Alice bristled at hearing her friend described that way, but held her tongue, knowing any response would be seen as a challenge.

196

'After you,' she said with a wave of a hand.

The games room was two-thirds full. The pool table and table tennis table had been pushed to one side and chairs laid out in an audience format.

She spotted Owen's tall figure sitting in the front row, with an empty seat next to him. Nanci made a beeline straight for him and Alice drifted behind her, curious to see how Owen would handle the charm offensive.

'Is this seat taken?' Nanci asked in a sweet voice that Alice would have almost believed if the woman hadn't signalled her intentions just moments before.

Owen glanced up and smiled politely, then his eyes slid over her shoulder and spotted Alice. She detected a hint of relief in them.

'Yes, I'm afraid it is. Hello, Alice, as promised I saved you a seat.'

Nanci shot her a rueful look then headed towards a seat in the third row.

'I'm glad you decided to come,' Owen said as Alice eased herself into the comfortable chair.

'I've always found Steve McQueen a good antidote to melancholy,' Alice replied.

'I'm surprised that melancholy is something you've ever been troubled with.'

'Memories will do that to you.'

Before he had a chance to comment further the lights dimmed and the movie started.

She'd seen it before, so Alice found herself zoning out after a while. She automatically glanced at her wrist, but her watch hadn't shown up and there was no way of knowing the exact time. Her phone was in her jacket, but people checking their phones while movies were playing was high on her list of annoying habits.

The matter was taken out of her hands though when she felt her phone vibrating. With a muttered "excuse me" she rose from her chair and left the room. Out in the hallway she slipped her phone out, expecting to see a text or missed call from Amanda. Instead it was a notification that there'd been some movement on the Teresa Cam. When she stared at the screen though there was nothing but the empty image of the area outside Teresa's door.

Frowning, Alice struggled to recall anything Troy might have said about rewinding or replaying. There was no big obvious button saying press me. She glared at the screen out of frustration, and when that didn't solve the problem she rang Troy. Unfortunately it went straight to voicemail.

She ended the call without leaving a message, then considered her options. From what she could tell there were four. Her first option was to ignore the notification and go back to watch the movie. She quickly dismissed that. Second option was to ask Owen to accompany her to Teresa's front door, but that would mean revealing the hidden camera and she wasn't quite ready to do that. Third option was to ring Vanessa and ask if she knew how to view the footage. Fourth option was the riskiest and despite her age, the most appealing.

With a glance back at the closed door, Alice walked as quickly as she could out of the complex and back to her building. Luckily there was plenty of lighting along the pathway. Management were less worried about muggers and more about elderly residents falling and breaking something. Whatever the reason Alice was grateful to be able to clearly see where she was going.

Punching the code into the front door she crossed the foyer to the elevator and pressed the button for Teresa's floor. When she stepped onto the landing everything seemed quiet. Cautiously she approached Teresa's door, and there was a buzzing from her pocket. She looked down and failed to hear the click of the door opening.

A figure barrelled into her, knocking her into the wall where she hit her head. As she fell awkwardly to the ground she saw someone rush through the door to the stairwell, then her vision blurred and she fainted.

TWENTY-ONE

London, June 1969

Alice didn't realise she was in trouble until the elevator doors closed. Then she noticed that she was riding up with three individuals that looked like they only cracked a smile when pulling wings off flies or kicking puppies.

That in itself was interesting, although not unusual. Most corporate types struck her as being capable of dark things.

It wasn't even the fact that the man to her left had pressed the door close button even though a couple were striding towards the doors and could easily have been accommodated in the space.

She'd met plenty that would have done the same. She'd even been guilty of it once or twice herself.

No, it was the subtle glance between the men, followed by the almost casual shuffle sideways. Now instead of her being in the middle, with clear space to the door, she was the centre point of a triangle, with two men in front and one behind.

Normally Alice would have backed herself against a man if it was one on one, but three to one were not odds she liked.

She glanced up at the arrow above the door as it crept around to the number two. She was on the fifth floor. Another glance at the numbered buttons showed none of the men were getting off on other floors.

Alice took a quick mental stock of her possessions. Nothing in her bag could be classified as a weapon.

The arrow past three and kept on climbing. Whatever was going to happen wasn't going to be on the elevator or they would have done it already. She had until the doors opened on five to think of a plan.

Halfway between four and five an idea came to her. She let the strap of her bag slip off her shoulder and grasped it in her hand.

As the doors slid slowly open she noticed the men in front rock slightly onto the balls of their feet in anticipation of a quick exit. She felt her own legs tense and her heart started racing.

The two men stepped out of the elevator and Alice took a step forward, then suddenly jumped to the side. The man behind her was caught out, already in the process of taking another step. He stumbled slightly. Alice swung her handbag, hitting him on the shoulder. He was almost out of the elevator when he caught the edge of the door with his hand. He started to turn and that's when she raised a heeled foot and kicked him in the backside. The force sent him sprawling into the other two and they all ended up in a tangle on the ground. Meanwhile she pressed the ground floor button and jammed her finger on the door close.

Agonisingly slowly the doors crept together as she watched one of the men rise to his knees. If he looked mean before, now his face suggested murder was the only thing on his mind. He lunged towards the elevator just as the doors came together. There was a thud from the other side followed by what sounded like an impressive curse word. Then the elevator smoothly began its descent.

Alice's heart thudded so loudly she couldn't hear herself think. She reached out and pressed the button for the first floor. Elevators weren't designed for speed and the three men looked fit enough to race down four flights of stairs in time to be waiting for her at the bottom.

With a soft ting, the doors opened and she rushed into the corridor. As she raced past the door leading to the stairwell she heard the clattering of shoes on stairs.

At the far end of the corridor was a second door, almost invisible to most of the hotel guests, bearing a sign stating *Cleaning Services*. (Most people who could afford to stay in the hotel weren't interested in anyone or anything involved with keeping it pristine.)

Through this door was a small room stocked with towels and toiletries, and at the other end of the room was a second elevator, a service elevator. It opened on every floor, except the ground floor.

Once she was safely inside, heading to the basement, Alice took several deep breaths and finally looked at the item in her hand. It was a man's brown leather wallet. As she'd shoved her assailant out of the elevator she'd lifted it from his jacket pocket.

There was forty pounds inside, which she slipped into her handbag, a driver's licence identifying the man as Brian Harrison, and one other item. A photograph of her. She was standing next to William, both of them smiling at the camera. They were outside sitting at a table, and behind them, in full stretch, was a man with a tennis racket.

Alice knew where it had been taken, and more importantly who had taken it. Richard Dankworth had just made his first move. She took a piece of paper from her handbag and stared at the numbers written on it.

It was her turn.

TWENTY-TWO

'You most certainly will not,' Alice said.

'It's standard procedure,' Tracey replied.

'I don't care, you will not under any circumstances inform my granddaughter of this.' She glared at the manager of the Silvermoon Retirement Village, a woman she would have described as harmlessly officious, and occasionally annoying.

Tracey glared back with a look mixing frustration with exasperation, and just a hint of desire to tell Alice where to go. Manners, and a desire to keep her job stayed her tongue.

They were in Alice's apartment, along with Janice, the resident nurse, Owen, and Teresa. Tracey was pacing back and forth in front of Alice who was sitting on the couch.

Alice stifled her irritation. She wasn't used to people fussing over her. She didn't like it. Her irritation erupted when there was a knock at the door and Vanessa rushed in.

'Who called you?' Alice asked.

The worry on Vanessa's face dissolved upon seeing Alice sitting up on the couch.

No one replied, but Owen's face turned a dark shade of red.

'Oh for goodness sake, I'm fine!' Alice snapped.

'You were found unconscious on the floor outside Teresa's apartment,' Janice reminded her. 'That doesn't sound fine.'

Alice had to admit that her head hurt, but she certainly wasn't going to tell any of them. Just like she was keeping the cause of her injury to herself. All she'd said was that she'd become bored watching the movie and had decided to visit Teresa, and when she arrived she'd felt a little funny and passed out. Which in hindsight was a mistake, because Tracey and Janice immediately wanted her to go to hospital and if she hadn't regained her sense in time to prevent it then she'd already be in the back of an ambulance.

Teresa had found her unconscious in the hallway and Alice realised she had only been out for a minute or so. The realisation gave her chills – Teresa must have just missed the intruder and while that meant she could have identified the person, it also meant she might have been in the firing line.

Alice had twenty years on her friend but had also had a tougher life. The closest Teresa had probably been to physical danger was when her cleaner had over-waxed the dining room floor of her mansion.

Alice stood (or rather sat) firm under the combined caring onslaught for the next five minutes, before Tracey and Janice eventually gave up in varying degrees of disgust and left.

The one concession Alice had made was that she wouldn't be alone overnight. Vanessa had quickly volunteered to stay with her, heading off a potentially awkward offer from both Teresa and Owen. Both hovered for a little while longer. Owen in particular appeared to watch Alice intently for any signs of imminent collapse. In the end Vanessa correctly interpreted the irritation on Alice's face and managed to usher the other two out with promises of updates should anything happen.

'They mean well,' Vanessa said into the silence.

'I know,' Alice sighed. 'But that doesn't mean all that pity isn't annoying.'

'It's not pity,' Vanessa crossed to the coffee table and started clearing up tea cups. 'It's concern. Whether you like it or not they care about you.'

'Of course I like it!' Alice glared for a moment, then seemed to realise what she said and her face relaxed into a rueful smile. 'I do appreciate having friends, and a slightly panicked village manager, but I have never abided fussing. I find it...'

'Irritating? Annoying? A pain in the—'

'Yes alright,' Alice waved a hand. 'You've made your point.'

Vanessa carried the cups to the kitchen bench. 'Good. Now tell me what really happened.'

It didn't take long, because there wasn't much to tell, but when she was finished Vanessa was frowning.

'Why didn't you tell Tracey? An assault on Silvermoon grounds is something she should know about.'

'It wasn't so much an assault as a bump.'

Vanessa stared at her from across the room and opened her mouth to say something that would irritate Alice even further.

Alice didn't want to snap at her, so she hurriedly cut her off. 'Look, I startled them. They must have heard the elevator or something. Once I was unconscious, they could have come back and finished me off. If they had wanted to hurt me they could have, but they didn't.'

Vanessa winced at her choice of words and her face drained of colour.

'Come and sit down,' Alice patted the couch. 'The last thing I want is to have to call Janice back for another fainting spell.'

Vanessa managed to move to the couch without collapsing, although her hands were a little shaky. Alice would have to toughen this girl up if she was going to teach her the art of the con.

'Listen, I'm fine. And now we know more than we did if I'd stayed at the movie. Take a deep breath, and let it out.' She watched Vanessa follow her instructions. 'And again.' By the third time, colour had returned to Vanessa's cheeks and she looked steadier. 'Right, now tell me what we've learned.'

Vanessa was quiet for a while. Alice was about to prompt her when she spoke. 'We know that Teresa wasn't crazy about someone being in her apartment.'

Alice nodded. 'Well done. What else?'

'We know that the person is a thief not a killer.'

Another nod. 'Although technically that's an assumption rather than a fact. It might just be they didn't think they had time to finish me off.' She saw Vanessa start to panic again and put a hand over hers. 'But I'm sure that wasn't the case. Anything else?'

Vanessa screwed up her face and started to shake her head, then paused. 'We can assume the person knew that Teresa wasn't at home, which means they knew she was going to be at the movie. Which means…'

'That it's likely that the person works here,' Alice finished.

'Or lives here,' suggested Vanessa.

'Possibly, but the person moved much too quickly to be a resident, so staff is more likely.'

'You know, working with you has coloured staff get-togethers in a whole new light. I can't help looking around the room and wondering who is going to be revealed as a murderer or thief,' Vanessa said sourly.

Alice gave her hand a squeeze and let go. 'Always best to think that at the start until you can assess things for yourself.'

'What sort of way is that to live your life?'

Alice slowly got to her feet and equally slowly walked to the bookshelf, where she took down a large book and brought it back to the couch. She handed it to Vanessa.

The title of the book was *The Great Apes of Madagascar.*

Vanessa looked at Alice.

'Open it,' Alice told her.

The spine cracked a little as she did. It had been a while since it had last been opened. In the centre of the book, nestled into an area cut out of the pages, was a small brass hip flask.

'I got this from an Austrian businessman in 1963 while I was working in Europe.' Alice lifted it out and gave it a little shake, listening to the satisfying slosh of liquid from inside. 'It contains Russian Vodka, probably aged into pure rocket fuel by now. The man I took it from had built his fortune on stolen Jewish gold from World War 2.'

'How horrible,' Vanessa said.

'Yes, which is why it was satisfying relieving him of a good chunk of his fortune, and this, as a souvenir. It hasn't always been an easy life, but it has occasionally been very enjoyable.'

'But how do you learn to trust people?'

'The same way you do,' Alice replied. 'By learning from my interactions with them. The only real difference is the stakes are usually higher for me. Or they were anyway,' she added wistfully.

'You sound like you miss it.'

Alice shrugged. 'Who doesn't miss their old life?'

'A lot of people,' Vanessa retorted.

Another shrug. It was true there were certain parts she didn't miss, but overall she wouldn't have traded her life for anything, with the possible exception of London and the Richard Dankworth incident. That part she would have been happy to skip.

'Of course, you're missing the most important piece of information,' she said to Vanessa. 'The whole reason I left the movie to begin with.'

Vanessa's blank look suddenly changed to excitement. 'The camera! We have video evidence of the person that assaulted you.'

'Bumped me, but yes, precisely.'

'Let's see it,' Vanessa was practically bouncing up and down next to her and Alice idly thought if she poked the girl with a sharp object she might fly around the room like a burst balloon.

'If I knew how to watch the blasted thing, I wouldn't have gone to Teresa's in the first place,' she said.

'I know how to,' Vanessa replied, pulling out her own phone. She tapped with her fingers and brought up an app that mirrored that of the one on Alice's phone.

'When did you get that?' Alice asked suspiciously.

Vanessa kept her eyes on the screen but her cheeks darkened slightly. 'I went back to the shop and asked Troy to put it on my phone too. Just in case, you know?'

Alice wavered between amused and annoyed. On one hand she applauded the initiative, but on the other hand she got the impression Vanessa hadn't intended to tell her she'd done it, and Alice was the only one in their relationship who wanted to keep secrets.

'In case?'

'You lost your phone or something. Ah, here it is.'

Alice parked the issue for future discussion. At the very least she needed to warn Vanessa about getting involved with Troy. Alice trusted him but he came with enough baggage to open his own luggage shop.

She turned her attention to the phone screen. Vanessa tapped the little arrow and the picture of the hallway outside Teresa's apartment began to move. Vanessa pressed something else and the video sped up.

Suddenly a figure appeared. Vanessa took her finger off but the figure had disappeared by the time the video returned to normal. Swearing under her breath she rewound, going too far, then after several more attempts got to the point of the figure arriving.

Unfortunately seeing it at normal speed didn't do much for identification purposes. The figure wore a plain hooded sweatshirt and was looking over their shoulder towards the stairs as they exited the elevator. By the time they looked forward their head was out of shot. Seconds later they had vanished through Teresa's door.

Alice sat back and considered what she'd seen. Even though the face wasn't visible, there were still things to learn from watching it. She thought about asking Vanessa to rewind it so she could watch it again, but decided she could do that later.

At the bottom of the screen was a clock. Alice did a quick calculation, then told Vanessa to forward it by ten minutes. There was a bit more fiddling but eventually they got there. They saw the elevator doors open and Alice stepped into view. She glanced straight at the video, then advanced towards the door, before suddenly looking down at her pocket.

'That's right. My phone made a noise.'

Suddenly video Alice was knocked towards the camera and there was the briefest of glimpses of the figure rushing past her and through the door to the stairs.

'That...' Vanessa's words were choked off as struggled to find the right insult. 'When I find out whoever that was I'll… I'll...' She proceeded to describe an act that had Alice nodding in appreciation.

'Physically that's impossible,' Alice pointed out.

'That's the point,' Vanessa replied.

'Come and sit down.' Vanessa paced a little bit more before flopping down into her seat. 'I appreciate that you care so much, but here's an important lesson and I want you to listen carefully. There's no place for anger in retaliation. That's the quickest way to failure.'

Vanessa took some deep breaths, then finally nodded. 'Did that ever happen when you were working? You let anger get in the way?'

Alice thought about avoiding the question, then she sighed. 'Just the once.'

'How did it go?'

'Badly.'

TWENTY-THREE

London, June 1969

'I'll kill you!'

Alice listened to the venom in the words and was thankful they were delivered down a phone line and not in person. She glanced towards the door and thought about locking it just in case.

After the attempted whatever-it-had-been earlier that week, she had changed hotels, going from luxury to quaint-but-rundown on the edge of the city.

Then she had put her plan into action.

Using the numbers from Richard's wallet at the tennis club as a starting point it didn't take much investigation to deduce the accounts weren't at Richard's usual bank. When she'd rung pretending to be his secretary with the correct account numbers, she learned he had three accounts containing considerable amounts of money.

The day after the attempt by the three men in the elevator, Alice had gone to the tennis club and used a five-pound-bribe to obtain a copy of Richard's signature. Members, especially of his level, never carried cash. It was thought that if you had to carry cash then you didn't have enough of it. William had always said that with a self-depreciating smile, even though he had more cash than most of London put together. Members simply signed for their drinks and food, and the bill was discretely paid, usually by a secretary or manservant.

Alice used the signature to forge a letter on fancy letterhead, asking for two thirds of the funds in each account to be transferred to another bank. Her hope was that since she wasn't closing the accounts there would be no alarm bells or nosy bank managers wanting to check with the account holder.

She needn't have worried. Between the letter, and her performance as a dizzy secretary with short skirt and low-cut blouse, the bank manager barely paused before completing the transfer. Thanks to the misogynistic world of 1960s London, no man dreamt of a woman being underhanded and devious. The swinging sixties hadn't yet reached the offices of the Lloyds Bank.

Alice had walked out of the bank fifty thousand pounds richer, and Richard was in for a very nasty surprise.

Which apparently he'd received the following day.

Alice had waited 24 hours before phoning Richard at his office and it was going about as well as could be expected.

'You're dead!' Richard ranted.

'Like William?' Alice shot back.

'What? He killed himself.'

'Bull! William was a good man and you killed him.'

'You're delusional.'

'And you're homicidal. William found out you were trying to buy his company out from underneath him and were planning to sack the staff. He wouldn't give you the shares you needed so you killed him. Now you can do what you want with the company.'

It was a shot in the dark, based on information gleaned from the chatty foreman at the factory after a few ales in the Fox and Hound after work.

Richard's silence was all the confirmation she needed.

'You can't prove that,' he said flatly.

He was right, but this had never been about winning a guilty verdict in a court of law. 'I don't need to prove it. You needed the money in those accounts to buy the shares. You couldn't do it until after the funeral because you were worried someone would point a finger in your direction. I just took away your opportunity. You killed William for nothing.'

She heard her anger in the last five words and fought to bring her emotions under control. Clear thought and white hot anger never mixed well.

'Look, this doesn't have to go badly,' Richard said, his tone calmer. 'Return the money and I'll let you keep ten percent for yourself. You can walk away with thousands of pounds.'

'Right now I can walk away with tens of thousands of pounds.'

'You didn't let me finish. You can walk away with all that money, free and clear. I won't look for you. I'll chalk it up to a bad business deal.'

Alice was quiet for a while, letting him think she was considering his offer. She had been expecting it and had no intention of taking him up on it.

'You won't come looking?' She allowed doubt to tinge her voice.

'Absolutely. You have my word.'

She smiled at the victory in his tone. 'Perhaps you're right. I didn't really think this through.'

'It's not surprising. This is business, not a place for a woman.'

Alice clenched her fist. She thought she'd like to shove her foot into his business with a great deal of force. 'Alright, I'll give it to you. But I'm not coming to you, and I don't want you to know where I'm staying.'

'Alright, where do you suggest we meet?'

'William's house in the country, at 10 tomorrow morning.' She held her breath, worried she had come across as too crisp and assured.

'Surely somewhere closer would be easier,' Richard replied impatiently.

'That's halfway between London and where I am,' she lied.

'Fine. Ten tomorrow morning.'

'And make sure you're alone, Richard. I don't trust you not to go back on your word.'

He had the good sense not to protest at this slight on his character. 'Don't be late, and don't make the mistake of changing your mind. If you run I'll look for you, even if it takes the rest of my life. No one robs Richard Dankworth.'

He hung up before she could reply.

If I ran it'd take the rest of your life to find me, she thought.

TWENTY-FOUR

Alice was pleased to discover that she was still alive the next morning, although her head did hurt a bit.

Despite the *trauma* (a word that others used, but not her) of the night before, she was still up in the morning before her nurse – Vanessa was lying on her back, a blanket half covering her body, and bed hair half covering her face.

Alice walked quietly into the kitchen and switched on the kettle. While she waited for the water to boil she set out two cups, put a teabag in each, and fetched the milk from the fridge. While she held the door open she glanced at the vegetable cooler, spotting a sliver of metal hidden behind a head of broccoli. She didn't eat broccoli, but there was always a fresh one in the fridge. It was exactly the right size and shape to hide the hip flask.

She closed the fridge door a little too hard.

Over on the couch Vanessa snorted and her body jerked. 'Wha… I'm up.' She half sat, then slumped back down. 'Almost.'

'Tea?'

'Coffee?' Vanessa replied hopefully.

'For that we'll have to take a trip to Charlie's.'

Vanessa groaned. 'That's sooo far. Okay, tea now. But you owe me a coffee.'

Alice looked at the bags under her eyes and felt a little guilty. 'What time did you get to sleep?'

Vanessa made it all the way to upright on the third attempt and yawned. 'I decided you weren't going to die on me around 4:00am.'

'I told you I was going to be fine,' Alice reminded her.

'You say a lot of things, most of them your own version of the truth,' Vanessa replied.

A fair assessment, Alice thought. She poured the tea and carried the cups to the couch. 'Can we look at the video again?'

'From last night?' Vanessa squinted at her then reached for her phone. 'What are we looking for now?'

'Just run it through.'

They sat in silence while the video played. Once the intruder was inside Teresa's apartment Alice asked for it to be rewound. She watched it three times, then indicated that Vanessa should let it roll. When they got to the part where Alice stepped out of the elevator, Vanessa paused it.

'Are you sure you want to see this again?'

Alice couldn't keep the amusement off her face. 'Do you think it'll upset my delicate disposition?'

'I'm not sure anyone under the age of 50 uses the word *disposition*, but come on. This could have gone badly. What if they'd hit you a little harder? What if they'd stuck around to finish the job?'

'Then I'd be dead, but I'm not, so park your *what-ifs* next to your *if-onlys* and let's move on.'

'Well, excuse me for caring' Vanessa shot back.

'That's alright, dear,' Alice replied, patting her arm. 'You'll grow out of it. Now play the damn video.'

Vanessa jabbed at the screen so hard Alice thought she'd go right through the phone.

Seconds later Alice was knocked into the wall.

There it was again, something that seemed different, but she couldn't put her finger on it. She got Vanessa to replay the same 10 seconds a few times. Muttering something about sadists, she complied.

'Actually if anything, this makes me a masochist, dear,' Alice remarked as her brain tried to piece together what was bugging her.

'What's the difference?'

'Mostly personal preference. Got it!' She yelled the last two words, causing Vanessa to jump.

'I stand by my comment,' Vanessa muttered darkly.

'We need to get to Teresa's.'

'It's seven in the morning. She'll be in bed.'

'Not for long,' Alice grinned.

As it turned out Teresa was up, and it seemed that she had been that way for a while judging by the bags under her eyes.

'You two are a matching set of luggage.'

'Very funny, Alice. How was I supposed to sleep when the intruder could have come back at any time and finished me off?'

'I was the one they started with,' Alice reminded her.

'Only because I wasn't here.'

Teresa looked set to escalate into full blown melodrama and Alice decided to cut it off but she was beaten to it.

'They could have broken in any time you were home, Teresa,' Vanessa said. 'The fact that they waited until you were out means they're not interested in hurting you. And yes, I'm aware I'm hurting my own argument,' she added to Alice.

'I suppose you're right,' Teresa said with a disappointed expression on her face. 'Why were they here then?'

Alice looked around the room. She tried to remember how it had looked the last time she was here so she could check any changes. Everything seemed the same, yet she was sure something was different.

'Look at it this way,' Alice said to Teresa. 'This proves you weren't crazy and someone *was* getting into your apartment. It also confirms that they were looking for something, and if I'm right…'

'…Then what?' Vanessa asked, when Alice didn't finish her sentence.

Alice stared at the carpet behind the couch. At one end there was an indent in the floor, like the couch had been shifted forward slightly. She put her hands on the back of the couch and pushed, but it barely moved. She asked Vanessa to do the same and she did get the piece of furniture to inch forward.

The couch was an older style wooden-framed three-seater that looked incredibly uncomfortable, but no doubt cost more than Vanessa's annual salary. Each of the old fashioned seats had space under it. If you lay on the floor you would have easily been able to see the other side, and a smaller more agile person could squirm under it and disappear entirely.

Alice was the smallest in the room, but she had no intention of squirming, lying, or anything else.

'Why did we do that?' Vanessa asked.

'There doesn't seem to be any reason to move the couch. Yet it had been moved. There's only a couple of reasons to do that, and one is to get to something underneath it.'

'Why?'

'Get down and find out,' Alice ordered Vanessa.

With a sigh, Vanessa knelt down and peered under the couch.

'Nothing here,' she reported.

'You can't possibly tell that from there. Get down properly.'

Vanessa pulled her head out and glared at Alice. 'I'm not a dog, you can't just order me around.'

'You're quite right, I do apologise,' Alice said. 'Why don't you hop up and I'll get down there instead.'

Vanessa rolled her eyes, then lay down on the floor and wriggled a little until her head and shoulders had disappeared from view.

'If I get stuck in here I'm going to kick you in the shins,' came her muffled voice.

'Can you see anything?' Teresa asked.

'No. Wait, hang on.' She wriggled her way out again. 'There was a nail or something sticking out of the bottom. This was hooked on it.' She held up a glove.

Still got it, Alice thought to herself. What she'd seen in the video, but wasn't sure she believed until now, was the thief with both their hands covered on the way into the apartment, and only one covered on the way out.

Alice took the glove and turned it over in her hands. It was black and leather and was the type that would have been mass produced in a factory. She looked inside and saw a label showing it was a medium sized glove. Unhelpfully the thief hadn't written their name on it.

'Why would they take their glove off?' Teresa asked. 'Do you think it got caught when they heard the elevator ding?'

Vanessa shook her head. 'There's no tear in the leather, and it was hanging by the little loop just inside the end. I think they took it off on purpose and hung it there out of the way.'

'What on earth for?'

'That's a very good question,' Alice admitted. 'By taking it off they risked their fingerprints being left behind. Although I doubt the police would think to dust for prints under the couch. I can think of only one reason why they would remove it – gloves are good for general tasks, but not for fiddly things. My guess is they were trying to do something that needed more dexterity.'

'Like what?' Teresa asked.

Alice thought it over. 'Teresa was this carpet here when you moved in?'

Her friend looked surprised. 'Of course it was. The carpet was new, why would I waste money changing it?'

Because you have money to waste, was the reply that sprang to mind, but instead Alice said, 'What about the couch? How long have you had that?'

Teresa looked at the couch thoughtfully. 'This thing? It's been in the family for years. I think my husband bought it for me for our wedding anniversary.'

'A couch?' Vanessa immediately turned red at saying her thought aloud.

Teresa smiled. 'My Gareth wasn't the most romantic man, but he tried hard and when it came to practical things he was the best. For our seventeenth wedding anniversary I had a broken ankle due to a silly mistake with a horse, and I'd mentioned to Gareth that our old couch was too hard to get up off with crutches. He went out and bought this thing.'

'I'm sorry, that was rude.'

Teresa patted Vanessa on the arm in a gesture that Alice interpreted to mean, 'It's fine, don't worry about it.' It also reminded her of all the times she patted Vanessa's arm or leg, and for an absurd moment she worried they were treating the girl more like a dog than a friend. She vowed to cease all patting immediately.

'Do you know where he got it from?' Alice asked.

'Of course. Kirkcaldie and Stains was the only place for quality furniture back then,' Teresa replied in a tone that suggested everyone should have known that and if you didn't then you probably couldn't afford quality furniture.

Kirkcaldie and Stains certainly was aimed at the more discerning customer. Unfortunately the 150 year old store closed down in 2016. Not that it would have been much use popping in and asking about a couch purchased decades earlier.

'What now?' Vanessa asked.

Alice rubbed the side of her face as she considered various plans of action. None of which seemed to lead any closer to an answer.

'Take a picture of the couch,' she ordered Vanessa. 'We'll send it off to some people to see if there is anything unusual about it.'

'But surely if they were after the couch they'd just have taken it, not got under it,' Teresa pointed out.

'I'll make sure to ask them when we catch them,' Alice replied.

She and Vanessa said good bye to Teresa and went back to Alice's apartment.

'Can I have a coffee now?' Vanessa asked.

'You only just had a cup of tea.'

'I don't understand your point. The day doesn't start until the first coffee has scalded my throat and eaten into my stomach lining.'

'That's quite a graphic description for someone who was a bit queasy watching a video of me getting knocked down.'

'Out. Knocked out. And that's what lack of coffee does. It turns me into a descriptive grump.'

'Alright, get dressed properly and I'll take you to Charlie's.'

For someone professing diminished capacity due to lack of caffeine, Vanessa was ready in a record time.

Like most cafés in the city, Charlie's was open early, not for the pre-work rush, but to accommodate the odd hours that retired people often kept. It wasn't unusual to find the place full at seven in the morning with similar conversations as could be found in any café – who's done what to whom, which politician is useless, and what they had planned for the day ahead.

This morning the place was mostly empty and it didn't take long before Vanessa had her hands wrapped around a large coffee cup, inhaling deeply like her lungs ran on the smell of lattes rather than oxygen.

Alice had to admit she did look more alert.

'When are you due back at work?' she asked.

Vanessa glanced at her watch, reminding Alice once again that she still hadn't located her own. 'In half an hour.'

'Are you sure you're awake enough for it?'

'This helps,' Vanessa lifted her cup. 'Just bring me one of these every couple of hours and I'll be fine.'

'What about a shower?'

'What's with the sudden interest in my personal hygiene?'

'We may be old, but the residents can still smell body odour from across the room.'

Vanessa pretended to sniff her arm and screw her face up in mock disgust before they both laughed.

'I was just thinking your job seems to get in the way of investigations,' Alice commented.

'Blimey, I hope you're not expecting this sort of thing to become a regular occurrence,' Vanessa replied with wide eyes.

Alice had been thinking exactly that. She didn't enjoy being knocked into walls, but the investigation had given her more energy and purpose than she'd had in years. 'Don't tell me you're not enjoying this,' she said.

'I'm sitting in a café at eight in the morning, haven't slept, haven't showered, and I spent the morning crawling around the floor under a piece of furniture, trying to work out why someone would break into Teresa's apartment.'

Alice stared at her, waiting.

'Fine,' Vanessa sighed. 'Of course I'm enjoying it. Life has been rut-like since I helped you find Betty's killer. Somehow sitting behind a desk doesn't hold the same level of fulfilment anymore.'

Alice shuddered at the thought of spending days behind a desk, having to be polite to people.

'Listen, thanks for the coffee, I'd better go shower.' Vanessa drained the dregs of her cup and stood up.

'Do you want to use my place?' Alice asked.

'No thanks. There's an employee locker room I can use. They encourage us to cycle or run to work. Tracey says it's to promote employee fitness and being kind to the environment.'

'But it's really….'

'So us lowly workers don't clog up the carpark with our old bangers.'

After Alice promised to supply her with both updates and caffeine throughout the day, Vanessa left to get ready for her shift.

Alice sat there for a while longer, taking her time to finish her tea and trying to focus on Teresa's problem, and not think about London. She'd thought she had everything covered back then. She'd been wrong.

TWENTY-FIVE

Oxfordshire, June 1969

At precisely 10:00am she heard car wheels crunching on the gravel driveway, and a soft skid as the driver braked. Car doors slammed shut, almost in unison, but with enough of a gap that she was able to figure out that there was more than one door slamming.

It could have been Richard's driver letting him out, but somehow Alice didn't think so. She had told him to come alone, and it had been 50-50 as to whether he'd follow her instructions. On one hand he might not want anyone else to know that he had been robbed – and by a woman. People like Richard relied on their position of power, and that position would erode if people thought he was a soft touch. Which is where the other hand came in. He couldn't risk being made a fool of and having her get away.

Through the slit of the open door she heard the front door open and close, and a soft murmuring of voices. He definitely wasn't alone. She pressed her eye to the gap. There were three of them, including Richard.

Even though there had been even odds he would bring men with him, Alice had planned for it. She glanced at her watch and hoped Edward was on time.

As the men stood in the entrance way, a phone rang in the room at the end of the hall. The phone that normally sat on the side table in the hallway had been removed.

The men looked in the direction of the sound. Richard took a step and one of the men went with him, but Richard stopped him with his hand.

'Check upstairs,' he said. 'You two stay here.'

Alice took a tiny step to the side, careful not to touch the door. She felt a soft rush of air as Richard strode past. She found herself holding her breath, wondering if the door was going to come flying open, knocking her backwards. When that didn't happen she gently pushed it shut, hoping the echoing footsteps in the hall would disguise the click it made.

As she turned the key there was another deafening click, but no resulting sound of alarm from outside. She withdrew the key and tossed it under a cushion on the couch.

TWENTY-SIX

'The cushions on the couch,' Alice murmured.

'What was that?'

She looked up and saw that Nanci was standing next to her table.

'I forgot to ask the cleaners about cushions on the couch,' Alice lied smoothly.

'Oh,' Nanci looked unsure, but she walked over to a table near the counter and Alice ducked out the front door.

TWENTY-SEVEN

London, June 1969

Hurrying to the door to the next room, Alice was in time to see Richard walk to William's desk and snatch up the phone receiver.

'Hello! Hello!'

She'd instructed Edward to wait until someone answered, and then hang up. And by the frustrated way Richard slammed the phone down, that's exactly what he'd done.

'Temper, temper!' Alice said loudly.

Richard whirled around, his surprise turning to anger. 'There you are,' he said, as if he'd been looking for her for hours rather than having just arrived.

'Your money's in there,' she said, stepping aside to let him see the open briefcase sitting on the side table. She'd had to move the furniture around a little to make sure this view worked. Judging by the look on his face, he could clearly see the pound notes sitting in bundles inside the case.

'I must admit,' he said as he brushed past her, 'I wasn't sure you'd show up.'

Once he was clear of the doorway she shut the door and locked it. By the time he got to the briefcase she'd taken three quick steps to the left, stopping at the edge of the window frame and taking a quick glance outside. Good, no one in sight.

She watched as Richard picked up a stack of notes and flicked through them.

'What the hell!' he exclaimed.

Only the top note was genuine. The rest was blank paper.

'You stupid…' He turned and stopped mid-insult when he saw she was holding a gun.

It wasn't hers (the truth was she'd never fired one before) but resolve kept her hand steady. Edward had shown her where William kept the pistol. She'd travelled to the house the previous night and found it in the top desk drawer. Alice had tested the pistol on the back lawn first thing this morning. The recoil and noise had shocked her, but the satisfying chunk of bark that flew off the innocent tree at least told her the gun worked.

Richard, too stupid to realise the threat (or too arrogant to consider it genuine) took a step towards her.

'There are three men right outside that door. You pull that trigger and you're as good as dead.' His face had turned red and his hands trembled with rage.

'Perhaps,' she replied in an unsteady voice. She cleared her throat and continued in a stronger tone. 'But that won't stop you bleeding out all over the carpet.'

He paused. 'What do you want? More money? You're not getting any, not from me.'

Alice shook her head. 'No, I already have your money. I want answers.'

'What sort of answers?'

He'd overcome his initial shock. His hands were steadier and his face was returning to its normal colour. She could see him considering his options, and had no doubt that all of them ended up with her dead.

'Why did you kill William?'

Richard laughed dismissively but she saw his hands shake a little, and his eyes darted from her to the door and back.

'William killed himself. Nothing to do with me.'

Alice shook her head. 'Try again.'

Richard cleared his throat and took a casual step sideways. Alice kept the barrel of the gun focused on his chest.

'What makes you think I had anything to do with his death?'

She just kept looking at him. One of the first things she'd learnt about people, especially people like Richard, was that if you gave them enough silence, they'd eventually fill it.

He looked at the door, then the gun, then at her, and Alice didn't need to be a mind reader to know his thoughts. 'You got it mostly right on the phone. I wanted to merge his company with mine. There might have been a few people out of a job, but I would have made millions of pounds.'

'And he wouldn't sell.'

'He kept going on about *tradition*, and then he laughed when I called him old fashioned and out of step.' His face showed disdain at being mocked by an inferior. 'He said that it was his responsibility to protect tradition.'

'That made you angry.'

'Of course it did, you stupid woman. He was standing in the way of my success, of *my* money. Just because of some insignificant factory workers.'

Alice added the stupid woman comment to the long list of reasons she was going to bury the man.

'How did you hang him? He must have struggled.' She was pleased to hear her voice was nice and steady once again.

'You really are clueless, aren't you? I didn't hang him. I strangled the idiot. Didn't mean to, but it got the job done.' He laughed with a hint of madness, making Alice shudder. She'd been hoping for a confession, but this had come too easily. She wondered how he thought this was going to end.

'But I couldn't have anyone thinking he was murdered,' Richard continued. 'Too many questions, and too great a possibility the police would look in my direction. So I strung him up. It wasn't difficult. No one else was in the house.'

Alice gripped the gun tighter and inched to the left so she was standing partly behind a chair. She was beginning to think she'd made a serious mistake.

Richard stopped talking and was looking at her shrewdly. 'The only remaining question is, what's going to happen now?'

Rodney Strong

TWENTY-EIGHT

'You realise that the last time you did that it almost ended badly.'

'Yes,' Alice replied, 'which is why this time we'll be better prepared.'

Vanessa stared at her from behind the reception desk. 'My dad always said that it's okay to make a mistake. It's just not okay to keep making the same mistake over and over.'

'A wise man,' Alice replied. 'But we're not making the same mistake. We're setting a trap for a thief. No one is going to get hurt.'

Vanessa made a face.

'That was an accident. This time I'll be prepared.'

'It's a stupid plan.'

It was Alice's turn to make a face and Vanessa immediately backtracked. 'I mean, it may not be your best idea. Surely there is another way.'

'Well, you've got nine hours to think of one. And besides, I didn't say you had to come. I was just telling you what the plan was.'

Vanessa looked outraged, bringing a sweet smile to Alice's face.

Realising she'd been manipulated Vanessa grumbled a bit more, before agreeing to help.

Satisfied, Alice walked over to the elevator. As she pressed the button her phone rang.

'Hello, Troy,' she said. Out of the corner of her eye she saw Vanessa's head pop up and she shook her head. She'd have to keep those two away from each other.

'Have I mentioned that I love it when you come to visit me, Alice?' He sounded pleased with himself, which meant he'd just done something clever.

'Only when you want something,' she replied.

'We all want something. In this case I want your begrudging thanks.'

The elevator arrived and she stepped inside, waving goodbye to Vanessa. 'Thank you, Troy.'

'You haven't heard what I did yet,' he said.

'Troy, we both know how this is going to go. You did something very clever that I'm not going to fully understand, and I'm going to tell you you're clever and then next time we'll do it all again.'

'Way to take the fun out of it. But you're welcome.' Alice could hear him smile. 'I sent a worm.'

'A worm.'

'A digital one anyway. Managed to trace the origin of the account transfer and use that to ping—.'

'Troy!'

He sighed. 'Sorry, I couldn't get Joshua's mum's money back. That's long gone. But I've infected the culprit's computer system so the whole thing will crash. They'll eventually get up and running again but it'll take a while.'

Alice didn't fully understand it but Troy sounded proud of his work and she definitely understood the bit about them being out of action for a while.

'Well done,' she said genuinely.

'Thanks.'

'Is there any way this can be traced back to you?'

Troy laughed. 'Nah. To them it'll look like someone in Russia infected them. Which is ironic since that's probably where they came from in the first place.'

The elevator doors dinged open and Alice stepped into the foyer outside her apartment. Maddy the cat was curled up by her door, like a furry welcome mat.

'How the…'

'It's pretty technical,' Troy misinterpreted her surprise.

'Alright, I'll get you the money to put into his mum's account. But it can't be connected to me in any way. Can you make it seem like the bank returned it?'

'Nah, that might raise questions. Leave it to me, I'll sort it.' There was a pause. 'Can I ask you a question?' he said hesitantly. 'Why are you doing this? You don't know this guy or his mother. People get scammed all the time.'

That sounded like a Vanessa question. Perhaps she and Troy had been talking to each other more than Alice had realised.

She unlocked her front door and stepped around the cat, who raised her head lazily.

'I simply don't like people wasting their potential.' *Why do you think I come to you?* she wanted to add, but sometimes it was better that people didn't know you were helping them. Egos had an annoying way of derailing plans.

'Fair enough. Send the money.' Troy disconnected.

Alice turned to see Maddy sitting up and looking at her expectantly. 'How on earth do you get up here?'

The cat opened her mouth, yawned, then stood, stretched, and walked through the open door.

'Oh, help yourself,' Alice muttered.

Maddy found a patch of sun beside the window, curled up and went to sleep.

Alice went into the kitchen to fix something for lunch. Her plan for tonight was simple. Subtly get the word out that Teresa was going to be out, then wait in her apartment for the thief to come back, jump out and shout *Gotcha!* (She'd leave the jumping part to Vanessa, although she doubted somehow she could get that girl to say *gotcha*.)

The plan seemed simple enough. Not much could go wrong. Although, as she knew, every plan, no matter how well conceived or executed, was always only one step away from disaster.

She pulled out William's hip flask from its hiding spot and held it between her hands.

TWENTY-NINE

Oxfordshire, June 1969

'I'll tell you what's going to happen. You're going to put down that gun and return my money to me, and then perhaps I'll let you walk out of here in one piece, Mrs Stratler.' He said it in such a commanding tone that for the briefest of moments she actually considered it. Then common sense kicked in.

She would never let a man tell her what to do (except during the war, and at least she'd been paid for that). She certainly wasn't going to start with Richard Dankworth.

Alice shook her head. 'None of those things are going to happen. If I put the gun down, you'll pick it up and shoot me.'

'I give you my word,' Richard said.

She laughed. 'Which means nothing.'

There was a knock at the door and someone called his name.

'In here,' Richard yelled.

The door handle rattled.

'Break it down!' Richard bellowed.

Alice used this distraction to take several quick paces to the left.

When he turned back, his face registered surprise and he rotated to face her head on again. 'What's going on?'

She reached behind her and felt the bump of book spines on the shelf.

The banging on the door got louder, then paused, then a louder thump, maybe from a shoulder. The door rattled but held.

'On the table in front of you is a piece of paper and a pen. You're going to write down your confession, everything you just said...'

Richard laughed. 'Don't be ridiculous, you stupid bitch, I'll—'

She pulled the trigger. There was a loud bang and the gun pulled upwards. The light fixture over his head shattered, raining glass onto him.

'Don't call me stupid,' she hissed, her heart thumping.

This time the gunshot was much louder inside than when she'd practiced in the field. Her ears rang a little and her hands were shaking. It took all her concentration to keep focussed on the man in front of her. She was vaguely aware that the thumping outside the door had stopped.

Richard looked astonished as he plucked a piece of glass out of his hair and looked at it like it was from another planet. 'You... you... shot me.'

'I shot *over* you,' Alice said, 'because you wouldn't shut up. Tell them you're alright.'

He looked at her blankly and she gestured towards the door with the gun. 'Stay where you are. I'm fine,' he yelled.

Alice nodded. 'Good. Now here.' She pulled the key out of her pocket and threw it to him.

Still unnerved by the gunshot, he fumbled before gripping it tightly in his hand. He frowned at it like he'd never seen a key before in is life.

'You're letting me go?'

'Well I'm not going to kill you... unless you make me. And part of me hopes you do make me, because I cared for William and you killed him.' She pointed the gun at his face, then trailed it down his body to between his legs, before lifting it up to his chest.

'Then what was the point of all this?'

'To get your confession.'

Richard opened his mouth to say something, then closed it again. She knew he was thinking that no one else had been around to hear it, so if she wasn't going to kill him then the whole exercise had been pointless.

As far as killing him went, Alice had never done that before. She much preferred intellectual sparring to the real sort. She wasn't sure if she

232

could actually kill him, but it was important that Richard didn't know that. As for the rest, time would tell if this exercise was pointless or not.

'Leave,' she said, her gun hand trembling. 'And forget about William's company. In exchange, I promise not to tell anyone that you killed him.' She thrust her chin forward defiantly, and gripped the gun with both hands.

Richard stared at her with narrow eyes then gave the tiniest nod. Spinning on his heels he marched to the door leading to the office and unlocked it with the key in his hand. Flinging the door open he turned to look at her, failing to keep a sneer off his face before moving towards the hallway.

Alice dropped the gun onto a seat and raced across the room. She slammed the door shut and quickly locked it before removing the key and running across to the coffee table.

Richard had been entirely focussed on her and, thanks to her deliberate positioning, he never once glanced at the wooden table she had moved from its usual position in the middle of the room. Or at the case resting on the table. She had left the lid half open. Even if he had looked at it he wouldn't have seen what was inside.

Alice switched off the tape recorder, stuffed the small microphone back into the case and snapped the lid shut.

Something heavy smashed into the hallway door with a *thud*. Almost immediately, the internal door shuddered. They weren't taking any chances that she would slip past them.

Alice examined the windows. There would be a short drop to the garden outside, then a long sprint across flat green lawn to the woods at the edge of the property. She flung one open, but had no doubt one of Richard's men had been dispatched to make sure she didn't get out that way.

She had his confession, but she was trapped.

At least that's what she wanted them to think.

THIRTY

The hardest part of the plan was preventing Teresa from attempting pantomime-level dramatics when letting everyone know that she was going to be out for the evening.

After giving a performance before a packed crowd at Charlie's, Alice had pulled Teresa aside and suggested she tone it down. The other advice she gave her friend was to only tell those people she *normally* told about her social events, otherwise the thief might guess that something was up.

It didn't help that Teresa had decided that the reason she wouldn't be home was that she was going to be the special guest of the US Ambassador to New Zealand this evening. By the time Alice heard the details it was too late and Teresa was already regaling people with the numerous dignitaries who would be present.

'Why couldn't she just say she was going to the movies like normal people?' Alice muttered to Vanessa.

'You're the last person who should talk about being normal.'

They were watching Teresa descend the steps outside the main building, dressed in an evening gown and enough jewels to make any thief salivate and any insurance company have heart failure.

She gracefully got into the back of the waiting limousine, the driver even tipping his hat as he held the door for her.

'Oh good grief. I can't watch any more,' Alice said disgustedly. She turned her back and walked to the elevator, Vanessa in tow.

'Where is she really going?' Vanessa asked as they stepped inside.

'No idea. But I have no doubt she will be the best dressed person there,' Alice said.

'Jealous?'

'Of being a walking jewellery store or riding in a limo? I've done both, and I actually met the US Ambassador to New Zealand. Although it was years ago, before he was the Ambassador. Or married.'

The elevator opened and they walked to Teresa's front door.

'I can never tell if you're joking or not,' Vanessa complained.

Alice unlocked Teresa's front door and paused. 'That's the point.'

Vanessa reached out to turn on the light and Alice stopped her. 'How is it going to look if the lights go on after every man and his dog has just seen her leave?'

'Good point.' Vanessa withdrew her hand.

Teresa had left her curtains open, as instructed, so it wasn't pitch black when they closed the door.

'Where are we going to hide?' Vanessa whispered.

'Why are you whispering?' Alice asked.

In the moonlight, she saw Vanessa shrug. 'It seemed appropriate,' Vanessa replied in a normal voice.

'Let's split up,' Alice suggested. 'You go behind the kitchen counter and I'll be in the bedroom. When they come in I want you to flick on all the lights you can. I'll do the same.'

'And the thief will freeze and throw their hands in the air and come quietly?'

Alice was impressed with the amount of sarcasm Vanessa was able to inject into those few words. Her education was coming along nicely.

'I'm hoping the thief will at least freeze, the hands up and coming quietly parts would be nice but unlikely.'

'Then how do we stop them from running?'

'Our intimidating stature.'

Grumbling under her breath, Vanessa went to her hiding spot while Alice took her place in the bedroom doorway. She closed the door enough so that she could easily step behind it to hide if needed, and equally easily step into the room.

The truth is there was nothing to stop the thief from bolting out the front door. But she was banking on the person being non-violent, and even if they did run, she would see enough to know who the intruder was. Her biggest concern was if she was wrong and he *was* violent, and she'd put Vanessa in danger.

As the minutes passed, Alice found her mind wandering and her knees protesting at standing in one spot. She forced herself to concentrate, and shifted from foot to foot to ease the discomfort in her joints.

The curtains in the bedroom were closed and it was darker in there than the lounge. She looked over her shoulder but could only see faint outlines. A prickle on the back of her neck made her squint in the darkness, suddenly sure she was being watched. What if the thief had arrived before them and was in the room with her?

The prickle turned into a bead of sweat on her forehead. She reached out for the light switch, ready to flood the room and banish the shadows, convinced she was being paranoid but at the same time trusting the niggle of doubt she felt.

As her fingers touched the switch she saw a sudden shaft of light pierced the lounge. Alice held her breath. There was a rustling sound and then the front door closed again.

A small, hand held light flicked on, pointed at the ground.

The thief had a bit of common sense then.

Alice peeked around the door in time to see a dark figure go straight to the couch. They knelt down and pointed the torch under the couch.

Suddenly the kitchen lights came on and Alice saw Vanessa standing behind the counter with an excited-but-terrified look on her face.

Startled, the thief stood and stared towards the kitchen. Alice could see they were dressed in black and had their head covered.

She flicked on the lounge lights.

The thief tried to whirl around, caught themselves on the back of the couch and ended up on the floor. Alice stepped into the room, but kept her distance as the figure scrambled to their feet and took a step towards the door.

'Stop,' Alice commanded. 'I know who you are,' she lied. 'There is no point in running. We can find you anywhere.'

The thief froze and turned to look at her.

Their eyes gave them away.

THIRTY-ONE

Oxfordshire, June 1969

Alice picked up the tape recorder and she approached the wall. A large portrait, almost as tall as her, of William's great grandfather was attached to the wall. Feeling along the right edge she felt part of the frame move a little. Pressing down she heard a click and one side of the painting came away from the wall. She swung it open and stepped through, pulling it closed behind her. She stood in the darkness, her thudding heart the only sound.

Fumbling with her foot she felt it nudge a hard object. She reached down and picked up a torch. She flicked it on, illuminating a narrow passage way that led towards the front of the house. William had shown her the secret door when he'd thought they had a future together. He swore it was a secret known only to the Partridge men and their loved ones.

She felt a pang of guilt. That was one of the reasons she'd decided to leave. While some women would have delighted at tricking a man into loving her, that had never been her intention. William was too sweet a man to have his heart played with. His money absolutely, but not his heart.

The passage carried on for several metres before leading to a set of stairs heading to the second floor. Although she had been assured the space was soundproof she made sure to keep her stride slow.

The stairs wound to the right and abruptly ended at a solid wall. This was the tricky part. There was no way to see whether anyone was in the room. She had to trust that all of Richard's men were downstairs looking for her.

She pushed firmly and the wall clicked open, sunlight flooding the passage. Alice quickly stepped through and closed the door behind her. She was in a small dressing room, adjacent to the main bedroom. William had taken great delight in telling her that his ancestors had used the secret passageway to conduct affairs with the downstairs maids. (Apparently that had been a family tradition as well.)

Alice looked into the bedroom and saw it was empty. Moving lightly she went to the door leading to the hall and cracked it open. The hall appeared empty. From downstairs she heard Richard bellowing. He must have found her gone from the room and was giving instructions to his men to search the grounds.

This was the flaw in her plan. She had known she could use the passage to get out of the locked room, but she was still in the house, and further from an exit than she had been before. Logic suggested she should find a hiding spot and stay there, so she had identified three possible places.

In the bedroom she rushed over to the window which looked out on the front of the house. Richard's car was parked neatly by the front door, with a driver casually leaning against the bonnet.

'Damn it,' Alice muttered.

The car was on the same side as the room downstairs, which meant the driver would have noticed her not escaping that way.

Suddenly hiding became less ideal. As she watched one of Richard's men came out of the house and spoke to the driver who stood up straight and shook his head.

She stepped back from the window and slipped into the hallway. Keeping her back to the wall she crept along to the third door on the left. All the doors were locked but this one, part of her contingency should things go wrong. Locked doors took time to investigate.

As she stepped into the room she heard heavy footsteps on the stairs.

It was too late to lock the door behind her.

THIRTY-TWO

The figure was still crouched, like he was waiting for a starter pistol to go off and signal his sprint for the door.

'Joshua, it's over,' Alice said.

'Joshua!' Vanessa exclaimed from the other side of the room.

For a moment longer he stayed bent over, then the man relaxed and stood, removing his mask.

'How did you know it was me?' He asked, ruffling his hair with a hand.

Alice stepped further into the room. 'Your eyes. It's a bit of a cliché that you can tell a lot about someone through their eyes, but I've found it to be mostly true. And a very handy skill to have.'

Vanessa joined them in the middle of the room. 'You can tell who someone is by their eyes? How?'

'Well, not just the eyes, but the area around them. The lines, the crinkles in the skin, combined with the eyes themselves tell you everything you need to know about a person. And they tell me that you are no thief. At least not a very good one.'

Joshua looked down at his hands. 'This is the first time I've done anything like this, I swear.'

'Don't swear. There's too much swearing in the world.'

'It doesn't mean…' Vanessa stopped when Alice looked at her. 'Let's sit down?'

Alice and Joshua sat on the couch. Vanessa perched on the arm of the chair opposite.

'I suppose you want to know why I'm doing this?' Joshua began.

Alice waved her hand. 'Oh, I know *why*. What I'd like to know is *what*.'

'Even *I* know *why*,' Vanessa chimed in. 'Your mum lost all that money and you were desperate to help her out so you decided to steal something.' She paused with a frown on her face. 'But I don't know what you were trying to steal either. There are plenty of expensive things in this apartment, you could have taken any of them.'

'I'm not a thief!' Joshua said indignantly.

'Not a very good one,' Alice said again.

'If I took something then Mrs Trusslock would have noticed and the finger would have been pointed at me. I did think about taking some of her diamond earrings,' he admitted. 'She has quite a few in there so I didn't think she would miss one pair. But…'

'You then had the problem of what to do with them,' Alice said.

'It's not like I know anyone who deals in stolen jewellery.'

'So you came up with another plan.'

'Yeah.' Joshua refused to meet their eyes. 'I wasn't proud of it, but I was talking to a mate from University one day about all the stuff in this apartment and I mentioned the old couch. We looked it up. One of these went for fifty thousand dollars at auction last year. They're designed by Arnold Herbert, he was famous for his furniture in the sixties and seventies. He used to do limited items which makes them more valuable, and this one is in perfect condition.'

'You were going to steal a couch? Don't you think Teresa would notice when it went missing?' Vanessa asked in disbelief.

Alice looked at the couch she was sitting on, and thought about why Joshua might have been under the couch.

'You needed a sample of the cloth,' she guessed.

Joshua nodded.

'I still don't get it. You thought you could take the couch and Teresa would happily walk around the place not noticing?' Vanessa said.

An idea came to Alice. 'You weren't just going to take it were you?'

Joshua shook his head.

'Because that would be obvious.'

'That's just what I said,' Vanessa replied.

'You better fill her in,' Alice said to Joshua.

'My mate. He's a furniture-maker. He can make anything. Reckoned we would be able to fool anyone, but he need to know the exact colour and material.'

'So you came here to cut a piece from beneath the couch, where it wouldn't be noticed,' Alice said.

'Yeah, he needed just a tiny bit.'

'But why not get it while you were cleaning the place? Why sneak around at night?'

'I never knew if she was going to come back, and there wasn't a good explanation for why I'd be under her couch with a knife.'

'You thought you could replace something that had been in her family for decades with something your friend whipped up in his garage?' Vanessa said.

'Give me a break. He has a fully equipped woodworking shop. I was desperate,' Joshua replied.

'And semi-smart,' Alice added. 'A dangerous combination.'

'I'm sorry about the other night. I tried to avoid you as I came out the door, and thought I'd only brushed you. It wasn't until the next day I heard I'd knocked you out. I'm glad you're okay.'

'No thanks to you,' Vanessa fired at him.

'No,' he replied miserably. 'My mum is going to kill me.'

'Why?'

He looked at Alice incredulously. 'Hello?' he waved his mask.

'You did something stupid,' she replied. 'But nothing was stolen, so no crime took place.'

'He broke into Teresa's apartment!' Vanessa argued.

'He had the security code for the door, so it was more an unauthorised entry than a break in,' Alice said.

'What's the difference?'

'About four years.'

Joshua looked horrified.

'And as there's been no actual theft or damage to Teresa's property we are now left with two options. Joshua, you come clean to Teresa and hope she doesn't want to press charges. Or…'

'I'm not going to like this, am I?'

'Or we lie and say no one showed up. Teresa is a bit freaked out for a few days worrying that someone is going to break in, then when it doesn't happen she'll relax and forget all about it.'

'I don't want you to lie for me,' Joshua said.

Alice sighed. 'For a thief you have quite a conscience.'

'My mother raised me right,' he replied.

'Sure she did,' Vanessa chimed in.

Joshua looked ashamed. 'I'm going to have to tell her what happened.'

Alice patted his arm. 'Let's not get carried away. Your mother will get her money back, and nothing has been stolen. There's no need for the truth here.'

'You want me to lie to my mum?'

Alice resisted the urge to question his inconsistent morals. 'Absolutely not. If your mother asks you if you've broken into anyone's apartment and attempted to steal anything then you must tell her the truth.'

'But she'll never ask... oh. Wait... what do you mean she's getting her money back?'

'I told you I'd get it taken care of.'

Joshua stared at her.

'But, you need to learn your lesson. You'll keep your job here for, oh I think six months will do it.'

'Fair enough,' he said with a sigh. 'I am so sorry. I felt helpless, and when I saw all the nice things the people here had my brain put two and two together and came up with crime.'

'Then the sooner we get you back to university the better,' Vanessa said.

Joshua opened his mouth and Alice stopped him with a wave of her hand.

'Learn when to keep your mouth closed, Joshua.'

He closed his mouth and didn't say another word until he was in the elevator. 'I don't know how to thank you,' he said to Alice.

'Neither do I... yet,' she replied.

Once he was gone Vanessa turned to her. 'Did you already know it was him?'

'Let's just say I assumed and hoped I was right.'

Vanessa shook her head. 'One day you're going to guess wrong and we're both going to be in trouble.'

Alice surprised her with a hug. 'I'm not going to tell you this life is all lollipops and roses, but there's danger in everything these days. If you do it right then the danger is part of the fun.'

'I keep telling you,' Vanessa said with an exasperated look on her face, 'I don't want to do what you did.'

'That's right, dear,' Alice gave her another quick hug. 'I'll see you in the morning.'

'Maybe I should walk you up to your apartment.'

Alice laughed. 'I doubt anything is going to happen between here and the next floor.'

Vanessa reluctantly said goodbye as Alice called the elevator back up and stepped inside.

THIRTY-THREE

Oxfordshire, June 1969

The door burst open. A man pushed his way into the room, closely followed by another. One looked to the left and the other the right. Between them they had a view of the entire room. Almost.

As soon as they stepped further inside, Alice crawled out from behind the privacy panel that was leaning against the wall next to the door. It was one of those free-standing things that women used to hide behind when they got changed. Alice had moved it in such a way that it wouldn't attract immediate suspicion, but would still be a useful hiding spot.

Alice slipped into the hallway, slammed the door shut behind her and turned the key.

Like the doors downstairs this one was built to withstand a lot of things. It wouldn't last forever but she only needed it to hold them until she was out of the house.

She turned and froze. Another of Richard's men stood a few feet away, equally as surprised to see her come out of the room two of his companions had just entered.

'Oi!' he yelled.

She tossed the case containing the recorder to him and he instinctively caught it with both hands. So she stepped forward and kicked him between the legs.

This is becoming a nasty habit, she thought as the man crumbled to the ground. Snatching the case back she sprinted away from the stairs to the other end of the hallway. Unlocking the last door she went inside and locked it behind her.

It was a small, servants' room. Specifically, a room that allowed servants to get things from the ground floor to the first floor without the family of the house seeing them.

Alice crossed to a sliding panel in the wall. Lifting it up she shuddered at the dumb waiter. Technically it was the tiny elevator, designed to carry food, but Edward had assured her it would hold her weight. He had been horrified to learn why she'd wanted to know.

She had checked it out earlier to make sure she could fit in there. She could, just. She sat down, pushing her bottom backwards and drawing her legs up, her head came forward so she was in a ball, and she inched into the elevator. Twisting her arm she reached out and pulled the door down.

It thudded on the case.

When she had tested it earlier, she hadn't had the case with her.

Outside the door she heard yelling and footsteps. Desperately she turned and pulled, looking for a way to create more space but a corner of the case still stuck out too far. She squeezed herself into the smallest ball she could, her knees scraping the side of her face as she saw the door handle turn and rattle.

She edged the case further in and tried to close the door once more. It hit the case, caught, then slid past it and clicked shut. Immediately a whirring sound started and the elevator began its agonisingly slow descent. As Alice held her breath, the elevator gave the tiniest jerk and stopped. She opened the door and began extracting herself from the small space. Finally she stood and stretched out the kinks. She was in the butler's pantry off the main kitchen, towards the back of the house.

Hurrying across to the back door she looked through the glass panels. All clear. She opened the door and went outside, her feet crunching on the gravel as she hurried to the corner of the house and peeked around.

Nobody there.

Staying hunched over, she raced to the next corner and saw the front of the house was clear as well. Richard's car stood empty, the driver's door open.

For a moment she hesitated, considering the likelihood that it was a trap. It was probably more likely the driver had been ordered to help search for her.

Aware of how exposed she was, Alice dashed for the car, each footstep on the gravel sounding as loud as the gunshot that still rung in her ears. When she was a few feet from the car she flung the case through the open door and jumped in after it.

The key was still in the ignition. Richard kept his cars immaculately serviced and the engine roared to life the first time. Pulling the door closed she put the car into gear.

'MAUREEN!' Richard stood at the front door, his fists raised, face blotted with fury.

Alice fumbled in her pocket and pulled something out. Unscrewing the lid, she raised William's hip flask and toasted Richard.

In reply the man screamed her name again and started towards the car. Alice stomped on the accelerator and the car wheels spun, then caught, shooting gravel out behind the car as it took off.

In the rear view mirror she saw Richard chase the car. For a brief moment he loomed close, then the car picked up speed and he fell behind.

Driving through the front gate Alice looked at the tape recorder. She would deliver it to Edward in London, who would take it to the police. Richard would be charged with murder. And by that time she would be out of the country.

After one more stop.

Alice knew that Richard had removed the rest of his money from the accounts she had accessed. However he had failed to realise that she'd anticipated this move, and a small bribe to the bank clerk had ensured she knew where the money had been moved to.

Richard wouldn't need the money where he was going anyway.

THIRTY-FOUR

Alice was feeling happy with herself when she walked into her apartment. No one had been injured, nothing was stolen, and she now had another favour in the bank.

She flicked on the kitchen lights and went in search of a hip flask. William's was sitting on the counter top but that was for special occasions and although this was a good day, it didn't rate in her top hundred.

'Hello, Maureen.'

Her head snapped up in time to see Richard Dankworth step through from bedroom door. Her legs wobbled and she leaned on the counter with her hands to avoid falling to the floor.

'Or should I say *Alice*?'

His face was the same, decades older of course, but the eyes held the same coldness as they had all those years ago. He held up his hand and her watch dangled between his fingers.

'I had intended to give it to one of my companions, but you looked so familiar… it nagged at me.' He came further into the living room. 'I honestly thought you'd be dead by now. Imagine my pure delight to find you still alive. Time has been cruel to you I see.'

'You poor dear, you haven't been plotting your revenge all this time have you?' Alice said. 'What a waste.'

'You took all my money. And tried to have me convicted of murder.'

'Yes, shame about that.'

After Alice had left the country, it had been harder to get information, but she'd managed to follow what happened to Richard. His lawyer had claimed that Richard had confessed out of fear for his life, a theory backed up by the sound of gunshot on the tape. When the mystery woman witness on the recording failed to come forward and testify, he was released. But although there had been no proof, the business world in London was a relatively small place. Richard had been left with nothing.

'It took me years to rebuild my fortune, and every day I fantasised about what I would do to you if I saw you again.'

Alice stifled a quip about fantasies, her eyes shifting around the apartment. She looked nervously at the door.

'How did you find me?' she asked.

'Vanessa. She had a name tag on her uniform when I bumped into you. Of course I got nowhere asking for Maureen Stratler, so I posed as a prospective resident. I claimed you were a long lost friend and I had the information in no time. Security here really is terrible. If you were going to be alive tomorrow, you should definitely complain.'

As he spoke, he took several casual steps forward until he was a metre away from the other side of the kitchen bench. Alice stayed where she was, although it was tempting to take a step back. There was no other exit to her apartment. Even if she made it into the spare room, it was just a different place to die.

He took another step towards her and her eyes came to rest on the hip flask in front of her. Richard followed her gaze.

'Wait, is that… William's? You kept it all these years?' He snatched it up. 'How fitting.'

He shook it slightly and unscrewed the lid. 'The last time we saw each other you toasted me with this. You thought you'd won. I guess you were wrong.' He raised the hip flask in mock salute. 'I win. I always win,' he said. 'When they find your cold dead corpse tomorrow morning, they will think your bitter old heart finally gave out on you.'

Richard took a swig and wiped his lips with the back of his hand. 'Are you ready?'

He put the hip flask in his jacket pocket and moved around the end of the bench.

Alice backed away and snatched up a saucepan from next to the stove.

There was just open space between them, and the sight of her wielding the saucepan didn't seem to faze him.

With a crash her front door flung open.

'Hey!' Vanessa shouted. 'Stop right there!'

Richard and Alice stared at her in surprise, then Richard laughed. 'I've waited too long to be stopped now.'

'I've called the police.'

'No matter. I'm old, I've got nothing to lose.'

He stepped towards Alice and swayed a little. His face was flushed and there was a hint of sweat on his forehead.

Vanessa crossed the room and stopped just out of reach behind him.

Richard ignored her, focussed solely on Alice, who raised the saucepan menacingly. She swung it at him, but Richard leaned back and as it passed his face, he plucked it from her grasp.

'Stop!' Vanessa said desperately.

Alice saw her grab Richard's arm. He stumbled slightly, then turned and brought the saucepan down onto her shoulder. She yelped and let go, clutching her injury.

'I've waited fifty years. I will not be stopped now by some stupid woman.'

He turned back to Alice, raising the saucepan, and for a brief second Alice thought she'd made yet another terrible mistake with Richard Dankworth.

Suddenly his face crumpled and he groaned in pain. Alice saw a foot withdraw from between his legs as he began a slow tumble to his knees.

'Don't call me stupid,' Vanessa said in a trembly, defiant voice.

Richard tried to get up, then clutched at his chest, and keeled over.

'Oh my god, I've killed him.'

Alice stepped over Richard's body and took Vanessa by the arm. 'He's not dead, dear. He's unconscious. Probably.'

'I just got angry, but I didn't mean to knock him out.' She looked over her shoulder as Alice lead her to the couch.

'*You* didn't.'

'But he's…'

'When I thought I saw him the other morning, I told Janice I was having trouble sleeping. She gave me some tablets, which I crushed up and put in that hip flask.'

Vanessa looked at her. 'You knew he would come?'

'Not at all, but it never hurts to plan. By the way, nice kick, dear. Where did you learn how to do that?'

Some colour was returning to Vanessa's cheeks and she gave a little smile. 'Karate lessons.'

'I didn't know you were learning karate. How long have you been doing that?'

Her smile widened. 'Since I started hanging out with you. After all, it never hurts to plan.'

Alice grinned. Another lesson nicely learned by Vanessa.

'What's going to happen to him now?' Vanessa asked.

'I could use this?' Alice said picking up the saucepan. 'Finish him off?'

Vanessa's eyebrows raised so high they almost disappeared into her fringe.

'Relax, I'm joking. You're going to call the police and we can have him charged with breaking and entering and attempted assault. And I'm going to sit down. I'm getting too old for this carry on.'

'Getting?' Vanessa called out as she made her way over to the couch.

THIRTY-FIVE

Oliver opened the front door and smiled. 'Thanks for coming. The kids will be happy,' he said.

'You're not?' Alice replied.

'Alice, it's my birthday. You will not put me off balance tonight. Where's Amanda?'

'Parking the car.'

Alice surprised him with a firm hug. I must be getting soft in my old age. Too many hugs lately, she thought.

'How's the investigation going?' she asked as he stepped aside to let her in.

'Slowly. Amanda said something happened at Silvermoon. Are you alright?'

Alice saw Reed and Rose come running towards her and she opened her arms to hug them.

'Oh yes. Nothing exciting ever happens there.'

THE END

Rodney Strong

Knitting Needles and Knives

A Silvermoon Retirement Village Cozy Mystery

ONƐ

'This is ridiculous!'

Vanessa took a tiny step back and let the ninety-eight year old vent her frustration. There hadn't been a lot of swear words in the rant, but there had been several words Vanessa didn't recognise which might have fallen into that category. Once Alice began to lose steam, Vanessa offered her the cup of tea she was holding.

'I don't want tea. I want to get off this couch!'

'You heard what the doctor said. You've sprained your ankle. You need to rest it for a few days.'

'A few days,' Alice scowled. 'A few days on the couch and I might not get up again.'

Vanessa offered the cup again and this time Alice grudgingly took it.

Retreating across the room to a safe distance, Vanessa asked, 'What on earth made you think you could kick that chair over?'

Alice pretended to sip the tea to hide her embarrassment. She had almost convinced herself that her injury was the result of an accident. It could have happened to anyone. Just a freak combination of wrong angles and incorrect force. The alternative was to admit that this was a consequence of her slowly creeping ever closer to triple figures.

She'd been in a bad mood since her granddaughter Amanda, and Oliver and his family had tricked her into having a birthday party. The party itself had been tolerable. All her friends from the Silvermoon Retirement Village had been there, but she'd always hated parties. And admitting she was getting older. And being the centre of attention.

In the three weeks since then, Alice had been moping around the retirement village, until yesterday when her dear friend Owen had tentatively suggested she snap out of it. Instead she'd snapped at him, immediately apologised and decided that he was probably right. Enough was enough. Until that morning in the dining room. Alice never ate there. (It was too institutional and besides, her apartment had a kitchen and there was a café in the complex if she didn't feel like cooking.) But that morning was the weekly poker game she and her fellow residents always held in the dining room. When Alice had entered, the first to arrive for once, she'd found a chair standing in the middle of the room. It was just a normal dining chair that someone had left out, but for some reason it had reminded Alice of a forty-year-old memory where a man had rushed towards her with a knife and she had disarmed him by kicking a chair into his path. Despite several subtle warning signals from her brain, she'd wanted to see if she could replicate the action (sans knife-wielding man). It had begun spectacularly well – until she'd lifted her foot off the ground. The moment her foot had connected with the chair, she lost her balance and stumbled sideways. She'd managed to stop herself falling to the floor by grabbing onto a nearby table, but by the time she'd gingerly lowered herself into a chair she realised she'd twisted the ankle she'd been balancing on.

Alice decided that her second mistake (after attempting the stunt in the first place) was telling Vanessa the truth about how it happened.

Calling Vanessa 'young' seemed a bit superfluous given that everyone was younger than Alice, but at twenty-four Vanessa was younger than most – and certainly younger than anyone else who frequented the Silvermoon Retirement Village. She was pretty, with long brown hair and an infectious smile and she was the Silvermoon front desk concierge – although Alice was surreptitiously working to change that. Vanessa was too bright and had too much potential to be running around after a bunch of oldies, and while Alice hadn't yet persuaded Vanessa to take up her own old profession, she felt Vanessa was definitely 'made for better things'.

For forty years Alice had been a professional con artist. This was known to but a few friends, including Vanessa. Alice wouldn't have said she'd been the best in the world, things like that never mattered to her, but she knew she'd been good. She'd earned enough to be better than comfortable and she had never been arrested. She'd also never had any patience for stupidity – even less so her own.

'Alice? Why?'

Alice waved a hand dismissively. 'The chair was closer than I thought,' she said, refusing to admit her foolishness.

'Well, you're lucky Tracey didn't insist on sending you to the hospital for an X-ray.'

Alice's mouth set in a line. Tracey was the Retirement Village manager. If she cared about the residents, she hid it well beneath her officious exterior. Apparently no one had explained to her that if you enjoyed strict timetables and careful planning, then a retirement village where the majority of residents were too old to give a damn about either of those things was not a suitable career move. That was all Alice's opinion of course as she knew from conversations with fellow residents that they found her highly efficient and good at her job.

'I'd like to see her try,' Alice said.

'She means well.'

'It's just a sprain. No need for hospitals.'

'Of course not,' Vanessa threw her hands up. 'You could be dying and you'd still say there was no need for a hospital.'

'If I'm dying there *would* be no need for a hospital,' Alice retorted.

She winked at Vanessa who blew out a sigh of frustration, before stomping across the apartment to the kitchen where she set about clearing the bench with as much clatter as she could muster. Far from feeling guilty, Alice considered this a small victory. She would apologise to Vanessa later, but for now she was happy to revel in the fact she could still get under her skin.

The real problem with Alice's injury was having to spend endless days laid up on the couch. She liked watching television and doing the occasional crossword, but the best thing about doing those things was the freedom to walk away when she got bored.

She shifted position on the couch and felt a twinge of pain in her ankle.

What I need is a good murder to take my mind off things, she thought irritably. *Or a bad one.*

TWO

The next day didn't bring her a murder, but it did bring her a cat. Maddy was the resident feline. No one knew who she belonged to and she conned food out of many of the residents, Alice included. Maddy had been involved in a recent mystery. Alice lived on the second floor of the main building at Silvermoon, and the cat kept finding her way onto the landing of the second floor. Alice would occasionally find her waiting outside her apartment door, with no clue how she'd managed to get there. Had she ridden up in the elevator? Or climbed the stairs and opened the fire door? Luckily that particular mystery had been solved at the same time as the never to be mentioned again birthday party.

Today there was no mystery. Maddy arrived in the arms of Owen. Tall and distinguished, dressed as usual in a shirt and tie, despite having been retired from his position at the bank for over two decades. His grey hair was short and immaculately groomed. He had moved into Silvermoon after his wife of fifty years died and he and Alice had slowly formed a friendship since then.

When she saw him on the security camera outside her apartment door, Alice considered pretending not to be home. Then she saw the paper bag in his hand.

'It's unlocked,' she called.

Owen opened the door and peered inside, hesitant despite having been invited. Alice wasn't sure what state he thought she might be in, but when she saw her on the couch with her bandaged ankle on a cushion he smiled and came all the way inside. Maddy wriggled out of his arms, dropped to the ground and stalked over to the patch of sun by the window, where she proceeded to clean her bottom.

'I thought you might like some company,' Owen said.

'You or the cat?'

'She was outside your door when I got here. We must have had the same idea.'

'That I needed looking after?' Alice's eyes flashed but Owen missed it as he settled his frame into the seat opposite her.

'That you might enjoy some conversation. Have you told Amanda about your... er... injury?'

Amanda was Alice's granddaughter and only living relative. Beautiful and talented, she'd easily followed in her grandmother's footsteps and was currently in places unknown. She usually checked in regularly, but Alice knew not to be worried if she ever went silent. Amanda could handle anything that might be thrown at her.

'No, and there's no need. It's just a sprained ankle, for Pete's sake. All my major organs and major limbs are doing what they're supposed to.'

'An ankle is probably included in the major limb category.'

Alice shot him a dirty look.

'Well, if you don't want conversation, how about a muffin from Charlie's?' Owen held up the paper bag.

Charlie's was the Village café and they usually had wonderful food. But the mention of their muffins made Alice hesitate. There was a suggestion box on the café counter where customers were encouraged to leave flavour combinaton suggestions for future muffins. Some had been absolutely delicious, like zucchini and cinnamon. Others, like apricot and basil, had not.

When Owen saw her hesitation, his smile widened. 'There are no suggestions on today's menu. You have your choice of blueberry or bran.'

'Blueberry,' Alice said quickly. 'Please,' she added.

Owen put both muffins on plates and carried them to the couch. Alice took a bite and sighed through her mouthful. The muffin was soft and full of flavour and just what she needed.

'I suppose I'm the talk of the village,' she said bitterly. 'A silly old woman trying to do things she has no right doing.'

'Some of them already thought you were that. In the last twelve months, you've solved one murder and almost been the victim of two others. Most women your age are content to crochet or knit.'

'Women my age?'

'My dear Alice, you know perfectly well that you are a unique individual,' chuckled Owen. 'In this case, however, most people think you simply lost your balance and fell to the ground, injuring yourself in the process. As you know, that sort of thing happens quite a bit for women your age, and men come to think of it.'

'Why would they think that?'

'Because that is what Vanessa is telling anyone who asks.'

Alice nodded. That girl was coming along nicely.

'Can I do anything for you?' Owen asked.

Alice raised her plate. 'You already have.'

Owen nodded slowly and took a bite of his own muffin. The look on his face made Alice suspect he had something else on his mind.

'Spit it out. The question, not the muffin,' she ordered.

His cheeks reddened as he swallowed. 'The thing is… you… uh, I mean we've never talked about… exactly what you used to do for a living. I mean, I think I know… uh… that it wasn't always exactly, er…'

'Legal?'

His cheeks darkened further. 'No.'

'What's raised this now?' she asked.

'Well, it's Rachel.'

'Your granddaughter.'

'Yes. I think she's in a spot of trouble, but she won't talk to me about it. I was hoping that perhaps you might…'

'Set her back on the straight and narrow?'

Owen frowned. 'You're mocking me.'

'Just a little,' Alice said gently.

Owen's frown deepened. She'd offended him.

Alice occasionally forgot how straightlaced Owen was. A lifetime of working his way up the executive ranks at the biggest bank in New

Zealand had developed in him a set of firm principles. A good number of those principles were in direct opposition to Alice's. Nevertheless, she was fond of him.

'Owen, I apologise. Why do you think Rachel is in trouble?'

He sighed and began to fidget with the end of his tie as he spoke. 'I don't think you've met Rachel. She's nineteen years old and has always been... problematic.' He sighed again.

'Good grief, Owen, *problematic* is a word for missed work deadlines or unexpected car trouble, not ill-behaved children.'

'I suppose. She was always a handful. My daughter and her husband had some alternative views to parenting.'

'You mean they let her do whatever she wanted.'

Owen scowled, confirming that Alice was right on the button. Knowing Owen the very thought of lax discipline for his granddaughter must have rankled considerably.

Alice's daughter had never shown the slightest interest in learning her profession, and Alice wass comfortable with that. But when she'd been tragically killed in an accident, Alice had found her granddaughter a more willing pupil. She'd instilled a strong work ethic and moral compass. Alice (and now Amanda too) had never conned anyone out of their life savings, and generally picked targets that could afford the loss or who were dishonest themselves. Not that she was any sort of Robin Hood. Alice may have robbed from the rich but the comparison ended there.

'You didn't come to me because she lacks discipline,' Alice said.

'No. She rang yesterday and asked if she could stay with me for a few days. I started to say no – you know Silvermoon's guest policy...'

Alice nodded. No overnight guests permitted. Management said it was to keep the residents safe, but Alice thought it was because they couldn't stand the thought of old people having a social life. She'd have done something about it, but so rarely had guests herself it had never been a priority.

'She sounded different. The usual bluster was gone. So, I said yes and she arrived last night. She's scared about something, Alice, and she refuses to talk to me.'

'You think she'll talk to me?'

Owen moved his fidgeting fingers from the end of his tie to the cuff of his shirt. 'One of your many skills is the ability to get people to tell you things. I thought…'

'Send her over.'

'Are you sure?' He'd been expecting more resistance.

'I've been stuck on this couch (if you don't count one long slow trip to the bathroom and back) for less than a day and I'm already bored out of my mind. Send her over.'

They chatted about other things while they waited, until there was a knock at the door. Alice's fingers twitched towards her phone, to check the hidden security camera. Door cameras weren't a standard installation and she preferred to keep her security precautions to herself. Owen got to his feet and went to let Rachel in.

She had short dark hair and multiple piercings through her left ear; she wore an oversized black T-shirt with a mildly offensive picture on it, and ripped jeans. Alice thought the girl was trying too hard.

Rachel locked eyes with Alice, staring defiantly, waiting for the old woman to look away first. But Alice had been stared down by considerably more intimidating people than this girl. She held her gaze steadily.

Owen interrupted their staring contest. 'Thank you for coming, Rachel. Oh for goodness sake, sit down.' He gestured to the seat he'd previously occupied. 'I'll be back in thirty minutes,' he said.

'You're leaving?' Rachel sounded worried.

'I don't think we'll need that long,' Alice smiled at Owen. 'Give us fifteen.'

Owen looked surprised, then nodded and walked briskly out of the apartment.

Rachel sat slumped in the armchair, picking at her fingernails. They sat in silence while Alice watched the clock on the oven. When two minutes had passed, she spoke.

'Your grandfather tells me your name is Rachel and you're nineteen years old.'

263

Rachel sneered. 'So?'

'That is what he told me about you. Now I will tell you what I know about you. Your parents were idiots.'

Rachel's eyes grew large, but she didn't protest.

'They decided the best way to raise a child was let you run free. But it wasn't as great as it sounded. You needed structure and boundaries, and the more they didn't give that to you, the louder you showed them you wanted it. The ear piercings, cutting all your hair off, those hideous clothes. You started wearing things you didn't even like just to make a statement. And you did some things – I'm guessing little things, nothing too felonious. Shoplifting? A bit of vandalism? And now you've done something you regret. Something that scared you and you don't know what to do.'

'Yeah right,' Rachel said. 'How could you possibly know all that?'

'Because I see things. You people today… you look at things, but you don't see them.'

'*You people?*'

Alice waved a hand dismissively. 'Anyone under sixty is *you people* to me.'

She watched while Rachel seemed to have an internal argument with herself. Finally, Rachel muttered, 'Even if you're right about some of those things – and I'm not saying you are – why would I talk to you?'

'Your grandfather is a good man. He asked me to talk to you and I said I would. So talk to me or don't, I don't really care. I'm doing this as a favour to him, and because I'm bored.'

'Even if I tell you, what could you do about it? You're ancient.'

Rachel's face flushed and Alice felt a glimmer of hope for the girl. Someone who didn't care what other people thought wouldn't be so easily embarrassed.

'Yes, I am ancient. Which means I've seen more than you could imagine. The worst that will happen is you tell me, and I, a feeble old woman, can't help you. You've lost nothing.'

A faint smile crossed Rachel's face. 'Something tells me feeble isn't a word people use around you.'

'No more than once.' Alice smiled back. 'Come on, dear. I'm sure things aren't as bad as you think they are.'

Rachel slumped further into her chair all traces of amusement gone. 'Someone is threatening to kill me.'

THREE

'Did you hear me?' Rachel asked when Alice didn't comment. 'I said, someone is threatening to kill me.'

'Yes, I heard you,' Alice said irritably. This was going to be tiresome if Rachel didn't get on with it.

'You don't seem shocked,' Rachel said.

'Would it help if I was? Get on with it. Who is making these threats?'

After a long pause, Rachel said, 'It's all bloody Colin's fault.'

Alice sighed and glanced at the bookcase. The third book on the second shelf was hollow and inside was a hip flask that would have made this conversation more bearable. But that probably wouldn't have made a great impression.

She refocussed on Rachel. 'Okay. Start at the beginning.'

Ten minutes later, Alice had a general picture of what had been going on.

'See? I told you so. You can't help me,' Rachel said miserably.

It had been far too long since Alice had been Rachel's age, and that had been during a world war, so her view of what was scary to a teenager wasn't going to be the same.

'I really don't see what all the fuss is about. It's pretty straightforward. If you do everything as I tell you, it should be easy enough to extract yourself from the situation with your heart still beating.'

'Really?' Rachel looked unconvinced.

'Trust me. You should tell Owen about it though.'

'No!'

'Why not?' Alice asked.

'Because… because he's my granddad. It's embarrassing. He wouldn't understand.'

Alice studied Rachel shrewdly. 'And because he's the only member of your family you respect?'

'Seriously, how do you do that?' Rachel complained.

Alice ignored the question. 'Alright, don't tell him all the details. But he's worried about you, so you need to tell him something.'

'Why? Can't we tell him after everything is sorted?'

'I'm not going to lie to my friend.'

Rachel's face darkened and she jumped to her feet.

'Oh, sit down,' Alice scowled. 'Young people – always so damn melodramatic. Look, just tell him that you and I are going to deal with it and he's not to worry.'

Rachel stood for a moment longer glaring at Alice.

'If you're not going to sit, you can go. Stay inside your grandfather's apartment until you hear from me.'

As soon as Rachel was gone, Alice dialled the concierge desk and asked Vanessa to pop up.

'Is everything okay?' Vanessa asked.

'Yes, but I need your help with something.'

'Alice,' Vanessa said. 'I can't just leave the desk whenever you call. I have a job to do,'

'Oh well, I suppose I could muddle through on my own. Where's that walking stick kept?'

Sure enough, Vanessa took the bait. 'Fine, I'll be up in a few minutes. But if I get fired, you pay my rent.'

'That's the plan,' Alice muttered.

Five minutes later, Vanessa unlocked Alice's front door. Silvermoon staff didn't normally have access to resident's apartments, but Vanessa was a friend, and it had been useful for her to be able to enter without Alice having to answer the door.

'What's up?' Vanessa asked.

'Owen's granddaughter needs our help.'

'The one who is staying with him?'

'How did you…?'

Vanessa grinned. 'You're not the only one who notices things.'

Alice frowned, but inside she was doing a little jig of approval. Noticing things was an important skill and one a lot of young people didn't have.

As Rachel had proven.

'So what's the story?'

'Rachel's rebellious teenage phase kicked in a little late. She met a man, Colin, who persuaded her to help him rob a house. Only it turned out to be a poor choice of house.'

'A poor choice…?' Vanessa repeated.

'Colin doesn't sound like the sort who'll be knocking on MENSA's door anytime soon. The owner of the house came home. Colin ran, leaving Rachel behind. She managed to get away, but the owner of the house was less than happy.'

'Why doesn't she go to the police?'

'Because according to Rachel, the owner of the house is the police.'

FOUR

Vanessa took a few minutes to digest Alice's statement. 'The police.'

Alice nodded.

'The police threatened to kill Rachel?'

'Not the police as a whole, just one particular officer who happened to live that that address.'

'Bugger,' Vanessa said again. 'Surely he didn't mean it? People say things in the heat of the moment they don't mean. I once agreed to try wasabi and immediately regretted that.'

Alice stared at her. 'You're comparing trying wasabi to making a death threat?'

'No. Not anymore.'

'You're right though, about things said in the heat of the moment. Often by men with no impulse control. But I never said the police officer was a man.'

'She's a woman?'

'That's the most common alternative, yes.'

'Not anymore,' Vanessa said again.

'What do you mean by that?'

'Never mind. Why does Rachel think she's serious?'

'Because Rachel is nineteen, Vanessa. How many people threatened to kill you at that age?'

Vanessa shrugged. 'Fair point. So Rachel can't go to the police because they're the ones threatening her. And Colin is after her as a loose end. She's stuck in the middle.'

'What makes you think Colin is going to come after her?'

'Because she can lead the police to him.'

Alice was impressed. 'We don't know for sure, but it seems likely that's right. Rachel certainly thinks he is. And so do I, because there's something else – Colin has gone missing. Either that or he's avoiding Rachel, which sounds too smart for him. The final sting in the tail is what they were hoping to steal. Rachel said the house had a laptop, television, PS4 – whatever that is – but Colin told her they were after only one thing. A book.'

'A book,' Vanessa repeated.

'Yes,' Alice's eyes sparkled. 'Now why would someone break into a house to steal a book?'

Vanessa frowned and chewed on the end of her ponytail. Alice sighed. She'd been trying to break Vanessa of that revealing habit for a while, so far without luck. It was a terrible tell.

'Only two reasons,' Vanessa finally replied. 'It's a very valuable book, or something is hidden inside it.'

'Excellent.' Alice beamed at her. 'Both options open up some possibilities don't they?'

'Does it?'

'Yes, it does. But none that are important now.'

'Was she wearing a mask or gloves?'

'She didn't say,' Alice said, annoyed at herself for not thinking to ask.

'If she was, then the cop shouldn't have been able to track her down.'

'Apparently as she was fleeing, the officer yelled that she was on tape. There must have been a hidden camera.'

'Even so—'

'And Colin and Rachel, our mastermind thieves, apparently referred to each other by their real names while they were searching the place.'

'Bugger,' Vanessa said once more.

'Yes, and several more words besides. Unfortunately, Rachel had some minor trouble with the police a few years ago, so her fingerprints and name are on record.'

'Double bugger.'

'Now do you see why I need your help?'

Vanessa shook her head. 'Not really.'

'I can give Rachel a new identity and help her move to a different city—'

'Do you know how to do that?'

'I do.' Alice tapped the side of her nose with a finger. 'But I think option two would be more suitable.'

'Which is?'

'I find out why the police officer reacted so badly to the break in, and then use that information as leverage to convince her to forget the whole thing.'

'What about Colin?'

'I may have been out of the game for a while, but shady characters are my area of expertise. You leave him to me.'

'Can I remind you that you're still stuck on the couch?'

'Did I ever tell you about the time I was locked in a trunk and loaded aboard a ship from Wellington to Sydney? That was a problem. This,' she patted her leg, 'is an inconvenience.'

Vanessa appeared unconvinced. 'What do you need me to do?'

'I'd like you to talk to Tracey's niece, that Detective Miller. See if you can get any information from her about the break in.'

'Why would she tell me anything?'

'She will if you ask the right questions. She's trying to prove herself. People like that usually trip over themselves to show how much they know. Just casually drop it into conversation.'

'How would I do that? I've only met her a handful of times and I don't even know where she works.'

Alice smiled. 'Indeed. So, while I was waiting for you to come up, I rang Tracey and suggested that her niece might like to come to the festival tomorrow to give us oldies a talk about safety.'

'You're sneaky.'

'Stating the obvious, dear,' replied Alice.

'Fine. Okay I can do that. But Alice, seriously, I can't keep leaving my desk to help you out. Tracey is already making snarky comments about my absences.'

'That is why you should come and work for me.'

'What are you talking about?' Vanessa stared. 'Work for you? Doing what?'

Alice waved her hand. 'I don't know yet, but I'd find a better use for your brain than sitting, smiling behind a desk.'

'You're serious.'

'I'm serious. I can afford it. And working for me would give you all sorts of opportunities that working here can't. Just think about it.'

Vanessa left the apartment looking a little shellshocked.

Alice hadn't meant to pitch the idea so abruptly. She had been thinking about it for a while but had planned to ease into the subject. If Vanessa didn't have to worry about her nine-to-five job, then she'd have more time to focus on the tutorials that she still wasn't fully aware Alice was giving her.

Alice made a couple more phone calls. Many of her contacts had retired – properly retired, unlike Alice, who was more retirement adjacent. Finally, she reached one who still had his fingers in a few pies. He promised to do some digging and to get back to her.

Once that was done, she sat for a moment with her phone in her lap. She had one more call to make. A cold wave went through her body. Murderers and thieves she could handle without raising her heart rate, but this call she'd been dreading. When she hung up, there was a tiny bead of sweat on her forehead.

Tomorrow was going to be one of the most difficult in years.

Tomorrow she would have to pretend to be interested in knitting.

FIVE

'I must say, I was…'

'Shocked?'

'Thrilled,' Freda continued, 'when you rang. I didn't realise knitting was something you were interested in.'

Freda and her husband Les were long-time residents of Silvermoon. They'd been married for longer than they hadn't and Freda could have challenged Alice for the title of thinnest, smallest woman in the Village. She was cheerful, with a quick smile and a kind word for all, while Les was a more sombre fellow.

The Silvermoon dining room had been transformed into a clattering cacophony of duelling knitting needles, with colourful skeins of wool cluttered over every table.

The Knitting Festival was an initiative by Rosie Wilson, a resident Alice barely knew. Rosie had one of those personalities most commonly described as *pleasant*, which Alice would have found insulting. It meant you weren't memorable enough for people to have formed a real opinion of you.

When Rosie had moved into the village just over a year ago, she had asked Tracey if management would mind her organising a knitting festival. Tracey had been surprisingly supportive. Alice supposed it fitted with her idea of old people. That first festival had been a raging success, with all the knitted items donated to the neonatal unit at Wellington Hospital. Alice had deliberately avoided last year's event. She could think of several uses for knitting needles, and knitting wasn't one of them. As far as she was concerned, *festival* seemed like a strong word to describe a group of people knitting in a room.

'Well, Freda, it looks like I'm not going to be very mobile for a while,' she indicated her bandaged ankle, which was propped on a cushion on the chair beside her, 'so I thought I needed to find a hobby.' Alice kept the internal cringe off her face. Frankly, the last thing she needed at her age was a hobby, especially one involving wool.

Freda nodded enthusiastically. 'Wonderful.' She glanced around and leaned closer, 'To be honest, I'm not such a big fan of knitting. But Les has decided he wants to build model trains and our entire living room is strewn with tiny bits of metal. I had to get out of there.'

Retirement had been the catalyst Les had needed to try every activity he hadn't during his working life. So far that included weightlifting, singing, and now apparently modelling. An unwanted image of Les on a catwalk sprang into Alice's mind and she shuddered.

'I know.' Freda mistook her response. 'He won't even travel on a real train so I don't know why he thinks it's a good idea to build a tiny one. Anyway. I have a spare pair of knitting needles here. What colour wool would you like? I have this nice blue.'

She handed Alice a ball of pale blue wool. Alice had to admit it felt soft and looked nice.

'I thought I might watch for a while at first,' Alice said. 'Just to get a feel for it.'

'Are you sure?' Freda waved a pair of long, white knitting needles at her.

Alice instinctively leaned back as they got a smidge too close to her face. 'They look lovely, but I'm sure.'

'Thank you. Do you see the elephant on the ends? That's Kamala. You know, the last elephant they had at the Wellington Zoo? They're quite unique you know, only ten sets were ever made. Les got one because he was friends with the zoo director at the time.' Freda placed the needles on the table and picked up her own knitting.

'So they're valuable?' Alice asked idly.

'As valuable as knitting needles can be. I'm not sure there is much of a demand for novelty items like these.'

'The craftsmanship is good. Is it real ivory?'

'Absolutely,' Freda replied with a nod.

Alice had been joking and when she glanced at Freda she saw her friend wink at her. Alice chuckled and put the needle back on the table just as a woman brushed past her. She didn't recognise the woman although she was wearing a staff uniform.

'Who's the new girl?' she asked Freda.

Freda stopped mid-sentence and peered at where Alice was looking.

'Her name is Glenda. She's the new arts coordinator. Started last week.'

Glenda was in her early fifties. A slim woman with short brown hair, she was smiling and laughing with some of the residents. After a moment, Alice lost interest and continued her scan of the room.

Dotted in amongst the residents were visitors – some younger relatives, some members of the community helping out for a good cause

Under normal circumstances, Alice would have been anywhere but here. Under abnormal circumstances too. But she'd promised to try to be a little more sociable around the village – more precisely, she had promised Oliver's daughter Rose. Alice had met Oliver two years ago and since then she'd come to know his family well. Rose and her big brother Reed now considered Alice a surrogate great grandmother.

At Alice's unwanted surprise party, Rose, in that way only an eight-year-old could, had calmly informed Alice that she was old and if she didn't use her brain it would turn into a vegetable. (Rose hadn't been specific about which vegetable.) When Rose had spotted the poster advertising the Knitting Festival on the noticeboard in the lobby, she had made Alice promise to attend. Alice had instantly agreed, thinking that between her birthday and the festival, she would find a reason why she wasn't able to attend. In fact, her sprained ankle had provided a perfect excuse. Rose, however, wasn't easily put off by minor ailments. Rose, via her father, had called the previous day and when Alice had said she wasn't going to be able to make it to the festival Rose had brought the full force of her eight-year-old logic to bear. Including an offer of Oliver coming to Silvermoon to carry Alice down to the dining room. Alice didn't think Oliver was silly enough to try it, but the threat had been enough for her to agree to go.

You don't lie to family.

Not much anyway.

'Are you paying attention?' Freda asked.

'Sorry, yes, show me again.'

Freda went through her instructions one more time and with a stifled sigh Alice picked up the Kamala knitting needles and attempted to follow Freda's movements. After a few minutes she threw them down on the table in disgust. Considering she could pick any lock on the market, she should have been able to pick up knitting straight away, but her fingers refused to move properly. It was incredibly frustrating, made even more so when Freda smiled at her gently.

'You're doing fine, Alice. Keep at it. You'll be knitting cardigans in no time.'

Why would she want to knit a cardigan? Alice stopped herself asking aloud. Learning not to take her frustrations out on other people was a relatively new skill for her. Her career had required a high degree of self restraint and she still mostly practiced that, but moving into Silvermoon had allowed a relaxing of her social skills. Freda was a friend and she didn't want to upset her.

'My hands are feeling a little sore.' It was a victimless crime to lie to her friend. Especially about knitting.

Freda accepted the excuse and was happy for Alice to sit next to her while they chatted about the other residents. Anyone else would have called it gossiping, but Alice preferred to see it as *gathering intel*.

Just as Alice was planning to make her excuses, her obligation to Rose fulfilled, Vanessa entered the dining room, followed by a tall woman dressed in a suit. Judith was in her early thirties, with short black hair and a stern expression that seemed to be a permanent fixture. Alice hadn't seen her look any other way in the few times they'd met.

Judith was Tracey's niece and had become a police detective the previous year. She had dismissed Alice's friend Betty's death as natural causes. Alice didn't hold that against her. The fact there hadn't been a knife sticking out of Betty's back had made it less obvious that she had been murdered.

Vanessa said something to Judith who surveyed the room and nodded.

'Excuse me, everyone,' Vanessa called. She had to repeat herself before the buzz of conversation died away and all eyes turned in her direction. 'We are lucky to have Judith join us today. Some of you will recognise her as Tracey's niece, but she's actually here in her capacity as a police detective to talk to us about safety. Judith?'

Judith stepped forward and flashed her teeth at the group in what Alice could only assume was meant to be a smile. As she began speaking, Vanessa walked over to Alice's chair.

'The doctor says you should be resting. I'll help you back to your apartment.' She winked in a way that was probably supposed to be subtle but was anything but. Alice added winking to her mental list of things they needed to work on.

They left Judith scaring the room with tales of criminals lurking in every shadow.

'I thought they idea was to make them feel safer,' Alice commented. 'Not believe they're about to be murdered on the way to the rose garden.'

'She might be overdoing it a bit,' Vanessa admitted, pressing the button to call the elevator.

'I take it you've discovered something.'

'Yes and no.' Vanessa waited until the elevator doors had closed before continuing. 'First I asked her how it was being a detective. That was a big mistake. It took me ten minutes to change the subject. Apparently, everyone from the cleaning lady to the Prime Minister of New Zealand is ecstatic about her promotion. Anyway, eventually I managed to get the conversation around to asking if the job had any downsides. Like, do criminals target police officer's homes?'

They stepped onto the landing to find Rachel waiting for them there.

'Sorry. I was going stir crazy waiting in Granddad's place. I thought I'd come and see what was happening.'

'Come on in. Vanessa was just giving me an update.'

'You mean you told her? But she's…' Rachel stared at Vanessa's uniform.

'I work in a retirement village. I'm hardly the cops,' Vanessa replied.

Alice led the way into the apartment. By the time she got to the couch her ankle was throbbing. Gritting her teeth, she masked her pain to avoid the inevitable 'you have to look after yourself' lecture from Vanessa.

The two women were eyeing each other up. Vanessa was older than Rachel and her expression was filled with the confidence provided by those few additional years. Rachel's face was a mixture of envy and hostility.

'Rachel, Vanessa can be trusted,' Alice said. 'So unless you're going to mark your territory, I suggest you sit down so we can get on with it.'

Rachel's eyes widened, but Vanessa smiled and sat on the couch next to Alice.

'If you hang around you'll learn there's not much of a filter between what's in Alice's head and what comes out her mouth.'

Rachel scowled a bit longer then flopped into the chair opposite. 'I suppose,' she mumbled.

'Right. Did you find out anything useful, Vanessa dear?' asked Alice.

'I found stuff out. I'm just not sure how useful it is. And you were right about Judith. As soon as I asked the right question, she let a couple of things slip. Turns out there's a senior police constable stationed at Wellington Central who came into work recently spouting off about someone breaking into her house.'

'She told you that?' Rachel said in disbelief.

'Sort of,' Vanessa grinned. 'I asked her who kept the police safe while they're keeping us safe. I asked as an example – like, if someone broke into a police officer's home, would she investigate, or would the officer investigate their own case?'

'Clever,' Alice nodded.

Vanessa nodded her acknowledgement of the compliment. 'Judith said detectives don't investigate burglaries, and it's not policy for constables to be assigned to cases involving their own property.'

'So who is going to investigate it?' Rachel asked.

'No one,' Vanessa replied. 'When someone asked what she was going to do about it she said she knew what the conviction rate was on burglaries and she didn't want to waste resources. Especially when nothing was taken.'

Rachel gave a little start.

'That sounds like a perfectly reasonable explanation for not pursuing things,' Alice said. 'But she was lying, wasn't she, Rachel?'

Rachel squirmed in her chair and tried to avoid Alice's gaze.

'What did you take?'

'It was nothing!'

Alice continued to stare.

'I mean, it was worth nothing. It was just a book.'

'What book?' Vanessa chimed in.

'What difference does that make? It's not valuable, it's just a stupid book.'

Alice sighed and held up a hand to stop Vanessa asking more questions. 'Where is it now?'

'In my room at Granddad's.'

'Go and get it.'

'Right now?' Rachel looked confused.

'Now.'

After Rachel left the apartment, Vanessa shook her head in disbelief. 'How are we supposed to help someone who hides things from us? This is crazy.'

'It's frustrating,' Alice agreed. 'But you'll find that most people you try to help will hide something from you, intentionally or not.'

Vanessa's eyes narrowed. 'How much do you hide from me?'

'Never more than necessary.'

Vanessa seemed less than satisfied with that answer but didn't press the issue. 'Did you have any luck with your side of things?' she asked instead.

'Not yet. I've made some phone calls and I'm waiting to hear back.'

Vanessa got up from the couch and went into the kitchen, where she filled a glass with water and brought it over with the small pill container that had been sitting on the counter.

'What's this for?'

'For the pain you're trying to keep off your face.'

Alice took the glass and swallowed the two pills Vanessa handed her. 'It just hurts a little bit,' she grumbled. Which wasn't true when she said it but was true by the time Rachel came back with the book.

Alice took it from her and studied it. 'This is what you thought was a valuable book?' she asked.

Rachel's face flushed and her eyes darted to the window. 'Colin said we were there to get a book. I panicked and grabbed the first book I could find.'

Alice flipped it over and read the blurb on the back. It didn't sound like her sort of thing. She looked at the cover again. *The Second Chance of Joshua Messer.* What sort of title was that? She flicked to the author bio page and saw that Rodney Strong was from Wellington. She'd ask Oliver if he'd heard of him. Why had the police officer cared about losing this book? She flicked back to the first page where there was a handwritten inscription. *I love you 99.*

Alice flicked through a few more pages, looking for anything out of the ordinary, but it looked like a normal book. She placed it on the arm of the couch and turned her attention back to Rachel. 'Have you tried to get hold of Colin again?'

Rachel shook her head. 'I've been getting calls from the same unknown number though.'

'Who is it?' Vanessa asked.

'I don't answer. I'm…' Rachel stopped and looked at her fingernails.

Afraid, Alice completed the sentence in her head.

'Being cautious,' suggested Vanessa.

Relief flashed across Rachel's face. 'Yeah, absolutely. I was being cautious. Who knows how many people are after me?'

'Do you have your phone with you?' Alice asked.

Rachel handed it over. It looked like a fancier version of Alice's. And she had no idea how it worked. She passed it to Vanessa who tapped on the screen then showed Alice the call log. There were six missed called from the same phone number in the last day.

'What does that mean?' Alice pointed at a symbol at the top of the screen.

Vanessa took the phone back. 'I missed that. Rachel, you've got a message.' She tapped a few times with her thumb, and a voice burst out of the phone.

'One new message. Message left today at 10.35am...'

Alice glanced at the clock on the oven. 11.45am.

A man's voice replaced the robotic woman. 'You had your chance. All you had to do was pick up the phone and none of this would have happened. I know where you are, Rachel. It would be a shame for something to happen to those old people you're with. Meet me outside reception in one hour with the book, or else.'

Rachel went pale and started shaking. Vanessa leapt to her feet and started for the door.

Alice looked thoughtfully at the book.

'Wait,' she called.

'You heard the man, an hour from then is right now.'

'There's a police detective downstairs.'

Vanessa stopped mid-stride. 'That's right. I forgot about Judith.'

'Take the stairs, and ring me on the phone before you go into the lobby. That way I can hear what's happening. If there's no one there, let Judith and Tracey know there's been a threat against a resident.'

'What about me?' Rachel asked. Her voice came out in a squeak and her breathing was short. Alice noticed that her first question was about herself rather than her grandfather. She remembered being that young – just – when self-preservation was your strongest instinct. Still, it annoyed Alice that the girl's concern hadn't been for Owen, the grandparent she'd endangered.

'No one knows exactly where you are. As long as you stay in this apartment for the time being, you'll be fine. Ring Owen and tell him to come up here. Just in case.'

Rachel's eyes confirmed Alice's suspicion that her grandfather's safety had never entered her thoughts. She snatched her phone off the coffee table and began dialling just as Alice's phone rang.

'I'm at the bottom of the stairs,' Vanessa whispered.

'Can you see anything?'

The lobby door had a small glass porthole allowing those coming down the stairs to see into the lobby. Vanessa had confided to Alice one time that management had added the window after someone had come out of the stairwell and bowled over a resident standing behind the door.

'Nothing in the lobby, hang on.'

There was a rustling sound, then some other sounds that were hard to decipher.

'There's a car outside the front door. I don't recognise it. I'll go take a look.'

'No! Go find Judith first.'

'Okay.' More rustling, then a sound that might have been a door opening, and murmuring.

'He's not answering his phone,' Rachel said.

A chill swept through Alice's body. She pushed the fear aside. There were many reasons Owen wouldn't be answering his phone. He could be in the bathroom, or the shower, or have gone for a walk. He could have been having a nap. His phone battery could have gone flat. (That happened to Alice so frequently she now had four chargers plugged in around the apartment so one was never far away.)

'Where was he when you came here?'

'At home.'

'Vanessa,' Alice called into her phone. There was no response but she could hear a muffled conversation going on.

'Vanessa!' she said more firmly.

'Yes, I'm here.'

'Change of plan, go to Owen's straight away.'

'Why? What's happened?'

'Take Judith with you.'

There was more rustling and muffled conversation then the phone clicked off.

'Damn,' Alice said.

'What?' What's going on?' Rachel asked.

'She hung up. That's alright. She and Judith are going to check on Owen. I'm sure he's perfectly fine.'

'This is all my fault.'

Alice didn't disagree.

The trip from Alice's apartment in the main building to the block of apartments behind it took Vanessa an extraordinary amount of time. Alice felt each second tick by and tried not to look at the clock.

When the front door opened, Alice and Rachel both jumped. Vanessa walked in, closely followed by Owen.

'You're alright,' Alice breathed a sigh of relief.

'Of course,' Owen said with a smile. 'At least I was until Vanessa hammered on my front door. I think she scared the whole block.'

'Why didn't you call me back?' Alice said to Vanessa.

'I didn't think of it,' she replied sheepishly.

Alice opened her mouth to chide her, but at the last moment switched to Owen. 'Why weren't you answering your phone?'

Owen sat down in his usual armchair and fixed her with a shrewd look. 'I was having a shower. Vanessa wouldn't tell me what the problem was, and poor Judith looked thoroughly confused, so why don't you enlighten me, Alice? What's going on?'

'What did you tell Judith?' Alice asked Vanessa. Now that Owen was sitting in front of her, she felt silly for overreacting.

'I told her that no one had heard from Owen for a while and I needed her to go with me to make sure he was alright. She must have thought I was a little cray-cray when he opened the door in his dressing gown.'

Owen's face went red, which Alice found amusing but she hid her smile and quickly changed the subject. She filled Owen in and when she finished Owen glared at his granddaughter.

'What have you done?' he said sternly.

Rachel's lip quivered. 'I'm sorry, Granddad.'

'There'll be plenty of time for blame after all this is sorted out,' Alice said firmly.

'You guys should see this,' Vanessa said, looking through the living room window.

Alice struggled to her feet with a hand from Owen and hobbled over to Vanessa. The window overlooked the front of the main building of the Retirement Village and down the hill to Wellington Harbour. On any day the view was spectacular, but today their eyes were drawn to an angry man standing beside a car arguing with a Tongan man in a Silvermoon employee uniform.

'Thank goodness Joshua was there,' Vanessa said.

The angry man was waving his hands in short sharp movements. Despite getting dangerously close to his face, Joshua didn't react. It wasn't the best angle, but Alice could see that the man had short black hair, wore a short-sleeved T-shirt and that both of his arms were covered in tattoos. He looked to be in his early twenties. Eventually he climbed into his car and drove down the driveway towards the Silvermoon entrance gates.

'Do you recognise him?' Alice asked Rachel.

Rachel nodded, her face pale. 'It's Colin. How did he find me?'

'He hasn't found you, not yet. Vanessa, will you go and ask Joshua to come up? Rachel, I think it best that you go back to Owen's apartment and wait there until we find out a bit more.'

When her apartment was empty again, Alice sank back onto the couch and glared at her ankle. She didn't get to ninety-eight without learning to ignore a few aches and pains, but this ankle injury was a tiresome bother.

By the time Vanessa returned with Joshua, Alice had managed to arrange herself on the couch so that her ankle was, if not comfortable, less annoying.

'Hi, Alice,' Joshua said in his soft voice. A broad Tongan man in his early twenties, he had come to Alice's attention the previous year through an unfortunate set of circumstances – which Alice had managed to resolve for him satisfactorily. He was studying law at university and working part-time as a custodian at the Village. That was part of the arrangement he and Alice had come to.

He kissed her on the cheek and sat opposite. 'How's the ankle?'

'Fine.' She waved her hand irritably.

'I'm sure that chair won't cause you any trouble again,' Joshua laughed.

Alice glared at him and he smiled back. She felt her lips twitch and changed tack. 'Tell me about the man you were arguing with?'

Joshua's mouth slipped into a frown. 'He was at the concierge desk giving Molly some grief, so I asked him to leave. He was looking for someone called Rachel Porter. I told him there was no one living here by that name.'

'You know everyone's name who lives here?' Vanessa asked.

'Nah,' he shrugged. 'But I would have told him that no matter whose name he said.'

Alice approved.

'I didn't like him. He had a vibe.'

'What sort of vibe?' asked Alice.

Joshua shifted in his chair and looked thoughtful. 'He was angry, but underneath I think he was scared. When I told him there was no Rachel here, he asked who her grandfather was. How would I know? Almost every man who lives here is someone's grandfather. Then he went on about needing a book. I suggested he leave.'

'You suggested?'

He turned to Vanessa with a cold expression. 'I'm pretty good at suggesting.' Then he broke into a chuckle. 'My mum is even better at suggesting than me. You're lucky she wasn't down there. Actually *he's* lucky she wasn't down there.'

Alice closed her eyes to think for a moment. When she opened them again the others were watching her carefully.

'Oh stop it,' she grumbled. 'Here's the thing, Joshua. Rachel Porter is Owen's granddaughter and she's staying with him for the moment. How would you like a job?'

'I have a job.' Joshua frowned at the news but he wasn't going to argue with Alice. 'Doing what?'

'Keep an eye on Owen and Rachel until I can sort this out for them.'

'I've already got a job,' he repeated. 'Two. Plus university.'

Alice fixed him with a stare. 'Perhaps if I talked to your mother we could come to some arrangement.' She watched him work through the implications of getting his mother involved and whether Alice was serious. She thought he was smart enough to know what she might mention to his mother.

Finally he gave a little shrug. 'Sure, what did you have in mind?'

Alice outlined her plan and Joshua agreed to help. She wasn't sure if it was fear of Alice or his mother that motivated him to agree, but Alice vowed to meet Joshua's mother as soon as she could. 'Vanessa will clear it with Tracey.'

'How am I supposed to do that?' asked Vanessa.

'I'm sure you'll think of something.'

'Gee thanks,' Vanessa muttered.

'Thank you both. Now, my ankle is feeling a bit sore so I might lie down for a while.'

Joshua jumped to his feet straight away, but Vanessa paused to look at Alice through narrowed eyes before standing up.

'Off you go,' Alice smiled encouragingly.

After they left, she dropped the smile. Her ankle *was* sore, but she was never going to let them know how much discomfort she was in. She closed her eyes for a moment.

And opened them two hours later.

Her foot felt better but her head was fuzzy. She blinked a few times to adjust her eyes to the sunshine coming through the windows. Her gaze fell on the book on the coffee table. She picked it up and leafed through it again. There was still nothing leaping out at her. It just looked like an ordinary book.

She turned to page one and began reading.

Eighty pages later her phone rang. She checked the screen, then answered it.

'I thought you were retired.'

'Technically I am,' she replied.

'You might want to turn that technicality into reality.'

Kevin Mackay was one of her longest acquaintances. She'd first met him forty years ago as her career was winding down and his was getting started. He wasn't quite on the same level as Alice had been in her prime, but he had both feet planted in the grey area between legal and illegal.

Like most of her business acquaintances, Kevin didn't know exactly where Alice lived. She kept that quiet. There were still a few people around that would have liked to nudge Alice towards the grave a little faster. (One of them was currently the Prime Minister of New Zealand.)

'Don't be melodramatic, Kevin. What did you find out?'

When he was finished, she begrudgingly conceded he wasn't being melodramatic after all. She thanked him and hung up.

Alice sat staring at the wall for a while. Finally, she leaned over and opened a drawer in the coffee table. Lifting the false bottom, she picked up the hip flask hidden beneath. It was small and silver and had a dent in the back, as if the flask had stopped a speeding projectile at some point. She took a swig and coughed as the sharp burn of whiskey hit her throat. Possibly she shouldn't be drinking while taking painkillers, but she considered whiskey an important part of the healing process. She examined the hip flask, brushing her finger over the dent. Now that had been a fun year.

Reluctantly she replaced it in the drawer and leaned back on the couch. Her head was clearer and she slotted Kevin's information alongside everything else she knew. She still didn't know everything she needed to, but it was becoming obvious that Rachel was in so far over her head she may as well be walking on the bottom of the ocean.

A knock at the door interrupted her thoughts. She checked the security camera via her phone and saw it was Glenda, the new arts coordinator.

Alice sighed. She didn't feel like playing nice with a stranger, but curiosity got the better of her, so she hobbled to the door and let her in.

'I just wanted to pop by and introduce myself. I'm doing the rounds,' Glenda smiled.

This was the closest Alice had been to the newcomer. She wore a loose-fitting blue top, with a necklace made of silver loops. Her fingernails were short and painted bright blue, and there as a wedding ring on her left hand.

'Nice to meet you,' Alice said.

'And you. I heard you're not very mobile at the moment, so I wanted to let you know about some of the upcoming activities I'm planning, just in case you'd like to come along.'

She handed Alice a list of activities and dates. At a glance, Alice saw nothing that remotely interested her, but she smiled and thanked Glenda. They chatted for a few more minutes before Glenda excused herself.

When she was gone, Alice called Vanessa to make sure she'd organised with Tracey for Joshua to be on the grounds after hours. Then she called Joshua to make sure he was ready for guard duty.

The Silvermoon Retirement Village was more secure than most facilities. The front gate was closed after dark so no cars could drive in, but there were no surveillance cameras or security patrols. The closest thing they had to a guard dog was Maddy the cat, which would have been comforting if Alice had been worried about being attack by birds.

Comforted that Joshua was on the job, and that even if Colin returned he'd have no idea where or even if Rachel was here, Alice spent the rest of the day reading *The Second Chance of Joshua Messer*. It was a good story, and she found herself sympathising with the main character. It was a coincidence that he had the same name as the Joshua she'd had in her apartment earlier. She always enjoyed stories more when she knew people with the same names as the characters. But she still couldn't see anything exceptional about the book. Perhaps there was nothing special about it. Perhaps the police officer was just angry that someone had broken into her house and stole something.

When she finished, she threw the book onto the coffee table and hobbled to her bathroom. Then she slipped into bed and switched off the light. She immediately fell asleep.

A loud noise woke her. It took a moment's fumble for the light switch, then a moment longer to check first the time (1.45am), then the camera on her phone. Joshua was outside, his fist hammering on the door.

As quick as she could she pulled on her dressing gown and, using her cane, made it to the front door.

The moment she opened it Joshua fell inside, narrowly avoiding Alice.

'What?' Alice asked. 'What's happened?'

'There's a… I think there's been a…'

'Take a deep breath and finish your sentence,' advised Alice.

'He's dead.'

SIX

It took Alice several more minutes to calm Joshua enough to get more details from him. She paused to put on slippers, then coaxed Joshua into leading her to the scene.

They made their way easily in the subtle outdoor lighting. The pathway to Owen's apartment building was lined with small bushes, and bench seats were placed at intervals. Apparently management thought old people needed a lot of rest on their journey between buildings.

Thirty metres from the door to Owen's building, Joshua stopped and pointed. A shadow stuck out from below a bush and it took Alice's eyes a moment to recognise that the shape was in fact two feet.

'Wait here,' she ordered.

Alice gripped her walking stick tightly as she cautiously approached the feet. As she neared, the feet developed a pair of legs, then a torso and finally a head. She immediately saw two problems. The first was that the man was undoubtedly dead. The second was that it was Colin, the man who had threatened to return for Rachel.

She felt Joshua step up next to her.

'Mum would never forgive me if I left you to do this alone,' he muttered.

Her eyes shifted up to Owen's apartment window. It was dark and there was no sign of movement.

Alice went closer and viewed the body clinically. Unlike Joshua, this wasn't her first dead body, nor her first murder victim. Although her career had been more about murdering people's bank accounts, there had been occasions when she'd stumbled into the wrong place at the wrong time. Colin's cause of death wasn't immediately obvious, but as she looked closer she noticed something clutched into his left hand.

'Get that will you?' She gestured with the tip of her cane.

'Shouldn't we preserve the… you know, the crime scene?'

'We'll put it back when we're done.'

Joshua hesitated so she pulled on his arm. 'Hurry up, before someone comes.'

He bent down and tugged the item free, quickly handing it to Alice and wiping his hand on his leg, as if afraid death was a virus he was going to catch.

It was a scrap of material, though difficult to make out the exact colour in the dim light.

'I'll put it back,' Joshua held out his hand.

'No, I'll do it,' Alice replied. She rubbed the material between her finger and thumb to smudge her and Joshua's fingerprints, then bent down and put the material back into the hand. His skin was still slightly warm. It was a cool night and Alice pulled her dressing gown tighter around her. He hadn't been dead long.

'Go and check that Rachel and Owen are alright.'

'I can't leave you here by yourself.'

'I'll be fine. The killer is long gone.'

'How do you know? They could be hiding.' He looked around him wildly.

'Trust me, there's no one out here now but the two of us. I'll be fine. Colin was obviously here to find Rachel so I need to know she's alright.'

Joshua's face showed he was torn, but he raced to the door of the apartment block and disappeared inside. Only then did Alice drop to her knees. (Getting back up might be a problem but she'd worry about that later.) As quickly as she could, Alice pocketed the scrap of material and searched the dead body's pockets. There was a wallet with a driver's licence telling her his full name was Colin Craze. She also found car keys, and a piece of paper with the number 12 on it. Owen's apartment number.

She screwed up the paper and slipped it into her dressing gown pocket. Her knees had started to ache. She placed her hand on the ground to shift some of the weight off her joints and felt her fingers touch something hard. Feeling around she uncovered a pocketknife with the blade extended, lying partially covered by leaves. Given how close it was to him she doubted it had been dropped by anyone other than Colin.

It was difficult to judge but she couldn't see any blood on the blade. Which meant he hadn't used it. It also meant no one had used it on him. So how had he died?

She looked up when a light came on in Owen's apartment and someone pulled the curtain back.

Silly, she thought. You're making yourself an easy target.

Alice figured she had about two minutes before Owen called the police and maybe five before he strode downstairs in a chivalrous attempt to shield her from the horror of the dead man.

She turned back to Colin. Something didn't seem right. He wasn't lying naturally. Not that there was much natural about murder, but…. she couldn't put her finger on it. Her sore ankle, the cold, and kneeling on the ground were all dragging her focus away.

Then she realised. His head was propped up slightly, like it was resting on something. She pulled the sleeve of her dressing gown down over her hand and reached out to tilt his head a little to the sidesaw a long thin piece of pale metal sticking out of his neck. She almost didn't recognise it. It was the end that reminded her. The sculptured end that she had admired earlier that day.

She knew what had killed him. But she didn't know why.

Colin had been killed by Freda's knitting needle.

SEVEN

'Why didn't you call me?!'

Alice sighed and rolled her neck. Her muscles were sore from the middle of the night excursion.

'What would you like me to have said?' she asked Vanessa. 'Come quickly, there's a dead body.'

'Yes!' Vanessa replied. She was pacing in Alice's kitchen, failing at her task of making a cup of tea.

'And what would you have done?'

'I don't know.' Vanessa stopped pacing and glared at Alice. 'Told you how crazy you were going out in the dark to investigate a body?'

'There was no danger,' Alice said calmly.

'You didn't know that!'

'Vanessa please sit down. There's no point agonising over the what-ifs. I'm here, I'm safe, so let's focus on the future, not the past.'

'The *what-ifs*?'

Alice gestured to the book on the coffee table. 'Sorry, I was reading that last night and they talk about *what-ifs* as a phenomenon. Anyway, let me ask you something. Do you recognise this?'

Alice retrieved something from her dressing gown pocket and showed it to Vanessa.

'What's this?' Vanessa took the scrap of material from Alice.

'It was in the dead man's hand.'

Vanessa looked horrified. 'You took something from a crime scene?'

'Yes, yes, but only because it would waste police time if they saw it.'

'What? How can you know that?'

'Look at the pattern and colour. Does it remind you of anything? Of anyone?'

Vanessa studied the scrap, turning it over in her hands. 'It looks familiar, but I can't place it.'

Alice shook her head in disappointment.

'Oh, I'm sorry we can't all identify the origin of something the size of a finger, Alice. I suppose you can tell me where this came from, where it was made, and who wore it.'

'Don't be silly. I have no idea where it was made. But I do know who wore it, and so do you. Rachel was wearing a T-Shirt that colour and pattern yesterday.'

Vanessa frowned. 'Rachel killed Colin? And you're covering it up?' she accused Alice.

'Honestly, Vanessa, have I taught you nothing? Rachel didn't kill Colin.'

'How do you know?'

'Because Joshua found her and Owen in his apartment. In the short time you've known her, do you think that girl could possibly commit murder, then pop back upstairs and go back to bed?'

'I've talked to her for about ten minutes!'

'Which should be plenty of time to decide whether she was capable of murder.'

'Well, I'm sorry, Alice, but I don't have your experience with thieves and murderers so it takes me a little longer to figure things out.'

'That's alright, Vanessa dear, we'll work on that.'

'Fine. If you don't think Rachel killed Colin then why did you take this?' She held up the material.

'Because the police have a nasty habit of becoming fixated on what is most convenient. Once they realise that Rachel had a motive to kill Colin, they won't look much further. We don't want to give them more evidence against her. We need them to look for the real killer.'

'And…' Vanessa looked troubled. 'And you said the killer used one of Freda's knitting needles? What does *that* mean?'

A knock at the door prevented Alice from answering that question. 'I have a feeling we are about to have an opportunity to find out. Get that will you, dear?'

Vanessa ushered Judith into the apartment, accompanied by a uniformed constable. The slim Indian woman was introduced as Constable Patel.

One advantage of being old is that the police believe you when you say you're in shock, so Alice had managed to avoid questions the night before. By the look on Judith's face, those questions were all about to be asked.

'Right, Alice. The more detail you can provide in your answers the quicker and easier this will go,' Judith said. She missed the narrowing of Alice's eyes and carried on. 'Why were you out in the grounds last night?'

'I couldn't sleep. It's part of getting old I'm afraid. I often go for a walk.'

'In the middle of the night? With a sprained ankle?' Judith looked pointedly at Alice's cane. 'Do you do that often?'

'I do the *oftens* as much as I can while I still can,' Alice said primly.

Constable Patel scribbled something into a notebook while Judith asked the next question.

'Were you alone?'

'Are you suggesting I was returning on a… Vanessa what does your generation call it? A walk of…?'

'Shame. Walk of shame.'

Judith's face turned pink. 'No, no, no, no, I wasn't… I didn't mean to suggest that…'

'That old people have sex?'

Constable Patel carefully laid her pencil on the top of her pad and placed her hands together.

A strangled sound escaped from Judith's open mouth.

Vanessa gave Alice a 'that's enough' look.

Feeling that she'd wrestled enough authority away from the detective to make things more even, Alice smiled and apologised. 'Just an old woman having some fun. To answer your question, Detective, yes I was alone when I started, but I met Joshua on my circuit around the building.'

Alice had considered telling Joshua to leave before the police got there, and if he hadn't been seen by Owen and Rachel she probably would have. But Owen was too straight to lie to the police. Instead she had decided on this alternative version of the truth.

'Ah yes, Joshua Leota,' Judith said while Patel flicked through her notebook. 'Any idea what he was doing on the grounds at that time of night? He's a custodian here, I understand.'

Judith checked something in the notebook before handing it back to Patel.

'I asked him to work after hours,' Vanessa said.

'Why exactly?'

'We don't have twenty-four hour security, although the front gate is locked after dark. There have been reports at some other retirement villages that residents are being targeted. I thought a night patrol might stop our residents from worrying.'

By luck Tracey had received a report from one of the other retirement villages the day before, so when Vanessa offered to ask Joshua to do a night patrol after he'd finished for the day she had agreed.

'Wouldn't a professional security company have been more appropriate?'

Vanessa nodded. 'Of course, but we didn't know if there was a need, you see. We thought we'd try this for a few days and see if the residents found it reassuring.'

Judith frowned, then turned back to Alice. 'Please talk me through what you did when you found the body. I imagine it must have been upsetting.'

Inconvenient certainly, Alice thought. 'It's never nice seeing a dead body,' she replied.

'That's right,' Judith pounced. 'You were there when your friend was murdered last year.' She smiled like she'd caught Alice out.

'I seem to recall being the only one who thought it was murder at the time.'

Judith had the decency to look slightly ashamed. She had been visiting her aunt when Alice's friend Betty died and had rather arrogantly declared her death to be natural causes based on Betty's age alone.

'Yes, well, anyway. If you could let me know what you did when you found the deceased?' Judith said in a gentler voice.

'I sent Joshua to make sure there was no one else on the grounds, and then I checked for a pulse.'

'Did you touch or remove anything from the body?'

'Goodness me no, I've watched enough crime shows to know not to… what's the phrase? *Contaminate* a crime scene.'

Judith nodded.

'May I ask? Do you know who the deceased gentleman was? Some poor soul who wandered onto the grounds by accident, I assume.'

'Enquiries are ongoing,' Judith replied.

'Absolutely. I'm sure you'll get to the bottom of it. I must say it is a comfort to know that Wellington's finest are on the job.' Alice beamed at Judith and Constable Patel with a smile so wide it hurt.

'Thank you,' Patel replied.

'Of course. You know, I think I was one of Wellington's first feminists, so I can't tell you how happy I am to see two young women representing law and order.'

Judith shifted in her seat, then nodded.

'Although I am a little surprised to see a police detective here for an accidental death,' Alice added.

'All suspicious deaths must be properly investigated,' Judith replied.

'Suspicious?' Alice clutched a hand to her chest and kept a straight face when she saw Vanessa roll her eyes. 'My goodness. You mean it could have been foul play? Was the man a… criminal?'

Vanessa made a choking sound which she turned into a cough.

'The man is known to us,' Constable Patel said.

Judith quietened her with a stern look. 'Did you recognise him?'

'I've never seen him before in my life,' replied Alice. That was mostly true. 'Oh dear. Was he a scoundrel? What if his accomplices come back? Are we safe?' Alice began twisting her fingers together nervously.

'Ms Atkinson, rest assured that there will be a police presence in the Village until we resolve the case,' said Judith. 'And although we don't know what Mr Craze was doing here, we have no reason to believe the residents are in any danger.'

'How can you possibly know that?'

'Obviously it is early in the investigation, but we have found the victim's car and a witness who was out walking his dog remembered that it was being parked when he passed at 10.30pm. The witness says Mr Craze was the only one in the car.'

Alice frowned. If Colin had parked at ten thirty and Joshua discovered his body just before twelve, what was he doing for ninety minutes?

'Is there anything more you can tell me?'

Can? Yes. will? No, Alice thought to herself.

She shook her head. 'This has all been very overwhelming, I think I need to lie down.'

Judith immediately stood up, no doubt spurred on by what her aunt would say if her visit prompted a medical event for one of the residents. 'We'll be in touch if we need anything else.'

After the police left, Alice let out a sigh and rolled her shoulders again.

'Pretending to be old is tiring,' she commented.

'You were laying it on thicker than my Dad puts jam on toast.'

'Perception, Vanessa dear. People see an old lady, they expect her to act like an old lady and say old lady things. Anything else and they get suspicious.'

'Have you spoken to Joshua or Rachel this morning?'

Alice frowned. 'I spoke with Owen and told him to make sure Rachel didn't leave his apartment. If the police interviewed him, he was to say his granddaughter was visiting. I've left a message for Joshua. To be honest, I'm feeling a little guilty about that. I thought if anyone showed up then Joshua would just frighten them off. I didn't think he'd be in any actual danger.'

Vanessa sat down in the chair recently vacated by Judith. 'You do that a bit.'

'What?'

'Send people into potentially dangerous situations without much thought for their safety.'

Alice's frown deepened. 'I don't send you any place I wouldn't go myself.'

'Alice, from what you've told me about your life, that's not exactly comforting.'

'You don't have to do everything I say,' grumbled Alice.

'No, I don't, but it's pretty hard to say no to you. And I know you have this fantastic notion that I'm going to follow in your footsteps, but all this,' she waved at the door, 'makes me really uncomfortable.'

'It's not like you haven't kept things from the police before. Besides we're not hiding anything important.'

Vanessa's eyes bulged. 'Nothing important! Only that you know exactly who the victim is, why he was here, and that he was clutching a strip of material worn by someone we know.'

'Exactly,' Alice beamed. 'Now we have another problem.'

'Another problem?' Vanessa repeated in disbelief.

'Yes. This,' she gestured to her ankle, 'is a tiny bit sore after last night, but I urgently need to speak with Rachel. Can you bring her over here without the police seeing?'

'Why don't you just call her?'

'It's harder to tell if someone is lying over the phone.'

'I suppose it is better for someone to lie to your face.'

'Precisely,' Alice agreed, choosing to ignore her sarcasm.

'Well, in case you haven't noticed there happens to be a crime scene between Owen's building and yours. How exactly am I supposed to get Rachel here without being seen?'

Alice thought for a moment. 'You're not. Have you ever heard of *hiding in plain sight*? That's what you're going to do.' She outlined her idea which Vanessa reluctantly agreed was workable.

Vanessa left to make the arrangements.

Meanwhile Alice picked up the book again and skipped past the inscription to read the dedication. It was absolute nonsense. To my wonderful wife 1, 20, and 210 times all the love. She flicked to the first page and read it top to bottom. Nothing leapt out at her. She turned to page 20. Again, nothing that suggested a hidden code or anything special about the page. By the time Vanessa returned with Rachel, she'd discounted page 210 as well. It was probably an inside joke between Mr and Mrs Strong.

There were bags under Rachel's eyes and she nervously chewed on a thumbnail as she sat on the edge of the armchair. The light green Silvermoon employee T-shirt she wore was several sizes too big.

'It was the only one we had,' Vanessa explained.

'Did you sleep?' Alice asked.

'Not after…' Rachel shuddered. All signs of her rebellious personality had been stripped away.

'Did you know Colin was coming?'

Rachel shrank back into her seat. 'No, of course not.' Her face lost the last little bit of colour and for a moment Alice thought she might pass out.

Alice sighed. She'd never get answers if the girl fainted. 'Vanessa, bottom drawer in the kitchen, in the box with the scales.'

Vanessa went into the kitchen and returned with a thin bronze-coloured hip flask.

'Drink,' Alice instructed, offering her the flask.

Rachel stared at it suspiciously, then opened it, sniffed, and finally took a small sip. She choked and coughed as the liquid hit her throat, and by the time she recovered there was a hint of colour back in her cheeks. 'What is this?'

'Fifty-year-old scotch,' replied Alice.

Rachel gingerly handed the flask back to Vanessa as if it was a bomb about to go off.

'Your parents live in Nelson, don't they?' Alice said.

Rachel nodded.

'And you have no other family in Wellington.'

It was a statement rather than a question. She'd already established that from Owen.

'No.'

'So how did Colin know to come here? How did he know about your grandfather?'

'You think I told him?'

'I think you wouldn't be the first young woman to have her head turned by the promise of danger, who said the wrong thing to the wrong person.'

'You think Colin and I had a thing?'

'A thing?' Alice looked at Vanessa.

'Were involved.'

'Ah. I'm suggesting that information like where your grandfather lives is more often shared between the sheets than on the streets.'

Rachel recovered her defiant look and shrugged. 'So what if we were?'

'And you met with him last night in the grounds.'

'How did you—?'

'Did you at least have the good sense to get rid of your torn top?'

'Of course. I'm not stupid. I threw it away.'

'Where?' Vanessa asked.

'In Granddad's rubbish bin.'

Genius. Vanessa and Alice exchanged looks. Rachel wasn't making this easy for them.

'You're lucky I took care of that little scrap of evidence already,' Alice scowled. 'What happened when you met Colin last night?'

'He kept ringing and leaving messages. I finally answered and he begged me to meet him outside Granddad's apartment building. I thought he was going to tell me he'd sorted it, but all he cared about was getting the damn book. When I told him I didn't have it anymore, he got mad and grabbed me. He had a knife.' Rachel shuddered at the memory. 'I seriously think he was going to cut me. It's just a stupid book. My top ripped when I broke free and ran inside. He was still alive when I left, I swear.'

'Don't swear,' Alice said. 'It's the second sign of a lack of intelligence.'

'What's the first?' Rachel asked.

'Constantly saying stupid things. Did Owen know you went out?'

Rachel shook her head. 'He was fast asleep. He woke up when that guy banged on the door. I think he woke a few of Granddad's neighbours up too.'

'You saw no one else while you were out?'

Another shake of her head.

'What time did you meet him?'

'Around eleven-thirty.'

'This is ridiculous,' Alice sighed.

'What?'

'If this was a murder mystery, you've just painted yourself as the prime suspect. Not only were you having *a thing*, as you say, with the victim, but you argued and struggled with him a short time before his death. You might as well wave a flag that says *I did it.*'

'But I didn't.' Rachel leapt to her feet.

Proving that was going to be tricky.

ƐIGHT

Alice sent Rachel back to Owen's apartment with a stern warning not to talk to anyone.

'Was I that clueless four years ago?' Vanessa wondered aloud as she made Alice a pot of tea.

'You've gained a great deal of intelligence since.'

'She's not a bad person.'

'Plenty of good people do stupid things,' Alice pointed out. 'She's not making it easy to help her though. If she was anyone other than Owen's granddaughter, I would tell her where to put her problems and walk away – well, hobble.'

'You wouldn't!'

'I'm too old to be helping people that don't want to be helped.'

'You keep helping me and I never asked for it.'

'Of course, you did,' Alice took the cup from her. 'Thank you, Vanessa dear. You may not have used the words, but you've been asking for help since you started working here.'

Vanessa sat in her usual seat and blew the steam off her own cup before trying a sip. 'I can't wait to hear this.'

'Why do you think you gravitated towards me? Of all the residents at Silvermoon, you chose to spend time with the one whose past is a bit shady.'

'Just a bit,' Vanessa choked.

Alice laughed. 'A lot.'

'You might find this hard to believe, Alice, but I hang around with you because I like you.'

Alice laughed. 'No one your age would spend time with an oldie like me if there wasn't an ulterior motive.'

'You know your trouble? You've spent too long with shady characters to see something genuine for what it is.'

Alice took another sip. She was enjoying sparring, and from the twinkle in her eye so was Vanessa, but it was time to get back to the matter at hand. There was something new bothering her about Colin's body. Something else that was out of place. Her eyes shifted to the coffee table where her phone sat.

Where was Colin's phone?

She asked Vanessa.

'Maybe he left it in his car?'

Alice frowned. 'Perhaps. But in all the time I've known you, your phone has never been further from her fingers than your pocket. Why would he use his phone to arrange a meeting with Rachel, then leave it in his car?'

'He wouldn't.' Vanessa matched her frown. 'So where is it?'

'It's possible he dropped it when he was stabbed. Which means the police have it. Or the killer took it.'

'But why?'

'In my experience,' Alice said as she shuffled to get into a more comfortable position, 'people take things for one of two reasons. Because they don't have one themselves and want one. Or because it's valuable. Are phones valuable?'

Vanessa shrugged. 'Depends on the phone, but some of them can cost up to two thousand.'

'So that's a possible motive. But if money was the reason they took the phone then the killer would have emptied Colin's wallet as well. It was full of cash, so the phone must be valuable for another reason.'

Vanessa took a sip before replying. 'It has something on it the killer didn't want anyone to see.'

'Exactly,' Alice beamed at her.

'What?'

'No idea. You know phones better than I do. What can you put on them?'

'Pretty much anything,' Vanessa admitted. 'Photos, videos, files. It could be in a text or email. Although an email would also be accessible in the cloud.'

Alice closed her eyes and tried to ignore the dull headache plucking away at her concentration.

'Are you alright?'

She opened her eyes again. 'Of course, I was just thinking. We're a little stuck right now. I need to think.'

Vanessa's eyes narrowed and she stood and went into the kitchen.

'What are you doing?'

'Getting you something to eat,' Vanessa replied. 'I'm guessing you haven't had anything this morning and that's why you have a headache.'

'What makes you think I have a headache?'

'Because you were rubbing your temples.'

Vanessa pulled a few things from the fridge and began making a sandwich. Alice didn't recall telling her hands to rub the side of her head. Was she that tired? Her stomach let out a loud growl and across the room Vanessa grinned.

'Oh, just give me the sandwich,' Alice snapped.

Vanessa handed Alice the plate with the sandwich on it. By the time Alice had complained about her using too much butter and too little filling, Vanessa was chuckling. She was still smiling when she left a short time later to get back to work. She let Owen in on her way out.

'I'm interrupting your lunch,' he said. 'I can come back later.'

'Or you can make yourself something and join me.'

A short time later they were chewing their food in companionable silence.

'I needed that,' Owen said as he wiped his mouth with a tissue from the box on the table.

'Don't tell Vanessa, but so did I,' replied Alice. Her headache had subsided and although her ankle was still throbbing, her brain was starting to kick back into gear.

'How are you doing?' she asked.

Owen sighed and straightened his tie. Despite everything that had happened the previous night, and the obvious lack of sleep etched on his face, he was still dressed in a business shirt and tie. A faint smile crossed Alice's face when she saw his cufflinks. Alice had given them to him at Christmas. They were small silver doves; very old and valuable. She'd acquired them sixty years ago in America. The man she'd taken them from had been a drug lord who was long since dead, so she didn't feel guilty giving her friend stolen jewellery. It did give her a small thrill to know her straightlaced friend was wearing her ill-gotten gains, but she would never tell him.

'I wish Catherine was still alive. She always knew what to do. I've faced boardrooms filled with hostile executives and barely raised a sweat, but trying to help a nineteen-year-old is beyond me.

'You've done the most important thing.'

'What's that?'

'You came to someone with more experience than you.'

Owen nodded. 'Ah yes. I outsourced.'

'*Outsourced*? Where do these words come from?'

One of the reasons Alice had stopped watching the news on television was all the new words that had crept into the modern vocabulary. And when the newsreaders started adding te reo Māori as well, things became even harder to understand. She approved of the te reo though, which at least was a proper language and had a legitimate reason for being there, but all the other jargon and gobbledygook was tiresome.

'I expect most of them began as mistakes,' Owen admitted. 'I'm not sure I like the idea of people sitting in rooms to come up with terms like *forward-thinking*, and *customer-centric*.'

Alice snorted. She was glad she'd grown up when women's place in the office was restricted to the secretarial pool. It had made her decision to avoid that life so much easier.

'I can't imagine you in an office,' Owen said, as if reading her mind. 'I pity the poor chap that tried to give you an order. Or attempted to press you into a compromising situation.'

'Believe me, they would have only tried it once,' Alice said with a smile.

'I know what you're doing.'

Alice raised her eyebrows.

'You're trying to distract me.'

'I'm not *trying* to do anything,' Alice replied with a wink.

'I trust you, Alice. I know you'll be able to help Rachel in ways that I can't, but I'm still worried.'

'Of course, you are. She's your granddaughter. I worry about Amanda all the time. As soon as you have children you sign yourself up to a lifetime of worry.'

'They should put *that* on the family planning posters,' Owen joked. The smile slipped from his face. 'Seriously though, Alice, how much trouble is she in?'

Alice chose her words carefully. 'She didn't murder anyone, so that's a positive.' She saw his shoulders relax a little, like he'd needed the words to help convince himself. 'But she stole something from a police officer and that's going to complicate matters. There's something else going on here and I don't quite understand it yet.'

'Perhaps I should take her away for a few days.'

'You could, but I think it might be better for Rachel to stay where I can keep an eye on her. I'm quite certain she hasn't told me everything she knows yet and I can't ask questions if she's not here.' Alice took a deep breath and continued. 'However, I wonder if you would consider taking a short trip, Owen. With this leg, I'm a little slower than usual so I can't protect you both.'

A smile twitched the corner of Owen's mouth as he assessed the tiny woman sitting opposite him. He was significantly taller than her and she could see him thinking the protecting was likely to be the other way around. Technically he was right. In a straight physical competition he was more likely to prevail, but she had three advantages that he either didn't know about or chose to ignore. One, she was a woman and men always underestimated women when it came to confrontations. Two, she was old, so the underestimation was doubled. And three, she knew enough about dirty fighting to fill all the books on a shelf in her bookcase. She preferred to keep that last one to herself.

'Humour me,' she said.

'I can't leave Rachel alone.'

'She won't be alone. She will be with me, staying in my spare room.'

'Are you sure about this?'

The short answer was no, she had no desire to have an almost-stranger stay in her home. But she had even less desire to see the girl killed, so if that meant sacrificing her personal space for a day or two then she'd grit her teeth and do it.

'I'm sure. Do you have anyone you can stay with?'

'I could check into a hotel.'

Alice shook her head. 'An old friend would be better. Think of it as a chance to catch up with someone.'

There was no immediate reason to think Owen was in danger. But someone was looking for Rachel, and eventually they would figure out that the best way to find her was through her grandfather. Maybe she was being overly cautious. Maybe nothing would come of it. But she hadn't gotten within spitting distance of a century on this planet by trusting maybes.

'I suppose I could visit John. He lives up the coast and has been asking me to come up to play golf for some time.'

'Perfect. Go and visit John and leave Rachel with me.'

It took several more minutes before Owen agreed. When he went back to his apartment to make arrangements, Alice called Oliver.

'How's the ankle?' Oliver asked.

'Still attached. How's the writing?'

'Slow. Summer school holidays are never productive – unless you count being forced to watch the same video forty times.'

'I do not.'

'No, neither does Jennifer. What can I do for you?'

'What makes you think I want anything?'

'Oh sorry, my mistake. So how's life? Read any good books lately?'

'No, but I keep one of yours beside my bed. It helps me sleep.'

They both laughed. Oliver was new enough in his writing career to still be sensitive to criticisms about his books, but he knew Alice enjoyed his work because she'd told him. And you don't lie to family.

Not often anyway.

'Alright, I do have a favour to ask. Heard of a book called *The Second Chance of Joshua Messer*?'

There was a pause while Oliver thought, then he said, 'Yeah, I've heard of it. It came out recently. There's some mystery around who wrote it.'

'Presumably Rodney Strong wrote it,' Alice replied with just the smallest trace of sarcasm. 'The author on the cover.'

'Well, that's the thing. There is no Rodney Strong, at least according to the article I read. He's a ghost. And before you ask, no, not one of my ghosts. I mean the book was ghost-written by someone uncredited.'

Oliver had a unique gift involving the spirit world. Alice preferred to deal with things she could use one of her five senses on, but it had become quickly apparent that Oliver's ghosts were genuine and he was not some whack job.

'What does that mean exactly?' asked Alice.

'It means the author doesn't want to be identified so they've used a fake name, or it was written by a number of people and they've just picked one of the group to name.'

'Why would someone not want it known they've written a book?'

'It's not common but it does happen. Sometimes an author writes in a different genre and doesn't want to confuse people by putting out a completely different type of book. Sometimes they have a conservative job or life and want to write something racy.'

'There's nothing racy in this book.'

'No. I don't know why that author did it, I'm just giving you reasons why writers have done it in the past.'

'Could you find out why this author did it?'

There was a pause. 'Is it important? Wait, of course it is, otherwise you wouldn't have called. I'll see what I can do, but I can't promise anything.'

'Thank you, Oliver. And sooner would be better.'

Another pause. 'I'll call you back this afternoon,' he said before clicking off.

Next Alice rang Freda and asked her to visit. They made plans for Freda to come by in an hour's time.

Shortly afterwards there was a knock on the door. Alice checked the camera and saw Owen and Rachel waiting outside. Rachel did not look happy to be there.

'It's open,' Alice called.

Owen placed two suitcases just inside the door before moving aside to let Rachel in.

'John was thrilled to get my call. He's sending his son to pick me up. He'll be here in an hour.'

'I don't see why I can't stay at your place,' Rachel grumbled.

Owen gave her an exasperated look and opened his mouth to reply, but Alice jumped in quickly. 'Because I need some help while I'm hobbled by this silly injury.'

'You're in a rest home. You can call for help at the touch of a button.'

'This is *not* a rest home.'

'Wat is it then?' ask Rachel.

'It's a retirement village.'

'What's the difference? Old people live here.'

'I wouldn't be caught dead in a rest home,' replied Alice.

'You're weird.'

'You have no idea. Put your things in the spare room.'

Alice expected Rachel to argue some more but she settled for an indifferent shrug. Underneath that indifference Alice recognised fear and even a little relief.

'Perhaps I should call John and cancel…' Owen said.

'We'll be fine. No one will know she's here, which means we'll both be safe,' Alice replied reassuringly.

Owen didn't appear convinced, but he finally agreed on the condition that they regularly check in with him.

After he'd gone Alice and Rachel eyed each other up.

'Why are you helping me? Do you have the hots for my granddad?'

Alice winced at the crude term. 'I prefer older men,' she replied.

Rachel thought for a moment, struggling to do the math. 'But that would mean…'

'Yes,' Alice nodded. 'As soon as a hundred-year-old man moves into the Village I'll be all over him.'

It was Rachel's turn to wince at Alice's directness.

'I'm helping Owen because he's my friend, dear, and when friends are in trouble you help any way you can. Did you know Colin well?'

'No. I mean I thought we knew each other pretty well, but I only met him a few weeks ago.'

'And do you often agree to break into houses at the request of recent acquaintances?'

Rachel's face flushed. 'No. Of course I don't. Colin was in trouble so I was helping him. Like you said, you help a friend any way you can.'

'What sort of trouble was he in?'

'I don't know,' Rachel admitted. 'He said he owed someone money and he didn't have it. Stealing something for them was the only way to get enough money to pay off his debt.'

'Who did he owe?'

'He never said.'

Which was alright. Alice already knew, thanks to Kevin.

'Does the name Justin Fry mean anything to you?'

Rachel shook her head.

'Justin Fry owns an accounting firm in the city. He's worth about one hundred million dollars.'

Rachel whistled.

'And he made the majority of that illegally. You appear to have entangled yourself with the Wellington mob.'

NINƐ

Alice had been hoping for more of a reaction than the blank look Rachel gave her.

'Like the Italian mob?' she tried again.

Still the blank look.

'Mob? Organised crime? Gangsters? Haven't you seen any movies from the last decade?'

'I don't really watch movies,' Rachel replied.

'Television?'

Rachel shook her head.

'Books?'

Rachel shrugged. 'I haven't read a book since college, and only then because they wouldn't let me pass English until I did.'

'What do you do to relax?'

'Watch videos, post on social media, that sort of stuff.'

It was Alice's turn to shake her head. At her age, every generation was a younger generation, but this lot coming through now might as well be a different species.

'Okay then. Justin Fry is a very bad man who has a lot of other bad men working for him. It appears that Colin owed the head bad man some money and the working theory is he thought there as something about this book that would allow him to pay his debt.'

'You don't have to talk to me like I'm stupid.'

Then don't be stupid, Alice barely managed to stop herself from saying. It wasn't Rachel's fault she didn't know things. But it was her fault she didn't seem to *want* to know things. Alice could tell by the defiant expression on Rachel's face that telling her that was not going to be helpful.

'My apologies. I don't have all the details, but here's what I can surmise. If Colin was killed by Justin Fry for making a mistake, then that should be the end of it, and you are no longer in danger. However…' she hurried on as a Rachel looked relieved. 'If Colin talked about you before he died, then you might be considered a loose end, in which case you're still at risk. Another theory, which is a little flimsier, is that this has nothing to do with Justin Fry. You robbed a corrupt police officer of something she was attached to and she's not going to stop until both you and Colin are dead and she's retrieved the book. In summary, you either have no one after you, or you are being hunted by one of two very annoyed, dangerous people.'

Rachel slouched, picking nervously at her fingernails. 'I thought you were supposed to make me feel better.'

'I never said anything of the sort. I promised your grandfather I would keep you physically well. Your mental wellbeing wasn't discussed.'

'You're not like any old lady I've ever met.'

'Thank you.'

There was a knock on the door.

'Could you get that please,' Alice asked. 'Oh, and Rachel, the first rule of being in this apartment is that occasionally I might need to say things that aren't always honest. It's important you don't react.'

Rachel nodded uncertainly and went to answer the door.

Freda was carrying a large bag that Alice recognised from the day before. It looked like someone had some spare carpet from the 1970s and had decided to make it into a bag. The pattern was a mix of browns and greens and whites and a knitting needle stuck out of the open top.

'I'm so glad you called,' Freda said as she sank into the end of the couch, careful not to disturb Alice's ankle. 'Les is in the middle of recreating the Wairarapa Express and he can't work out why he has extra wheels. You don't want to talk about trains, do you?'

'Good grief, no. Trains are for getting you from point A to point B, and for complaining about when they don't run on schedule. End of topic.' The last train Alice had travelled on had been the Orient Express, and although she hadn't seen a murder or Hercule Poirot, there had been several other aspects that had made her eager to get off.

'Good,' Freda sighed with relief. 'I must say, Alice, you are surprising me this week. First attending the Knitting Festival. Then asking me to bring my knitting over today. Once could be put down to idle curiosity, but twice makes me suspicious.' Her eyes narrowed, but the crinkle showed she was joking. 'I've heard knitting can help keep your fingers nimble. That could be useful for all sorts of activities… like taking things that aren't yours?'

Alice stared at her. Freda and Les were even more law-abiding than Owen, good church folk who'd worked hard all their lives and had stolen nothing more than an extra kiss or few minutes in bed. Alice certainly hadn't told them anything about her past.

'Teresa may have let something slip after a second sherry one night,' Freda said mildly. 'Don't be angry with her, she was instantly mortified and begged me not to say anything to anyone. And I haven't.' Freda looked up and saw Rachel leaning against the kitchen bench, listening intently. 'Oh dear. I should say, I hadn't.'

'Rachel, if I suggest you go into your room and close the door, what are the chances you won't eavesdrop on the rest of the conversation?'

Rachel shrugged, 'Not great.'

'I'm so sorry.'

'It's fine, you haven't revealed anything other than a suspicion, have you, Freda?'

Freda shook her head.

'So no need to be upset about broken confidences.'

Freda's face relaxed.

On the other hand, I will need to have a word with Teresa, Alice thought.

Teresa was another resident at Silvermoon, and the richest, with the exception of perhaps Alice. She didn't flaunt her wealth, but there was definitely no mistaking it, from her jewellery to her fancy clothes. They were fancy enough to say, *look at me I have money*, but not so fancy as to say, *look at me I could buy this place*. Although she probably could.

Alice and Teresa had had a rocky start to their relationship, but eventually developed an easy friendship. The biggest issue Alice had with Teresa was her unfortunate taste for gossip.

'She really didn't tell me much,' Freda rushed to defend her friend.

'What exactly did she tell you?' said Alice.

'That you used to steal things.'

Alice scowled at the clumsy description.

'Oh dear, now I've offended you.'

Alice softened her face. 'I suppose technically Teresa is correct. Although that's like saying a Michelin-starred chef works in a kitchen.'

Freda's eyes popped. 'It's true?'

'It's a little more involved than that but yes technically it's true. Though, I never broke into people's houses and took things.' She looked directly at Rachel who suddenly found an imaginary stain on her T-shirt that required her attention.

And if they were talking technicalities then what she'd just said was true. She'd never *broken* into anyone's house. She'd usually been invited.

'I must say this is very exciting. I've never known anyone with a criminal background,' Freda said.

Alice held up her hand. 'Technically criminals are people who have been convicted of a crime. I was never caught.'

'Actually, criminals are also those who have committed a crime,' replied Freda. 'I looked it up before coming here.'

Bugger. I had hoped to spend the rest of my days here, but it seems I'll have to move, thought Alice.

'Anyway, knitting,' Alice changed the subject. 'I'd like to give it a go after all.'

'Wonderful. We can start with something simple and you'll be knitting your granddaughter a jersey in no time.'

Alice smiled at the thought of Amanda's response to receiving a hand-knitted jersey. She'd be worried about Alice's sudden burst of domesticity. Freda took the smile as a sign to continue.

'Here, you can borrow these.'

She handed Alice a pair of silver knitting needles.

'These are lovely,' Alice exclaimed. 'Although I really liked the ones with the little elephants at the ends that you showed me yesterday at the festival.'

Freda frowned. 'I like those ones as well, but after the festival I couldn't find them. I can't for the life of me understand where they've gone. Of course, I don't think you took them,' Freda hurriedly added.

I bet, Alice thought bitterly. That was one of the reasons she never told her friends at the Village what she used to do. Everyone confused the sophisticated art of con artistry with common thievery. 'No, of course not,' Alice smiled.

'I remember having them at the festival. I definitely put them back into my bag.'

'Maybe they fell out,' Alice suggested.

'I'm sure I would have noticed.'

'You're very observant.' Alice reassured her. 'Perhaps someone borrowed them while you weren't looking.'

'Yes, I'm sure that's it.' Freda looked relieved. 'I don't know why they wouldn't have just asked me... but maybe I was distracted and they needed them urgently. They'll show up.'

One of them might, anyway.

'I suppose they're unique enough that no one else would mistake them for theirs?'

Freda looked startled at the question. 'Well, I didn't have my name on them if that's what you're asking.'

Alice thought. 'Did you show them to anyone else yesterday?'

'Apart from you? No, I don't think... oh, wait...'

'Yes?'

'Rosie and Glenda came over after you left and were admiring the baby sweater I was knitting. But I'm sure neither of them would have taken my needles. Why would they?'

'Maybe they really wanted to knit,' Rachel piped up.

Alice and Freda turned to look at her, surprised to see she was still there.

'I suppose so,' Freda said dubiously.

Alice shot Rachel a warning look. 'I'm sure we'll find them, Freda. The important thing to remember is that you had them, then you didn't, and the last time you saw them was during the day at the knitting festival.'

'Yes, you're right. Anyway let's get started. I'll show you how to cast on.'

'I'll just go check out my room,' Rachel said.

'Oh no, you can learn to knit too. Good for your fingers like Freda said,' Alice told her.

'But I've got to, um, unpack.'

'Sit.' Alice pointed to the armchair opposite.

Reluctantly Rachel walked across the room and threw herself into the chair. Freda handed her a ball of light blue wool, and two pale pink knitting needles.

Alice actually enjoyed the next hour. By the end of the afternoon she had a basic rhythm going and even had a few lines of a scarf completed. Rachel couldn't keep the smile off her face when she held up her long line of blue.

'Shall I leave it here for you?' Freda suggested.

The smile vanished from Rachel's face and she shrugged indifferently. Alice couldn't help noticing her eyes drift to the wool in her lap.

Apparently she wasn't the only observant one.

'I don't need that wool for the next day or so. Just leave it on the table if you are too busy to get to it again. I'm sure the hospital will be happy to wait for the blankets.'

'Hospital?' Rachel asked.

'Oh yes, we're knitting blankets for the neonatal unit. They always need more.'

Alice kept her face blank as she marvelled at Freda's artful manipulation. She'd obviously had experience with her own children.

'Anyway, I can finish it if you don't get back to it.'

Freda turned to view Alice's efforts. 'Would you like to keep yours as well?'

Alice wanted to say, *yes of course*, but showing enthusiasm would be giving too much away. Instead she settled for a smile and nod of her head.

After Freda was gone Alice and Rachel stared at each other.

'Was she serious? About the hospital?' Rachel asked.

'I'd imagine so. Freda isn't the sort to lie.'

'Oh.' Rachel frowned and rubbed her face with her hand. 'I might go and lie down for a while. I'm pretty tired.'

She disappeared into her room. Alice noted that she took the knitting with her. She frowned as she wondered how Freda's knitting needle had travelled from the dining room into the back of Colin Craze's neck. And what had he been doing in the hour between parking his car and meeting with Rachel?

Alice sighed and scowled at her ankle. She needed answers and they weren't going to just drop into her lap while she sat in her apartment with her foot up. She needed to go out and find them.

TƐN

'Absolutely not!'

'Do you want to go out or not?' Vanessa asked calmly.

'Not that badly.'

'You haven't been resting, which means your injury is going to take longer to heal. Do you want to be laid up for even longer?'

Alice stared at the offending item Vanessa had brought into her apartment.

'But a wheelchair is so…'

'Oh, I'm really interested to see how you finish that sentence,' Vanessa said.

Alice glared at her. 'I've never used a wheelchair in my life. I'm not an invalid.'

'Oh really?' Vanessa eyed the bandaged ankle.

Alice grumbled some more before finally lowering herself into it. She caught Vanessa stifling a smile and almost stood up again, but the chair was quite comfortable. Then she thought of Vanessa having to push her around and all resistance evaporated. If she was going to sit in this humiliating thing, at least there was an upside.

It was her own fault. She had asked Vanessa for help, not thinking for a moment that she might suggest a wheelchair. Alice was kicking herself for not thinking it was an option. Of course, it was the only logical choice, apart from perhaps having Joshua carry her around on his back. Her lips twitched at that thought.

'Where are you going?' Rachel asked. She was in the kitchen making herself a sandwich with what little there was left in Alice's fridge.

Alice usually got a weekly food delivery but it wasn't due until tomorrow and she hadn't anticipated so many guests.

'Put the butter away when you're done,' Alice said.

'I was going to.'

'Good. And don't look through my things while I'm gone. In fact, Vanessa can you call Joshua. He can push me around and you can stay here and supervise Rachel.'

'You don't trust me,' Rachel said.

'Why do I have to stay?' Vanessa chimed in. 'I mean, it makes more sense that Joshua stays with her.'

'I don't need anyone to stay with me!'

'Because if Joshua stays then I'd have two strangers in my apartment instead of one.'

'But I always help you.' Vanessa's face showed her disappointment.

Alice silently cursed the slowness of her companion to understand the unspoken reason she wanted her to stay.

'I'll be fine by myself,' Rachel said, her eye roll adding the unspoken *I'm not a baby.*

'Of course, you will, but I have an issue with allowing people in my apartment when I'm not here,' Alice told her. 'Vanessa, please. It'll give you and Rachel a chance to get to know each other better.'

Finally Vanessa understood, and it was good that her back was to Rachel as there was nothing subtle about her reaction.

Fortunately, Joshua had a free hour between cleaning jobs and was more than happy to help out. 'As long as it doesn't involve any more midnight corpses.'

Alice had given a non-committal reply. She never planned on corpses, but she found that they popped up whether you wanted them to or not.

'Is it a good idea to leave those two alone?' Joshua asked as he wheeled Alice across the ground floor lobby. They were heading to the dining room. Alice considered it as good a place to start as any.

'They'll be fine. I hope,' she said. 'What's the worst that could happen?'

Joshua laughed. 'I don't know, but the look on their faces was like my mum's cat and the neighbour's dog when they're eyeing each other up. It usually ends with one chasing the other up the tree.'

'Joshua?'

'Yes.'

'For your own safety, I wouldn't use that analogy with Rachel and Vanessa in the room.'

Joshua thought about it, then nodded. 'I can see how that could be bad for me. So, what exactly are we looking for?'

Alice surveyed the empty room. Tables and chairs had been arranged for dinner, but for now Alice and Joshua were the only ones there. Alice wasn't actually sure what she hoped to find. The cleaning crew came in every morning before breakfast to vacuum and dust. Anything left behind after the knitting festival was long gone.

'Help me up,' Alice said.

'No way. Vanessa will kill me if she knew I let you walk around.'

'Who are you more afraid of?' Alice fixed him with a stare.

'Fine. But if she finds out, I'm blaming you.'

'Of course, dear.'

Alice shuffled around in a slow circle. She was trying to picture the room as it had been the previous morning, especially who was present. With a sigh she sank into the wheelchair and asked Joshua to push her over to the table where she'd sat with Freda. Once she had the chair positioned in the same spot as yesterday, Alice scanned the room again. It was no use. Nothing leapt out at her. She had to admit that she'd been too distracted by the pain in her ankle and the boredom of listening to everyone talk about knitting.

'Do you know where I can find Glenda, the new arts coordinator?' she asked Joshua.

'I'm not sure. She has an office in the Olympic complex, she could be there.' The Olympic complex was the nickname residents had for the building which housed the swimming pool and gym. There was also a games room and a massage therapy room.

'Then onwards, James.'

'What?'

'It means *let's go*,' Alice pointed to the exit door.

'Who's James?'

'Never mind. You're too young to understand.'

It was only a short distance in the bright sunlight from the main building to the Olympic complex, but to Alice it seemed to take forever. She fought the urge to hurry Joshua up. The longer she was outside, the more likely it was one of her friends would see her in the wheelchair. Then there'd be questions and looks filled with sympathy, all of which would make Alice want to kick something. That that's what put her in the wheelchair in the first place only made her madder.

They managed to get through the doors of the complex without being seen. And then her luck ran out. As they were coming in, Teresa appeared from the corridor that ran through the middle of the building. She was carrying a small gym bag in one hand and a towel in the other, although her hair and make-up were so perfect it seemed unlikely she'd used either item.

'Alice! Is everything alright?'

'Fine, Teresa. I was just going a little stir crazy in my apartment and this is the only way Vanessa would let me out.' She adopted a woeful expression and Teresa laughed.

'If I didn't know you better, I would believe your sad sack look.'

'Well, what about you?' Alice shot back. 'Don't tell me you've taken up physical exercise.'

'You don't think it's important to stay in shape at our age?' asked Teresa with an innocent look.

Alice returned it with a sceptical one of her own.

Teresa glanced at her hands, then smiled ruefully. 'Alright you caught me. There's a new water aerobics instructor.'

'What's his name?'

'Simon. He's only fifteen years younger than me and quite a dish.'

Alice sighed. Teresa's wealth made her a potential magnet for charlatans and con artists. She would have to check this Simon out. Teresa could generally take care of herself, but Alice considered herself the Village expert on shady characters. There was no harm in sizing Simon up.

'Do you wear your make-up in the pool?' she asked.

'Of course,' Teresa looked shocked. 'You don't put your head under for water aerobics, so no need to go *au naturel*. I assume you're involved with the dead body they found yesterday.'

'Mrs Garvey' Joshua exclaimed.

Alice held up her hand to indicate it was alright. '*Involved* is a strong word. I have some knowledge of what's going on, but I trust the police will get to the bottom of it.'

Before Teresa could ask a follow up question a man walked up behind her. He appeared to be in his late fifties, his face was rugged and handsome and he clearly took care of himself. When he smiled she had to admit that if she'd been forty years younger she'd be tempted. She hadn't seen him before so assumed this was the reason for Teresa's sudden quest for fitness.

'Hello, ladies.' He acknowledged Joshua with the barest of nods.

Alice saw Joshua's hand tighten on the handle of the wheelchair.

'I'm Simon Hall. Nice work today, Teresa.' He offered his hand and when Alice took it he shook gently before letting go. Alice approved. She'd always said you could tell a lot about a person by the way they shook hands, especially with a woman. Some men avoided it all together, others squeezed hard in an attempt to exert dominance. The gentlemen treated everyone equally. Alice should have been reassured by this initial gesture, but her gut instinct told her to watch Simon closely.

'This is my friend, Alice,' Teresa said.

'Pleasure to meet you, Alice. Teresa, I'll see you tomorrow morning. Enjoy your day, ladies.'

Teresa watched him go and Alice watched her. She was definitely smitten, and smitten people were always less cautious.

'Isn't he handsome?' Teresa said.

'Mmm,' Alice replied.

'Anyway, back to this body you found. I don't know how you do it, Alice. You always seem to be in the wrong place at the wrong time.'

'Or the right time, depending on your point of view,' Alice replied.

'Rumour has it you were there as well, Joshua,' Teresa turned to him.

'Teresa, I'd love to stay and chat, but I left Vanessa in my apartment and I'm worried she might break something if I'm away too long. Or worse, tidy up. We must be on our way.'

Teresa made her promise to tell her all about it later before exiting through the main door.

'Why didn't you want her talking to me about finding the body?' Joshua asked.

'Teresa's worst fault is a propensity for gossip. Telling her anything would be the same thing as taking out a full-page ad in the local paper. The less she knows, the less she can tell.'

'Oh.'

Joshua pushed Alice down the corridor and stopped outside a door. The sign said Glenda Murphy, Arts Coordinator. He knocked and a muffled voice said, 'Come in'. Joshua opened the door to reveal a tiny room, barely big enough for a desk and two chairs.

'Hello, come on in,' Glenda said. 'I'm afraid there isn't much room, but at least I can tell my children I have my own office. I meant to say the other day that I saw you at the knitting festival. It's great that you came, but I noticed you weren't actually knitting.'

Alice shrugged. 'It's not a hobby I ever picked up. I was there for moral support and scintillating conversation.'

'Indeed. Well, the babies can't wear scintillating conversation but if it made the ladies more productive then I approve.'

I don't need your approval. Alice gritted her teeth. 'Do you knit?'

'Of course,' Glenda replied. 'My mother made sure I learned. I'd like to think it was out of maternal instinct but the truth is money was tight when we were growing up, and we got by wearing knitted jerseys for years.'

Alice knew something about difficult childhoods. She never took her current good fortune for granted.

'I'm not sure I'd be able to pick it up now,' Alice said. 'I'm so absent minded these days.'

'Oh?'

'Yes, Freda loaned me a pair of knitting needles, white ones with a small figure of an elephant on the end. Anyway she's misplaced them and

I worry that I might have put them somewhere without remembering.' She adopted a look that was concern mixed with anxiety, but she watched Glenda carefully.

'Oh dear. Have you asked Freda?' Glenda said.

'No, I haven't.' Alice dropped her eyes in shame. 'I didn't want to admit that I'd lost them.'

She flicked her eyes back up in time to see something fleetingly cross Glenda's face. Was it relief? She couldn't be completely sure.

'I'm sure they'll turn up. You probably just put them down somewhere. I'm sure if you explain to Freda how you lost them she would be absolutely fine.'

Alice smiled. 'I'm sure you're right. Anyway, I just wanted to meet you and say hello.'

Glenda bobbed her head up and down and pulled a piece of paper out of the top drawer of her desk. She passed it to Alice. It was a list of dates and events.

'Just in case you lost the last one.'

It looked the same list Glenda had given her when she'd visited Alice's apartment, but Alice said thank you and Joshua wheeled her back down the corridor and out into the sunshine.

'Thoughts?' Alice asked.

'About what?' replied Joshua.

'About Glenda.'

'What about her?'

'Head to Charlie's please.' She waited until he started pushing her towards the café before continuing. 'What are your impressions of Glenda? Is she trustworthy? Honest? Duplicitous?'

'Oh, well, I wasn't really paying attention to her.'

'What were you doing?'

Joshua didn't reply and Alice turned her head to see him wearing an embarrassed look.

'Spit it out,' she said.

'I was thinking about a girl.'

'It's been a long time since anyone called me a girl. Thank you.'

'I didn't mean…'

'Relax,' Alice laughed. 'I'm just toying with you. We can talk about your lady friend later, but for now, remember this. Always pay attention to what's happening in front of you. Nothing is more important than the information you can find out from the room you're in.'

'So what did you learn?'

They reached the café and Joshua manoeuvred the wheelchair next to a table, before sitting down on a chair opposite.

Alice sighed. The art of observation was on the way to extinction. There would be fewer problems in the world if everyone just asked the right questions and kept their eyes open. (Although she had to admit if more people had done that while she had been working she wouldn't have been half as successful as she was.)

'Is Glenda an only child?'

Joshua stared at her. 'How am I supposed to know?'

'She told you. She said her mother taught her how to knit because money was tight "when *we* were growing up". Not when *I* was growing up. So she has at least one sibling.'

'Oh my gosh, how on earth did you notice that one word?'

'Because I was listening for it,' Alice snapped. 'Now pay attention. Glenda is married, she wears a simple wedding band, no sparkle, and her necklace was nice but plain. What does that tell us?'

Joshua looked like his teacher had just announced a pop quiz in a subject he'd never heard of. 'That she likes wearing jewellery?'

Alice sighed, then caught herself before she could say anything caustic. It wasn't Joshua's fault he didn't notice the important things. Probably had his head filled with useless things like chemistry and social studies, or whatever else they taught in schools these days. Vanessa had been just as slow to pick up this skill. Alice blamed phones. Her granddaughter had tried showing her all the wonderful ways that phones could make her life better, but all Alice could see was more ways to waste what little time she had left trying to remember which application did what. She mainly used her phone for making calls, occasionally send a text message, and most importantly to check the hidden camera outside her front door.

'This girl you like. Does she wear jewellery?'

Joshua scrunched up his face as he tried to remember. 'Yeah, she has this ring on her right hand. And earrings of course.'

'There's no of course. Not every woman wears earrings. What sort?'

'Sort? Um, I didn't know they came in sorts.'

Alice resisted the urge to reach across the table and slap him. 'Are they small studs, little dots of metal, or loops, or dangly ones?'

'Oh. Right, I get you. They're gold studs.'

'There you go. You've just learned something about her.'

'I have?'

'She wears practical earrings, she's sensible, but they're gold so they aren't just something she threw on, she took time to choose them.'

'But, they're just… earrings.'

'Of course you're right. Don't listen to the ramblings of an old woman. Could you be a dear and get me a coffee? A trim flat white, please. Just put it on my account. And get yourself something too.'

The good thing about Charlie's café being part of the Silvermoon Retirement Village was that the owners had set up a system so residents could charge purchases to their account and pay it off at the end of the month. Alice didn't usually use her account as she didn't like debt, even if it was just for a coffee and muffin. But today she hadn't intended to come to the café so didn't have any money.

While she waited for Joshua to come back with her coffee, Alice closed her eyes and enjoyed the feeling on the sun on her face. Her brain was still running at speed. Glenda knew something about the knitting needles. She'd jumped on the opportunity that Alice gave her to suggest it was Alice herself who lost them. But what could possibly be her motive to kill Colin? It seemed unlikely.

'Alice?'

She opened her eyes. Joshua was standing over her, looking concerned.

'Stop that. Enough people look at me like I've got both feet in the grave. I closed my eyes to think, not because I'm heading toward the light.'

'Er, okay, sorry I was just going to say they were out of trim milk so I got you regular. I hope that's alright.'

'Oh. That's fine, thank you.'

He put her drink on the table in front of her and sat opposite. 'The murder is all everyone is talking about in there.'

Alice turned to look through the window. Half of the tables were occupied and by the look of the hand waving and excited expressions there were some animated conversations going on.

'Hear anything useful?' she asked.

Joshua shrugged. 'Nobody knew anything, just that the police were here in the middle of the night and there was a body. General agreement seems to be that it wasn't a resident who was killed.'

Before Alice could ask another question, Joshua's cell phone rang. He checked the screen before answering it. A one-sided conversation followed and when he hung up he looked worried.

'Tracy wants me to come to her office. She says it's to discuss last night.'

'When?'

'Now.'

'Alright, let's go.'

'I'll take you home first,' Joshua said as he stood up.

'Not on your life. You were only there last night because of me. If there's going to be trouble because of it, then I'm going to make sure it doesn't come down on you.'

'Alice, you—'

'Zip it. Get the coffees to go.'

She was pleased to note he didn't try any further argument.

'You don't have to come with me.'

'Oh yes I do.'

This will be fun.

ELEVEN

Tracey's office was located down a short corridor behind the concierge desk in the main building. Alice had only been inside once before, soon after she came to live at Silvermoon. At the time, she'd been surprised at how big it was. Big enough for a desk, chairs, and a couch. On the wall behind the desk were two framed diplomas proudly proclaiming Tracey's credentials in management.

Tracey was surprised to see Alice. 'This is an employment matter, Alice. It would be better for you to wait outside, or perhaps Joshua could take you back to your apartment. I'm sure you're tired.' Which summed up Tracey's thoughts on old people. They must constantly be tired and need to rest.

'That's alright, if I need to I'll nod off in my chair,' Alice replied.

'I really think it would be better for this discussion to be private,' Tracey pressed on.

'If it's alright, I would like Alice to stay,' Joshua said.

'Why?'

'Vanessa made me promise to take care of her while she was out, and I'd like to keep an eye on her.'

Tracey frowned. 'Very well, as long as you understand that confidential matters pertaining to your employment will be discussed. If you're comfortable with Alice being present, then that's fine.'

Joshua nodded and looked nervously at Alice who smiled reassuringly back at him.

'Last night you were on the grounds after hours. Vanessa persuaded me that we needed to trial some additional security because of break ins at other retirement facilities. Is that an accurate synopsis?'

'Yes ma'am.'

'Your actions last night have put management in a difficult position. We are a business, one that relies entirely on people wanting to come and live here. Although you were authorised to be here after dark, you are not a security guard. The liability alone makes this awkward. Then there is the fact that we cannot possibly be seen to employ a murder suspect.'

'What? I didn't kill anyone.'

'Which is why I said *suspect*. It's a matter of image. I'm sorry, Joshua, but I have no choice but to immediately terminate your employment.'

'But…but…' Joshua stammered.

'That's not entirely true,' Alice said.

The other two turned to look at her.

'You do have a choice. You could choose to stand behind your staff. After all, Joshua had to undergo a police check to get his job here.'

'Yes, well—'

'And he's loved by the residents. I assume you've had nothing but glowing reviews of his work.'

'Of course, his standard of work is not in question, it's—'

'A matter of image.'

'Exactly,' replied Tracey.

'Like the image of an employer who doesn't take care of their employees?'

'That's not what—'

'The fact is there is no question that Joshua had anything to do with the body last night, other than being the one to find it. He could be in shock. You should be offering him counselling. Firing him could turn into a public relations nightmare, don't you think? *Silvermoon Retirement Village fires traumatised employee.*'

'I…I don't see why the press would be involved.'

'It happens so easily these days. The wrong word to the wrong person and suddenly it's all over… the face-thing. What's it called?'

'Book,' Joshua said.

Something in Alice's mind shifted. 'Facebook.' Alice beamed at Tracey. 'I'll ask my granddaughter. She has Facebook.'

Tracey's shoulders slumped. 'I can't have him seen working, though. At least until all this is resolved.'

'I understand,' Alice nodded. 'So Joshua will be working for me in the meantime. As you can see,' she tapped the chair, 'getting around is a bit tricky for me. I need a strong young person to help, and I can't take Vanessa away from her duties every time I want a bit of sun.'

'That's not…I need to remove him from Village property.'

Alice sighed. She could see this conversation dragging out. She decided to end it. 'Joshua, could you wait outside for a moment please.'

Joshua and Tracey both looked confused, but he stood up and left the room.

'There's something you should know, dear,' Alice began.

Three minutes later Joshua was called back into the room, where Tracey informed him that he would be suspended from his duties until the police investigation was over, however was free to work for Alice. Her face was paler than usual and she spoke with a subdued tone.

'What did you say to her?' Joshua asked in the elevator to Alice's apartment.

'Never you mind.'

'You didn't…threaten her, did you?'

'Look at me. Do you honestly think I could threaten anyone?' Alice shrunk down to make herself appear smaller. The elevator doors opened and Joshua pushed her onto the landing.

'I suppose not,' he smiled.

They looked at her front door as the sound of raised voices came from the other side.

Quickly Alice unlocked and pushed open the door. Inside the apartment they found Vanessa and Rachel standing nose to nose, mid-argument.

'That's stupid,' Rachel snapped.

'No, you're stupid.'

'What's going on?' Alice had to raise her voice to make sure she was heard.

Both girls turned and immediately stepped away from each other. 'Well?'

'Nothing,' Vanessa said calmly.

'Nothing!' Rachel glared at her. 'Do you know what she just said to me?'

'Obviously not, as I wasn't here. Vanessa?' Alice said.

'It's simple—'

'Wait.' Alice climbed slowly to her feet and shuffled over to the couch. The first step was the hardest as her ankle had stiffened up, but she managed to get there without falling. As soon as she was seated with her injured foot up on a pillow, she waved for Vanessa to continue.

'It's simple—'

'You're simple!'

'What are you? Twelve?' Vanessa sniffed.

Rachel's face turned a lovely shade of purple.

'Oh, sit down both of you. You're giving me a headache.' She waited until they were seated as far away from each other as they could before she continued.

'Alright. Rachel, tell me what you were arguing about.'

'She,' Rachel scowled at Vanessa, 'said that all this was my fault, and that if I had better taste in men I wouldn't be in this mess.'

Alice raised an eyebrow at Vanessa who shrugged.

'Words to that effect,' she confirmed.

'Do *you* think this is my fault?' Rachel demanded of Alice.

'Mostly.' Rachel looked like she was about to erupt again so Alice held up a hand and continued. 'Are you seriously trying to suggest that you should take none of the blame for this?'

Rachel opened and closed her mouth a few times, then slumped into her chair.

'Precisely. Now Vanessa might not have used the most tactful language, but she has a good point.'

Rachel stood up abruptly. 'I'm going to take a shower.' She disappeared into her bedroom, reappearing a few moments later with a handful of clothes and a towel. She closed the bathroom door and they heard the water running.

'Did you have to be so blunt?' Alice asked.

'I was just doing what you asked me to do,' protested Vanessa.

'You asked her to make Rachel mad?' Joshua asked.

'Explain.'

'You left me with her to see if I could find out anything else. Yes, it took me a while to get your message, but I figured it out eventually. The only problem is she doesn't like me. Don't know why, I'm very likeable.' She flashed a smile at Joshua who grinned back. 'So I thought I would take a leaf from your book, Alice.' Her smiled broadened. 'I annoyed her into a fight in the hope that she would let something slip.'

'Very nice. Did you get any information?'

Vanessa winked. 'I think I might have to use that technique again. It was fun.'

'Don't gloat, dear. I'll be the judge of whether you've found out anything useful.'

'Spoilsport,' Vanessa muttered. 'While she was ranting about how she's an excellent judge of character and how I'm a miserable old hag that no one will ever love, she let slip that this wasn't the first time she and Colin had… what would you call it, Alice? Pulled a job?'

'I would never use the phrase *pulled a job*,' Alice scowled. 'It's so… common.'

'Huh?' Joshua looked confused.

'It's an inside joke,' Vanessa told him.

Joshua looked like he had more questions but Alice got in first.

'What else did she tell you?'

Vanessa shrugged. 'Nothing. She shut up pretty quick when she realised what she'd said. When I pressed her that's when the shouting started.'

'The young lady lied? I'm shocked.' Alice smiled.

'You're not mad?' asked Joshua.

'I'm not surprised. Rachel strikes me as someone who has become accustomed to the necessity of lying on a regular basis.'

'I thought her parents were liberal with their rules. Why would she have had to lie?'

'They are,' Alice said. 'At least according to Owen, but then I suspect his style of parenting would be considered draconian by today's standards. The truth is probably somewhere in the middle. Besides upbringing doesn't necessarily have anything to do with one's ability to deceive. Sometimes it's genetic.'

'Is that what it is for you? Genetic?' asked Vanessa.

'More like well-practised.'

'I have no idea what you two are talking about,' complained Joshua.

'As it should be, dear.'

'What are you going to do about Rachel lying to you?'

Alice cocked her head to the side and listened. The shower had turned off and while she waited for Rachel to emerge from the bathroom she considered Joshua's question. The problem with liars, as she unfortunately knew all too well, was that if you confronted them their first instinct was to lie more.

'Alice?'

'I'm going to make her a cup of tea.'

TWELVE

'What's this?'

Rachel was staring at the cup in front of her as if the steaming liquid was some strange concoction she'd never seen before.

'Tea,' replied Alice. 'First brewed in the sixteenth century, sometimes served with cookies. Like these.' She opened the round old fashioned biscuit tin next to her teacup and slid it over the bench to Rachel. There were four kinds of cookies and she made a silent bet with herself which one Rachel would choose. Sure enough, a round chocolate-covered Toffee Pop was quickly devoured.

Alice waited until Rachel was chewing the last bite of cookie before she casually said, 'Men, eh? Always getting us in trouble.'

Rachel stopped mid chew. She nodded.

'I knew this boy once who made my heart flutter. All Robert had to do was smile and I'd agree to do anything for him. One day he told me someone had taken something of his mother's. Stolen it right out of her handbag. He asked me to help get it back for him, because he knew who took it. Mark Carrington. Mark was the local…alley cat, I suppose you'd call him. Dirty, mean, would soon as spit on your hand than take anything offered. He was eleven. We were nine. I was scared of him. Everyone was, even some of the adults. But I agreed to help my friend.'

'Because he made your heart flutter,' said Rachel.

'Because he made my heart flutter.' Alice smiled. 'But I had another reason as well.'

'What?'

'Later. Anyway despite looking and acting like he lived on the streets, Mark actually lived in one of the nicer houses in Thorndon. They even had a maid. So we knew where to find him. We just needed a plan to get inside.'

'What did Mark take?'

'A brooch. Robert told me it was his mother's favourite piece of jewellery and she was distraught at having lost it. The plan was pretty simple. I would go to the front door and distract whoever was home, while Robert snuck in the back and searched for the brooch. I could be pretty charming, and it was easy to come up with some story about losing my hair ribbon in their garden. I think I had everyone looking for it with me, including Mark. He might have been wild and mean outside the house, but when his father sternly told him to help he jumped right to it. Eventually we found the ribbon and I thanked them and left.'

'You found it? I thought the ribbon was an excuse.'

'It was, but I'd planted it in a rose bush before I knocked on the door.' Alice smiled to herself. 'Even back then I knew the devil was in the detail. I met Robert in the park down the road and he proudly showed me the knife he'd stolen.'

'Knife? I thought it was a brooch.'

'So did I. It turned out Robert was worse than Mark. He hid his meanness on the inside. There was no brooch. Robert had seen Mark buy a brand new pocketknife and he was jealous, so he made up the whole story so he could steal it.'

'That's horrible. What an ar—'

Alice held up her hand. 'Accurate, but it was a long time ago so don't waste a good swear word on him.'

'What did you do?'

'What could I do? I was an accomplice. If I told anyone, Robert would say the whole thing had been my idea, that I'd wanted to steal the knife. I'm sorry to say, back then boys were believed a lot more readily than girls. I couldn't do anything. Except learn from my mistake.'

'Trusting a boy,' Rachel nodded.

'No,' Alice sighed, 'letting my emotions dictate my actions. I can't say I never did it again, but it opened my eyes to what it meant to trust someone. Like you trusted Colin.'

Rachel quickly picked up her cup and took a sip to hide her face.

'He asked you to break into a house and steal something. There's a certain level of trust that goes with that. Him asking; you agreeing. That's a level of trust that isn't usually given quickly.'

'Who says I trusted him?'

'Whether you did or not is by the by. I'm talking about him trusting you. He obviously trusted you enough to confide his plan to break into the house and steal the book. Unless…' Alice adopted a thoughtful look, watching Rachel out of the corner of her eye to see if she'd take the bait.

'Unless what?'

'Well, it's a bit mean to say and I'm sure it's not the case, but… unless he didn't trust you. Unless he was manipulating you.'

Rachel slammed her cup down, her eyes blazing. Hot tea sloshed from her cup onto her hand. She snatched the hand away and clutched it to her chest, grimacing with pain.

'Run it under cold water,' Alice said.

Rachel looked like she was about to argue, but then the pain, and hopefully common sense, took over and she quickly rounded the counter and turned on the cold water tap. She winced as water hit her skin and started to pull her hand back. Alice grasped it and forced it back under.

'You were about to say…?'

'He wasn't manipulating me,' Rachel scowled.

'It's nothing to be ashamed of, dear. It happens to us all at some point.'

'Not me! I was the one in control. If anything, I was manipulating him.'

'Come now, dear, I appreciate hubris as much as the next old lady, but it's nothing to be ashamed about.'

'I didn't fall for anything. He thought I was there to help him, but I was going to double cross Colin. That's why I let him leave the house first. Shannon and I had it all worked out.'

'Shannon?'

Rachel clamped her mouth shut and her eyes darted around the room.

'Shannon is the police officer,' Alice guessed. 'The one who's house you broke into. Only you didn't break into it, did you? She let you in.'

Rachel's face drained of colour and she glanced at the front door as if readying herself for a dash for freedom.

'Okay, off you go. Good luck,' Alice waved at the door.

'What?'

'You're not a prisoner, Rachel. You're here so I can help you, but you've not been honest with me so obviously you don't want my help. There's the door. Good luck.'

Rachel licked her lips nervously, her eyes moving between Alice and the front door. 'I can just go?'

'Of course. I'll just tell Owen that you're way smarter than I am, and that you decided you could handle the police, the gangsters, and the murderer by yourself.' Alice patted Rachel's arm.

Rachel actually started towards the door, making Alice wonder if she'd pushed too hard. But halfway across the room, she stopped. Alice waited and after a moment Rachel turned, with fear and uncertainty on her face.

'What do I do?' she asked in a wavery voice.

'Make better decisions,' Alice replied. 'The first of which is to come back, finish your tea, and tell me the truth. The whole truth this time.'

The whole truth took twenty minutes and by the time Rachel finished Alice had to summon all her self-control to avoid wasting a good many swear words on her.

'You won't tell my granddad?'

I think your granddad would be horrified, Alice thought. 'No, I think it's best kept between us.'

'She did what?' Vanessa stared in amazement.

Alice didn't feel guilty including Joshua and Vanessa in the definition of 'us'. They were already involved and it seemed right that they were kept informed. Unfortunately, Rachel hadn't agreed and had immediately stormed to her room in a huff when Alice had announced her intention to tell them.

'She made her own deal,' Alice repeated.

'With the person whose house she was robbing.'

'Apparently our budding thief decided she might get a better deal if she knocked on the door of the house the day before the break-in to tell the owner of the plan.'

'I don't know much about that sort of thing but it doesn't sound like a good plan to tell the person you're robbing about it before you rob them,' said Joshua.

'Colin thought he had her under his thumb and she didn't like that. She thought she could get a reward by ratting him out.'

'What went wrong?'

'Unfortunately, she didn't know that the owner of the house was a police officer, who promptly threatened to arrest her on the spot. Our little idiot immediately spilled everything including, I suspect, her lunch.'

'Why wasn't she arrested?'

Alice turned to Vanessa. 'Because Officer Shannon decided to let the robbery take place as planned, and "catch them" in the act.' Alice wagged her fingers in air quotes. 'Did I use that right?'

Vanessa gave her a thumbs-up.

'Shannon didn't explain her entire plan to Rachel so I don't know exactly why, but I have a theory.' Alice lapsed into silence while she considered, and after a short while realised the other two were staring at her. 'What? Oh yes. Well one theory is that Shannon needed something over Colin, possibly to turn him into a confidential informant. Colin wasn't the smartest but he had some shady friends, so having someone spying on them might have been handy for her.' Even as she said it aloud Alice was discarding that theory as unlikely.

'And the other theory, the one you like more?' Vanessa asked.

Alice gave her a sour look, unhappy to have been read so easily. 'Theory two – Officer Shannon is a dirty cop and wants some information on the man Colin owes money to. Perhaps she thought she could leverage him.'

'That sounds a little like both options are the same,' Joshua commented.

'No,' Vanessa replied. 'One is all official, the second is off the books. Am I right?'

Alice nodded.

'I feel kind of sorry for him.' Joshua frowned. 'Either way, Colin was stuffed.'

'So it would seem,' Alice agreed.

'So what went wrong?' Vanessa repeated.

'Colin was slipperier than Shannon thought and he escaped out the back door. Meanwhile Rachel panicked so she grabbed a book from the kitchen table and ran for it.'

'How did Rachel know which book to take? Surely there was more than one book in the house.'

'I think that might be Rachel's worse piece of luck. There was a whole bookshelf of books, but this one was out on the table. Rachel was too scared to stop and take a proper look but she said it looked like Shannon was going through the book and making notes.'

'What do you think?' asked Vanessa. 'She was a petrified kid in a highly stressful situation. Maybe what she saw was a shopping list.'

'I know what I saw!'

They all turned to see Rachel standing in the bedroom doorway. She'd obviously been listening and her face was red with anger. 'And I'm not a kid!'

Alice held up her hand to stop the next outburst. 'If you two want to go at it again do it outside. Having you snap like puppies squabbling over a chew toy is tiring and distracting.'

Everyone stared.

'Puppies?' repeated Vanessa in a strangled voice.

'You'd prefer cats?'

'I'd prefer not to be compared to any animal, thanks.'

'But she called me—' Rachel started.

Joshua interrupted. 'It occurs to me that you're a smart person, Rachel.'

Rachel stared at him in amazement. 'I am,' she said firmly.

'And a smart person would know when to be quiet.'

Alice watched Rachel trying to work through that statement and come out the other side with some dignity.

'I'm sure of what I saw,' she said quietly to Alice.

'Of course, dear,' Alice replied.

Her eyes went to the book on her coffee table and as if on cue her phone rang. Not her cell phone, the landline. The display indicated it was the concierge desk.

'Mrs Atkinson?' came the bubbly voice of Vanessa's colleague Molly. 'There's a visitor for you in the lobby. Shall I send them up?'

Alice looked at Vanessa. Much as she enjoyed her company and needed her help, things ran much more smoothly when she was at her post.

'Absolutely not. Who is it, Molly?'

'Oh yes, sorry. It's Detective Miller'

'Then by all means send her up.'

Alice hung up. 'We're about to get a nosy visitor. Take the book, go into the spare room and close the door,' she said to Rachel. 'Joshua, go with her.'

'Who's here?' Rachel immediately stood up, panic on her face.

'Just go into the room and be quiet and everything will be fine.'

Joshua immediately did as Alice asked and Rachel followed a moment later.

'Police?' Vanessa asked,

'How did you know?'

'They'd be the only reason you'd want Rachel and Joshua to disappear.'

Alice nodded approvingly. 'Get the door will you, please, Vanessa?'

There hadn't been a knock, but by the time Vanessa crossed the room and opened the front door the elevator doors were opening.

'Vanessa, good to see you again,' she heard Judith say.

Vanessa stepped aside to allow the visitor to enter, and Alice saw there were visitors, plural. Judith was accompanied once again by a uniformed constable. Not Constable Patel this time.

'Alice, how's the ankle? I just had a couple more questions, if you don't mind. This is Senior Police Constable Jamieson.'

The constable smiled and crossed the distance between them with her hand outstretched. 'Call me Shannon,' she said.

THIRTEEN

'Pleased to meet you,' Alice replied without missing a beat. 'Why don't you sit down.'

Vanessa retook her seat on the couch next to Alice, while the two police officers sat in the armchairs opposite.

'How can I help you?'

'We just had some follow up questions about the night you found the victim,' Judith said.

'Of course. Would you like something to drink? A cup of tea?'

'No thank you,' Judith replied, all business. She nodded to Shannon who pulled out a notebook and pen. Alice didn't miss the narrowed eyes she shot at her superior. Here was someone who didn't like being told what to do.

'Now you said you were going for a walk when you came across Joshua Leota and the deceased.'

'That's right.'

'Where was Mr Leota in relation to the victim?'

'I'm not sure I understand your question,' Alice replied.

'Was he standing over the victim, kneeling next to him?' asked Judith.

'Oh, I see. He was standing next to the body.'

Shannon scribbled something on her pad, then leaned forward. 'Was he carrying anything?'

Alice pretended to think while she considered the purpose of the question.

'Well, it was a little dark. He could have had something small in his hand, but I don't think so.'

Shannon sat back in her chair and mostly managed to keep the disappointed look off her face. Alice decided to push back a little.

'Do you think Joshua stole something from the man?' She widened her eyes in shock.

'We're exploring all options,' Judith assured her.

'I definitely would have noticed something big, like a bag or book or something like that.' Alice was looking at Judith when she spoke, but saw Shannon flinch when she mentioned the book.

'Why did you say a book?' Shannon said.

Alice waved at the bookshelf behind her. 'I was looking at the bookshelf. I read a lot.' She smiled at Shannon.

Shannon stared back for a moment, before she relaxed into her chair and returned the smile.

'After you found the victim, was Joshua out of your sight for any period of time?' Judith asked.

'Why all the questions about Joshua? Surely you don't think *he* murdered anyone,' protested Vanessa.

'We can't discount anything until we have all the facts.'

'That's crazy.'

'I appreciate that Joshua is your friend, Vanessa, but it's my job to ask these questions.'

'Fine, but I don't like it.'

Alice gave her arm a squeeze.

'Have you seen anyone hanging around the Village recently. Someone new or unfamiliar?' Shannon asked.

'People come and go all the time,' Alice replied. 'Family visiting, that sort of thing. It would be hard to know if anyone was out of place.'

'What about you?'

Vanessa laughed. 'Do you know how many visitors come to the Village every day?'

'What about the victim? Had he been here before?'

'I don't know what he looked like,' Vanessa shrugged. 'I never saw the body.'

Judith pulled her phone out, tapped the screen then turned it around to show Vanessa a candid photo of Colin – luckily taken while he was alive.

'I've never seen him before.'

'What about you?' Judith passed the phone to Alice. 'Had you seen him before finding his body?'

Alice shook her head and handed the phone back. 'No. Do you think he'd been on the grounds before?'

Judith put her phone back into her jacket pocket. 'We spoke with the girl downstairs earlier. Are you aware that Mr Craze was at the village earlier in the day, and that it was Joshua Leota that escorted him to his car. Apparently they had words.'

Alice's eyes widened. 'Really I had no idea. Why would that man come here? Is he related to someone who lives here?'

'Not a relative, no. But it's possible he was here to see someone he knew,' Judith confirmed.

'Oh dear. How terrible for them.'

'If you don't mind me saying, finding a body doesn't seem to have affected you too much,' Shannon said. Her tone suggested she expected old ladies to be quivering messes on the couch at the sight of blood.

Alice fixed her with a steady gaze. 'Occupational hazard. At my age I'm closer to death than life.'

'Actually,' Judith retrieved her phone again and brought up another picture, 'you were at the knitting thing the other day. Do you recognise this?'

She showed the picture first to Vanessa, who shook her head, then to Alice. The photo was a close-up of Freda's knitting needle, undoubtedly the one found in the back of Colin's neck. While she peered at the picture, Alice's eyes flicked to Judith's fingers gripping the phone. Her fingertips were white.

As Alice leaned back in her seat she casually shook her head, taking in Shannon's posture and Judith's face as she moved her head. Suddenly she sat straighter. 'Actually yes! Sorry, I do recognise it. It was at the knitting festival. I saw someone using one just like it. It has a little elephant on it, doesn't it?'

A brief look of disappointment passed between the police officers and Alice knew she'd passed whatever sort of test they'd set.

'Do you know who it belonged to?'

'I think it was Freda's. She was sitting at the same table as me. Where did you find it?'

Judith put her phone away and Shannon closed her notebook.

'Just one more question, Alice,' Judith said casually. 'Do you know where Joshua Leota is right now?'

'Should I?'

'Aunt Tracey said you were employing him until our investigation is resolved.'

'Yes, he's helping me to get around, but that doesn't mean I'm his keeper. As I am at home, I didn't need him for a few hours. I assume he's at university, or at home with his mother.'

'Vanessa? What about you?'

Vanessa shrugged. 'No idea. He's not working for me.'

'Alright, well thank you. We'll be in touch if we need anything further.'

Vanessa saw the visitors out the door then rounded on Alice.

'How could you tell them the knitting needle belonged to Freda!'

'They already knew. It was a test, to see if I would lie to them.'

The spare bedroom door opened and Joshua and Rachel came out.

'How could you possibly know that?' demanded Vanessa.

'Judith. Fingers.'

Vanessa exchanged bewildered looks with the other two.

'Do sit down, dear. You know your pacing makes me tired.' Alice waited for them to sit before continuing. 'Judith was holding the phone too tightly. The first time she held it up her fingers were relaxed, the second time the tips were squished and pale. She was tense. Same with Shannon. When I started to shake my head she was holding her pen so tightly I thought it might snap. They were trying to trap me.'

'Why?' Rachel asked.

'It's a pretty standard police tactic. Catch someone in a simple lie and you start to expose what else they're lying to you about. Suddenly everything I told them was at risk of being a lie. Maybe I *had* seen Colin before, maybe I *did* know where Joshua was.'

'Technically you did know where I was.'

Alice shrugged. 'But they didn't know that. Anyway it doesn't matter that they know the knitting needle is Freda's. There isn't a person on the planet that would think Freda capable of murder. Not with a knitting needle anyway.'

'I suppose she's more a poison sort of person,' Vanessa said sarcastically.

'Most women are, dear.'

'I'm not!'

'Me either,' Rachel added.

Me either, Alice thought. I'd use a more direct approach if the necessity ever arose.

'They'll talk to Freda, she'll tell them the needle went missing at the festival and they'll leave her alone.'

'Are you going to warn her?' Joshua asked.

Alice shook her head. 'Better I don't. Her responses will be more genuine, and like I said, she didn't kill Colin so she has nothing to worry about.' She noticed that Rachel was rocking back and forth lightly in her chair, her face drained of colour. 'Are you alright?'

'I didn't expect to be that close to her again,' replied Rachel.

'Ah yes, of course,' Alice nodded.

'How could you see that just from her asking a few questions?' asked Joshua. 'We were listening at the door,' he added sheepishly.

Alice nodded approvingly. 'She was fishing, looking to see if the book, and you,' she looked at Rachel, 'were at Silvermoon.'

'What if she'd realised I was in the next room?' Rachel leaned forward and put her head between her knees.

'If you're going to be sick, use the kitchen sink or the bathroom, not my carpet,' Alice said sharply.

'Slow deep breaths,' Vanessa told her. 'Just focus on breathing. No point thinking about what could have happened. She didn't find you. You're okay.'

Slowly the colour returned to Rachel's face and she offered Vanessa a wan smile. 'Thanks.'

'You're welcome. Sometimes, it's better to be helpful,' she said to Alice.

'I was helpful. I offered her two alternatives to being sick on my carpet.'

Vanessa rolled her eyes.

'Does it mean anything? That woman coming here, does it mean anything?'

Alice considered Joshua's question.

'It means that what was taken from her house is important enough for her to get herself assigned to this case so she can look for it. We knew there was more to the book than there appears. It would seem that we underestimated how much more. Unless…'

'What?' asked Rachel.

'Unless you took something else.'

'I didn't!'

'Are you sure?'

'I swear, the only thing I grabbed was the book. You have to believe me.'

Alice considered the irony of someone who had lied repeatedly asking her to believe she was now telling the truth. She decided to give her the benefit of the doubt. 'Alright, maybe something you saw then. Was there anything in the house that looked out of the ordinary?'

Rachel shook her head.

'Are you sure?'

'I'm sure.'

'Mmm.'

'You don't believe me,' Rachel said bitterly.

'Your track record isn't great, and no, in this instance I don't believe you. Only,' she held up her hand, 'because you answered too quickly. You were in a high stress situation with a lot going on. Seems to me that you would need to consider it before deciding you didn't see anything unusual.'

'But I'm really observant.'

'What colour is the bed cover in the spare bedroom?' Alice asked.

Rachel's mouth opened as she struggled for a response. 'Red.'

'Blue.'

'Oh. Fine, I get it. So what if I did see something else. I don't remember it.'

'You will, it'll come to you in time. Now onto the next task. We need to—'

A knock on the door interrupted her. There hadn't been a call from the concierge desk, so it must be a visit from another resident. Joshua and Rachel raced to the spare room and once they were hidden, Vanessa opened the front door.

'Oh, hello. Vanessa isn't it? I was hoping to have a quick word with Alice if she's available.'

Vanessa looked over her shoulder to where Alice was hidden from view behind the door. Alice raised her hand and waved her in.

'Of course,' Vanessa said to the visitor. 'Come in.'

She stepped aside And Alice was surprised to see that the visitor was Rosie, the resident who'd organised the knitting festival.

Rosie stood in the entrance way, twisting her hands together and looking around the room. 'I'm sorry to barge in uninvited.'

'Please sit down,' Alice indicated the chair opposite her. 'Vanessa, more tea I think. Unless you prefer coffee?'

'I do prefer coffee, but unfortunately these days it doesn't prefer me. Tea would be lovely, thank you.'

While Vanessa busied herself in the kitchen, Alice studied her visitor. Rosie appeared to be in her late sixties, tall and thin, with brown hair and glasses. She wore jeans and a T-shirt with a bird on the front. Alice didn't know what sort of bird it was, wildlife wasn't her speciality.

'I've been wanting to stop by and say hello for a while,' Rosie said, 'but something has always got in the way. Also,' she dropped her eyes and let out a little laugh, 'to be honest I was a little intimidated.'

'Why?' Alice replied.

'Oh well,' Rosie looked at her, 'you have quite the reputation around Silvermoon so I kept putting off coming and introducing myself, and suddenly it's a year later, and here we are.'

Alice liked having a reputation, as long as it remained inside Silvermoon. She didn't want tales making their way into the wider community. The statute of limitations had run out on most but not all of the things she'd done in her life.

'And what does my reputation say about me?'

'I can think of a few things,' Vanessa quipped as she placed a cup of tea on the table in front of Rosie.

'So can I,' Alice fixed her with a steely gaze which Vanessa ignored.

'Just that you're a no-nonsense sort who doesn't suffer fools. Also I should never play poker against you, and you're secretive about your past.'

Alice leaned back and smiled. 'Most of that is true, although I'm not secretive about my past. It's just not exciting to talk about.'

Vanessa choked on her drink and Alice looked at her with a raised eyebrow as she coughed. 'Are you alright Vanessa?'

'Tea, wrong way,' Vanessa said bringing her coughing under control.

'I know what you mean,' Rosie said. 'My life was a bit boring too. Only...'

Alice waited for Rosie to summon the courage to finish her sentence.

'That reputation I spoke of. People say that you're good at... helping people.'

That caught Alice by surprise. She'd hoped to be described as stern or aloof or determined. Helping people hadn't appeared on her list of possible reasons for a reputation.

'I do seem to have certain skills in that area,' she reluctantly admitted.

Rosie sighed with relief. 'Only I have a slightly delicate situation that I would be grateful to have your help with.' She glanced at Vanessa.

'You can speak in front of her,' Alice said. 'Since I'm a little restricted in my movements, I'll probably need her assistance to help you anyway.'

Rosie's cheeks reddened. 'Oh dear. This is rather embarrassing.'

Alice waited while Rosie had an internal argument. Finally her face cleared and Rosie sat up a little straighter.

'The thing is, when I said my life was a little boring, there was one thing I did when I was younger, much younger… It seemed like a bit of fun and no one would know it was me…'

Her hands were working double time and Alice almost expected them to become permanently interlocked any second.

'The thing is… the thing is I once posed for an artist. He painted this beautiful painting of me…'

'Naked.'

'How did you know?'

'You're not acting like someone who was painted fully clothed.'

Rosie ceased working her hands and raised them to her chin. 'I never considered myself pretty, so I thought perhaps the artist could, you know, touch up a few things. I had a few drinks before I did it and when he suggested I take my dress off I drowned my inhibitions in another wine and thought why not.'

'Very sensible,' Alice said. 'The only thing wrong with what you've said so far was about not considering yourself pretty. That sort of self-doubt won't do anyone any good.'

Rosie's cheeks darkened further and she self-consciously tucked a stray hair behind her ear.

'I wouldn't have had the courage to do what you did, no matter how many drinks I'd had,' Vanessa gave her an admiring look.

Rosie shook her head slightly but the colour in her cheeks lightened and she looked pleased with the assessment. 'It was when I was single. Before I met my husband. Anyway, I always kept the painting in my bedroom at home, where no one could see it. Alistair, my husband, he never knew it was me. He used to say the woman in the painting was beautiful. He never told me…he would sometimes have a drink. He wasn't a bad man, but he would have a drink and talk about the woman in the picture and tell me I'd never be as beautiful as her.'

Alice decided it was a good thing that Alistair wasn't still around.

'You never told him it was you?'

'Oh no! He was a church going man, he would have…I don't know how he would have reacted, but it wouldn't be good. When I moved here I hung it in my bedroom again, because, well you know, if anyone found out that I'd posed…'

'Naked? In the altogether? *Au naturel*?' Alice suggested.

'In your birthday suit? Buck naked? Wearing only a smile?' Vanessa chimed in.

Rosie stared at both of them, then burst out laughing.

'You do realise that women have been posing nude since the beginning of time,' said Alice.

'I'm not that old,' Rosie shot back. Fresh laughter erupted.

'Right,' Alice said when they were all under control, 'so you want me to find out who took the painting?'

Rosie looked at her in astonishment. 'How on earth could you know that?'

'You were obviously embarrassed to talk about it, so the only reason you would was if someone was blackmailing you about it, or if someone had taken it. Or both.'

'I was in the games room the other night playing bridge, and when I came home my door was unlocked. I thought perhaps I had forgotten to lock it, so I went inside.'

'You should have called the office,' Vanessa said.

'I know, but sometimes I think I've done something and then it turns out I haven't. Like pay the power bill. Anyway, nothing was missing, not that I have much that would attract burglars. But when I went into the bedroom, I saw immediately that my painting was gone. You see I like to look at it, as a reminder... it's silly really.'

'What night was this?' Alice asked, although she thought she could guess.

'The night they found that man who passed away. What if someone finds the painting and realises it's me? I'll have to move.'

Alice held up her hand. 'Don't call the moving company just yet.'

'Can you help me?'

Alice thought about it. Aside from protecting Rachel, keeping Joshua away from the police, finding out who killed Colin, and trying to work out the importance of the book, she didn't have much going on.

'Of course I will,' she smiled.

'We will,' Vanessa chimed in.

Relief flooded across Rosie's face.

I need four of me, Alice thought. She looked at Vanessa.

She'd have to settle for one and a half.

FOURTEEN

'Do you think Colin took it?' Rachel asked.

They were sitting in the same arrangement as before. Rosie had left, reassured that Alice would try to find her painting and wouldn't reveal its subject to anyone.

All Alice had told Rachel and Joshua was that a valuable painting was missing. She was thankful to learn that they hadn't been listening at the door this time. She didn't agree with Rosie's need to feel ashamed at posing nude, but she was sympathetic. While she'd never done it herself, her best friend Violet Tumbleton had been painted by the man that Alice had subsequently married. In fact, her married name had been the same as the writer of the book they were trying to decipher. She hadn't thought about that before. Her John Strong had no living relatives, at least as far as she knew, and Strong was a common enough name.

'A painting goes missing on the same night as a thief is found dead on the grounds? I wouldn't be very helpful to Rosie if I didn't at least consider the probability those two things are connected.'

'But why would he take the painting and nothing else?' asked Vanessa.

'Who said he only took the painting? Remember we have a missing hour between when he parked his car and when he was found dead. That's a lot of time to break into people's homes.'

'No one else has reported anything missing,' Joshua pointed out.

'True. Perhaps no one else was robbed. Or, perhaps no one else has noticed they've been robbed. Rosie noticed because the painting was special to her and she looked at it every night. If the thief had taken a piece of jewellery it might have taken her days or weeks to notice.'

'Speaking from experience?'

Alice scowled at Vanessa.

'So how can we find out?' Rachel asked. 'Knock on everyone's door and ask if anything is missing?'

'That's one way. Although they might not want to tell us what was taken.'

Alice thought, then a smile crossed her face. 'But as there was a murder on the grounds, and the victim was a known thief, it would be prudent for Silvermoon management to talk to the residents and see how they're feeling. And if in the course of that conversation it arose that something had been taken from their homes, then that might be useful.'

She saw Rachel and Joshua nodding. Vanessa seemed less excited, having immediately understood that she was the 'management' part of the plan.

Vanessa stood up. 'I'll let you know how I get on.'

'While you're out and about, if you see the police leaving can you let me know? I need to go out and ask some questions of my own but Joshua can't leave the apartment with them hanging around.'

'Yessir! Anything else, sir!'

'Yes, a little less cheek.'

Vanessa chuckled as she spun on the spot and strode over to the front door.

Rachel turned to Alice and said, 'I don't get it. If Colin took that painting, where is it? Did the killer take it with them?'

'That's a good question,' Alice replied.

By the look on Rachel's face she didn't hear that very often.

'Let's make some assumptions, although I'm not a fan of them. It's just a fancy way of saying you don't know enough. But for argument's sake, let's assume Colin took the painting. And let's also assume that the killer took it with them after they murdered him. Does that mean that his death had nothing to do with you?'

'Maybe Rosie killed him,' suggested Joshua. 'She obviously loves the painting. Maybe she came home and saw him sneaking out of her place with it. She followed him and killed him to get it back.'

Alice shook her head. 'She doesn't have the painting, Joshua. And why would she then come to me asking for help to find it? There would be no need to tell anyone the painting existed.'

'Oh, yeah, good point.'

'So, until we find evidence to the contrary we have to believe that someone else killed Colin, and if he had the painting with him, then taking it was a crime of opportunity.'

'So what now?' asked Rachel.

'We wait until Vanessa gives us the all clear, or reports back about whether anyone else had something taken that night. You two should have something to eat.'

'I'm not hungry,' Joshua said.

Alice looked him up and down. 'You're a young, active man, how is that possible?'

'Alright,' he grinned, 'I'm a little hungry.'

She waved towards the kitchen. 'Anything you can find to eat is yours.'

'Do you want anything?'

'No, I'm really not hungry.'

'How is that possible?' he laughed.

'Because I'm *not* a young, active man.'

Alice's phone rang. It was Oliver.

'Sorry it took a little longer to get some info than I thought.'

'That's fine. What did you find out?'

'Not a lot I'm afraid. I did a bit of research and talked to my publisher. She asked around. Turns out that there are only a few people in the world who know the identity of Rodney Strong, including Kowhai Press, his publisher. And they're not telling anyone. I did find out that they're prolific, like really prolific. What gets published is only a fraction of what goes to his publisher. Apparently there are dozens of manuscripts locked away in an office somewhere.'

'Why weren't they published?'

'Don't know, but the numbers I heard make me feel like a tortoise.'

'Can you get a look at one of them?'

Oliver laughed. 'Not a chance. They're not with my publisher. I can't just walk into his publisher's office and ask to take a look.'

'No, I guess not.'

She was pretty sure she could pull it off, but she had less faith in Oliver's ability to bluff his way through a situation. Besides, she wasn't actually sure how the book fit in yet and she didn't want to arouse suspicion by poking around asking too many questions. She thought about the book, trying to remember anything else that might help.

'What about the publisher? What do you know about them?'

'They're a small unit based in Wellington. They put out about four books a year.'

Alice thought some more. 'Do you know any of their other titles?'

'No, but it'll be on their website. I can look it up.'

'Do that and send me a text message with the info.'

'Yes, ma'am.'

'And can you find out who owns Kowhai Press?'

'Yes ma'am,' Oliver repeated.

Oliver hung up before Alice could call him out on his cheek. That was two people in the space of ten minutes who'd treated her like a commanding officer. She couldn't help grinning. She had no problem being bossy. No sense breaking a habit of a lifetime.

'Why do you want to know the history of the publishing company?' Rachel asked.

'Following a hunch. It might be nothing. It might be that the books are a red herring and have nothing to do with any of this.'

'Or it might be that they are important,' finished Rachel.

'Exactly. I want to know if there have been previous books put out, and if we can get a hold of them, whether they have the same sort of messages in them, with the numbers.'

'You think these aren't one-offs?'

'I don't know. There's too much I don't know right now and it's irritating.'

A loud song began playing from Joshua's pants and he pulled out his phone. 'It's my mother.'

He'd barely pressed the button to accept the call when everyone in the room could hear the sharp tones of his mother. Her voice was clear enough for Alice to realise she was speaking Tongan, and loud enough to establish she wasn't asking how his day was going. Joshua's face was part panic, part resignation. When she paused, presumably to take a breath, he said something. The only word Alice recognised was his name. Another burst from his mother was followed by a two-word reply from Joshua. He looked at Alice apologetically. 'She wants to talk to you.' He hesitantly held out the phone.

'If you're going to yell at me can you do it in English, please? My Tongan is virtually non-existent.'

There was a sharp intake of breath from Joshua and silence from the other end of the phone.

'No yelling,' came the reply. 'Yelling is for my boy – and my husband when he does something wrong.'

'So a lot of yelling then,' Alice commented.

Loud laughter erupted from the phone. Alice winced and held the phone away from her ear.

'You're funny. Joshua didn't tell me you were funny. He used some other words.'

'I can imagine,' Alice said.

'No need to imagine, I'll tell you.'

'I'm sure it's nothing I haven't heard before.'

'Probably not. My boy isn't that imaginative. He tells me you're keeping him out of trouble.'

'I'm trying.'

'Good, because he also tells me you were the one who got him into trouble in the first place.'

Alice looked at Joshua, who sat rigid in his chair.

'He's been quite chatty then, hasn't he?'

'He's a good boy.'

'Yes, he is,' replied Alice.

'But sometimes he's a little too nice for his own good. That's when he needs someone to take care of him.'

Alice stayed silent. She wasn't sure where this was going.

'The police came to see me. They're looking for him. He told me about finding the man the other night.'

'Did you tell the police where he is?'

'How can I tell them something I don't know? Besides, I didn't like the look of them.'

'Does that assessment relate to police in general or just the ones that came to see you.'

'Eh? I have respect for police. They do a good job. But I know bad people when I see them, and that woman was bad people.'

'Let me guess, about five-foot-four, blonde, intense stare?'

'She's been to see you?'

'Yes, and I agree with you.'

'Joshua said you were a smart lady. Is he in danger?'

Alice deliberately didn't look at Joshua when she answered. 'Not as long as he does what I say.'

'Good. You send him home when this is done. And you come with him and I'll make you dinner. Joshua says you're too skinny. Now put him back on.'

Joshua was berated by his mother for another minute before he hung up.

'I like her,' Alice said with a smile. Then the smile slipped from her face. There was something wrong. She looked around the apartment for inspiration but the nagging feeling wouldn't materialise into anything useful.

When Joshua's phone rang again, her eyes snapped to the table where it sat.

'Turn it off!' she snapped as he reached for it.

'What?' He snatched his hand back as if she'd stabbed at him.

'Turn it off now!'

Quickly he picked up the phone and jabbed with his fingers. The ringing stopped.

'What's wrong?' Rachel asked.

Alice wasn't one hundred percent sure. Something Amanda had told her, or she'd seen on a television show. 'Something about phones,' she murmured.

'What?'

'The police can track phones,' Alice said. 'What does that mean exactly?'

Joshua and Rachel had mirrored looks of horror and they both stared at the phone like a police officer was going to climb out of it and arrest them.

'Well?'

Rachel gave a little start, then shook her head. 'It means they can find your location by using cell towers to work out where your phone is.'

'What do you mean find your location? How close? Like could they tell Joshua is in this apartment?'

'I don't think so,' Rachel frowned. 'I think they'll be able to see he's in the Village somewhere. I don't think they can get closer than that.'

'That's bad enough,' Alice said darkly. It was one thing trying to juggle all these things at once, but to have to contend with modern technology as well... People she understood, basic human nature hadn't changed in her nine decades on the planet, but beyond what Amanda had shown her out of necessity, Alice was badly out of touch with technology.

'Why didn't you tell me they could do that?' she grumbled.

'S-s-sorry, I didn't think... Why would the police want to track me?'

'Maybe they aren't,' replied Alice. 'Or maybe they consider you their lead suspect in Colin's murder. The point is we don't know.'

Joshua nodded wordlessly. Alice sighed. She was supposed to be helping these two, not terrifying them. But sometimes a healthy dose of fear helped.

Alice felt a sudden, overwhelming desire to be alone. There were too many people in her apartment. Short of turning them loose to get in even more trouble, she wasn't going to get any alone time.

Her own phone pinged with a message from Vanessa confirming that the police were gone, apart from a single constable guarding the murder scene at the back of Alice's building.

Alice decided it was safe to go for a little excursion. Rachel wasn't happy about staying inside, especially as the sun was streaming in through the windows.

'It's so boring here,' Rachel complained.

'Do some more knitting.'

Luckily the recent scare around the police visit and tracking phones was enough to prevent any further argument.

Joshua didn't say anything but Alice caught a glimpse of his face in the mirrored surface of the elevator and she could tell he was nervous.

'Just take me into the rose garden, Joshua, then you can come back and stay out of sight.'

'How will you get back?'

'I'll text you when I'm ready.'

'But you told me to turn my phone off,' Joshua reminded her.

'Then I'll send up smoke signals,' snapped Alice.

'What are those?'

Alice took a deep breath and let it out slowly. It wasn't his fault he knew nothing.

Luckily, there was no one else in the rose garden. It consisted of rose bushes shaped in a rough square directly opposite the main building, with back to back bench seats in the middle of the garden. All the roses were in bloom and everywhere she looked was bursting with blues and reds and yellows. She knew several of the residents took a lot of pride in maintaining the garden, but Alice had never been a stop and smell the roses sort of girl.

Its main advantage was that it was relatively secluded. While anyone looking out the window of their apartment might be able to see her, from the ground she was partially hidden by the bushes, which meant she could work in peace.

From the bag she held on her lap she pulled the book. The frustrating book that she had a nagging feeling was the key to everything that had happened. It was well written but not a masterpiece, and certainly not worth killing for. She studied the inscription once more.

I love you 99

Strange. She turned to the dedication page.

To my wonderful wife, 1, 20, and 210 times all the love.

All *the* love, not all *my* love. That was unusual. And the numbers? She was sure they related to page numbers but there was nothing out of the ordinary on those pages. She flicked to the first page and re-read it. Nothing leapt out. The first word was 'I'. The twentieth word was 'was' and the two-hundred-and-tenth word was 'several'.

'I was several,' Alice said out loud.

She went to the twentieth page and tried the same exercise, ending up with, 'took Joshua he'.

She could sense herself getting frustrated. She was, better at setting puzzles than trying to solve them.

Alice turned back to the first page in the book, the title page, which just had the title and author name on it. No place for hidden messages there. The next page was the imprint page, with standard copyright information, the publisher, the editor and cover designer. None of the names meant anything to her.

She closed the book and stared moodily as a bee flit from one flower to another. The sun was warm and beyond the boundary fences the world was muted. This wasn't such a bad place to sit after all.

'There you are.' Vanessa sat on the bench beside Alice's wheelchair. 'It's beautiful isn't it?'

'If you like that sort of thing,' Alice said.

'What's got you grumpy...ier than normal.'

Alice was too relaxed to do anything other than give her companion a gentle slap on the arm. 'It's this stupid book. I can't work it out.'

'Can I see it? Maybe I can figure something out,' Vanessa asked.

When Alice handed it to Vanessa, she turned the book over in her hands before flicking through the pages. She even held a page up to the sunlight. 'Just in case,' she said with pink cheeks.

'Good idea.'

After a few more minutes of examination Vanessa handed the book back to Alice.

'Keep it,' Alice ordered. 'Have a proper look later. How did you go with canvassing?'

Vanessa closed her eyes and raised her face to the sun. She wriggled into a more comfortable position before answering.

'Well, I freaked out the Baskins. They insisted I wait while they examined every item in their apartment to see if anything was missing.'

'Was there?'

'Only the time I'll never get back. Harold thought his favourite watch was gone until Karen told him it was on his wrist.'

'You can't even blame age for that one. I understand Harold was never very observant. It took him five years to realise Karen was flirting with him.'

Vanessa looked impressed. 'That's a new level of obliviousness – that's a hard word to say, *obliviousness*.'

'Vanessa, focus.'

'Right, anyway, I went to ten apartments. Two people weren't home, but of the others I found four that were missing something valuable. And do you know what they all had in common?'

'They weren't home the night of the murder.'

Vanessa's face fell. 'How could you possibly know that?'

'Lucky guess.'

'Sure,' Vanessa said in a disbelieving tone.

'It stands to reason. One thing went missing, other people had missing things, logic suggests the pattern was the same. In this instance I'd hazard a guess that they were all in the games room at the time of the thefts. Close your mouth dear, that bee might fly in.'

'Seriously, how do you do that?'

'It's not hard, dear. I'm sure if you hadn't been in such a hurry to show off what you'd learned you would have worked it out yourself.'

'Way to make me feel good.'

'Sulking is as pointless as gloating, Vanessa. You did a good job gathering information, but remember to analyse what you find out, otherwise it doesn't mean anything.'

'Yes, ma'am.'

'Stop that.'

Vanessa laughed, and Alice knew the moment had passed. She was going to have to work on the girl's confidence.

'Where's your list of what was taken?' asked Alice.

Vanessa pulled out her phone and tapped the screen before showing it to Alice.

She was pleased to see that Vanessa had added the painting to the top of the list. Apart from that there was a silver cup, a gold bracelet, and a small statue of a penguin.

Alice blinked when she read the last item. 'A penguin?'

'I had the same look on my face. But according to Frances Wilkins it's made of crystal and is quite expensive.'

Alice shrugged. It wasn't like she hadn't acquired some uniquely shaped objects in her time.

'So apart from the painting, all of these things could easily be hidden in a bag,' she mused.

'Which doesn't help us figure out where they might be.'

'Or who took them.'

'I thought we'd decided that Colin took them?'

'No,' Alice replied, 'we decided that it was likely Colin took the items, but we also need to consider that someone else could have taken them.'

'You mean someone else was on the grounds that night?'

Alice gave her a look and a moment later Vanessa's eyes grew bigger.

'No! Surely no one at Silvermoon would steal from other residents?'

Alice gave her a different look and Vanessa slumped into her seat. 'Damn.'

'I'm not saying they did, but we can't rule out they didn't. Not yet.'

'So what do we do now?'

'We know the people who were robbed were all in the games room. We need to find out exactly who was there that night, and more importantly, who wasn't there.'

'More questioning then,' sighed Vanessa.

'I'm afraid so. Don't consider it questioning, think of it as getting to know the people you see every day a little better.'

'Are you coming with me?'

'I already know these people as well as I need to.'

'Then what will you be doing while I get to know people better?'

Alice thought about that. She felt like one of those people spinning plates on the top of sticks – she was trying to keep them all spinning, but she didn't know which one to focus on.

'I don't know,' she finally said.

'Would you like me take you home?'

She wanted to say yes, to go home and lay down on her bed and sleep away the fuzziness and confusion that was picking at her mind. But a lifetime of stubbornness kicked in, refusing to give life to the fear that the fuzziness and confusion might not be due to tiredness, but old age finally catching up with her. And Rachel would be there.

'Alice?'

It was no use, there was just nothing coming, no obvious next step.

'Yes, please,' she said, defeated. She noticed the look of concern from Vanessa but couldn't muster a rebuke.

On the short walk back to her building, Alice managed to sink into new depths of moodiness, that the sun, several attempts from Vanessa, and a bright hello from two friends walking briskly past, could not dispel.

As Vanessa wheeled her through the front doors of the lobby, Alice's phone pinged. She had received a text from Oliver with the list of books put out by Rodney Strong's publisher last year.

'Stop!' Alice read the message again. 'New plan. We're going on a road trip.'

'What? Where too?'

'The closest bookshop.'

'What's going on?'

Alice passed her phone up to Vanessa who scanned the message before passing it back.

'I can get those for you.'

'I think an outing would do me good. I'll just need to fetch my purse from upstairs first.'

'Are you sure?'

'Less talking more doing,' Alice ordered. Something about the thought of an outing was enough for Alice to feel better, even if it was just a trip to the bookstore.

'Feeling better?'

'I don't know what you're talking about,' she replied. 'And stop grinning, you look like a crazy person.'

Vanessa laughed. 'Maybe we should go to the pub while we're out, have a couple of drinks.'

Alice pressed the button for her floor. 'Dear, I'd drink you under the table.'

FIFTEEN

The short trip turned into a longer trip as they trapsed from shop to shop looking for the books. None of the big stores had them, and Alice grew more and more frustrated, until they finally found a small independent bookshop that had recently opened. They had all three titles on the shelf.

By the time they'd purchased the books and returned to the car Alice was ready to go home. Partly she was tired from the excursion, even though she was sitting for almost all of it. And partly because of the looks she was getting from passers-by. She became painfully aware that to most of them she was a frail old woman in a wheelchair, one foot in the grave. The fact she could have put all of them in their place verbally, and some of them physically, was the only thing stopping her from sinking back into the dark mood she'd been in earlier.

While Vanessa drove up the hill towards home, Alice tore open the paper bag and pulled out the first book. The cover seemed to be of a painting, the title "Hidden Desires" didn't seem like the sort of thing she would want to read.

She flicked through to the dedication page. It read:

"To my husband, 100 times my love."

'Do any of these authors write normal things,' she muttered as she moved onto the next book.

She ignored the cover and went straight to the dedication page:

"33 years together, but feels like 12."

A thought formed in Alice's mind and she quickly moved onto the last book. The dedication read:

"To my beautiful wife Margaret, you make my 70 year old bones feel 23 again".

The thought deepened as Vanessa turned down the street towards Silvermoon.

'You've gone quiet on me,' Vanessa said.

'I'm thinking, you should try it more.'

'Oh I think all the time, I'm thinking something right now for example.'

Alice shot her a look, then beamed.

'Fair enough. Sorry. I think I might have worked out the books.'

They passed through the front gate and headed up the long tree lined driveway. As they approached the main building, Alice spotted a shiny red convertible parked out front. The vanity number plate read "84LNCH".

'Now that's a car I could see myself driving around Wellington.'

So could I, if it was sixty years ago, Alice thought.

'Too flashy for my tastes,' she said out loud.

Vanessa helped Alice out of the car, where she insisted on hobbling up the steps by herself. She thought her ankle might be a little better than it had been. She'd be stalking the grounds of Silvermoon again in no time. She snorted at the image of her as some sort of predator terrorising the villagers.

She was halfway across the lobby when Tracey emerged from the corridor behind the concierge desk. With her was a short, distinguished gentleman wearing a grey, pinstriped suit.

'Oh good, Alice. Can I have a moment?' Tracey hurried on as if afraid to give Alice the chance to say no. 'This is Alice, she is one of our oldest residents, oh, I mean longest residents, although she is the oldest as well. Alice, Justin here is looking to move into Silvermoon and wanted to look around.'

He held out his hand. 'Justin, nice to meet you.' He was in his late fifties, far too young for Silvermoon. Although there was no official age limit, the youngest current resident was Mary who was sixty-eight.

Without hesitation Alice shook his hand. The handshake was firm and brief. The shake of a man happy to treat women as equals.

'I know what you're thinking,' Justin said.

Alice raised an eyebrow.

'You're thinking I'm too young to live in a retirement village. And you're right, but I'm used to the best in my life, and Silvermoon has the reputation of being the best in the city, possibly even the country. When I learned there was a waiting list, I thought I'd better put my name down now.' He was smiling as he said it and Alice found herself smiling back.

'Although,' Justin's smile faltered. 'I heard that you recently had a murder on the premises, so perhaps this isn't the place for me.'

More than one over the years, thought Alice.

'I can assure you that this facility is safe,' Tracey told him. 'The man who died had nothing to do with Silvermoon. He was a common thief.'

'Oh, do you have a problem with burglaries here…?'

'Alice! Tell Justin that Silvermoon is a safe place.'

Her tone was urgent and Alice wondered why Tracey was so worried about losing this potential resident. It wasn't like Silvermoon was short of money – or residents.

'Tracey is right. Silvermoon is an exceptionally quiet village.'

Alice plastered on her best bland look and after a moment Justin's eyes slid away, dismissing the old woman.

'I'm relieved to hear that. Shall we continue the tour?' he said to Tracey.

She shepherded him out the front door quickly. Alice was watching them descend the steps to the driveway when Vanessa walked through the door.

'Who's that?'

'That, my dear Vanessa, is Justin Fry. A very, very dangerous man.'

Vanessa's mouth dropped open as she turned to stare out the front windows. 'And you let Tracey go off with him?'

'Relax, he's not here to kill anyone. I'm sure he has people for that.'

'That doesn't make me feel better. What's he doing here?'

Alice had been wondering the same thing. 'It could be he's genuinely looking for somewhere to live when he retires,' she said as she hobbled over to the elevator.

'But…'

'But it's likely there's more going on than we realised.'

The doors closed and the elevator began its smooth ride up.

'Why do you look so happy?' Vanessa asked her.

'Because we've met all the major players. Now I can start sorting it all out.'

'You've worked something out already, haven't you? With the books?'

'I have,' Alice confirmed. 'I'm just not quite sure what yet. I need to look at all four books together.'

She punched in the code for the front door and opened it to a rich smell of baking.

'Hey,' Rachel called from the kitchen. 'I got bored so I raided your pantry. Do you know you had this hiding in a box of baking powder?' She held up a small leather covered hip flask.

'Oh, is that where it was? I was wondering where I'd put it,' Alice smiled. Now I'm going to have to hide it again, she thought.

'What's that smell?' asked Vanessa. 'It's amazing.'

Rachel's face broke into a smile. 'Thanks. I made chocolate-chip cookies. Alice didn't have all the ingredients, so I had to improvise. They're a family recipe.'

The kitchen was a bomb site, with containers and bowls stacked all over the counter. Alice scanned the rest of the apartment to see if the mess had leaked out. Nothing else looked out of place.

'Don't worry. I'll clean up,' Rachel said.

The spare bedroom door opened and Joshua emerged with a towel draped around his shoulders and wet hair.

'You won't let me go home, and I needed a shower,' he explained.

'If we're going to be prisoners here then we might as well be clean and fed prisoners,' Rachel added cheerfully.

Alice let that one go, crossing to the couch and pasting a blank look on her face as she propped her foot up on a cushion. Walking from the car had been a terrible idea. Her ankle throbbed and, as if in sympathy, her opposite knee had started aching as well.

If she'd been alone in the apartment she would have groaned, then gone in search of the nearest hip flask. With a full apartment she wasn't going to give Vanessa the satisfaction of an 'I told you so'. Instead she focused on the smell of the cookies. Alice had never been a domestic goddess – or in fact any form of deity when it came to cooking and cleaning. She had kept her daughter and Amanda fed and clothed and educated, but from memory she couldn't conjure a single time when cookies had been baked. She'd even outsourced the making of birthday cakes, rationalising that if her ten-year-old granddaughter wanted a cake that looked like a horse, then it should probably resemble a horse, at least if you looked at it the right way. Now she wondered if she'd deprived Amanda of an important childhood memory by not teaching her how to make a scone, or a pavlova, or a loaf of bread.

That thought troubled her for a minute or two, then she shelved it. She was ninety-eight years old. If she was going to go looking for regrets she might as well lay down on the bed and never get up again.

The beeping of the oven drew her attention and she watched Rachel take the baking sheet out, resting it on the rack Alice had completely forgotten she owned.

Perhaps I should go through my cupboards, she thought.

There was a knock at the door. With a resigned look, Rachel abandoned her cookies and disappeared into the bedroom, followed by Joshua. Vanessa opened the front door.

'Hello, Vanessa. Can we speak with Alice, please?'

Alice frowned. Why was Tracey here? Who was 'we'? She gestured for Vanessa to let them in. Tracey entered, closely followed by Justin Fry.

'Sorry to bother you, Alice, but Mr Fry was wanting to look at one of the apartments and he suggested since you'd already been introduced you might not mind him having a look around.'

Alice noticed he was already doing that, his eyes scanning the space, resting on the cluttered bench.

She could see him forming a story as he turned towards her.

'What a wonderful smell,' Tracey exclaimed. 'I didn't know you baked, Alice.'

'And so quickly too, it seems like only a short while ago we saw you downstairs,' Justin added.

'It's a dormant habit,' explained Alice, boldly.

'My fault,' Vanessa said. 'I convinced Alice this morning that baking something might take her mind off her ankle. We got halfway through preparing the mixture when I realised she didn't have any baking powder. You saw us as we were coming back from the shops.'

'I don't recall you carrying anything.' Justin turned to Alice, with a mildly quizzical expression.

'You expect her to be carrying shopping? She shouldn't have even been walking,' Vanessa said. 'The doctor told her to take it easy.' She glared at Alice.

'I have been taking it easy,' Alice snapped. 'I just walked from the car to the apartment.'

'Anyway,' Vanessa turned back to the others, 'I carried the things up and we've just finished making the cookies.'

Justin stared for a moment before nodding and giving Vanessa a dazzling smile. 'Of course.' He resumed his inspection of the apartment. 'What's through that door?' He pointed to the spare bedroom.

'That's the second bedroom,' Alice said.

'Mind if I take a look?' He started across the room before she could reply.

'I'd prefer you didn't,' Alice said calmly.

Justin stopped and looked back.

'Alice, really…' Tracey began.

'Forgive me, Justin. I've been going through my wardrobe and there are certain garments – under garments shall we say, laid out on the bed. Of course, if you have no problem looking at an old lady's underwear then be my guest.' She leaned back in her seat and closed her eyes. If Justin called her bluff then she'd have a problem. Perhaps she could feign surprise at two young people having a tryst in her apartment. There was also the distinct possibility that Justin would recognise Rachel, in which case Alice would have just handed the girl over to the last person in the world she should see.

'Well,' she heard Justin say. 'I expect it looks just like a bedroom.'

Alice opened her eyes and smiled at him. 'Just like any other room with a bed in it.'

'This is a lovely space. I could easily see myself living here in the future.'

'Not exactly here,' Vanessa said. 'This is Alice's place.'

'Of course,' Justin gave a wink. 'Although, no one lives forever, do they?' He said it lightly, but to Alice it sounded sinister. He was sending her a message, one that had nothing to do with her age.

'No,' she agreed. 'Although I seem to have managed better than most.'

'Thank you for allowing me into your home, Alice. Perhaps I'll see you again.'

'Anything is possible,' Alice replied.

She and Justin locked eyes and after a moment he raised an eyebrow, as if surprised that the little old lady in front of wouldn't be intimidated.

He gave a slight nod, then followed Tracey out of the apartment.

'What was that?' asked Vanessa once the front door was closed and locked.

'What, dear?'

'That stare.' Vanessa began pacing back and forth. 'It's like, you know he's a bad man, you know he can do bad things, but you look at him like he's a naughty boy you want to send to his room.'

'I only know his reputation, and admittedly that's impressive, but I've met more dangerous men than him. And I believe you kicked one once.'

Vanessa's face flushed but she looked pleased at being reminded. As she should, Alice thought, it had been a particularly brave move.

'Besides, I learnt a lot in those few seconds.'

'Oh, I can't wait to hear what,' Rachel said from the doorway.

I might have to start charging for all these lessons, Alice thought wryly. 'Vanessa?'

Vanessa resumed her pacing as she thought. Meanwhile Joshua and Rachel leaned on the kitchen counter and watched.

'He was trying to alpha male you,' she began. 'But he didn't need to. There's no way he could have considered you a threat –because he doesn't know you,' she hurried on. 'So he must do it out of habit. He's used to intimidating people, or at least to being the superior one in the room. Or maybe it's a male thing? Does he just consider all women inferior?'

Alice shrugged. 'Possibly. People like that rarely think the other sex is an equal, but in this case I'd imagine that Justin Fry considers himself superior to everyone in the room. And on most occasions, he's probably right.'

Vanessa paused by the window. Grey clouds had begun to fill the sky and the apartment was growing darker.

'You chose to show him you weren't afraid of him. You tipped your hand as someone he has to watch. Why would you do that?'

Alice waited patiently for her to work it out.

'It wasn't your ego, was it?'

'Ouch,' Alice pretended to wince, although Vanessa was partially right. Alice's ego had prevented her from looking away. She'd grown up in a time when women were routinely considered inferior by men. She'd set more than one of them straight, but the constant battle had left her with a built-in aversion to letting a man win a fight just because he was a man. When she was younger, some had tried to label her a feminist, but she didn't enjoy that any more than being called a con artist or an old woman. Besides, she'd put a few women in their places over the years as well.

'Alright,' Alice admitted, 'it was partially ego, but also I wanted to see how he would react.' Looking around the room she saw that Joshua and Rachel looked confused. 'Because?' she asked Vanessa.

'Because you were testing him. As far as he knows, you're just a harmless little old lady. So what would he do when you refused to be cowed by him. Would it rattle him? Would he get angry? Or would he shrug it off? If he got angry then you'd know he was more dangerous because he doesn't have control of his emotions.'

Alice nodded approvingly. 'Spot on, well almost. It's not always true that the ones with no self-control are the most dangerous. Sometimes the ones with no emotion at all are the ones you don't want to turn your back on.'

Vanessa frowned and looked at the others. 'Does that mean he's a threat to Rachel?'

'Let's just say,' Alice replied, 'that for now he's down the list of potential threats.'

'Great,' Rachel said. 'I'd have felt a lot better if you hadn't said *for now.*'

'I think he was on a fact-finding mission. He wanted to get the lay of the land. I don't know what he'll do next, but his visit has made resolving this thing more urgent.'

'By *this thing* you mean Colin's murder?' asked Joshua.

'The murder and the books. I found that interesting.' When the others continued to look confused, Alice sighed and waved at the coffee table. 'The books we bought today were in full view and he didn't react.'

'Maybe he's good at poker?'

Alice shook her head. '*I'm* good at poker. He didn't give the books a second look. If they had something to do with him, I would have expected some reaction, no matter how tiny.'

'Which means there's something else,' Vanessa said.

'Yes, it seems Rachel stumbled into something more complicated than we first thought.' In the kitchen Rachel's face had gone pale, and she looked like she was about to be sick.

'Have a cookie, dear. The chocolate will help your nerves.'

Rachel reluctantly picked up a cookie and took a tiny bite. When that went down okay she took a bigger bite and slowly the colour came back to her face.

Joshua snagged a cookie from the baking rack and shoved the entire thing into his mouth. 'So, any clues from these?' He picked up one of the books from the coffee table, immediately smearing chocolate across the cover. 'Sorry,' he mumbled through the mouthful of crumbs and licked his thumb.

'Where's the other book?' Alice asked.

'In the bedroom.'

Alice waited. He dropped the book he was holding. 'I'll go get it.'

While he was gone, Alice asked Vanessa to find a piece of paper and pen. She opened the first book to the dedication and copied the message down, before doing the same with the other three books. When she had everything noted down on one page she started looking for common words or numbers. When nothing jumped out, she wrote all the numbers from the individual inscriptions together underneath the messages until she had a list of 12 random numbers. Looking up she saw the others had taken a book each and were in various parts of the room reading. Rachel was stretched out on the floor reading *The Code of Jasper* and making the most of the single ray of sunshine that had managed to break through the clouds. Vanessa was still in her armchair opposite Alice, comparing the imprint pages of *Second Chances* and *Hidden Desires*. Joshua had returned with *The Second Chance of Joshua Messer* and was leaning on the kitchen counter paging through it.

'What do you make of these?' Alice handed Vanessa the list of inscriptions and numbers.

Vanessa studied the page. 'Coordinates to buried treasure? Secret code? The combination to a safe?'

'Helpful,' Alice told her.

Vanessa held out her hand for the pen, then studied the sheet of paper for a moment. She began scribbling intently.

'Maybe…' she mumbled, pulling out her phone and looking something up. With a frown she scribbled some more, then tapped at her phone again. Over the next five minutes she repeated the pattern several times.

'Not coordinates,' she finally said, straightening up and rolling her shoulders back. 'Unless the baddies have a secret liar in England or the middle of the Indian Ocean.'

'Unlikely,' Alice replied. 'I have a feeling we're dealing with local rather than international criminal masterminds.'

Vanessa grinned. 'It could be a secret code. There are a lot of number cyphers out there. You must know some.'

'Vanessa, how many times must I tell you? I was a con artist, not a spy.'

'You were a con artist?' Rachel looked up from her book.

Alice groaned internally. This was what happened when she didn't have time to think, she let things slip out.

'Yes, and I'd appreciate it if you didn't tell anyone, including your grandfather. He has rather linear views of the world. Anyway, I never needed to learn secret codes.'

She looked at Joshua who was pretending to read his book.

'Alright, you each get two questions, then we will drop the subject forever, understood?'

'Yes,' Rachel said, sitting up.

'Yes,' Joshua rapidly closed his book.

'Yes,' Vanessa added.

'Not you,' Alice replied.

Vanessa tried her best to look disappointed, but a cheeky smile spoiled the effect.

'What's was the most expensive thing you took worth?' asked Rachel.

'Did you ever steal anything famous?' was Joshua's first question.

'Are you wanted by Interpol?'

'Did you ever steal from anyone who couldn't afford it?'

The last question was from Joshua. Something in his tone made Alice study his face before answering.

'Alright. Two million dollars, yes, no, and no. And point of order, I never *stole* anything. I persuaded the owners that their items would be more appreciated as part of someone else's collection.'

'Yours,' Vanessa clarified.

'Mostly,' admitted Alice. 'But not always. A lot of the time I moved the items on to other owners. Look, I'm not going to lie and say that everyone I worked with was a bad person. I was actually quite fond of some of them. And yes some of the things I ended up with would have left them feeling a bit poorer and quite upset, but no one went bankrupt as a result. I know what it is to be poor, Joshua. It's not a situation any decent person would wish on another.'

Joshua seemed relieved, confirming Alice's suspicion that he was a little too law-abiding to be drawn into her long term plans. Never mind, Vanessa was coming along nicely.

'So, you were like Robin Hood,' Rachel said.

'Yes, except I'm not a man, fictional, or a thief. And I definitely wouldn't live in a forest. Although I did have to survive for a week in the Italian mountains with just a tent and a knife.'

'Are you serious?'

Alice nodded at Rachel. That had been a particularly unpleasant seven days. She never considered herself a particularly vain person, but a week without a shower had been hideous. Afterwards, she'd been tempted to cut all her hair off, the knots had knots, but thankfully she had been talked out of it.

'Anyway,' she shook herself out of the memory. 'If we're done with my past, can we get back to the present? I need to work at the numbers some more. Vanessa, you and Joshua search the grounds again. Start at the last place you know something was taken from, and work from there towards where the body was found.'

'What about the police?' Vanessa asked, looking at Joshua.

'The constable on duty will no doubt be bored and not interested at all to hear that you're looking for your lost earring.'

'Got it.'

'And it's unlikely they'll have Joshua's description. Unless the detectives have bumped him up from a witness to a suspect in the last few hours. You'll be fine, Joshua.'

Joshua nodded but didn't look convinced.

'I would, however, change your shirt if you can.'

'I'll put my baseball cap on as well.'

'Don't do that,' Alice replied with a pained expression. 'Nothing says I'm trying to disguise my appearance like a baseball cap and sunglasses. You might as well carry a sign that says *look at me*.'

'No cap, got it. Any other advice?'

'Yes, you've done nothing wrong, so don't act so guilty. Police aren't interested in people who carry on about their business. If you see the constable, smile and say hi, then get on with what you're doing.'

'Okay, I can do that.'

'Any advice for me?' asked Vanessa.

'Plenty, but we're in company.'

Vanessa was still laughing as she and Joshua left the apartment.

SIXTEEN

'I was just wondering if you'd had any luck, you know, with my er, problem.'

'I haven't found it yet,' said Alice to Rosie, 'but I believe it's still here in the Village.' She had nothing to back up that statement other than a hunch, but better to give Rosie hope and admit she was wrong later.

'Thank you. It's been weighing on me. The thought that someone might see a painting of me without… you know.' Rosie gave a nervous laugh. She looked thinner in the face than last time she'd visited Alice.

'I promise I'll let you know as soon as I find out anything.'

Rosie thanked her several times, then left Alice alone.

As someone who had always been confident enough in her body to use it to her benefit over the years Alice couldn't summon much sympathy for the departed visitor. A body wasn't something to be ashamed of. Although Alice could understand wanting a painting back.

She stared moodily at her phone, feeling like throwing it across the room. Luckily she saw sense, sparing herself the embarrassment of having to ask Vanessa to go out and buy her a new one.

'My mum says irritation is a sign of not looking at things the right way,' Rachel said from the doorway of the spare bedroom.

'Your mother sounds like an annoying person,' Alice grumbled. 'Sorry, that was harsh.'

'But true. Mum is an annoying person. Which is probably why I got into this mess in the first place,' Rachel replied with a sigh.

Alice studied the girl sitting opposite. 'It's a mother's job to be annoying, at least for a while, then when you get a bit older it'll be her job to be indispensable.'

'Was your mother like that?'

Alice's mother had been dead for sixty years and most of the memories she had of her were as faded as the black and white photos buried in a drawer somewhere. 'My mother thought her job in life was to raise a good girl who would turn into a good wife and bear good grandchildren. I guess I only ticked one of those boxes and my mother wasn't around long enough to appreciate her granddaughter. She seemed more interested in her job than me.'

'What did she do?'

'She was a maid for a wealthy family. They treated her like rubbish and she still showed up every day. Sometimes I think that's why I've been so determined all my life not to let anyone run over me.'

Rachel nodded slowly. 'Mum seems to think that discipline is asking me if I'm alright when I do something wrong.'

'What a monster.'

Rachel laughed. 'Alright it isn't that bad, but sometimes I had to ground myself because she wasn't going to do it.'

'I applaud your dedication.'

'Don't. My groundings never lasted more than an hour.'

They both laughed and Alice almost missed her phone ringing. It was Oliver.

'I was going to send you an email but realised I don't know your address.'

'Silvermoon Retirement Village.'

'No, I mean your email address,' Oliver said.

'Oh, well I don't have one.'

'Okay. Well, the publishing company has only been around for four years. The first year it only published one book, but from then on it's been producing four books a year. I have a list. Do you want to hear it?'

'No. Can you get me copies of the books. I've got this year's ones but not the earlier ones?'

'I can try but I've already asked my bookshop contacts and none of the books are in stock anymore.'

'Mmm, I probably don't need all of them, just the ones before this current lot.'

Oliver sighed down the phone. 'I'll see what I can do. And if I can't get all the books?'

Alice tapped her finger on her knee as she thought. 'Is there another way to see the dedications at the front?'

'Maybe. I've got an idea. Oh and as to who owns it? It's registered to another company called UHC Enterprises. UHC Enterprises has two directors listed, a D Russell and G Watson.'

Neither of the names meant anything to Alice.

'Sorry, I know you were banking on some answers.'

Oliver hung up with a promise to get back to her if he found anything else out.

'What does it mean?' Rachel asked when Alice filled her in.

'Again, maybe nothing. I need to get back to these numbers.' She waved to the piece of paper on the table. A thought struck her. Something Oliver had said. Quickly she retrieved the paper and studied the numbers again.

She rearranged them several times, slowly working from the beginning based on what she knew of the New Zealand banking system. Suddenly everything clicked into place. 'It's a bank account number,' Alice said.

'Let me see.'

Rachel scrambled out of her seat and came around to kneel next to the couch. 'Weird. What a strange way to hide a bank account.'

'Indeed it is.' Alice's eyes shone as she considered the implications of the discovery.

'Why do you look so happy? We don't know whose bank account it is.'

'I'm happy because we're making progress and the more we know, the less we don't know.'

Rachel screwed up her face in confusion. 'What does that mean?'

'Mysteries, like most things in life, have a finite number of pieces to them. When you start all the pieces are turned face down. The more pieces you can turn over the clearer the picture becomes.'

'Like a jigsaw puzzle.'

'I suppose. Never liked those though. Can't see the point in putting something together when you already know what it's supposed to look like. I mean it's right on the box.'

'You can get jigsaws without the pictures on them. So you don't know what you're making.'

Alice raised her eyebrows. 'Can you? What's the point in that?'

Rachel seemed surprised by the question. 'Well, I guess to making it more challenging.'

'Mmm, anyway. We have a bank account. Not just any bank account either. One that someone went to an awful lot of trouble to keep hidden.'

'It seems a bit over the top if you ask me. Wouldn't it be easier to just write it all down somewhere? Or email it?'

'Of course it would be easier. But also less secure. A piece of paper can get lost. An email deleted. This way is much more secure.'

'Unless the book is stolen.'

'Yes but who's going to steal a novel?' Alice looked at Rachel pointedly. 'Do you remember seeing any of these other books in the house?'

Rachel began to shake her head, then her eyes fixed on one of the covers and her expression turned thoughtful. 'Maybe that one?'

'Are you asking me or telling me.'

'That one, for sure.'

Alice nodded. 'Which means it's highly likely the other two books were there as well.'

'Okay, there's something else I don't get. If the same dedication is in all the books, then what's the big deal if one of them goes missing? You can just go and buy another copy.'

Alice picked up *The Second Chance of Joshua Messer* and turned to the handwritten inscription. 'Because of this. Something tells me this is the key. Having a bank account number is only half the solution. You can't just turn up at a bank and access it. There's something in this inscription. And you stole it. Tell me something, where was it in the house?'

'It was on the dining table.'

'What was it on?'

'I just said, the dining table,' Rachel rolled her yes.

'Yes, but what was it on?' Alice repeated through gritted teeth. Eye rolling was the surest way to get on her few remaining nerves. 'Was there a shopping bag nearby?'

'Oh, actually now you mention it the book was sitting on top of a brown paper bag from the Writers Plot bookshop. There was a receipt sticking out of the book as well, but that must have slipped out while I was running.'

'So maybe the reason Shannon Jamieson is so eager to get the book back is because she hadn't read the key yet. She can't access whatever is in the account.'

Rachel's face went pale again. Alice wished she'd just faint and get it over with. All this blood draining from the face couldn't be good for you.

'She won't stop until she gets it.'

'No, but we already knew that. This doesn't change anything from that point of view, but it does give us a lot more information. And some leverage.'

Alice's phone rang before she could expand on her comment. 'That was quick.'

'Power of the internet, Alice,' Oliver replied. 'All the books are available as e-books on Amazon so it was easy to look up the info you wanted. I just checked the preview pages. Got a pen?'

He quickly rattled off a series of numbers, then repeated them more slowly. Alice read them back to him to make sure she'd written them correctly.

'Thanks, Oliver.'

The numbers were completely different to the ones from this year's books. She had the end result, the bank account, so she worked back from there, using the dedications to see if it fit. It didn't. A thought began forming in Alice's mind. She shelved it for the time being. Some things were starting to make sense, but there were still too many blank spots.

'Why are you helping me, Alice? And don't say it's because of my granddad.'

Alice sighed. She had too little time left in the world to waste it repeating herself. 'What answer would satisfy you?' she asked.

'The truth.'

'The truth is I'm helping because I can, and because I like Owen, and because I was once a girl your age in a bit of strife and I wish someone had helped me.'

'Oh. Okay.'

'Now go away, I need a rest.'

Rachel shot to her feet and disappeared into her room, stopping to grab one of the books off the coffee table.

Alice shuffled down on the couch so her head rested on the cushion. Her ankle throbbed and she briefly fantasised about the painkillers sitting on the kitchen bench. Perhaps she should have asked Rachel to fetch them before sending her away. She thought of calling out, but stubbornness held her tongue. If she just lay there for a while she was certain the pain would subside.

She'd barely closed her eyes when the front door burst open. Instantly sitting up, she saw Vanessa standing in the doorway, breathing heavily, her eyes wild.

'We have a problem.'

'Where's Joshua?' asked Alice.

'That's the problem. The police are interviewing him.'

'Take a breath.'

She waited for Vanessa to comply.

'Where is he?'

'Downstairs. She's using Tracey's office.'

'She?'

'Senior Police Constable Shannon Jamieson.'

Alice pushed aside the feeling of apprehension and struggled to her feet. 'Let's go.'

'What are you going to do?' asked Vanessa.

'What needs to be done,' Alice replied grimly.

SEVENTEEN

It was hard to work out who was more surprised when Alice quietly opened the door to Tracey's office and stepped inside. She'd asked Vanessa to wait outside, determined not to put more people in the firing line. She was already beating herself up for misjudging the safety of Joshua being able to wander the grounds.

'This is official police business,' Shannon said sternly.

She was out of uniform, wearing a blue T-shirt and a jean jacket. She sat behind Tracey's desk, while Joshua sat in the same seat as the previous day when Tracey had tried to fire him.

'No, it's not,' Alice said. She walked to the seat next to Joshua and eased herself into it.

'If it was official police business then you'd be conducting this interview at the police station.'

'It's not an interview. I'm just asking Mr Leota some questions.'

'Well then, no harm in me sitting in then,' Alice beamed.

'I don't mind,' Joshua said.

Shannon frowned, but seemed to realise she had no grounds for objection. 'I was just asking why we haven't been able to find him.'

'But you have found him, and here we are,' replied Alice.

'That's not what… Why were you hiding from the police when you knew we wanted to talk to you?'

'I was—'

'Hiding? Goodness me what a silly thought,' Alice tittered. 'Joshua was working for me. I insisted that his phone was turned off while he was on duty. I like to be the centre of attention.' She beamed again, putting on her best vacant expression.

Shannon's face showed her frustration. 'Alright, fine. I want to know if you left anything out the other day when you told us about finding the body.'

'Like what?'

'Like whether you saw anyone else that night. Maybe someone with Mr Craze?

'He was already dead when I found him,' Joshua said.

'Maybe he was. Or maybe you surprised him and there was a struggle and you stabbed him with the closest thing you had to a weapon.'

'A knitting needle?' Joshua said in disbelief. 'You think I was carrying a knitting needle just in case I was attacked.'

Shannon waved her hand irritably. 'Who knows why you were carrying it. Maybe you found it in the grounds. Wasn't there some sort of knitting event earlier in the day?'

'I didn't kill him.'

'Alright. Let's say I believe you. Was anyone else there?'

'Gracious, you think there was a gang of thieves?' Alice tried to look worried, hoping she wasn't overdoing it.

'Not a gang. But Colin was known to work with an accomplice. A young girl, about nineteen, with short dark hair. Have you seen her?'

'No,' Alice replied. 'Is she dangerous?'

'Have *you*?' Shannon looked straight at Joshua.

Joshua glanced at Alice, a tiny bead of sweat appearing on his forehead.

'Are you asking this young man if he's *ever* seen a nineteen-year-old girl with short hair?' Alice asked.

'Oh yes, I've seen plenty,' Joshua said to Shannon. 'Half the girls at university have short hair.'

'I meant that night.'

'Why would a girl from university be at the Silvermoon Retirement Village?' asked Alice.

Shannon fired a frustrated look at her and then said through gritted teeth. 'Perhaps it would be easier if you waited outside.'

'Oh, I would,' Alice nodded vigorously, 'but it's my ankle you see, it's a bit sore and I think I should rest it a while longer.'

'Mr Leota, so you didn't see anyone else the night you found Mr Craze's body?'

Joshua shook his head.

'The bushes are quite short around there.' Alice offered.

'What?' Shannon said in exasperation.

'If you were thinking that someone might have been hiding. The bushes are quite short. Maybe a small person, or a large dog. Did you see a large dog, Joshua?'

Joshua smothered a smile as he shook his head once more.

Shannon drew a card from her jacket pocket and passed it to Joshua.

'Call me if you think of anything else, Mr Leota.'

'Goodness, I'll need to lend you my cardholder, Joshua. All these police officers giving you their business cards. Is the other officer not working on the case anymore? It was Detective Miller, wasn't it? Isn't she Tracey's niece, Joshua?'

'Yes, I think so.'

'Yes, she's still on the case,' answered Shannon, 'but I'm pursuing this particular line of enquiry so I'd appreciate it if you would contact me in the first instance.'

Joshua promised he would and Shannon gave Alice a curt nod and stalked out of the office.

'Thanks,' Joshua mumbled. 'I didn't know what to do. She came out of nowhere and nabbed me before I could slip away.'

'No harm done, dear.'

The door opened and Vanessa poked her head in. 'She's gone. Got into a car and drove away.'

'She's desperate. Coming here off duty and pretending its police business. That's risky. This is about more than getting the book back,' Alice said. 'There's something we're missing.'

'Speaking of missing…' Vanessa perched on the edge of Tracey's desk. 'We didn't find any of the stolen stuff.'

'Perhaps Colin didn't take those things after all.' Alice frowned. 'If he had there was no reason for him to hide them. Unless the person who killed him took them.'

'So maybe his death doesn't have anything to do with Rachel. What if one of the things he took led to his death? Or what if there was another thief out that night and Colin stumbled into them and was killed for it.'

Alice nodded at Vanessa thoughtfully. 'It could be we're dealing with two separate crimes. And it just occurs to me that we didn't ask Rosie an important question.'

'What's Rosie got to do with this?' asked Joshua.

'That's not important, dear.'

'But you just said it was an important question!'

'I mean it's nothing for you to worry about.'

Joshua slumped in his seat. 'Yeah, why should I worry? The police just think I killed someone.'

'Save the overacting for the stage, dear. The police don't think you killed Colin, otherwise you'd be down at the police station already. Right.' Alice stood up a little too quickly and paused as the brief wave of dizziness subsided. She should have known better, sudden movements usually had consequences these days.

'Right,' she said again. 'I'm a little tired of sitting around waiting for pieces of the puzzle to present themselves to me. Time to go on the offensive.'

'I trust you don't mean that literally,' Vanessa said.

'Don't worry,' Alice reassured her. 'I'm not planning on kicking any doors down.' She looked at Vanessa's shoes. 'But you might want to put some boots on.'

EIGHTEEN

The offensive started at Alice's apartment, with her sitting on the couch, leg raised, cushion behind her back and a cup of tea in her hand. A teacup, really, because what was in it was most definitely not tea. For this exercise she had raided the hip flask hidden in a small hollow in the back of her bed's headboard.

The coffee table was clear except for a large sheet of white paper, which Vanessa was currently drawing on.

'It just has to be a rough map, Vanessa. You don't need to colour in all the different rose bushes.'

Vanessa ignored her and kept filling in details onto the plan of the Village. Alice swallowed her irritation along with a mouthful of whiskey. It was her own fault. Alice was a skilled painter, a talent taught to her by her husband who had been among other things, a master forger. She could have whipped up the plan in no time, but she had decided to let Vanessa do it, wrongly assuming the girl would draw a couple of squares and some squiggles for trees. Instead, Vanessa seemed to be channelling her inner architect, trying to get the proportions right, colour coordinating bushes and trees.

'That will do,' Alice insisted.

Reluctantly Vanessa put down her coloured pencil and sat back from her work.

Alice asked Joshua to push the table a little closer to the couch, and then she picked up a black pencil.

'Right. At 10.30pm Colin parks his car in the neighbouring street out here.' She made a mark on the edge of the paper. 'At midnight his body is found here.' A cross was added to the map.

'Oh, for goodness sake Vanessa,' Alice said when she saw her pained expression. 'What did you think we were going to do with the map? Now which apartments had things taken from them?'

Vanessa took the pencil from Alice and made several marks.

Alice frowned. 'Those are furthest from the entrance. He would have had to go past Owen's apartment to get to them.'

'Maybe he thought he'd start at the end and work his way back to Granddad's place,' Rachel suggested.

'Maybe,' Alice tapped the pencil against her lips thoughtfully. 'What sort of thief was Colin?'

'Oh,' Rachel said in surprise. 'I don't know. He seemed pretty good, but I guess he wasn't as good as he thought he was.'

'What makes you say that?' asked Alice.

'Well he didn't do very well breaking into the cop's house. He didn't even make sure she was out all night.'

'So he wasn't a great planner.'

Rachel shrugged. 'He wasn't a great planner in any other part of his life so why would stealing stuff be any different.'

Alice stared at the map. 'Do you know what I would do if I was going to break into apartments?'

'I thought you weren't a thief?'

'I wasn't,' she said. 'But that doesn't mean there weren't occasions when entering someone's house without their knowledge wasn't required. Anyway, do you know the first thing I would have done?'

The blank looks were slightly disappointing but probably a good thing, Alice thought. Especially from Rachel. It meant she hadn't gone too far down the felony route.

'If I was going somewhere like this, I'd scout things out first. Which means I…?'

'Would visit the place earlier,' Vanessa filled the silence. 'You'd want to case the joint.'

Alice grimaced at the cliché. 'I'd visit the place earlier,' she confirmed. 'Why?'

'So you'd know where to go?' said Joshua.

'Yes, but that's not the only reason. Think about it. This is a high-risk situation, the chances of being seen are greater because there are always people around. Every second I'm on the grounds increases the likelihood I'm going to be discovered. And it's dark, even with all the lights along the walkways, if I'm not familiar with the surroundings it's going to slow me down. What else?'

Vanessa snapped her fingers. 'How would you know it's worth the risk? How would you know there's anything worth taking from these places?'

'Exactly,' Alice beamed. 'The higher the risk the more reward I want. This is a retirement village, admittedly one of the better ones, but how do I know if there's anything worth taking from here? Maybe all these old fogies have is a bunch of rubbish.'

'Old fogies,' Vanessa laughed. 'You do know you're the oldest fogie here.'

'But I don't have a bunch of rubbish,' Alice replied.

'What you're saying is Colin may have came here before that night,' said Joshua.

Alice shook her head. 'No, I don't think so. There aren't that many strangers wandering the grounds on a daily basis that it wouldn't have looked suspicious to see one peering through windows. No, I'm becoming more convinced this is an inside job.'

'What! You can't think a resident or staff had anything to do with this.'

'Well, let me ask you this. Were the taken items displayed in plain sight? Or hidden away somewhere?'

'I don't…' Vanessa frowned.

'Someone had to see inside the apartments. And there's something else that doesn't make sense. Colin had a piece of paper in his pocket with the number 12 on it. Your grandfather's apartment number,' Alice said to Rachel. 'Remember his voicemail? He was desperate to get that book. Why would he waste time breaking into all those apartments if he already knew where to find you. No, the more I think about it, the more I'm convinced we're looking for two different people. A thief, and a murderer.'

'And we're no closer to identifying either of them,' Rachel said glumly.

'I suspect we're closer than you think.'

'What do you know that we don't?' Vanessa asked.

'Many things. Goodness, I can't believe how stupid I've been. I still need you to check one thing for me. Just ask one question.'

She told them the question and Vanessa seemed troubled but agreed.

Fifteen minutes later they had their answer.

NINTEEN

'I honestly don't know what you're talking about.'

'I think you do.'

Glenda licked her lips and looked around her shoebox office. She and Alex were crammed in around her desk, while Vanessa waited in the corridor outside.

'You think I broke into multiple apartments and stole things?'

'Why not? You'd visited each of the apartments, I checked. Part of your, *introduce yourself* tour. I'm assuming I would have noticed something missing from my place at some point.'

'Can I suggest you see a doctor, Alice, because these delusions could point to a serious mental problem.'

'I am worried about a mental problem,' Alice admitted. 'I should have seen it sooner, but I've been a little distracted. I had a look at your personnel file, you've had quite a few jobs over the past six years.'

'How did you see that? That file is confidential.'

Alice was impressed by the indignant look on Glenda's face, but wasn't going to fall for the obvious attempt to change the subject.

'I'm guessing if I track down some of your old colleagues they'll tell me the same thing. That you left under a cloud of suspicion relating to thefts from—'

Glenda leaned back in her chair and laughed. Her hands were tightly clenched into fists and her eyes darted to the filing cabinet in the corner of the office. 'You can see yourself out. I'm very busy, but you can rest assured that I'll be taking this up with Tracey. Reading employee files is a gross breach of privacy.'

Alice stayed where she was and continued speaking as if Glenda hadn't interrupted. 'What I don't know is *why* you steal things. Is it for cash? Or is it some compulsion to take things that belong to other people?'

She was thankful that Vanessa wasn't in the room to point out the irony of her questions.

'Seriously, Alice, I think you need to get your medication checked.'

'Undoubtedly. What I don't understand is why you killed Colin.'

'What?'

'It's quite a leap from petty thief to murderer.'

Glenda's face lost all its colour as she stammered out a protest. 'I didn't kill anyone.'

'Maybe. That's for the police to decide. And while they're talking to you about that, I wonder what they might find in that filing cabinet over there.'

'Okay, okay, stop.' Glenda seemed to be having an internal battle. Finally she licked her lips and said, 'look I admit I took some things, but I did not kill anyone. I'm not a murderer. I'm a vegetarian. Please, you have to believe me.'

'I don't *have* to do anything, but let's for a moment say I did believe you. Tell me exactly what happened that night.'

Glenda fumbled open her desk drawer and pulled out a small bottle half-filled with clear liquid. She took a deep swallow, then replaced the bottle.

'I was organising the games in this building. It was a great cover because I didn't need to be here all the time and it meant I knew who was here and away from their apartment. I'd slip out for five minutes, race across to the apartment blocks, take something, and store it in here before going back to the games room.'

Alice nodded. It actually was pretty clever.

'That night, on my last trip, it must have been just after ten thirty, I saw someone lurking behind the main building. He seemed to be waiting for someone, but I didn't stick around. He saw me, and that was enough to tell me my night was done. I went home. He was still alive when I left him. I didn't know who he was. I'd never seen him before, so I had no motive to kill him.'

'Did you see anyone else?'

Glenda shook her head, then paused and looked thoughtful. 'I didn't see anyone but I heard someone call out. The voice was quiet but I'm pretty sure.'

Alice considered this before asking her follow up question. 'Did you take Freda's knitting needles?'

Glenda nodded glumly. 'I panicked when you asked about them the other day, especially when they were sitting just a few feet away. Freda was one of the last ones to leave that day, so it was easy to distract her and swipe them from her bag.'

'Why take them? They're knitting needles. Are they really so collectable?'

'The elephant figures on the ends are made from ivory, which is banned in pretty much every country. They're highly valuable.'

Alice shook her head. 'Freda bought them in 1983 at Wellington Zoo. There's no way they're ivory.'

Glenda looked stunned. 'But I heard...'

'You heard two friends sharing a joke. You realise,' Alice said, 'that you just confessed to murder.'

'What? I did not. I told you I didn't kill anyone.'

'Then how did one of Freda's knitting needles – stolen by you – end up as the murder weapon?'

Glenda leapt to her feet. 'That's not possible. They're here. I'll show you.' She took a key from her pocket and unlocked the top drawer of the filing cabinet. She pulled out a rectangular flat wooden box which she placed on the desk. 'Everything I took is in here.'

She opened the box using a smaller key and lifted the lid off. Alice stood up to see better. The box was filled with items Alice recognised from Vanessa's descriptions. She rummaged amongst them but couldn't find the knitting needles.

'They're not here.'

Glenda grabbed the box from Alice and conducted her own search, with the same result. She slumped back into her seat, distress all over her features. 'That's impossible. I put them in there myself.'

'Well, either you took them out yourself and used one to murder Colin,' Alice said, 'or someone came into your office when you weren't here, broke into your filing cabinet and your wooden box, took the needles, then locked both things and left again. Which do you think is more believable?'

'I didn't kill anyone!'

'Unfortunately for you that is the sort of thing a murderer would say.'

Glenda's distress turned to panic. 'Now hang on. I'll admit to taking those things, I'll even go to the police and tell them, but I did not kill anyone. I won't go to prison for murder.'

'Then I need something more than a vague statement about a voice calling out.'

'I don't know anything else. I only heard about three words.'

Alice waited for her to divulge the three words, then sighed when Glenda's mouth stayed quiet. She did so despise having to drag information out of people. 'Well?'

'Oh. She said, *Hey, you.*'

'Are you sure that's what she said?' Alice frowned.

'Pretty sure.'

Damn.

TWENTY

'Is she telling the truth? About not being the murderer?' Vanessa asked.

'She seemed genuinely shocked when I suggested it. And why admit she took the murder weapon? No, I'm inclined to believe her – for now.'

Vanessa wheeled Alice into the lobby just as Tracey emerged from her office.

'Oh, Alice. Good. Can I talk to you?' Tracey came over to them.

'I have something to do right now, Tracey, can it wait?'

'No, it needs to be now,' Tracey wrung her hands together.

'What is it?'

'In my office, please.'

Alice stifled her irritation. She wanted to get upstairs and have a particularly stern conversation, and it would be more effective if she was still feeling cross when she had it. 'Fine, let's go.'

Tracey stayed where she was. 'This might be a conversation for just the two of us.'

'Oh for goodness sake. Vanessa can hear anything you have to say.'

Once they were in her office with the door closed, Tracey sat behind her desk and picked up a rubber band, which she began to twist around her fingers. 'I had a call this morning from someone wanting to buy Silvermoon.'

Alice wasn't surprised. There were rumours of regular probes by some of the bigger retirement village chains wanting to absorb Silvermoon into their brand.

'Did you give the usual response?' Alice said.

Tracey nodded. 'I told them the owners weren't interested in selling but they still wanted the offer presented to the owner.'

'Why are you telling Alice?' Vanessa asked.

'Oh for goodness sake, Vanessa, don't be slow.'

Vanessa's mouth dropped open. 'You? You own Silvermoon?'

'Of course I do. Consider the offer received and rejected.'

'Don't you want to know how much they offered?' The rubber band in Tracey's hands snapped. 'The thing is, this isn't the first time they've contacted me. I took the first offer to the lawyers – um, your lawyers, I guess. Now they've come back with a higher offer.'

'What's the offer?' Alice asked.

Tracey said a number that had Vanessa choking in her seat. Alice nodded thoughtfully. If she cared about money it would have been extremely tempting. And if Amanda cared about Alice's money then it would have been more tempting. But Alice was too close to the grave to care about accruing more wealth, and Amanda was determined to make her own.

Alice shook her head. 'My decision stands. But thank you for telling me, Tracey.'

Tracey looked relieved. 'Should I, would it be better… in future…?'

'Knowing I'm the owner doesn't change the process. Continue to communicate through my lawyers as you normally do.'

Alice indicated to Vanessa she was ready to leave but stopped her at the door. 'Out of curiosity, who made the offer?'

Tracey checked a piece of paper on her desk. 'A company called Rooproop Enterprises.'

Alice had never heard of them. 'On second thought, if you receive any further approaches from them bring them straight to me.'

'Of course,' replied Tracey.

Vanessa waited until they were in the elevator before bursting out with, 'What the actual H-E-double-hockey-sticks?'

Alice looked at her.

'I've been researching different ways to say swearwords,' Vanessa shrugged. 'You own frigging Silvermoon? Why did I not know that?'

'Because nobody knows that. Tracey only found out because she was going to fire Joshua and I had to pull rank. You are not to tell *anybody*, do you understand?'

Vanessa sighed. 'I guess I'll add it to the list of secrets I'm keeping about you.'

'Good girl. Now back to more important things like murder investigations.'

'But it wasn't important,' Rachel was almost in tears. 'He was still alive when I left him.'

'That seems to be a common theme,' Alice muttered. They were back in her apartment and she was asking the questions she should have asked much earlier.

'Tell me exactly what happened,' she said.

Rachel sniffed and Joshua passed her a tissue from the box on the coffee table. She blew her nose then scrunched the tissue up in her fist.

'Colin texted me to say he was on the grounds. Said either I came down to him or he'd come up and meet my granddad. So I went down and we talked and I told him I didn't have the book and that he needed to leave.'

'And?' Alice said when she fell silent.

'I swear, that's all that happened.'

'I need to know exactly what was said.'

Rachel shoved the used tissue into her jeans pocket and plucked a fresh one from the box. She began tearing tiny pieces off and balling them up between her finger and thumb. 'I got to the door to Granddad's building and checked to see if anyone was around. I saw Colin. There was a woman as well.'

'There was a woman? Where?'

'She was walking away.'

'Walking away like she'd been talking to Colin?' asked Alice.

Rachel frowned, then shook her head. 'I don't think so. She was quite far away from him.'

Alice gestured for her to continue.

'I called out to him and we talked. He wanted the book.' She snorted. 'He didn't even care about me, just about the stupid book. Tried to tell me that it was the key to us getting rich. Only he slipped up and said it was the key to *him* getting rich, before he realised what he said. Idiot.'

Alice agreed. 'Did he say *how* the book was going to get him rich?' she asked.

'No. Just that the book was worth millions, but I mean, look at it, it's just a paperback.'

So that bank account had millions in it, Alice thought. She thought she knew exactly who the money belonged to – Justin Fry. It was the only explanation. That was the reason Justin Fry came to Silvermoon that afternoon. He wanted his money back.

She pushed the idea aside and returned to Rachel. 'What happened when he asked for the book?'

'I said he was crazy and told him to leave me alone. He grabbed my arm, and pulled out his knife. I thought he was going to kill me. But there was a noise and my shirt ripped and I took off inside.'

'What sort of noise?' Joshua asked.

Rachel shrugged. 'I don't know. A noise.'

Alice felt a headache forming behind her eyes. 'Was it a noise like an elephant walking through a china shop? Or like a rolled up piece of paper hitting a carpeted floor?'

'That's…I mean that's a big range,' replied Rachel.

'That was my point, dear. Telling me you heard a sound is only marginally less helpful than *not* telling me you heard a sound at all. Details, girl, I need details,' Alice slapped her own knee.

'Okay, okay, I get it. Jeez. Let me think.'

Alice wanted to slap her knee again, or something else, while the seconds dragged out.

'It was almost like footsteps, but the noise was really short. Like maybe they stopped.'

Alice closed her eyes and counted to ten. When she opened them again she was still cross. 'I should ring Shannon Jamieson and hand you over to her.'

Rachel leapt to her feet, closely followed by Joshua. 'You can't—.'

'No!'

'Oh stop it, both of you,' Alice snapped. 'I said I should, not I would.'

Slowly they sat back down.

'What time was this conversation with Colin?'

Rachel thought carefully before replying. 'At 11.35pm.'

'And the conversation lasted only a few minutes?'

Rachel nodded.

'Then there was a short window of about fifteen minutes between when you went back upstairs and when Joshua found the body.'

'Does that help us?' asked Vanessa.

'It might. Because it pretty much rules out an accident. Quarter of an hour minutes might be plenty of time in a dark alleyway to come across someone and decide to kill them, but your average thug doesn't tend to hang out at Silvermoon. Someone waited until everyone had left and took their chance.'

'Maybe they followed Colin from his car?' Joshua said.

Alice shook her head. 'I think we're too far into this investigation for maybes.'

She thought for a while but kept coming back to the fact they were dealing with two different crimes, and her focus was being pulled between them. She couldn't escape the hunch that if they solved one of them, the other would become clearer. It was a question of motive – was it murder or money? And how did the knitting needles get from Glenda's office cabinet into the back of Colin's neck. And where was the matching needle in the pair?

She reached for her phone.

There was a knock at the door and Vanessa answered to find Owen standing there.

'What are you doing here?' Alice asked.

'Rachel, thank goodness you're alright.' Owen rushed into the room and embraced his startled granddaughter.

'Why wouldn't I be alright?' Rachel's voice was muffled by Owen's hug.

Finally, he let her go and studied her face before turning to Alice. 'I may have made a mistake in coming here.'

TWENTY-ONE

Owen straightened his tie, then pulled at the cuffs of his shirt.

'Granddad, what's going on?'

Alice narrowed her eyes and ran through the possibilities in her head. 'Who called you?' she asked.

'I don't know, but she said Rachel had been hurt and was asking for me.'

'Why didn't you call me here to check?' asked Rachel.

'I tried—'

'Irrelevant,' Alice snapped. 'We need to move. Now!' By the time she'd struggled to her feet, Vanessa was the only one moving. The others were staring at her in astonishment. 'Vanessa, fill them in.'

'Someone figured out the best way to find Rachel was to have Owen lead them to her. If they're not already here, then they're on their way.' Vanessa scooped the books off the coffee table and shoved them into Joshua's arms. 'Move!' she snapped at Rachel.

Too slowly for Alice's liking they hustled out of the apartment. The display above the elevator showed the car was at the ground floor. Before they could press the button to summon it, the display changed from G to 1.

'Stairs,' Alice ordered.

The others hustled through the stairwell door and Vanessa started to push the wheelchair through.

'No, I'll stall them,' Alice said.

'I'm not leaving you—'

'Take the others to the games room.'

Vanessa hesitated, and Alice pushed her through the door. 'Go.'

Without seeing if she obeyed, Alice quickly turned the chair around, then shuffled forward out of the chair and eased herself to the ground. As the elevator doors began to open, she let out a groan.

'Are you alright?'

Alice permitted herself the tiniest of smiles. 'I think so. Constable Jamieson, wasn't it?'

Shannon loomed over Alice, a strange look on her face as she looked around the small landing, before reaching down and helping Alice back into the wheelchair.

'What happened?'

'Stubbornness, I'm afraid,' Alice replied. 'I can't abide the thought I need help getting anywhere, so I tried to do it by myself. It didn't go well, as you can see.'

Shannon gave her a smile that didn't reach her eyes. 'Are you alone?'

'More often than not these days. A consequence of getting old.'

'Would you mind if I have a look inside your apartment?'

'Well, I can't see why you would want to, but you are a police officer so I trust you have a good reason.'

Alice opened her front door and Shannon pushed her wheelchair inside. Alice noticed that the woman moved quickly through the door and stepped to the right, probably in case someone was waiting to leap out at her.

'Were you coming to see me for a reason?' Alice asked.

Shannon didn't answer as she scanned the room. She stepped further in and Alice watched as she turned her head, first towards Alice's bedroom, then to the spare room.

'Your apartment is beautiful,' said Shannon. She started towards the spare room door, which was slightly ajar. As she neared, Alice couldn't help noticing Shannon slip her hand into her jacket pocket and pull something out. She kept her hand in front of her so Alice couldn't see what she was holding.

'Is there anything in particular you're looking for?' Alice said.

Shannon pushed open the door and leapt into the room, only to reappear a few seconds later, her hand back in her jacket pocket.

'If you told me what you were looking for, perhaps I could help.'

'There have been reports of suspicious individuals hanging around the complex.'

Alice bit her tongue to subdue the sarcastic comment that formed there. Instead she said, 'There are plenty of suspicious-looking people residing at Silvermoon. I hope you don't intend to arrest us all.'

Shannon crossed the room and repeated her move into Alice's bedroom. When she reappeared her face was a mix of frustration and disappointment.

'I understand you're a friend of Owen. When was the last time you saw him?'

'I suppose it's been a few days.' Alice pretended to be puzzled. 'He's out of town visiting friends, I believe.' She gave a little laugh. 'I do hope you're not considering Owen a suspicious individual. Although I think he'd be quietly chuffed,' she chuckled.

Shannon crossed to Alice and stood close enough that Alice had to tilt her neck up to see her face.

'What about his granddaughter? When did you last see her?'

Alice noticed that Shannon kept her hand firmly inside her pocket. She could have been holding a small gun. There wasn't enough of an outline for it to be a full-sized pistol or revolver. More likely a knife or canister of pepper spray.

'I've never met his granddaughter. Owen has often said how disappointed he is that his family doesn't come and visit more often.'

'I don't believe you.'

'That's your prerogative.'

'Where is she?' A bead of sweat had formed on Shannon's forehead. Alice kept her apartment at a comfortable temperature so she didn't think the moisture had anything to do with the heat.

'Who?'

'Rachel! Owen's granddaughter. Where is she?'

'I told you I don't know her.'

'You're lying,' Shannon snapped. She whipped her hand out of her pocket. It held a nasty-looking knife. Although, as she studied it, Alice decided that any knife when brandished like this one would be considered nasty.

'Let's stay calm, shall we?' Alice said.

'I need to know where she is.'

'Then you shouldn't have pulled a knife on me, dear. There's no way I would tell you now, even if I knew,' Alice added.

Shannon waved the blade closer to Alice's face.

'Please don't do that,' Alice said. She tried to keep her voice steady but her heart was beating unhealthily fast. She took a couple of deep breaths to slow it down. If she was going to act, she didn't need shaky hands sabotaging her.

'I need to find the girl,' Shannon hissed.

'Why? What's she done?'

'She stole something. I need it back.'

More sweat joined the first droplet and Shannon's face was bright red. Alice became concerned she might be having a stroke or heart attack. There were some pieces of the puzzle Alice still wanted, which might not be provided if the woman dropped dead of natural causes.

'The book,' Alice said.

Shannon straightened in surprise. 'Yes. Where is it? Is it here?'

She whirled around. For a moment her back was to Alice.

If Alice had been thirty years younger, she would have jumped up and disarmed the woman easily. But age and injury put paid to that possibility.

'Is it here?' Shannon spun back, grabbing Alice by the arm. 'Give it to me.'

Her fingers bit into Alice's skin and she brought the knife close enough to touch Alice's chest.

I've had enough of this, Alice thought. 'Do you know what you should never do when you're holding a knife to someone?' she said.

Shannon looked confused at the abrupt change in subject.

'You should never get so close you can't see their hands.' Alice grasped the thumb on the hand holding the knife and twisted it sharply.

Shannon yelped and dropped the knife, Alice deftly catching it by the handle.

Shannon clutched her injured hand to her chest and stared at Alice in disbelief.

'There, now we can have a civilised conversation.'

'Who are you?'

'I'm someone interested in resolving this mess without anyone getting hurt. Well, hurt much.'

Shannon flexed her thumb. Anger replaced pain on her face and she balled her hand into a fist.

'Don't be silly. Unlike you, I'm more than proficient with this, but I'd prefer not to have to get blood stains out of my carpet.'

Shannon stood breathing heavily. It seemed like she was preparing to launch herself at Alice, despite the knife, but slowly everything drained from her face except for an expression of desperation and defeat. 'I need that book.'

'For the money.'

Alice enjoyed the shocked reaction. 'I know whose money it is, I just wonder what on earth convinced you that stealing from Justin Fry was a good idea.'

'How could you possibly...?'

'I might be old but I can put two and two together and come up with the right number. Colin said the numbers were worth millions. But the numbers are worthless without the handwritten ones in the book Rachel stole. They're the key to the whole thing. I'm guessing an access code of some sort. And without that you can't get the money. What I don't understand is why go through all this complicated stuff with the numbers and the books? Why not just give the numbers?'

'I don't know what you're talking about. I've never heard of Justin Fry.'

'If you want to lie then I can't help you, dear.'

'Help me? You just tried to break my thumb.'

'And you just threatened me with a knife so let's not quibble over semantics.'

'I...I...'

Shannon rushed forward. Alice held out the knife but Shannon raced past her and through the front door.

'That's annoying. I had more questions to ask,' Alice muttered.

Struggling to her feet she reached out and pushed the front door firmly closed, waiting to hear the click of the lock before settling back into the wheelchair.

She studied the knife, but it had no distinguishing features beyond a folding blade and black handle. It looked like it would cause a lot of damage if the pointy end went into a body. Alice folded the blade and slipped the knife into her pants pocket. It was only then she leaned forward, placed her elbows on her knees and released the shakes she'd been holding inside. She wasn't concerned for herself, she had long ago accepted her close proximity to the grave. But she had come to feel she had more reasons to stave off death, and three of them were currently hiding in the games room.

Alice took a deep breath and held it as long as she could before slowly letting it out. By the time her lungs were empty, the shakes had stopped and she was back in control. 'Getting soft in my old age.'

Standing up, she retrieved a cane from beside the door and hobbled out of her apartment.

She exited her building, seeing no sign of Shannon or her police car, and slowly made her way to the Olympic complex. When Alice got to the games room she found Rachel, Owen, and Joshua.

'Where's Vanessa?' asked Alice.

'She went back for you,' Owen said. 'Didn't you see her?'

TWENTY-TWO

'I'm coming with you,' Joshua said.

'No,' Alice said. 'I need you here in case anyone comes back.'

'I don't need a guard,' Owen protested.

Alice stifled the urge to be blunt and point out that the closest Owen had ever been to physical violence in his life was punching holes into paper then pushing it across the desk.

'I'd feel happier if Joshua stayed.'

'What about you?'

'I'll be fine,' Alice said. 'The most likely scenario is that Vanessa got waylaid by another resident. There's no reason to believe she's in any danger.'

'Then there's no reason why we shouldn't all go,' Owen said.

Never argue with a banker, Alice thought.

'It's called not putting all our eggs into one basket,' she said. 'Or in this case, all our potential hostages in one location.'

'Isn't that what you just did with us?' Rachel asked.

'I thought you said she was fine,' Joshua said at the same time.

'I said it was the most likely scenario. Look, we could argue for a while and then you do as I ask, or we can skip all that and you can just do as I ask now.'

As she hobbled alone down the corridor, Alice paused outside Glenda's office. Something had occurred to her – one of many questions she should have thought to ask sooner. She knocked and poked her head inside, but the office was empty. Alice made a mental note to come back later. She would have picked the lock to the filing cabinet and answered the question herself, but she didn't think she had time.

As Alice stepped through the front entrance to the Olympic complex she considered her options. It was possible Shannon had taken Vanessa, but the timing was off. She would have had to grab Vanessa in a public place and take her somewhere private, all in the space of the few minutes between leaving Alice's apartment, and Alice arriving at the ground floor. That was the problem with any scenario. While Silvermoon wasn't exactly the Wellington train station during peak hour, it also wasn't a cemetery at night. There were usually people around, going for walks or sitting on one of the many benches dotted around the grounds. Taking Vanessa without witnesses would have been difficult.

Alice decided to start at the concierge desk. It was usually Vanessa's base but in her absence there was always someone else on and they might have seen Vanessa.

Halfway back to the building Alice's phone buzzed. It was Vanessa.

'Where are you?' Alice asked.

'In Tracey's office. Could you pop in for a minute?'

'Sure, I'll be right there.'

'Thank you, Ms Atkinson.'

By the time Alice opened Tracey's office door her hobble had worsened, and she was leaning heavily on the cane.

Vanessa was sitting in one of the visitor chairs, with a large man looming over her. Justin Fry sat behind the desk, his fingers rapping lightly on the desktop.

'Ah, Alice, please come in.'

Alice crossed to the second visitor chair and sat with a sigh of relief. She studied Vanessa's face, and was satisfied that she didn't appear to be injured or terrified.

'The gorilla is a bit unnecessary, don't you think?'

'Careful, Carl is very sensitive.'

'So he'll beat you up but feel bad about it afterwards?' suggested Alice.

Justin's lips twitched. 'The girl, where is she?'

'The girl isn't important,' Alice replied. 'She doesn't have what you need. I do.'

'Oh? And what is it I need?'

Alice made a point of looking at Carl who returned her look with features set in concrete. She held his gaze long enough to show she wasn't intimidated, then slowly winked at him before turning back to Justin Fry. 'You need your money back, and I can get it for you.'

Justin's face was as expressionless as his employee's, and despite his smaller stature, it was even more unsettling. Alice had played too much poker over the years to reveal anything other than boredom in her own.

'Carl, wait outside.'

Carl moved instantly, which Alice found an interesting indication of the control Justin Fry had over his underlings.

'Are you alright, dear?'

Vanessa nodded ruefully. 'Sorry, he…,' she jerked her head in Justin's direction, '…stopped me in the lobby and asked for my help. Then gorilla-man appeared and they brought me in here.'

'But they didn't hurt you?'

'No, the arm-twisting was more implied.'

'You see Alice? I'm not a violent man, but you are correct. Some money has been taken from me and I want it back.'

'Not just some money, a lot of money,' Alice said. 'For a number of years at my guess.'

A pained expression crossed his face. His fingers stopped tapping and curled into fists. 'Do you know what a reputation is, Alice?'

'Hard to build, easy to lose.'

The man nodded appreciatively. 'I see you have some experience with reputations. Mine has been carefully carved over a number of years, and should it be known that someone has stolen from me, then my reputation, my entire business, would be at risk. I won't allow that to happen.'

'Is that why you killed Colin?'

'Who?'

'Sorry, you're right, what I meant to say is, is that why you had Colin killed? You'd never have done it yourself, of course.'

'Again, I say, who?'

'If you don't know who Colin is, then how do you know who the girl is?' asked Alice.

'I want my money. If you can get it for me, then I suggest you do it now.'

'It's not that easy—'

'Stop!' Justin slammed his fist onto the desk. Instantly the office door was thrown open and Alice felt a rush of air signalling Carl's return. Justin held up his hand and there was a click as the door closed again. 'You were about to tell me that it's complicated, that you need more time. I want my money *now*. Either you can get it, or you can't. And if you can't then you're of no use to me. Let me make myself clear. If the girl is on this property, I will tear down every door, rip apart every room, until I find her. Am I clear?'

Alice saw Vanessa's face go pale. She wanted to reach out and give her a reassuring pat but both of her hands were currently in her pockets. She decided enough was enough and pulled her left hand out to show Justin her phone.

'Is this where you threaten to call the police?' Justin sneered.

'No, this is where I tell you that everything said in this room has just been recorded on my granddaughter's voicemail.' She held up the phone to show the call in progress. 'So let me be clear. If you want your money, you will come back in two hours, alone, and meet me in the games room in the Olympic Complex. I will ensure you get your money back, and you will promise to leave Rachel and her family alone, forever. She didn't take your money. She was just unlucky enough to steal the thing everyone seems to need to access it.'

'Or how about I take your phone from you, send my men to retrieve the recording, and hurt you until you give me what I want.'

Alice sighed. This wasn't going as she'd hoped, but it wasn't unexpected. 'Your man is pretty fast.'

Justin nodded.

'How fast is he?'

She pulled her other hand out and clicking the button, the knife blade sprang free. She flipped the knife into the air and deftly caught the blade between her thumb and finger. Inwardly she gave a jump for joy at pulling the manoeuvre off. She hadn't done it in decades. 'Is he fast enough to stop me throwing this knife through your throat?'

Justin's eyes betrayed his surprise.

'I might not have the strength I once did, but there's only a few feet between us, and this is a light knife. Two hours. Just give me two hours then it can all be over and everybody gets what they want.'

For a long moment nobody moved, then Justin gave a curt nod and stood up. 'Fine, you can have two hours.'

He rounded the desk and paused just out of arms reach. 'Why did you record us? How did you know to bring the knife?' he asked.

'Vanessa would never call me Ms Atkinson.'

Justin nodded again, then left without saying another word.

'Cool trick,' Vanessa cleared her throat. 'Would you really have killed him?'

Alice carefully folded the blade and put the knife back in her pocket. 'Honestly, I was more likely to hit you than him if I threw it. I was taught that flipped blade trick by a man in a circus in the 1950s. Our lessons never got as far as throwing.'

'Damn, as if I needed any reminder never to play poker against you. Why did you tell him you needed two hours?'

'Because I need that long to organise things.'

Vanessa's eyes narrowed as she studied Alice. 'What are you cooking up?'

Alice feigned innocence. 'I know I should come up with some witty cooking metaphor right now, but I hate cooking, was never good at it. I've always been good at manipulating people though. Time to put an end to all this nonsense.'

'Just like that,' said Vanessa.

'Just like that,' Alice confirmed with a wink.

TWENTY-THREE

Two hours later Justin Fry walked into a room full of people. To give him credit he only paused for a fraction before walking over to where Alice was seated.

'Well?'

'Please sit down.'

Justin scanned the room, then took a seat opposite Alice.

'I wasn't expecting an audience,' he commented.

'No, but everyone in the room is involved in this situation in some way so it seems appropriate that they are all here.'

Justin's eyes scanned the room once more but either he was a better poker player than Alice thought, or he really didn't recognise anyone.

'So this is what? A denouement?' Justin asked. 'A grand reveal?'

Alice shrugged. 'It worked for Agatha Christie.'

Justin waved a hand impatiently. 'Alright then, get on with it.'

Alice took a deep breath. All going, well this whole thing would be wrapped up nicely and she would get her apartment back. All her visitors had well and truly overstayed their welcome.

'Someone in your organisation is stealing money from you and has been for the last four years. Someone with a sense of theatrics and a pathological need for security. They use different bank account numbers every year, hiding the numbers in the dedications of four published books. There's never any direct communication linking them to the bank account. Smart, but complicated. I don't know how much has been taken but I'm guessing it's in the millions. You only recently learned about the theft, which implies either a lack of oversight on your part, or that you make so much money you didn't miss a million here or there.'

Justin's expression didn't change beyond a slight narrowing of his eyes. 'May I see your phone?' he said.

Alice pulled her phone from her pocket and passed it over. Justin touched the screen, then passed it back and gave a slight nod for her to continue.

'As I said, two alternatives there, but I suspect the latter,' Alice continued. 'That must be nice. Anyway, things were going well for the embezzler, they had a partner who would decipher the bank account and who would transfer the money elsewhere. Do you know if you search the right websites you can get a list of employees? Anyway the scam went smoothly for several years, but this year something went wrong. I thought Colin owed you money. That's what he told Rachel. But that's not true is it Justin? You're not a loan shark, and Colin was too low brow to lend money too. I think it was something else. Then it came to me. Colin was a confidential informant for the police. But what if he was feeding information the other way as well.'

She paused but apart from the tiniest movement in his eyebrow Justin remained passive.

'When Colin found out about the scheme he concocted a plan to steal the book containing the cypher needed to access the bank account. He saw this as a way to get out from between two rather nasty people. He broke into the house of Constable Shannon McAlpine. I'm not one hundred percent sure how she's connected to the other thieves. Maybe she decided to double cross her partners, or maybe she somehow found out about the scam and decided to take the money for herself. Whichever it was Colin broke into her house but she was home. Sadly he was a cowardly weasel who ran, leaving Rachel behind.'

There was a gasp from the corner of the room where Rachel was trying to her best to hide behind Owen.

'He already knew who you were, Rachel. Better to meet you in a room full of people.'

Justin turned to study Rachel before bringing his gaze back to Alice. He gave a slight nod for her to continue.

'Have you met Constable McAlpine?' Alice indicated Shannon who sat bolt upright in her chair.

'No, but I know her reputation,' Justin's face was stony.

'Yes, well Colin, being the greedy man he was, planned to keep all the money for himself, so he didn't tell Rachel exactly what she was there to take. He just said it was a valuable book. She claims she grabbed the right one by accident, but I suspect that's another in a long list of her lies. She knew which book to take because he told her the title, he just didn't tell her why it was valuable.'

That had been one of the things bothering Alice. Of all the things in Shannon's house, how had Rachel happened to pick up the one thing she was there to find? (In the 1970s Alice had met a brilliant mathematician who could rattle off statistical probability like others rattled off shopping lists. He would have said the likelihood was improbable that Rachel would pick the right book – although not impossible.)

Looking at Rachel's face, Alice knew her guess had been correct. The girl had lied from the beginning so it hadn't been a stretch to suggest she'd been lying about other things.

'When it all went sideways Rachel got scared and came here to hide out with her grandfather. Somehow Colin found out where she was (she probably told him herself) and came to get the book. Only to wind up dead. The way I see it, there are three suspects: Rachel herself…'

Everyone in the room turned to look at Rachel who was clutching Owen's arm.

'Now see here, Alice—'

Alice held up her hand to cut off Owen's protest.

'…which is unlikely. For one, she had no access to the murder weapon. Second, she doesn't come across as a stone-cold killer. It takes nerve to stick around after you've murdered someone and nothing about Rachel suggests that she has any.'

'Gee, thanks,' Rachel muttered.

'You'd prefer I think you're a psychopath?' Alice raised her eyebrows.

'No! I just meant… Never mind.' Rachel shrunk back down behind Owen.

'So, let us eliminate Rachel as a suspect. We then turn to Constable Shannon Jamieson and theory number two. Shannon was desperate to get the book back, *and* she knew Colin. In fact, I expect that's how Colin heard about the books in the first place. Shannon must have let it slip.'

'What makes you think I knew him?' Shannon asked.

'Common sense.' And a phone call she'd made to Kevin Mackay. Her friend had been able to find answers to a couple of questions she'd had. 'A scheme like this, stealing from Justin Fry…' she enjoyed the slight wince on the man's face as she said it. '…works only if few people know about it. It's not impossible Colin found out some other way, but he was a low-level criminal. It's more likely that he was your informant.'

This Kevin had confirmed. According to Kevin, Colin had been working for Shannon as an informer since she'd busted him for petty theft four years earlier.

'So Shannon let it slip and Colin saw a chance to take the money for himself. He thought he was being smart getting Rachel to do the actual robbery, but he didn't know Rachel was double crossing him. Robbing a police officer was a step too far for her, so she talked to Shannon. But that went wrong when Rachel panicked and took the one thing she shouldn't have. I'd guess Shannon only left the book out as bait. As a cop Shannon had the resources to track Rachel through her family. She found Colin, confronted him, and killed him.'

Alice waited for an outburst of professed innocence, but Shannon just shook her head.

'I can see how you got there. It's a good theory, but way off the truth. The first I knew about Colin being here was when his body was called in. And I'm not stupid. Why would I kill him without first finding out where the book was? It doesn't make sense.'

'Only if we assume you kept your cool. But as our earlier meeting in my apartment showed, you're not always great at that are you, Constable?'

Shannon scowled, telling everyone in the room that Alice had hit her mark.

'Then we have theory number three, that Justin Fry found out that he had an embezzler and came to get his money back.' Alice paused.

'This is fascinating.' Justin leaned back in his chair and smiled. 'Please continue.'

'Justin runs a successful accounting firm. One of the biggest in Wellington. Losing money is bad for business.' Alice thought suggesting exactly how Justin Fry made his money might be hazardous to her health and to the others in the audience, so she deliberately avoided mentioning that part. 'He would want to keep the problem as quiet as possible,' Alice continued.

'Murder isn't exactly quiet,' Justin pointed out.

'On the contrary, murder can be very quiet. It's the aftermath that's noisy. No one heard a thing, despite a witness seeing Colin alive a few minutes before the body was discovered.'

'Perhaps the person who discovered the body was the killer,' suggested Justin.

Alice smiled, 'The only way I could be more sure that's not the case was if I had discovered the body myself.'

'As you said, I'm a businessman. I'm not in the habit of wandering around in the middle of the night murdering people.'

No, you're more likely to do it in the daytime, Alice thought.

'I suppose a successful person like yourself would have people for that,' she said.

'I have a driver, a cleaner, and a personal assistant, but I don't have a killer on my payroll. And while all this theorising is fascinating, I came here because you said you could get my money back.'

Alice pulled a slip of paper out of her pocket and passed it to him. 'It may not be everything, but the majority of your money should still be in that bank account.'

Justin glanced at the paper. 'Where's the access code?'

'I wanted to ensure we came to an agreement. You get your money, and no action is to be taken against Rachel or her grandfather. She was a simpleminded pawn as you can plainly see.'

'Agreed,' Justin said instantly. He and Alice held each other's gaze. Justin was the first to look away.

Alice withdrew a second piece of paper containing the five digit pin code. Once she decided the written inscription was an access code she worked at it, eventually converting the number of letters in each word into a number and arriving at 14399. She decided not to tell Justin that she was sure it worked because she'd accessed the account just before coming to the meeting.

Justin stood up and placed the papers in his jacket pocket. 'This has been educational, but I have other matters to attend to.'

'You can't let him leave,' Vanessa protested. 'He's a murder suspect!'

He turned towards her and Vanessa took a tiny step backwards. 'Alice was incorrect in one point. The aftermath of a murder isn't always noisy. I'm a businessman, I don't solve problems, I make them disappear.'

To Alice the inference was crystal clear. Justin would never be so sloppy as to leave a body lying around. She hadn't thought he had anything to do with Colin's murder. She'd just wanted to see his reaction when she'd implied it.

'One question before you go. If you don't mind,' Alice added politely.

Justin's impatient expression made it clear that one question was all she was going to get.

'When you came here earlier you were intent on finding Rachel. Why? How did you know about her?'

'That's two questions.'

Alice shrugged. 'Two parts to the same question.'

Justin pursed his lips and pulled at this shirt sleeves. 'Does it matter? She's safe and I have my money back.'

Alice kept her face expressionless as she and Justin locked eyes again.

'I was warned about you,' Justin finally said.

Alice frowned slightly.

'A man in my position meets a lot of people. So let's leave it at that. Thank you for returning my property.'

He gave Shannon a look that seemed to say, 'You and I will be having a cosy little chat soon.' Shannon's face suggested she hoped that would be twenty years in the future.

Justin left, taking most of the tension in the room with him.

The silence grew past relieved and into uncomfortable.

'I'm leaving too,' Shannon finally said as she got to her feet. 'I don't even know why I was here.'

Because I promised to give you the book, Alice thought. Greed had been all Alice had needed to exploit to get Shannon rushing back to Silvermoon.

'There's still the matter of Colin's murder. We haven't finished debating your innocence,' Alice reminded her.

'You've got nothing on me. Just a bunch of theories,' Shannon said spitefully. 'I'm a police officer. What you're implying is close to libel.'

Before Alice could reply, Joshua piped up from the corner of the room. 'Actually, it's slander. Libel is written, slander is spoken.'

Shannon rounded on him. 'And you're still a person of interest in a police investigation. I've got half a mind to haul you down to the station right now.'

Alice bit back a quip about how having half a mind is what got Shannon into trouble in the first place. 'I think you'll be a little busy for that,' she said.

Shannon whirled back to face her.

'There's the little matter of stealing from a criminal.'

'I'm a police officer and you're a bunch of nobodies. You've got no proof of anything.'

Alice sighed. 'Sometimes being underestimated is a double-edged sword, dear. People mistake you for being stupid. Everything said in this room has been heard by the police.'

'No it wasn't.' Shannon's eyes darted to where Alice's phone sat on the table. 'I saw him check. If you were making a recording, he would have seen it.'

'Quite right,' Alice said sadly. 'Except he only checked my phone.' She turned to Vanessa who held up her hand with her phone showing a call in progress.

'Give me that!' Shannon lunged at Vanessa, grabbing her by the wrist. Vanessa pulled Shannon closer, then twisted her body and sent the woman up into the air and down on top of a table.

The door to the room burst open and Judith rushed in, closely followed by two uniformed constables. They lifted Shannon off her feet, gripping her firmly by the arms.

'Did you see that? She assaulted a police officer.'

'Quite proficiently I'd say,' Alice remarked.

'Judith, I can explain,' Shannon said.

'Good. Let's go back to the station and you can tell me all about it,' replied Judith. She waited until the constables had escorted Shannon from the room before turning to Alice. 'You promised me a murderer.'

Alice shrugged. 'Things didn't go quite as I'd hoped, but I eliminated some suspects for you.'

Judith shook her head disbelievingly. 'All you've done is give me a mountain of work and even more things to unravel.'

'And a crooked cop. And one other thing.'

'What?' Judith glanced at the door impatiently.

'If I were you, I'd look for an employee of Justin Fry who has disappeared. Someone on the inside of his organisation was stealing from him. You heard him. He makes problems disappear. Someone in his business goes missing, you've already got the motive. And I can do one better. D Russell and G Watson.'

'Who are they?'

'The directors of the publishing company that produced the books. Mr Russell works for Justin, so I'd start there.'

Judith looked thoughtful, then turned and left without another word.

'She could have said thanks,' Vanessa said.

'I'm not sure she knows how,' replied Alice.

Owen cleared his throat. 'So, just to be clear. Rachel is out of danger now?'

Alice nodded. 'I believe so. The police will undoubtedly have more questions for her about Colin, but Justin has given us his assurance and I think we can believe him. Meanwhile Shannon will be too busy to worry about Rachel. But let's be clear,' she addressed the last part directly to the girl. 'You just dodged a train-sized bullet. You could have easily ended up the same way as Colin, or worse. Despite what people tell you, second chances come along all the time. But third chances are rare. Don't screw this up.'

'Don't worry, she won't,' Owen said firmly. He took his granddaughter by the arm. 'It's time I took a more hands-on approach with my grandchildren.'

Rachel threw her arms around Owen. When she finally let go and turned to Alice there was a tear in the corner of her eye. She sniffed and wiped her face with the back of her hand.

'Look,' she said snatching a pale blue wool scarf from off the table where she had been sitting. 'Turns out I sort of enjoy knitting. Can you get it to your friend, you know for the hospital.'

'I'll make sure she gets it,' Alice replied.

'Thanks. I owe you.'

'We both do,' Owen said.

'I'm too old for IOUs,' Alice said with a flap of her hand.

Owen seemed to be struggling for more words, but in the end he walked over and briefly gripped her shoulder before escorting Rachel through the door.

'I hate to address the elephant in the room,' Vanessa said. 'But there's still a murderer on the loose.'

'I know that,' Alice scowled. 'Damn, Agatha Christie, making the whole thing look so simple.'

'What do we do now?' Joshua pulled up a chair opposite her.

Alice didn't answer. She was staring at the wall.

'Alice?'

She kept staring, not at the wall, but at what was on it.

'Alice?'

'Come with me.' She held out a hand and Vanessa helped her up. Alice led the way into the corridor.

'Where are we going?' Joshua asked.

Alice pushed open Glenda's door, startling the woman behind the desk.

'One question,' Alice barked.

'You scared me.'

'Get over it. One question. Did you take a painting?'

'What?'

'When you stole all those other things, did you break into Rosie's apartment and steal a painting?'

Glenda didn't answer immediately, but her eyes flicked to the filing cabinet. Alice crossed to it and pulled on the top drawer but it was locked. 'Key!'

Glenda fumbled in her pocket and pulled out a bunch of keys. She handed them to Alice who selected one that looked the right size. The drawer was empty.

'Where is everything?' Alice asked.

'I returned it,' replied Glenda.

Alice looked at Glenda and asked again, 'Where is everything?'

Glenda held her gaze for a long time, then her eyes slid to the bottom drawer of the filing cabinet.

Alice pulled the drawer out to find it full of items. She immediately saw there was no painting there.

'Where is Rosie's painting?'

Glenda sighed. 'Behind the cabinet.'

Alice signalled to Joshua who pulled the cabinet away from the wall and fished around behind it with his hand. He withdrew a large, framed painting and handed it to Alice. She studied the canvas. The artist obviously had some skill. The woman was slightly turned away, her hair fell over her face concealing her identity, but she was clearly beautiful. Alice felt a pang of sadness as she recalled how her best friend Violet had been painted in a similar pose by her husband John. She touched her finger to the surface and let herself miss them. Then she shrugged it off and glared at Glenda.

'I've had enough lying. Tell me the truth. The knitting needles. Did they really disappear from here?'

Glenda shook her head and scrunched up her face, as if knowing the words she was about to say would bring fresh wrath from Alice. 'No. I took them with me that night.'

'Why?' asked Vanessa.

Glenda licked her lips and continued. 'It's a trick I've used before. I take something with me, and if someone catches me and asks why I'm wandering around the grounds, I say I found it on the path and I'm on the way to return them.'

'So what happened to the knitting needles?'

'I saw the man, like I told you, but then I heard a sound behind me, like someone was coming from there as well. I panicked and dropped the needles in the grass.'

'Why didn't you tell me that before?' Alice said.

'Are you kidding? One of the needles turned out to be the murder weapon. There was no way I was going to admit I had them that night.'

'Your fingerprints would have been all over them anyway,' Alice rolled her eyes. 'You said originally that you were out at ten. Is that true?'

'It might have been later than that. Like closer to midnight.

Alice stared at her, barely bothering to hide her fury. 'You're fired. Get out.'

'But...I... you can't fire me. I don't work for you,' Glenda blustered.

'Actually, you do. I own the Silvermoon Retirement Village. Get your bag now, and Joshua will escort you off my property. And Glenda? If I see you again, we're going to have a big problem.'

She didn't wait to see how Glenda reacted, but marched out of the office with Vanessa in tow.

TWENTY-FOUR

'I can't believe I'm going to say this to a ninety-eight-year-old invalid but can you please slow down!'

Alice ignored her and continued towards the apartment building.

'At least let me carry the painting,' Vanessa said.

Alice gripped it tighter, as if Vanessa had been trying to tug it from her hands rather than offering to carry it.

A short time later she knocked on Rosie's door. There was a delay, then the door opened. Rosie's eyes went straight to the painting.

'You found it!' She clapped her hands in delight and snatched the painting from Alice. 'Thank you, thank you. Oh my gosh thank you. Please come in.'

She didn't speak again until they were all settled into the big squashy tan couch. Rosie kept sneaking glances at the painting, the smile never leaving her face. 'I thought it was lost forever, especially when that man...' Rosie cut herself off and looking guiltily at them.

'When that man... didn't have it?' Alice suggested.

'Yes,' Rosie nodded. 'I was sure he had it, but he insisted he didn't.'

'Is that why you killed him?' Alice said gently.

'Well, I didn't mean to, but he laughed at me. He said... he said who would want a painting of an old woman like me. I was so ashamed. But I wanted my painting back. He... he was so rude. He told me to toddle back to my rocking chair and then he turned away like he was dismissing me. I got mad and I saw the knitting needle lying on the grass, so I snatched it up and then suddenly he was lying on the ground and... and I could see he didn't have my painting. So, I went home. I waited for the police to come and lock me up. But they didn't come. And I needed my painting back, you understand. That's why I asked for your help, Alice. I knew if anyone could find it you could. And you did.'

Rosie beamed at Alice. She rose from her seat and carried the painting into the bedroom.

'Did you know?' Vanessa whispered urgently.

'I wondered,' Alice replied.

Before they could continue, Rosie reappeared without the painting. Alice suspected it was back in its place on her bedroom wall.

'Of course, now I have a problem. I only just got my painting back. I can't risk losing it again.' Rosie pulled her hand from behind her back. She was holding the second knitting needle. She lunged towards Vanessa, who threw herself back against the couch, but there was nowhere to go. The point of the needle went straight for Vanessa's eye.

Alice's cane came up, hitting Rosie's hand, and the needle went over Vanessa's head and into the cushion behind her.

Vanessa shoved Rosie and the older woman stumbled backwards, colliding with an armchair, and falling to the ground. There was a loud snap followed by an equally loud wail.

Alice leaned over and patted Vanessa on the arm.

'She… she tried to kill me,' Vanessa said in disbelief.

'Yes, dear, but only because you were closer.'

Vanessa took in a ragged breath and let it out with a short laugh. 'Oh good, is that why.'

Rosie's wailing had receded to a whimpering.

'Why don't you go and see if Judith is still on the grounds,' Alice said.

'And leave you alone with Lizzie Borden?'

'I'll be fine. But I'm impressed you know who Lizzie Borden is.'

'There was a show on Netflix.'

'What's a Netflix?'

'Alice!'

Alice laughed. She knew if she exasperated Vanessa enough, she would forget to worry about her near-death experience, and it seemed to have worked.

Vanessa went to find Judith.

Rosie managed to sit herself up and lean against the television cabinet.

'She broke my ankle,' she whined.

'You broke your own ankle,' Alice replied. 'Don't worry. You're going to get a lot of opportunities to rest it after they lock you up. Be thankful I'm not as fit as I used to be or that ankle would be the least of your problems.'

'But isn't my painting beautiful? Didn't I look pretty in it? All I wanted was my painting. I needed it.'

Alice sighed. She had thought there was hope for Rosie, but perhaps not.

'Oh, Rosie, you were already pretty. But there's nothing quite as ugly as a murderer.'

TWENTY-FIVE

'Was she, you know, a bit crazy?'

Alice shook her head at Joshua.

'I think Rosie had been worn down by her life. Her husband had spent years putting her down. All her confidence was gone, and that painting was the only thing that made her feel good about herself. I think when it went missing something in her snapped.'

Alice, Vanessa, and Joshua were sitting in Alice's apartment. The doctor had just been to inform Alice that she would need several further days of complete rest. He'd threatened to put her on restricted bed rest and had scolded her for aggravating the injury. She'd restrained herself from telling him that she'd only done it to catch a thief and solve a murder.

'Do I have to start calling you boss?'

'Please don't. As I've said repeatedly, I'd prefer that no one else knows. I could do without the complications.'

Vanessa grinned at her. 'Can I get a raise?'

'No.'

'How about next Monday off work?'

'Vanessa!'

'Oh fine.'

'My mum wanted to thank you,' Joshua chimed in.

Alice waved her hand dismissively. 'I'm only sorry it took me so long to sort it all out.'

'She wanted me to invite you to dinner.'

Alice cocked her head to the side. 'Why does that make you nervous?'

'Are you kidding me? The thought of you two in the same room is terrifying. You're both bad enough separately, but together…'

'Good,' Alice smiled. 'Alright, that's one good thing that's come out of this. Vanessa, since you now know that I'm technically paying your salary anyway, why don't you quit your concierge job and come to work for me full-time.'

Vanessa looked surprised, then her eyes narrowed in suspicion. 'And do what?'

'You're bright and resourceful, but you lack the necessary skills. I'm going to teach you everything I know.'

Vanessa didn't answer for a while. When she did, she looked troubled. 'I don't think I'm cut out for a life of crime.'

'Who asked you to be? Most of these skills can be used in a wide range of careers – almost all of them legal,' Alice added with a twinkle.

'I have already learned a lot from you,' Vanessa said.

'That's just a fraction. But as this damn ankle has reminded me, I'm running out of time to pass on my wisdom.'

'If this is about your legacy, didn't you already teach Amanda everything you know?'

'This is not about my legacy,' replied Alice. 'It's about your future.'

Vanessa chewed at her hair.

'Do you know that using some of the things I've shown you, you've helped catch three killers?'

Alice wanted to say more but she clamped her mouth shut. It was Vanessa's decision, and she knew if she pushed too hard then Vanessa might panic and make the wrong choice.

'Okay. I'm in.'

THE END

Acknowledgements

The business of writing a book is definitely a team effort. Although my name is on the cover, it wouldn't exist without the support and effort of the following:

My wonderful wife Sarah who is always encouraging and tells me off for over committing

My equally wonderful editor Anna Golden who takes the rough edges off my words

Debbie Weaver for designed the book cover

Knitting Needles and Knives

Rodney Strong

Made in the USA
Monee, IL
01 April 2024

56144269R00243